RED
MIST

Ant Middleton was the frontman for Channel 4's hit show, *SAS: Who Dares Wins*, among other major series, and is a hugely bestselling non-fiction author. Born in Portsmouth and raised in rural France, Ant set his sights on a career in the armed forces and didn't stop striving until he achieved his goal. Over the course of his career he has served in the Special Boat Service, the Royal Marines and 9 Parachute Squadron Royal, achieving what is known as the 'Holy Trinity' of the UK's Elite Forces.

Also by Ant Middleton

Fiction
Cold Justice

Non-fiction
SAS: Who Dares Wins
First Man In
The Fear Bubble
Zero Negativity
Mental Fitness
The Wall

Children's
Mission Total Resilience

ANT MIDDLETON

RED MIST

SPHERE

SPHERE

First published in Great Britain in 2022 by Sphere
This paperback edition published in 2023 by Sphere

1 3 5 7 9 10 8 6 4 2

A CIP catalogue record for this book
is available from the British Library.

ISBN 9-7807-5158-047-1

Typeset in Sabon by M Rules
Printed and bound in Great Britain by
Clays Ltd, Elcograf S.p.A.

Papers used by Sphere are from well-managed forests
and other responsible sources.

Sphere
An imprint of
Little, Brown Book Group
Carmelite House
50 Victoria Embankment
London EC4Y 0DZ

An Hachette UK Company
www.hachette.co.uk

www.littlebrown.co.uk

My brother Michael Middleton, who is Mallory x1000! I'm proud of how far you've come and who you've become but we've got so much further to go together! Keep pushing …

APPELBURG, SWITZERLAND

An unseasonal chill hung in the air. The night sky was almost completely clear, other than a sharp wedge of black cloud that cut through the centre of the full moon like a spear.

Nicolas Devereaux lowered his gaze from the stars. The summit of the mountain cast a shadow over most of the grounds, leaving only the patch of grass closest to the sprawling house doused in milky moonlight. Nicolas gripped the SIG P210 and, for the hundredth time, wondered what the hell he had got himself into.

They couldn't have been serious, could they? This was just another test. Jonas, the lanky ex-soldier who was lurking somewhere out here, had to be in on the joke. Like the way stage psychics put a plant in the audience to give credibility to their powers of clairvoyance. Nicolas had taken Océane to see one of those guys in Pigalle last year. The psychic put on a good show, but Nicolas hadn't been fooled. No, this had to be a joke. They were hazing him, seeing how far he would go.

So why did it feel so much like he was being hunted for real?

He left the cover of a thick stand of azaleas, aiming to cut across an open stretch of grass to a set of stone steps that led up to one of the other levels. Platforms and staircases and statues and fountains. The place reminded Nicolas of a video game more than a garden. He got the impression that it had been designed that way.

He wondered if that had been at the instruction of the man who was his host tonight. The tall, salt-and-pepper-haired Swiss who pointedly did not introduce himself when they met; whose handshake was bone-crushingly firm. The man whose staff referred to him only as *le patron*. Boss.

Two or three paces from the staircase, Nicolas sensed movement in the corner of his eye. He moved instinctively, ducking and thrusting his body forwards as he heard the snap of a gunshot in the still air. The stone sculpture that had been behind his head a moment ago cracked, dust spraying out from the clean wedge that had just been blown out of it by the bullet.

Not a joke. Not a game. This was for real.

He heard Jonas's deep voice throw out a curse. There was real anger behind it. Maybe Nicolas didn't want to hurt anybody, but it didn't sound as though his opponent shared that impulse.

Nicolas crouched behind the stone banister lining the staircase and peered between the supports. Jonas was still in the position from where he had fired. Nicolas could see his shadow disturbing the line of the bushes.

Suddenly, there was a flash of light from the opposite end of the garden. Nicolas turned to train his gun on the source of the light; a flashing array of spotlights. Music blared out. Brahms, he thought. Another distraction.

The lights winked out and the music faded. Nicolas turned and saw from the shadows that Jonas had not yet moved. Most likely, he had also been surprised by the light show.

Jonas would have to break cover sooner or later. To approach Nicolas's position, he would have to come straight across the open stretch of grass, or circle around the bushes on the perimeter. Nicolas thought the first approach was unlikely. But if he went around the bushes, Nicolas would be able to track his movement. There were two places where the foliage thinned out, almost like windows in a green wall. All he would have to do would be to wait and time his shot just right.

He risked taking his eyes from Jonas's position for a moment to size up the nearest gap. Barely thirty metres. No wind. He could make the shot with his eyes closed.

Wait, was he crazy? He had never met this man before the party earlier in the evening. He knew nothing of him, beyond a vague, instinctive dislike. Was he really going to shoot him?

But Jonas had shot at him. He had shot to kill, too. A slightly more skilled marksman would have succeeded.

Nicolas looked around. There had to be a way out of here. The garden was large; difficult to get a sense of its exact dimensions in the dark, with all of the foliage and the stone-work. But from everything he had seen so far, there was no obvious way out. The mountain rose above them on one side. The different levels and extensions of the house towered and sprawled out on the opposite side. On the remaining sides were stone walls at least fifteen feet high.

They were in a box. And if what the man who owned this land had said was true, only one of them was leaving the box.

Nicolas was brought back to the task in hand when he heard the whisper of soft rubber soles on grass.

As expected, Jonas was taking the route around the perimeter. He probably didn't realise there were gaps in the bushes where he could be seen. Nicolas waited for him to pass the first window, gauging his speed. The older man was moving quickly, confidently. Nicolas trained his gun on the second window and waited. He focused on the spot where Jonas would appear in seconds. Pinpointing the area he wanted the bullet to hit to the centimetre. He breathed in and waited.

Jonas's silhouette appeared, passing the second window.

Nicolas squeezed the trigger.

The gun kicked, the silhouette jerked and went down.

Nicolas let the breath out.

He stood up, keeping the gun aimed at the window.

Arc lights switched on, much brighter than before, bathing the garden in a sudden nuclear glare.

Nicolas crouched down behind the stone banister again, shading his eyes with his free hand against the dazzling white light from the house.

He saw the silhouettes of three men walking out from the house across the grass, their shadows elongated. They looked like extra-terrestrials emerging from a spaceship.

He heard the boss's voice, but didn't know which of the three had spoken. 'You can come out now, Nicolas.'

Hesitantly, Nicolas stood up, keeping the gun raised. The three men reached the spot where Jonas had fallen.

Nicolas walked out onto the grass, half-expecting to be shot down. He still couldn't see the faces of the three men against the light, but their body language was relaxed, matter of fact. The game was over.

The three of them stood around Jonas, lying prone on the ground. He recognised *le patron*'s figure now. He was the man in the middle, the edges of his suit sharp against the light. The other two flanking him were dressed in bulkier gear, both holding automatic rifles. He looked up as Nicolas approached. The two men on either side turned almost casually to cover Nicolas with their weapons.

A low moan drifted up from Jonas, like an animal in distress. He was clutching his shoulder, dark red blood gleaming between his fingers in the white light. The man to the left of the boss approached. He nodded at the gun in Nicolas's hand. Nicolas handed it over.

'You shot to wound,' the boss commented, perusing the man on the ground like a mechanic evaluating the work of an apprentice. There was no judgement in the tone, but no doubt either. He knew.

Nicolas opened his mouth to say something about it being a tough angle, then thought better of it.

His host sighed and stepped forward, extending a hand. Nicolas took it, felt the firm grip again.

'Congratulations. Join me for a drink?'

In the corner of his eye, Nicolas saw the man who had taken his gun adjust his rifle slightly.

Nicolas gestured down at Jonas. 'He'll be okay?' His voice sounded shaky, like he had just been in a car accident. He couldn't help it.

His host glanced back down at Jonas, as though he had already forgotten all about the bleeding man at his feet. Jonas stared back up at him. He was hyperventilating now, the breath hissing in and out from between his teeth. The fingers of the hand gripping tight against the wound looked white as bone against the red. Like a skeleton's fingers.

'That wound is treatable. Come.'

He put a hand on Nicolas's shoulder and gently guided him around so that they were facing the house. Nicolas saw him exchange a glance with the second man with a rifle, and then an almost imperceptible nod.

They started walking, the boss's hand still on his shoulder. As they got close to the house, two shots rang out.

Nicolas flinched. His host did not react, beyond giving his shoulder a slight squeeze.

'A good hunt, Nicolas. We'll have that drink. And then we'll talk.'

TWO MONTHS LATER

SUNDAY

1

ST-JEAN-DES-PERTES, NORMANDY

Up until the moment the two guys pulled up in the shiny red Renault Alaskan, shattering the tranquillity with aggressive revs and a radio turned up way too loud, it had been a very pleasant afternoon.

It was a proper French village tavern: white stone walls, a thatched roof, exposed oak beams inside. Mallory was sitting at the table furthest from the bar, by the window that overlooked the Vire as it flowed endlessly by. The place was sublimely quiet. No conversation, no music. If he closed his eyes, he could hear nothing but the flow of water and occasional birdsong.

The job was complete, and today had seen an early finish after four days of back-breaking work. Mallory could barely feel the chill of his beer glass through the new calluses on his hands. He was tired, but it wasn't an unpleasant feeling. He had worked hard, bonded with the rest of the crew, and they had finished the task more quickly than the stony-eyed foreman Philippe had predicted. The Corsican, usually so sour-faced, had even cracked the first smile Mallory had seen on him.

Mallory had tried his hand at a lot of jobs for the first time over the last year, since he'd stepped out of the passenger seat of the long-haul lorry that had carried him from Caen. He had done his share of digging while in the military, but this was the first time he had dug a well. It had been tough work, but he had enjoyed it. It was soothing to clear his mind and focus on nothing but the spade. Dig, shovel, toss, repeat, with the hole growing deeper imperceptibly. The repetition of work that kept the thoughts away.

In the age of peace and quiet before the red truck showed up, Mallory had been wondering what the old man in the corner was upset about.

He looked to be in his seventies or eighties. He was solidly built, wide across the shoulders, with a thick bushy beard that was mostly grey with traces of red. He was dressed like most of the men of his vintage Mallory had encountered in this part of France: dark trousers and a loose cotton shirt. The top two buttons were open, showing a thatch of grey chest hair. He wasn't demonstratively upset. He wasn't sobbing uncontrollably, or rending his garments, or even knocking back that wine he was nursing, but still, Mallory could tell something was wrong. It was a faraway stare that he recognised.

Mallory made a point of minding his own business, as far as was possible, but something about the old man made him curious. He was of half a mind to walk over and strike up a conversation. They were the only two customers. Or rather, the only two drinkers. A young mother wearing pink and black jogging clothes was spooning mush from a Tupperware container into her baby's mouth at a table at the other end of the bar.

All of that went out of Mallory's mind when the red truck rolled to a stop, some kind of raucous French rock band blaring out of the radio.

The old man didn't react. His thousand-yard stare didn't waver, even as the baby spat a mouthful of its food out to wail in displeasure, and the young mum shot an infuriated look in the direction of the car park. Mallory shifted in his seat a little so he could see past the brick pillar in the middle of the room and watch as two men got out.

They were both young, late twenties, perhaps. The driver was over six feet tall and the August sunshine glinted off his shaved head. He stepped out of the truck unhurriedly. He was dressed in camouflage trousers and a white sleeveless T-shirt with the logo of a beer company on it. The passenger seemed in more of a hurry, skirting around the bonnet of the truck like he was worried he might be left behind. He was four or five inches shorter and quite a bit skinnier than his friend, and wore a faded denim baseball cap. They looked similar enough to be brothers, but maybe that was more about their dress and demeanour than anything else. The passenger caught up with the driver and matched his pace as they entered the bar.

Mallory picked his glass up and swirled the remnants of his beer as he watched them approach. The driver raised a hand in greeting to the bartender, who was polishing glasses. He acknowledged the two of them with a wary nod. They stopped halfway across the floor and looked at the old man. If he noticed them, he did not react. Then, as one, they turned the other way and looked at the woman and the baby. She definitely noticed them, but avoided their gaze. The driver kept looking at her while the passenger turned his head to inspect the bottles on the shelf behind the bar. So far, they had taken the time to look at everything and everyone in the place except Mallory.

That was how he knew there was about to be trouble.

They reached the bar, both of them still studiously avoiding Mallory's gaze. The passenger in the truck, the one wearing the denim cap, jutted his chin in the direction of the bartender. 'Laurent. *L'habituel*, eh?'

The usual.

Mallory's French wasn't anywhere close to fluent yet, but it had come a long way over the long, hot summer.

The bartender muttered something that was a little too fast for Mallory to catch, but he was pretty sure it didn't translate as 'Right away, sir.'

The driver came up with a rejoinder, then smiled and pulled a roll of euros out of his pocket, waving them to show the bartender he was good for a round.

Mallory rolled his shoulders and put his hands on his thighs. He wanted to be ready for the fight he knew was coming. He reminded himself he wasn't looking for trouble. A familiar tingle at the back of his neck suggested that wasn't the whole truth.

The bartender started pouring a couple of beers. Finally, the two men looked over at Mallory. They did it simultaneously, as though responding to a wordless signal.

Mallory felt his pulse slow a little as they approached his table, an almost relaxed feeling. That worried him, because it meant something else was about to take over. As soon as the first punch was thrown, his body would react, and for the duration, proportionality and morality and consequences would cease to be factors. He hoped the two of them would go down easy. It wouldn't do any of them any good to prolong the fight.

The shaved-headed driver broke into a grin as he reached him. He reached a beefy hand out for the chair opposite Mallory and pulled it out, twisting it around so that the back was facing the table, straddled the chair and sat down heavily, resting his forearms on the chair back.

'Bonjour.'

Mallory didn't reply right away. He just stared back at the driver, keeping his own face impassive in contrast to the belligerent grin on the other man's face. The second man had stayed on his feet. He stood a couple of feet back from the table, between Mallory and the door, his hands clasped behind his back like a weekend yacht captain.

After leaving a pause long enough for the grin to start fading, Mallory returned the greeting.

'Bonjour.'

'You are not from here,' the driver said, switching to English.

'I'm not.'

Without taking his eyes off Mallory, he raised his voice. Addressing someone else. He was asking the bartender if he knew this *anglais*, investing the last word with a heavy dose of contempt. After a pause the bartender answered. He called the driver Remy. Said he didn't want any trouble. Mallory had enough French to grasp all of this, but in truth he didn't require it. The tone of voice and body language told him everything he needed to know.

It confirmed he wasn't walking out of here without blood being spilled. Part of him wanted to warn them, but he knew such a warning would have the opposite effect. It would only make the situation worse.

He tried to focus on something mental rather than physical. The two men wanted a fight, so there was going to be a fight. But he was curious as to why.

'You have a problem with people who aren't from here?' Mallory asked mildly.

Remy grinned. 'I don't have a problem, friend. Hugo here sometimes has a problem with people who aren't from here.'

The passenger, Hugo apparently, took the conversational baton and leaned on the table, getting in Mallory's face in a way his companion had not done so far.

'Remy's uncle's house was broken into last night.'

Hugo's accent was thicker. He was less sure of the words.

'I'm sorry to hear that,' Mallory said. 'Has he notified the police?'

Remy put a hand on his friend's forearm, tapping it lightly. Hugo held Mallory's gaze for a moment before straightening up and taking a step back from the table. Easy to tell who the boss was.

'Of course we spoke to the police,' Remy said, through a smile that did not reach his eyes. Then even the pretence of good humour vanished. 'They said it was probably someone ... not from here.'

Mallory took his time, not wanting to let this guy dictate the rhythm of the conversation. If you could call it a conversation. He glanced around the bar, careful not to let either of the two men completely out of his sight. Laurent the bartender was still polishing a glass that had been clean and dry two minutes ago. The woman on the other side of the room had stopped feeding her baby. Even the baby seemed to be watching. Its mouth hung open, its pale blue eyes mesmerised by the trio in the corner of the bar. The only person not paying attention was the old man in the corner, who was staring into the bottom of his wine glass as though the sediment could tell the future.

Mallory was pretty sure he could tell the future too. It was going to start with him letting them make the first move, and progress to both of them lying face down on the floor.

He cleared his throat. 'Doesn't sound like a very thorough investigation, if I'm being honest,' he said, keeping his face entirely straight.

The two of them exchanged a glance. The one standing, Hugo, looked a little unsure of himself for the first time. The driver, Remy, seemed unmoved. He considered Mallory's suggestion and smiled again, letting a brief laugh out through his nostrils.

'We think they're right. We think it was someone just like you.'

'Someone just like me,' Mallory repeated. He wanted to keep them talking for a minute, until the time for talking was over.

'There have been other break-ins,' Remy continued. 'How long have you been in St-Jean? A week? There have been three break-ins in a week.'

Mallory sighed heavily and rolled his head around. He wanted them to know he wasn't intimidated, but he was tiring of the conversation. The movement also gave him a chance to take stock of his surroundings. What happened next would happen quickly, so he wanted to block out each move in advance.

15

He was literally backed against the wall. Deliberately so. He made a point of always sitting with his back protected and a clear view of the doorway. But once the punches started flying, he didn't want to be boxed in. So the second thing he would do would be to flip the table. The second thing, because the first thing he would have to do would be to get Remy to move his thick, hairy forearms from the table.

There were a couple of ways to accomplish that. He could throw the last of his drink in Remy's face. Remy would automatically bring his hands up to protect his eyes. But that wouldn't accomplish exactly the right effect, because Remy's friend was standing by, ready to move.

So he had to take out Remy's friend first. The further target.

Without taking his eyes from Remy's, Mallory considered the wine bottle in the centre of the table with the stubby candlestick jammed into the neck. He thought about how it would feel in his hand. The weight of it. The dried wax against the palm of his hand. He visualised grabbing it with one movement and hurling it in Hugo's face. Bottom first. The glass probably wouldn't break, but the nose might.

That would accomplish the other goal. Remy and Hugo were positioned close enough together that in the split second, Remy would not know whether the bottle was aimed at him or his friend. He would get his arms up. And then Mallory would flip the table.

The table would push Remy back and prevent him from grabbing Mallory as he rose.

From there, it would be routine. He would take out Remy first, smacking his face off the brick pillar that he would be lined up with perfectly after the table had pushed him back. Then, depending on whether the bottle had knocked Hugo out already, he could finish the job with an elbow to the bridge of the nose. It would be a smooth transition into that move from slamming Remy into the pillar.

These calculations took Mallory a fraction of a second. He wasn't worried that he was rusty, or in any doubt he could take these two losers. What he was worried about was unintended consequences. Collateral damage. He was worried about what he would do when he *stopped* thinking.

The old man was close by. What if he had a weak heart, couldn't take sudden shocks? The woman and the child were on the other side of the bar, but it wasn't that big a place. A chair could get thrown. Glass might get smashed. The bartender might feel the need to intervene, and he would definitely get hurt.

Mallory told himself he had to stay in control and contained, to make sure this was finished as quickly and efficiently as possible.

Remy was waiting for him to say something, perhaps mistaking Mallory's hesitation for fear. Eventually he relented and spoke. 'I think it's time to step outside.'

Mallory shook his head slowly. He spoke without thinking about it, like something dark and ugly inside of him was using his voice.

'I like it inside.'

He could see in the eyes of Remy and his companion that they knew what was coming next. They didn't know it was going to happen a beat sooner than they expected.

'Why?' Remy said, grinning.

Mallory's hand went for the bottle like he was reaching for the neck of a snake. The thing inside of him started to take over.

But he froze when he heard the voice from the far corner.

2

'*Arrêtez!*'

The old man had spoken, and his voice sounded like Charlton Heston in one of the Bible movies they used to show on TV on Easter weekends.

Mallory felt the building urge inside of him subside a little, like a pot abruptly turned down low just as it was about to boil over.

He kept his eyes on the two men. He needn't have worried. Both of them were staring back at the old man.

If you had asked Mallory to make a prediction ten minutes before, he wouldn't have been entirely confident that the old guy was capable of standing unaided, but capable he was. He had stood up straight, unwavering. He was glaring at the two men, his eyes blazing above the bushy white beard.

Remy looked back at Mallory, almost questioningly. It was a look that said, 'Do *you* know what's going on?' Seeing no help there, he turned back to the old man, brow furrowed. The laidback intimidation with which he had spoken to Mallory was gone. Now he looked like a kid on his first day behind the till at McDonald's trying to deal with an angry customer.

'*Monsieur*—' he began, and was promptly cut off by a barrage of Gallic invective that was too fast and too rapid-fire for Mallory to parse.

Remy held a hand up, like he was trying to physically ward off the torrent of words, and tried to interrupt. The old man wasn't having it. He had advanced across the room and was pointing out of the door at the truck.

'*Sortez!*'

Hugo stepped forward. He had recovered from his surprise and looked ready to lay the old man out. Mallory would intercept him before he got that far, but watching the scene, he wondered if his help was required. Hugo started yelling back at him, tossing in a few curse words that Mallory recognised. The old man responded by taking two quick steps forward.

As though coordinated, Mallory and Remy stepped in, getting in front of the old man and Hugo respectively.

Remy shook his head at his friend. He looked askance at Mallory.

'Maybe we talk later, my friend, huh?'

'Maybe we do,' Mallory said.

Remy gave him a hard stare and turned around. Hugo hesitated, hands dropped to his sides now, but he looked as though he was straining against the urge to launch himself forward again.

Remy called his name without turning or breaking stride, and Hugo spat another curse and turned on his heel to scamper after his friend.

'There's a good boy,' Mallory said, just loud enough for him to hear. Hugo stiffened, but didn't turn again.

Mallory watched as the two of them exited the bar and

got back in the truck. Hugo slammed the door so hard the window dropped down in its frame halfway. Remy gave Mallory one more look that was heavy with meaning and pulled the truck out of the space, kicking up a cloud of fine yellow dust that hung in the air long after the sound of the engine and the too-loud radio had faded to nothing.

It was as though the oxygen in the bar had suddenly returned after being steadily sucked out. The mother feeding her child started packing her various accoutrements away, getting ready to go now that the path to the door was clear. She avoided looking in Mallory's direction. Behind the bar, Laurent finally seemed satisfied with the gleam on the glass he was polishing and placed it carefully on a shelf.

Mallory turned to the old man, not sure what he would say. He decided to keep it simple. '*Merci, monsieur.*'

'*Anglais?*' the old man said.

'Yes,' Mallory confirmed.

'Those boys are *motherfuckers.*'

He looked extremely pleased with his grasp of the language.

Mallory broke into a grin. 'I got that impression.'

He asked if the old man would like another drink and he shrugged in the affirmative. Mallory gestured for him to sit back down at his table while he ordered. In contrast to his movements a few moments before, the weight of years seemed to have returned to the old man's limbs. He shuffled over to his chair and sat down heavily. As he moved, Mallory noticed there was an old tattoo protruding from under the sleeve of his cream shirt. He recognised the design, and it might go some way towards explaining why the man had commanded so much authority, and how he had managed to stare down two physically fit men a third his age.

Laurent raised an eyebrow when Mallory asked him for another bottle of whatever the old man was drinking. Without comment, he reached under the bar and dusted off a bottle, then produced two wine glasses. He uncorked the bottle with a practised hand and worked the cork off the screw before pushing the bottle across the bar. It had a plain label with the name of the town on it.

Mallory paid cash and took the wine over to the table. He had to stop to let the woman and baby past on their way to the door. The woman ignored him and addressed the old man in the corner. She called him stupid, said he could have got himself killed. The old man responded with a defensive shrug of his shoulders and a bewildered look at Mallory.

She rolled her eyes and pushed the buggy past Mallory.

Mallory crossed the room to the table, glancing back the way the woman had gone.

'You know her?'

'Celine,' the old man responded. 'A friend of my granddaughter.'

Mallory sat down and placed the bottle and the glasses on the table. 'Something tells me your granddaughter will be getting a full report.'

The old man said nothing. His eyes were on the bottle.

Mallory reached for it, but the old man beat him to it with surprising alacrity, lifting it and pouring expertly. He raised his glass. Mallory reciprocated and they clinked.

'Serge.'

'Mallory. Pleased to meet you, Serge.'

'Mallory,' Serge repeated, accenting the y as most of his countrymen did. *Mall-or-ee.* He considered for a moment and then added, 'Do you cause this much trouble wherever you go?'

3

The wine was good. Then again, most of the wine was good in France.

'Who were they?' Mallory asked as he watched Serge take a gulp from his glass. 'The motherfuckers.'

Serge swallowed and wiped his lips with the linen napkin from the table. 'Remy, his father is the mayor.'

Mallory understood immediately. In small towns like this, the mayor's word was law.

'Thinks he owns the place, huh?'

Serge gave him an approving look. 'His father does own it. His son only thinks he does. They look for trouble. They don't like people like you.'

'Brits?'

Serge snorted. 'People from anywhere else. Outsiders.'

Mallory nodded. 'Was he telling the truth about the break-ins? Or was that just an excuse to beat me up?'

Serge shrugged dismissively. The short sleeve of his shirt rode up again, revealing more of the tattoo. It was faded from black to blue.

'Where did you serve?' Mallory asked, taking his index finger off the wine glass he was holding to point at the ink.

Serge looked down at his arm as though he had forgotten the tattoo was there, and then carefully lifted the sleeve up to show the whole design: a star overlaid on the image of a parachute, with wings extending on both sides.

It was the regimental badge of the Deuxième Parachutist. The airborne regiment of the French Foreign Legion. Judging by his age, Mallory was guessing the answer to his question would be Algeria.

'*Algérie*,' Serge confirmed. He narrowed his eyes. Mallory caught the unspoken question.

'Afghanistan, Iraq ...' he answered. 'The usual.'

'Complicated wars,' Serge commented.

'Aren't they all?'

Serge considered this and then nodded. 'How long have you been out?'

'Almost two years now.'

The two of them sat in silence for a couple of minutes. It wasn't an uncomfortable silence, far from it. Two men from different countries, from different eras, considering how their life experiences might not be all that different.

Eventually, Mallory broke the silence. 'Why did you step in there? I could have handled that.'

Serge snorted. 'And how would you have handled it? Put them in the hospital?' He gestured over at the bar with his wine glass. 'Break some of Laurent's shitty furniture?'

'Hey,' the bartender cut in. '*Je parle anglais*.'

Serge waved the comment away. 'Those boys are idiots. No need to ...' He paused and grasped for the right word, looking satisfied when he came up with it. '*Engage*.'

'You solved my problem, but maybe you created one for yourself. Are you worried about that girl telling your daughter?'

'Granddaughter,' he snapped. He pointed at Mallory. 'Don't ask me about her again or this will be a short conversation.'

Mallory held his hands up in apology and changed the subject. But he was intrigued now. He poured Serge another glass.

The afternoon shadows lengthened as the two men talked. Serge talked about his years in the Deuxième Parachutist, about the fighting in the Aurès Mountains in '56. Mallory told Serge about the cross training he had done with French special forces, and that he had a pair of those wings too, through a combined exercise. They compared gruelling training exercise stories: being buried in the sand up to your neck, carrying ridiculous loads on your back over the Brecon Beacons.

Serge lifted his shirt and hitched down his trousers to show Mallory the four-inch scar where shrapnel had hit him fighting rebels in Chad, in 1969. The man next to him had been eviscerated. He told Mallory there was still shrapnel inside him.

'Must be fun at airports.'

'I don't fly,' Serge said. 'I don't go anywhere.'

'Why not?'

'I have been to enough places. I have seen enough,' he said, staring out of the window at the river. His focus shifted back to Mallory suddenly. 'You have not had enough?'

Mallory considered the question before answering. He knew there was a part of him that could never have enough, no matter how much he wished otherwise. He looked away from Serge's gaze, kept his voice light with an effort.

'I haven't.'

Serge considered this for a moment. 'You are still young, so young.' His eyes wandered to the flowing water again, and when he spoke, it was as though he was talking to himself. He said a single word.

'Océane.'

Mallory waited for him to say something else. He was about to ask him which ocean he was talking about when Serge spoke again.

'I love her with all my heart, but I cannot help her.'

'Océane is your granddaughter.'

'Yes. She is beautiful. Very smart.' He dug in his pocket and produced a battered phone, the screen spider-webbed with cracks. He shook it until it woke and showed Mallory the screen saver. If this was Océane, then he was at least half right about her.

She stood with her back to the River Seine and a clear blue sky. That it was the Seine was evident from the fact the Eiffel Tower was framed in the background. She appeared to be in her mid to late twenties with long, straight, jet-black hair and hazel eyes. There was a very slight family resemblance, but it was mostly in the look in her eyes. She was staring away from the photographer, and the set of her jaw made it look as though she was preparing to take some considered action.

Serge was staring sorrowfully at the back of the phone as Mallory examined the picture. There was a heavy sense of loss in his stare, and Mallory knew this was what he'd been dwelling on earlier, when Mallory had been wondering about him.

'What happened to her?' Mallory said, suddenly wondering if he was looking at a photograph of a dead woman.

Serge blinked. 'I do not know.'

'You don't know?'

Serge drained the last of the wine from his glass and raised himself up, steadying his hand on the table. Again, it seemed to require more effort than when he had risen to confront the two young men earlier. It was as though he had expended his reserves of energy for the day and needed to recharge. He walked to the door and stepped outside. Mallory followed him. Just beyond the door there was a long covered roof with colourful hanging baskets suspended from the beams. The blossoms smelled sweet in the evening air.

Serge waited for Mallory to join him and pointed to a spot a mile or so away, where the main road stretched across the side of a gentle hill like a scalpel cut.

'You see that road?'

Mallory had travelled along the road in the passenger seat of the lorry on which he had hitched before being dropped in this town.

'Fifteen years ago, my son and his wife – Océane's parents – were returning from Lyons. The driver of a ...' He searched for the words in English, and couldn't find them. '*Camion de bois.*'

'A lumber truck.'

'*Oui.* He was drunk, drove into the opposite lane. They were both killed instantly. Océane was in the back of the car. She survived.' Serge shook his head and put a hand on one of the upright oak beams supporting the roof covering the outdoor area. 'She was in a coma for three weeks. The doctors, they were not sure she would live. But she did. It was a miracle. After many more weeks, she was allowed to come home to me. It was hard.'

'It must have been,' Mallory said quietly. 'Was there anyone else?'

'No one else. Just the two of us.'

'You did it, though, you took care of her.'

Serge smiled briefly. 'No. She took care of *me*.'

That brought a reciprocal smile to Mallory's lips, which faded as he realised that Serge didn't look like anyone had been taking care of him for a while.

Serge took a crumpled pack of Winston cigarettes from his hip pocket and fitted one to his lips.

The bartender called his name and Serge ignored him as he took out his lighter and sparked up. He inhaled deeply, paying no attention to the bartender's remonstrations.

'Océane was a good girl. She kept the house, she cooked, she went to school every day.' He sighed. 'She shouldn't have had to do so much, but she said it made her happy to take care of me. Perhaps she felt that she had to be her parents as well as herself.'

Mallory didn't get the sense that the older man expected him to say anything. Perhaps he was just thankful for the opportunity to talk for the first time in a while. Mallory didn't know why he had chosen him. Perhaps it was the shared military background, or just the more recent confrontation they had shared in the bar, but he didn't think that was it. He thought Serge had decided to open up to him for the same reason as Remy and his friend had targeted him for their attentions. He was an outsider. Someone who didn't come with the baggage of being from the town.

'Do you know the date, Mallory?'

Mallory looked at him in surprise. It was the first time Serge had broken his monologue to address him directly. He had to think about it. Dates had become fuzzy in the last few months.

'It's the seventh of August, I think.'

Serge raised a weary eyebrow. '*Sept août*. It is later than I thought. It has been eight weeks since I spoke to Océane. Eight weeks since she told me I was an old fool and she never wished to speak to me again.'

'What happened?'

'Perhaps she was right. Perhaps I am an old fool. But I am an old fool who wants the best for his child. I was angry too. I said things I should have not said. I said I no longer had a granddaughter. I regret this now.'

'Never too late to give her a call,' Mallory said. Adding quickly, 'In the morning, perhaps.'

'I have tried to call many times,' Serge said. 'She does not answer. With each day that passes, I worry more. I worry that perhaps she *cannot* answer.'

That brought Mallory up short. 'You think something could have happened to her? That she could have harmed herself?'

Serge stopped and leaned on a barrier that overlooked a drop to the street that ran below, twenty yards down the hill.

'She would not harm herself. Her boyfriend, though. I begin to fear that is a different story.'

4

MALAKOFF, PARIS

Nicolas Devereaux stepped out of the air-conditioned chill of the pool bar and into the humidity of the night. It had still been light when he entered an hour ago, but darkness had fallen quickly while he was in the windowless back room. It felt as though someone had thrown a warm, wet towel over his head as soon as he stepped outside the door.

His silver Audi A1 was parked at the far side of the car park. He was relieved to see it still had wheels and intact windows. There was a group of five shady-looking teenage boys on the corner, all kitted out in ostentatious trainers and sportswear. Five pairs of eyes watched him as he passed. One called out to him, asking if he needed any *taz* in a tone that sounded more like an invitation to fight than a sales pitch.

Nicolas waved his hand in a 'thanks but no thanks' gesture. He quickened his pace and heard a low mutter followed by a shrill cackle.

The five of them were little more than kids, acting tougher

than they were. They might not have been so quick to taunt Nicolas if they'd known what he was carrying in the sports bag slung over his shoulder. Until the fat man with the blood-shot eyes inside had given the gun to him, none of this had felt real. But ever since that June night in the garden, he had known that this was all too real.

The Audi was parked in the furthest corner of the car park, away from the lights. In normal circumstances, he would park as close as possible to the building so that he could keep an eye on it. Shit, in normal circumstances, he would think twice before parking anywhere in this part of town. But these were not normal circumstances.

The chatter of the tough guys dropped away into the back-ground. Maybe they weren't even drug dealers, just bored teenagers. Nicolas looked around before tapping the key in his pocket to unlock the car. The lights flashed and the doors unlocked with a clunk. He went around to the back and opened the trunk. A shriek of sirens cut through the night air as a police car two junctions away picked up speed, heading towards him, its lights flashing. Nicolas felt as though a cold hand had reached into his chest and grabbed his heart.

But the police car gained speed instead of slowing, flashing by him so fast that he couldn't see the features of the two policemen. The car reached the corner, slowed, and turned into traffic.

Nicolas gazed back over at the line of stores. The group of young toughs had scattered, and were warily returning to their posts.

He let out the breath he had been holding and opened the lid of the trunk all the way. The only other thing in there was a small backpack he had stuffed with a couple of changes of clothes. He wouldn't be staying long where he was going. In three days he would be done, he told himself. One way or another.

And then he made the mistake of dwelling on the last four words to cross his mind: *one way or another.*

He turned around again. The kids on the corner were no longer paying him any attention. They were circling a couple of teenage girls dressed for a night out. The girls looked unworried, enjoying – or at least unfazed by – the attention. There were no other moving vehicles on the street and the sound of the police siren had been lost in the night.

Nicolas unzipped the bag and took out the Stoeger STR-9S pistol. It felt good in his hand; the weight, the curve of the grip. He was a little surprised they had given him exactly what he had suggested.

The gun would do the job, that wasn't in question. The real question: could *he* do the job?

He would have to. *One way or another.*

In three days, either a man would die by his hand, or Océane would pay the price.

5

ST-JEAN-DES-PERTES

The lighting was low, and the warm, fragrant night air was seeping through the open window. Serge looked like he was on the verge of collapsing into a drunken coma, and Mallory wasn't far behind the older man. The wine was potent stuff.

The bartender collected their empties and pointed at the clock.

'*Fermeture*. Closing time.'

Mallory held up a hand in acknowledgement and raised his gaze to look out of the window. It was fully dark outside. The moonlight glinted off the ripples on the surface of the river. He realised he had no idea where Serge lived.

'Mate,' Mallory said, nudging him. 'We need to get you home. You far from here?'

Serge batted Mallory's hand away and mumbled something unintelligible in French.

Mallory looked up at the bartender for help.

'He says he has no home,' Laurent translated.

'Right. You got any idea where he lives?'

Instead of answering, Laurent pointed at the clock again.

'What does that mean?'

'It means I finished five minutes ago. It means it's not my problem.'

'Very helpful, cheers.'

Mallory patted Serge down and found a wallet and a door key. There was an old driving licence in the wallet, creased and warped around the edges. It had expired eight years ago. Maybe the address would be out of date. Then again, Serge said he had lived in the town all his life, and he didn't seem like the kind of guy who liked change. *I have seen enough.*

'Rue de St Germain,' Mallory read.

Laurent sighed and pointed up the road. 'Walk about eight hundred metres, turn right, up the hill, just by the church.'

With the Laurent's grudging help, Mallory got Serge to his feet and pulled one of his arms around his neck so that he could walk him outside. The door closed firmly behind them.

The night air seemed to revive Serge a little. After they had gone a short distance, he was walking more steadily, so that Mallory didn't have to support him as much. He would mumble in French, occasionally looking up to remember to switch into English for Mallory's benefit. He was slurring his words so much that it didn't make much difference. Mallory caught a few words here and there. He mentioned Océane a few times.

They took the narrow road on the right that the bartender had indicated. It climbed at a steep incline and Mallory could see the silhouette of a church steeple against the deep blue of the summer night sky. Serge was out of breath by the time they reached the top of the hill, and they had to stop and rest for a moment. Mallory looked back the way they had come, down to the road that ran alongside the river, and across to the other bank where the streetlights picked out the line of the main road. There wasn't a car in sight.

'Thank you, Mallory. I will go alone from here.'

Mallory was amused by his dramatic stoicism. 'I didn't walk all the way up that bloody hill to leave you here. I'm going to make sure you get home. By strength and guile, as we say.'

Serge laughed a little and tapped his forehead, muttering a motto that Mallory vaguely recognised: '*À la manière de nos Anciens.*'

The house was a little grander than Mallory had anticipated. A large villa with wood-shuttered windows and a wrought-iron balcony over the front door. Serge reached into his pocket and his brow furrowed. Mallory gently patted the pocket on the other side and Serge tried that one, finding his door key.

The house was entirely in darkness. Serge seemed exhausted now. Mallory glanced around for a light switch but couldn't find it. He lifted Serge's arm around him and guided him along the hall towards the stairs.

The upper floor was approached via a winding staircase in the corner of the living room. The gaps between stairs were open, ready to twist an ankle if you looked at them the wrong way. Mallory was glad he had insisted on accompanying Serge the whole way. He didn't fancy the old guy's chances navigating these in his condition. Then again, he didn't think this was the first time Serge had arrived home three sheets to the wind.

When they reached the short landing at the top of the

stairs, Serge grunted and moved towards the nearer of the four doors. Mallory got him braced against the wall and opened the door. There was a bed in the middle of the room and an old dresser. Around both sides of the bed were stacked piles of books and magazines. There was a desk with a partly completed ship in a bottle, a work in progress.

Mallory helped Serge out of his trousers and helped him get into bed.

'She is a good girl,' Serge mumbled in French, as he lay down on top of the covers. Mallory didn't have to ask who he was referring to. In less than a minute, the older man was snoring, his chest rising and falling. Mallory stood by the door for a minute, wondering if this was the only peace he could get: the oblivion of too much wine every night.

His concern for his granddaughter was real and acute. Anyone could see that. It wouldn't do any good to try to persuade him that he didn't have to worry, that it was natural for young people to leave and go out in the world. And that arguments between those who love each other are natural, too.

He closed the door over, leaving it a little ajar. His head was clearer after the fresh air and exercise, but he wasn't sure of the way to the hostel where he was staying. It might be easier to retrace his steps back to the bar and go from there.

As he turned back into the hall, he heard a soft chime. It came from one of the other bedrooms. He opened the door. The light of the full moon was streaming in on this side, illuminating the room. It was a contrast with Serge's bedroom, and he knew immediately this must be Océane's.

There was a hardwood floor and a metal-frame bed in the centre of the room, still made up with light-coloured sheets. Bookshelves lined the entirety of one wall. There was a triangular window that was open a crack. A small knot of windchimes hanging from the apex of the triangle was the source of the noise he had heard.

Positioned below the window was a desk with a small vanity mirror and a few accoutrements neatly positioned on top.

The bedroom felt very different from the rest of the house. Walking into it was like stepping through a portal into a separate location miles away. Where there was clutter and dust in Serge's part of the house, this room was tidy. Instead of the smell of mustiness and old cigar smoke, this room smelled subtly of perfume and fresh linen. A light breeze circulated from the window, teasing the chimes occasionally. Océane had been gone for months, but in that time, Serge had been careful not to let the rest of the house encroach on this space. Maybe that was a good sign. Deep down, he believed she was coming home.

The room seemed to chart different phases in her life: a row of well-loved soft toys were lined up on a shelf next to a trophy with an engraved plate declaring that Océane Fontaine had come second in her lower-secondary school gymnastics competition a decade and a half ago.

There were framed pictures on top of a bookcase that were more recent. Some were of Océane with female friends, and a couple with a dark-haired young man. Mallory glanced at them, assuming this was the troublesome boyfriend. He started to close the door and then something on the desk caught his eye.

It was a notepad, lying open. One of the visible pages was entirely covered with writing, the other down to half the page. He hesitated, and then curiosity got the better of him.

Other than the soft, regular snoring emanating from

Serge's room, there was no sound. The night outside was entirely silent. You could believe you were in a farmhouse in the middle of nowhere, rather than in the heart of a small town. People retired for the night early in St-Jean-des-Pertes.

The handwriting on the notepad was in a clear, feminine cursive. There was a date at the top of the left-hand page: 12 *juin*. His eye was drawn to the page on the right, where the narrative on the previous page continued for three lines and then there was a gap.

And then eight words that really stuck out.

J'aime Nicolas. Mais j'ai peur qu'il me tue.

I love Nicolas. But I fear he will kill me.

MONDAY

6

There was no regular bus service that stopped in St-Jean-des-Pertes, but Mallory was able to persuade the manager of his hostel to give him a lift to the next town, where he could get a bus to Vire-Normandie and onwards to Paris. The only downside to that was he had to be up at the crack of dawn, just as the sun was peeking over the treetops that lined the hill rising above the hostel. An early start wasn't usually a problem, but after a morning of hard manual labour followed by an afternoon and evening of hard drinking, it wouldn't have been his first choice.

Yves, the hostel manager, was a taciturn man at the best of times, and Mallory was thankful for the absence of chit-chat as they traversed the narrow road out of town. He leaned against the window and rested his eyes, asking himself again why he was doing this.

As though in answer, the image of his hand gripping the bottle neck in the bar appeared in his mind's eye. He had been a split second from beating the shit out of those two idiots yesterday. Maybe killing one or both of them. If Serge hadn't interrupted him, there would have been a lot of blood spilled in that bar.

It gave the lie to the complacency that had been building in him over the summer, and he realised the physical work he had been seeking out was a poor substitute for what he really craved.

That was why he was hitching this ride out of town. The two guys from yesterday would come looking for him. Wounded pride demanded it. And when they did, Mallory wouldn't hold back.

Maybe this was the real driver behind the Good Samaritan act. He remembered last year; helping Donno's mum and his brother. That had entailed more than a little roughness too, of course, but it had channelled that energy somewhere worthwhile, given him a goal to keep him on the rails. Perhaps that was what Serge had unwittingly done for him now.

The entry in Océane's diary might mean nothing, or it might mean everything, but either way he had to know. He would find her, make sure she was all right, and perhaps even persuade her to contact her grandfather to reconcile. He didn't doubt that Serge might be hard to live with, but he felt a strange urge to protect the old man. Perhaps it was simply a desire to pay him back for getting him out of that corner yesterday, saving him from his own worst impulses.

Mallory decided not to tell Serge where he was going. Doing so would only raise his hopes or deepen his concerns, and Mallory didn't want to do either. Instead, he left a short note on the dining-room table thanking Serge for his company and promising to drop by next time he was in town.

Once Yves's truck was out on the highway, the smooth motion and the hum of the engine started to lull him to sleep.

He jolted awake as they pulled to a stop. Opening his eyes, Mallory saw that they had arrived at the bus station. An ugly one-storey concrete structure with a coffee shop on one side of the entrance and a news kiosk on the other. Mallory thanked Yves and got out, lifting the backpack that contained his worldly belongings from the back seat.

At the desk inside, a pissed-off looking cashier with orange-dyed hair and thick-rimmed glasses sold him his ticket without saying a word. He bought an espresso from the coffee shop and waited the twenty minutes for the bus to Vire-Normandie to show up. The injection of caffeine helped, along with the fresh air. He felt his mind begin to sharpen as the daylight bled reluctantly into the overcast sky.

The bus pulled into the station, made a wide circle and pulled to a stop beside the first bay. Mallory boarded and sat at the back, force of habit again. Difficult for someone to attack you from behind in the back seat. Then again, Mallory had always been one of the kids who took the back of the bus in school, so perhaps the instinct was innate, rather than a product of training and experience.

Now that his head was clearer, he was surprised to find he wasn't questioning his decision to go to Paris. If the entry in the diary was as concerning as it looked, then someone needed to check in on Océane. If she wouldn't take calls from her grandfather, then perhaps it would have to be a stranger. And there was another consideration. The job Mallory had been paid for in St-Jean was done, so it was time to move on. That would have been true even without the encouragement from the two pricks yesterday.

He had a few weeks before his ninety days ran out and he had to return to the UK, and he had always meant to go back to Paris. This would kill two birds with one stone. He would eat some nice food, walk the streets, see the sights. And along the way, he would see if he could find Océane Fontaine and make sure everything was five by five. He sat back in his seat and watched as the Normandy landscape rolled by. This part of France wasn't so different from back home: rolling green fields and small, rustic towns.

The bus reached Vire-Normandie in forty minutes. A quick change and Mallory was on the move again. Fields gave way to a series of bigger towns and then to the autoroute heading south to the big city. They passed a sign that showed the distance: *Paris 206*. He would be in town in time for lunch, and then he'd begin the search for Océane.

A thinking exercise, after weeks of hard manual labour. It would be a welcome change of pace. And if Nicolas turned out to be a threat to Océane, it would be nothing he couldn't handle.

7

RIVE GAUCHE, PARIS

By the time the well-dressed man sitting alone at Table *Janvier* signalled for her attention, Océane Fontaine was regretting picking up her phone. Her manager, Guillaume, had called her at 6 a.m. on what was supposed to be her first day off in over a week. He needed her to come in, as two of the other waitresses had tested positive and were isolating.

Guillaume would not take no for an answer, so she crawled out of bed and took a test, almost hoping to see a second line appear. It did not. When she reached Les Douze Mois she found she was the only waitress who had turned up.

Guillaume thanked her briefly and then sprang the next problem on her. The morning's seafood delivery had not yet appeared, and there was a reservation book full of people expecting lobster for lunch. But they muddled through, and the time passed quickly and uneventfully, except for the infant son of one customer using his spoon as a trebuchet to fire a scoop of chocolate ice cream onto her black blouse. When the darkly handsome man asked her if she was ready to take his order, she assumed it was a passive-aggressive rebuke.

'I'll be right there,' she snapped, unable to keep the irritation out of her voice.

She regretted it immediately. The customer looked well heeled, even by the usual standards of Les Douze Mois. He sat alone at Table *Janvier* – all of the twelve tables at Les Douze Mois were named, and styled, for months of the year – and wore a perfectly fitted black suit over a cornflower-blue shirt. His skin was tanned and his hair was mostly grey with a few lines of jet black still visible, probably in his fifties. He had the look of one who had been an athlete or a dancer in his youth. She apologised for snapping, but the man was already waving away the apology.

'No, mademoiselle, it is I who should apologise to you. Take all the time you need. I am in no hurry.' His accent wasn't local. He spoke French with the hint of another accent, Swiss, perhaps. He leaned back and gestured out of the window at the Seine. 'I have the sunshine, I have the beautiful morning, I have this espresso. I have everything I need for some time.'

Océane smiled and reached for her notepad to take Monsieur Janvier's order. She scrawled a number one at the top. At best, the clientele in Les Douze Mois were brusquely polite. It was rare indeed for one of them to go out of his way to give her space, even put her at ease in a stressful moment.

She rattled through the specials of the morning, apologising that the lobster was unavailable. The man listened intently, his expression making it look as though he was carefully weighing her suggestions, and then said that he would require only two poached eggs and three slices of toast, browned a little longer than standard, and another cup of coffee.

She gave the order to the kitchen and then responded to the snapped fingers of a tourist at another table. An American, she was pretty sure. When she had dealt with him, she had a moment to breathe. The man in the suit wasn't looking out at the view any more. He was consulting a black notebook, holding it open with his left hand on the table while he made some notes with his right hand.

The morning rush had passed, and it was starting to quieten down. Even the rude American seemed mollified for the moment. The secret to making it as a waitress in an establishment like Les Douze Mois, Océane reminded herself for the hundredth time, was not letting yourself get rattled. Some days that was harder than others.

Even with the staff shortage and the absence of lobster, she had weathered tougher shifts than this.

She sanitised her hands. As she was rubbing the alcohol until it evaporated, she decided that it was her personal life that was piling on the stress. Nicolas had been odd for months. Their argument three weeks ago had been the last straw. Only now did she realise that she was no longer on speaking terms with the two men she was closest to.

Océane had thought, off and on, about calling her grandfather for weeks now, but with every day it became harder to pick up the phone. She regretted changing her number, because it meant that the ball was entirely in her court. Not that she thought *grand-père* would be any faster than her to pick up the phone, make the first move, admit fault. There was a reason she was so stubborn. It ran in the family. No, if a reconciliation was on the cards, she decided it would have to be in person. She had considered making the journey home to St-Jean on her last holiday, but other things had got in the way. Nicolas had been one of those things.

Ah, Nicolas. She felt less guilty about that. She had no doubt that the fault was overwhelmingly on her boyfriend's side. In the past few months, he had become a different person to the bright, funny, just-the-right-side-of-arrogant man of the world she had met at that premiere in Cannes. If she closed her eyes, she could feel the warm September night air on her skin, smell the lamb kebabs roasting in the charcoal oven. Nicolas had raised an eyebrow and told her that she looked like trouble.

The sound of the bell that signalled a ready order brought her back to the here and now. She collected the order for Table *Janvier* and took it over to him, laying it in front of him and asking if he needed anything else.

Monsieur Janvier said that he did not, and then added, 'If you don't mind me saying, you seem a little stressed.'

'You could say that,' Océane said. 'I told you about the lobster and—'

'You know Nicolas Devereaux, do you not?'

That caught her by surprise. The breaking of the boundary between work and personal was a surprise. How did this guy know Nicolas?

'That's right. He's my ... friend.' She forced the polite smile to stay on her face. 'Do you know Nicolas?'

'I know someone who knows Nicolas,' Monsieur Janvier said, a playful look in his eye.

'And you know that I know Nicolas.'

'I had dinner with my friend last night and mentioned I was coming here. He said Nicolas's girlfriend works here, and that she is the most beautiful waitress.'

Océane laughed. 'He's wrong, Simone is sick today. But flattery is always nice. And I'm not his girlfriend.'

'Nicolas is doing some work for us,' the man said. 'An important job, you understand.'

Océane said nothing, because she didn't understand. She didn't know what sort of work Nicolas would be doing with a man like this, or his friends.

'He is under pressure. He mentioned the two of you had a ... disagreement.'

'Did he?' Océane's voice was icy.

Janvier held up a hand in apology. 'He did not go into details. He asked me to apologise to you in person. He'll be back in Paris in perhaps three days, no more than four. You received the flowers?'

'What flowers?'

Janvier looked apologetic. 'The flowers delivered to the apartment this morning.'

'I'm ... I'm not staying with Nicolas at the moment.'

'Then we must make sure they come to you. I'll have them brought to your address, or here, if you would prefer?'

'No, thank you,' she said. 'That won't be necessary.'

'As you wish,' Monsieur Janvier said. 'I'll let you get back to work now.'

'Bon appétit,' Océane said.

On the way back to the kitchen, she passed Henri, the doorman, who was drinking coffee at the bar waiting for his shift to start. He was dressed in his grey suit and watching her approach with his usual hungry leer.

'Who's Monsieur Janvier?' he asked. 'You like the silver foxes more than us young guys, hmmm?'

'I like stomach flu more than guys like you, Henri,' she said, flashing her fakest customer service smile.

Henri shrugged and looked back at the customer, who was still looking down at his notes.

'Everyone's a critic. He seemed to know you.'

'He's nobody,' Océane said. 'A friend of a friend of a friend.'

8

Mallory yawned and rubbed an ache out of his neck as the bus pulled to a stop outside Paris Montparnasse station just after the stroke of noon. The outside world had seemed to shift and change on the journey from the heart of Normandy: gradually at first, and then more and more rapidly. There were more cars on the road, more people on the streets, more buildings jostling for position and blotting out more of the sky. More everything.

Mallory felt a little like a diver gradually descending further into the depths, acclimatising to the different levels of pressure. As the air brakes hissed and the doors opened and the driver called out the stop, he felt ready to enter the metropolis.

In fact, Paris was a city he had visited twice before. The first time on a school trip at fourteen, during which he got drunk for the first time, then again years later between deployments in Afghanistan. That had involved drinking too: an enjoyable forty-eight-hour interlude of which he had only misty recollections. He hoped his third visit would be a little more sedate.

There was a coffee shop across the road from the curved glass and steel façade of the station. Mallory bought a baguette sandwich and a Coke, plus a double espresso to knock the haze off the early start and the lengthy bus ride out of his brain. He sat at one of the tables on the pavement and watched the traffic crawl by as he ate. Fumes hung in the air, horns cut through the drone of engines and the rapid-fire conversations of the pedestrians walking briskly past. It had been too long since he had been in a big city. The noise, the smells, the visual overload was a world away from the last few weeks in the Normandy countryside. He relished the change, just as he had relished the peace and quiet. This was what life was about. Change. Contrasts. Difference.

Mallory checked his watch, a Bremont Argonaut bracelet that had survived unscathed through multiple deployments in Afghanistan. He wondered if Serge was awake yet. Something told him that the old man was a late sleeper. Perhaps he would have some good news later today.

Mallory finished his sandwich and sipped the espresso. He took out his phone and scrolled through the snaps he had taken last night of the pictures in Océane's room and the one Serge kept on his mantelpiece downstairs. Most of the ones on display in her room had been recent, suggesting she had flitted back and forth between Paris and St-Jean before falling out with her grandfather. The photograph Serge had shown him on his phone had been no fluke. Océane was very photogenic. In every picture, whether posed shots, selfies or candid pictures, she had a kind of effortless poise. Serge had mentioned something about her modelling, and Mallory could believe it. No wonder she had been drawn to one of the most glamorous cities in the world.

There were three pictures in particular that Mallory thought might give him a chance of finding Océane.

The first showed Océane on a wide Parisian avenue. Perhaps she was posing, but Mallory thought it was more likely the photographer had snapped her in an unguarded moment. She was leaning with her shoulder against one of the trees that jutted from the pavement. In the background, the trees marched away from the camera, spaced evenly apart. Océane had her phone in one hand and was looking down at it. With her other hand, she was adjusting the high-heeled shoe on her left foot. It looked almost like an image from a fashion shoot. Only the fact it was very slightly out of focus suggested that this was a candid shot, and not one of a series of posed pictures. She wore black. The heels were black, her tights were black, and the well-cut dress was black.

Mallory was no fashionista, but he could tell that the dress was a uniform of some kind. There was a small, subtle logo on the left breast, but it too was out of focus, so it wasn't possible to make out. It looked like the uniform someone at a classy hotel or a salon might wear.

The shops lining the street visible in the background were mostly names and brands that might appear on a hundred streets in the French capital. BNP Paribas. A pharmacy. A restaurant with an awning and street tables, but no visible name. The omnipresent golden arches of McDonald's. But there was one coffee shop called *Tatou* according to the green neon sign in the window. A quick google told him there was a Tatou on Rue de Turbigo, in the 3rd arrondissement. Comparing the map to the combination of chain businesses visible in the photograph, he was able to say with reasonable certainty that the photograph had been taken somewhere around number 400. There were plenty of hotels and salons around there, but no way to narrow them down.

He swiped to the next photograph – the first of two showing Océane with the man Mallory assumed was her boyfriend, Nicolas. It showed the couple at a bar, and this time both of them knew they were being photographed. They were staring into the camera and displaying two sets of shiny white teeth. So far, Mallory had found nothing in the background of this shot to give him a hint to where it was taken. There was a bar and a line of bottles on underlit shelves. The place was modern: lots of grey and glass. It was busy, from the elbows and shoulders of other patrons creeping into the shot. It could be anywhere in Paris. Anywhere in the world, probably.

In the picture, Nicolas had his arm around Océane. They were both dressed to the nines. Him in a dark blue suit and white open-necked shirt, her in another dress – sea-green this time – and with her hair up. Nicolas was a head taller than Océane. He had black hair and was deeply tanned. A little older than Océane, probably, but not much. Early thirties, perhaps. In contrast to Océane's smile, Nicolas's grin seemed slightly smug to Mallory's eye. Based on this picture, he didn't like the guy.

The third picture, like the first one, gave a clue to a location, and this one was potentially important.

This photograph had been taken inside. There was a window and part of a kitchen counter and a coffee mug visible in the background. An apartment, rather than a hotel room. Mallory assumed the apartment belonged to Nicolas, based on what Serge had said. '*She goes to stay with him in Paris.*' He remembered how he had spat the name of his capital city, as though he was an evangelist preacher talking about Sodom and Gomorrah.

In this picture, Nicolas was wearing board shorts and a white T-shirt. Océane was wearing a nightdress, and from the angle of her body, she was the one taking the selfie.

They seemed happy. Wide smiles, relaxed body language. That didn't really mean anything about their wider relationship. In Mallory's experience, people didn't document the fights with selfies. But he wasn't interested in the expressions here. What he was interested in was the background, specifically the window.

It was tall and thin, divided by mullions into six sections, framing the view outside.

In the bottom of the window could be seen the top floor and roof of the building across the street, suggesting that the apartment where the picture had been taken was also on the top floor. Hanging below the windows there was some kind of red fabric that could have been part of a flag or a banner. Above the rooftop, in the near distance, there was what looked like the clock tower of a church.

So far, Mallory had had no luck identifying the building. Google informed him there were more than two hundred churches in Paris.

'*Bien, monsieur?*'

Mallory glanced up as the café waiter cleared his cup away. He had close-cropped hair and wore a tight-fitting, white short-sleeve shirt.

'*Très bien.*' He held up the phone and pointed to the tower in the background. He tried to remember the word for church. As he was fumbling for the word, the waiter answered in English. 'You are looking for this church?'

'You know where it is?'

He shrugged. 'Atheist. If you want to know a club on the other hand . . .'

'Actually ...' Mallory tapped the screen and showed the waiter the other picture, the one in the bar.

'No, sorry. It's an expensive place, though.'

'How do you know that?'

He pointed to one of the bottles. 'That liqueur is three hundred euros a shot.'

Mallory whistled. 'Think I'll stick to the coffee, mate.'

He left a tip – respectable, but less than three hundred euros – and picked up his backpack. There was a Metro below the main station and Line 4 would take him north. In the absence of any better place to start looking at two hundred churches, he decided to start on Rue de Turbigo.

9

The Metro was cleaner than Mallory remembered from his previous trips. Maybe it was just that he was older and more observant, but there seemed to be more police at the stations than there used to be. That made him generally uneasy. As a rule, police tended not to like Mallory. With a couple of honourable exceptions, the feeling was mutual. Even though the car was only two-thirds full, he stood by one of the doorways and kept an eye on the other passengers for the duration of the ride.

Alighting at Réaumur-Sébastopol, he followed the signs to the exit and climbed up to the street. A busker was playing Soundgarden's 'Black Hole Sun' on an acoustic guitar and singing in a thick French accent. A school party of teenagers followed their teacher along the road, probably en route to the Louvre or Notre-Dame. Mallory took his time so he could keep an eye on the streets while raising his gaze periodically to see if any of the taller buildings looked familiar.

He spent the next forty minutes walking the length of Rue de Turbigo and the smaller streets surrounding it, alternating between checking the map on his phone for nearby churches and scanning the skyline. Nothing fitted the bill.

At a busy diagonal intersection between two main roads, Mallory stopped and watched as a large van parked outside a wine merchant and proceeded to unload three heavy crates. When the delivery was complete, the burly moustached driver, wearing a yellow hi-vis vest, paused on his way to the cab to berate the female driver of a Saab who had stopped, blocking his path. She leaned out of the window and swore back at him, gesturing at the line of traffic blocking her way. Mallory smiled to himself. Perhaps he had lingered too long in the countryside. He felt himself feeding off the energy and aggression of the city, like it was supercharging his batteries. That was something he needed to keep an eye on. Without consciously thinking about it, he had started to hope that this Nicolas needed sorting out.

The line of traffic finally cleared with a last chorus of horns and backing vocals from pissed-off Parisians, and the Saab moved, and the van driver pulled away. As the van moved out of Mallory's line of sight, it unveiled a building, like a curtain being drawn back on the stage. A gothic tower rose at one side of the building.

He had passed the church tower ten minutes ago, but he now realised he had been at the wrong angle. It looked completely different from this position, and very familiar.

Mallory took his phone out and compared it. No doubt about it, this was the church.

Five minutes later, Mallory was standing outside what he was reasonably sure was the apartment building where Océane had taken the selfie of herself and Nicolas. He consulted his watch. It was just before half past one. Not bad: under ninety minutes to find a single apartment building in a city that had to contain tens of thousands of them.

If this was the right place, of course.

The building rose up six storeys. It was the classic eighteenth-century Parisian design, with grey stone walls and tall windows behind balconies with wrought-iron railings. Years ago, killing time between missions at base in Helmand, Mallory had read a lengthy magazine article about Haussmann, the architect who had renovated Paris. One of his innovations had been the wide boulevards, designed to make it more difficult for mobs to assemble. Another was the apartment buildings which lined the boulevards, intentionally of the same design to create a unified urban landscape. The buildings were one of the most characteristic features of Paris, and this had made the thought of tracking down one single apartment all the more daunting. But the tower of Saint-Nicolas-des-Champs predated the Haussmann renovations; it was a unique landmark.

He examined the picture on his phone again, comparing the image with the building directly opposite. A hotel, in fact, and the small glimpse of red fabric in the picture was part of a vertical flag hanging down the side of the building with the hotel's name in gold.

This was the building. But which apartment?

Mallory had been watching the main door for ten minutes when he saw movement behind the glass pane in the ornate blue main door to the building. He moved towards the steps as the door opened. A grey-haired man in an expensive-looking suit appeared at the door, his eyes on the road, perhaps looking for a cab. Mallory stepped in close enough that the two of them collided.

He apologised and pointed at the building, before consulting the phrase book he had in his hand, making sure his French sounded a lot worse than it was.

'*Ici une* . . . Airbnb?'

The taxi driver beeped his horn. The man in the suit rolled his eyes but held the door open for Mallory.

Mallory tucked his phrase book under his arm and put his hands together in a gesture of thanks. '*Merci beaucoup*, mate. *Bonjour*.'

Another eyeroll and the man hurried down the steps towards his taxi. Mallory stuffed the phrase book in his back pocket. It was possible he would need it later, either because he genuinely needed to look something up, or because he wanted to look like a dumb tourist.

Inside, the foyer had a high ceiling. The floor was tiled in terracotta and there was a slight musty smell that contrasted with the suffocating traffic fumes outside. Three feet from the entrance, he saw what he had been hoping for. A set of mail drawers attached to the wall, organised by apartment number. Some of them had names attached, some were completely blank. Some of the residents had carefully printed labels, a couple had masking tape with a name scrawled in biro. Two apartment numbers on the top row. One of them had no label, the other one had a name: N. Devereaux.

The stairwell wound tightly around the core of the building. Mallory ascended the first four flights quickly, slowing as he got closer to the top floor and wondering for the first time what exactly he was going to say if someone answered the door.

He had decided against a direct approach. Banging on the door and dragging Océane out to ask if she was okay probably wasn't going to achieve anything worthwhile. Threatening Nicolas, when he had nothing to go on other than an old man's suspicions, even less so. At best Nicolas would call the police. At worst he would take it out on Océane. No. In general, Mallory liked to assault a problem head on, but sometimes some lateral thinking was called for.

His plan was to knock on the door and use the excuse that he was a tourist looking for his Airbnb again. If Océane was there, he could get a look at her, enough to make sure she was okay, at least for the moment. If Nicolas was alone, he would try to get a measure of the man up close. But if no one was in, that might be even better.

He had slowed his pace on the last two landings to take a better look at the doors. They had old-fashioned locks. As he rounded the corner for the last half flight, he took his wallet from his back pocket and took two lengths of rigid steel out of it. In his former life, he had to go through a lot of locked doors. Most of that time, entry was accomplished by physical brute force or by an explosive charge, but there were occasions when a little more finesse was needed, and those skills might serve him better in a classy French apartment building.

Mallory reached the top-floor landing and secreted the picks in the palm of his right hand as he made it into a fist to knock.

And then he stopped with his fist in the air, like he was making a revolutionary salute.

The door was ajar.

10

Mallory dropped his fist. He slid the picks into his pocket and glanced back at the apartment door opposite. No peephole. If Nicolas had a nosy neighbour, they would have to open the door a crack.

He took a step forward and put his ear to the gap. Nothing but the distant sound of the traffic outside. A window was open. He nudged the door open further with the back of his hand. It swung gently back without a sound, opening on a short vestibule and a long hallway with white walls and floorboards varnished in a dark brown.

There was a large bouquet of flowers on the floor next to the door. Fresh and fragrant, a recent delivery. The attached card said, *à Océane*. Definitely the right apartment.

The hallway was neat and tidy. A small table with a vase containing pink geraniums stood undisturbed at the side. Someone here clearly liked flowers. On the face of it, there was nothing amiss. Perhaps someone had just forgotten to close the door fully as they left. But Mallory had a familiar tingle at the base of his neck. The last time he had ignored that warning had been more than two years ago, in Faryab Province, Afghanistan. Three men had paid the price with their lives, and Mallory had been lucky to escape with his own.

Carefully, he lifted his backpack off and lowered it to the floor softly. He opened it, pressing his thumb against the zip to silence the buzz as it travelled along the teeth.

Keeping his eyes on the hallway as he reached into the bag to push past the balled-up clothing, he wrapped his hand around the comfortingly solid steel casing of the Maglite torch he always carried. A torch doesn't invite the kind of questions at security that a pistol or a hunting knife would, but it can be just as deadly in the right hands.

Mallory straightened up, gripping the torch.

He advanced down the hallway, passing two bedrooms and a bathroom. The door at the end opened onto an open-plan space, divided by a counter into a living room and kitchen. The window was open, the traffic noise filtering up from below and the curtains swaying slightly in the breeze. He recognised the kitchen units from the photograph. The window and the view were the same.

The living space had a couch and a television and a wide glass coffee table. The place was neat. Perhaps Nicolas didn't spend much of his time here. There was a piece of paper crumpled on the coffee table. Mallory unfolded it and saw it was a to-do list. Scanning it, he decided it was a pre-travel preparation list. Most of the items, reminders to pack clothes, to book the hotel, to charge phone, were crossed off. The bottom two items were

Maxim, 7 p.m.
Récupérer, 9 p.m.

A name and an action. *Récupérer* meant to retrieve or collect something. Mallory was wondering who or what Nicolas had to collect for his trip when he heard a slight rustle and turned around. The breeze had rattled the venetian blind on the opposite side of the room.

There were framed posters and pictures on the wall. French movies he had never heard of. A photograph of Nicolas on a shooting range holding a pistol outstretched. He looked as though he knew what to do with it.

On the far side of the room was a small desk by the window with the blind. Mallory walked over to it and stopped as he got closer. There were two drawers built into the top of the desk. They had been removed. One of them was full. The other was half empty, the contents arranged neatly beside it – the way someone would search a drawer if they wanted to replace items in a manner that would not alert the owner to the fact there had been a search. One of the items that had been placed on the desk was a photograph of a man in a grey suit and sunglasses. Someone had crossed out his face with a red felt-tip pen.

Mallory turned and moved back to the door to the hall. It was as he had left it, the door still ajar.

He moved to the first door, nudging it open.

Bedroom. Empty.

The second door. Bathroom. The shower cubicle had an opaque glass door. He reached for it and opened it.

Empty.

There was a soft exhalation and the click of a heel on the wooden floor outside. Mallory whipped around just in time to angle his body out of the way of the blade.

11

The guy on the other end of the knife was big. Taller than Mallory, almost as wide as the doorway. Ducking under the swipe of the blade, Mallory pushed past him as his momentum took him into the bathroom. He turned on a sixpence, leading with the knife again. Mallory reached to grab his wrist, but he jerked back, the blade seeming to dance in his palm, and cut a score across the back of Mallory's hand. He snatched his hand away and backed down the hallway. The adrenaline was building. More than adrenaline, a feeling of release. He fought the urge. He needed to keep control.

The knifeman came at him fast, not wanting to let him turn around and run for the door. A black leather satchel was at his side, the strap crossing his chest. He wore a black, long-sleeve T-shirt. Jet black hair tied in a ponytail. Brown eyes utterly focused on the job.

Mallory made a split-second decision. Turning and trying to run would just get him stabbed in the spine. He set his feet and watched the blade.

His assailant adjusted his grip on the knife, swept it back

and forward, feinting with his other hand. Mallory took two more steps back and then anticipated the direction of the next swipe. He raised the Maglite to block the swipe and felt the blade glance off it an inch from his fingers.

With his other hand, he reached out and swept the glass vase full of geraniums from the table, sending it straight at the guy's head. He got his arm up in time, but the vase shattered on his forearm, sending water and flowers raining down.

'*Pička ti materina!*'

Serbian, Mallory thought. Something about his mother. No time to get offended right now.

Mallory dodged a blind swipe and went on the offensive, jabbing the Maglite at his opponent's face. The Serbian somehow anticipated that move, even though his eyes were closed against the impact of the broken glass and the water. The Serbian managed to block it again, but had to use his other hand, the one with the knife. The impact knocked it from his hand and Mallory heard a thunk as it embedded itself in the wood floor.

Mallory heard himself let out a yell of anger as he charged and tackled the Serbian, slamming him into the wall. He was no longer thinking about each move. Something else was in control. The other man twisted around and managed to free himself.

Mallory pressed forward, blocking the man's path back to where the knife was sticking out of the floor. He swung the torch at his head. The Serbian ducked, avoiding it by a hair, and fell back into the living room, then ducked another of Mallory's swings and managed to get the fingers of his right hand around Mallory's wrist. The two grappled. The Serbian gripped the strap of his satchel and tried to wrap it around Mallory's throat. Mallory got a hand up in time to jam it before he could pull the strap tight, but he felt himself being pulled backwards. The Serbian had six inches on Mallory and at least twenty pounds. On strength alone, this was going to be a tough one. So Mallory used his size against him, pivoting and swinging them both around.

They crashed through the glass coffee table, scattering the cups and magazines across the floor. Mallory rolled off and got to his feet. The Serbian had mirrored his action and they were standing across the shattered glass remains, poised for action. A shard from the table had cut the Serbian across the cheek. A dark line of blood was running down his face and neck.

Whoever this guy was, he looked nothing like Nicolas. And Mallory already knew he didn't belong here.

Mallory tensed for the next attack, and then the Serbian did something he didn't expect. He turned and ran.

Mallory followed, grabbing for his shirt as he reached the doorway. The Serbian twisted and pulled the shelving unit by the door down on Mallory, who caught it and pushed it aside, hearing trinkets and glasses smash on the floor, clambering over the shelves as the Serbian ducked into the main bedroom.

Mallory made it in a moment later in time to see him exit by the window.

Six storeys down, was he insane?

But Mallory leaned out and realised the Serbian had swung down to the next floor and was climbing onto the balcony. Mallory scanned the balcony and the drop, calculating how he had done it and how to follow, and then changed his mind.

He ran back out into the hallway and got the door open.

He raced down the steps. The door to the apartment below was already open, running footsteps already on the stairs. At that moment he heard a surprised female scream and a clatter. Mallory increased his speed of descent, taking four stairs at a time, trusting in his natural coordination not to miss a step and turn his ankle.

He passed a woman cursing on her knees as she started to pick up an upturned laundry basket. A terracotta plant pot had been knocked over in the collision. She raised her head as he appeared and sent a few French swear words he hadn't encountered before in his direction.

Mallory heard the urgent chatter of the Serbian's boots on the stone stairs as he peered over the banister. From this angle he could see the foot of the stairs in the foyer. He watched as the shadow of the man passed the second-floor landing, then the first.

He lifted the fallen plant pot and listened for the footsteps taking the last flight, trying to time it just right.

It wasn't a large pot, but it was solid, filled with soil, had to weigh three or four pounds. Not much from up close, but enough to cause his sparring partner some problems with thirty feet of velocity built up.

Mallory let go. It dropped straight down. Mallory watched as it tipped to one side, the fluorescent light from the stairwell shining off the bright green leaves. He heard the last footsteps and saw the shadow lengthen on the tile floor of the foyer, just ahead of the pot.

The Serbian appeared, directly beneath.

And then at the last moment, some instinct made him look up. He managed to move just enough that the pot smacked off his left shoulder instead of his head. Mallory heard a cry of pain simultaneous with the smash of the pot hitting the tiles, earth and foliage spraying everywhere.

The Serbian swayed on his feet, clutching his arm. He looked up the gap between the stairwell and locked eyes with Mallory, the pain and anger white-hot even from a distance.

'Come on back,' Mallory said under his breath.

But in the next moment, he was gone.

12

By the time Mallory reached the ground floor and stepped out onto the doorstep, the Serbian had disappeared. He closed the door again and went upstairs. The woman with the laundry basket was nowhere to be seen when Mallory reached the third floor, sparing him an awkward conversation. He carried on up to the top and stepped cautiously inside Nicolas's apartment again. He wasn't expecting anyone else to jump out and attack him, but 'better safe than sorry' had saved his neck five minutes before, so it was a motto he was sticking to.

The knife was still jutting from the floor. Mallory bent and pulled it out. The sharp blade had buried itself deeply in the wood, leaving a scar in the polished surface. He held it up to the light to examine it. Decent kit. The brand of a stylised tree on the hilt told him it was a Böker. It had a three-and-a-half-inch steel blade and a handle that terminated in a steel ring. He remembered the way it had seemed to float in the Serbian's hand, changing position and direction fluidly. Mallory knew the design was based on the Indonesian *karambit* knife. Not the sort of thing an opportunist burglar would carry, even in a neighbourhood as classy as this one.

Not bothering to be quiet this time, he moved from room to room. He flung cupboard doors open and checked under beds and in the shower cubicle. When he was satisfied that there was no one else around, he returned to the living room.

Something he hadn't had time to register in all the excitement: a faint burning smell. It took him a couple of moments of looking around before he located the source. In the kitchen sink there was a burned sheaf of papers.

Part of one of the pages had escaped the flames. A roughly circular section burned on all sides. Mallory picked it out of the sink and carefully flattened it on the counter. Bits of charred edging flaked off, and he had to be careful not to tear the damp paper. It was thick, off-white notepaper, not standard printer paper. There was some handwriting on it, running into the curved edge where the flame had burned itself out. There were almost no complete words. There was a euro amount.

€50 ...

Fifty euros? Five hundred grand? Five million?

The next identifiable words made it likely it wasn't just fifty.

... preuve de décès ...

... Chance ...

... 10 août ...

Mallory stared at the notepaper, trying to work out what the hell it had said before it had been burned. It seemed to offer a monetary figure for something that translated as 'proof of death'. A hit? Who the hell was Nicolas? Certainly not just the dodgy boyfriend Mallory had come looking for.

And that second part. *Chance*. That needed no translation, but what could the rest of the sentence be?

You only get one chance?

This is your last chance?

Then Mallory looked closer. It was impossible to tell what word had come before Chance, but he could see what he was pretty sure was the edge of a letter *e*. There was no full stop, meaning, if the grammar of the author of this note was as good as his penmanship, that Chance, with a capital C, could be a proper name.

Chance. Was this 'Chance' the target?

Then there was the date. The tenth was only two days from now: Wednesday.

Mallory looked around for something to keep the scrap of paper safe in and found a torn open envelope in the waste-paper bin. He carefully slipped the paper inside and tucked it into his pocket. He didn't want to spend much more time in here, just in case the Serbian came back with another sharp knife. Or with friends. Mallory had come out of that scrape all right, but he didn't relish the prospect of a rematch.

One thing was clear: Nicolas was either in trouble, or he *was* trouble.

The peal of the insistent two-tone French police siren drifted into the room through the open window. Not close, maybe not even approaching this building, but a reminder that it was time to leave.

Mallory hurried down the stairs and left by the main entrance, letting the door swing shut behind him this time. He walked west along Rue Réaumur, slipping into the crowds on the pavement the way the man he had pursued earlier must have done.

Mallory made a point of not looking back until he had passed two cross streets, but he didn't hear the sirens any more. He slowed his pace to his normal clip and felt his pulse start to return to normal. The visit to Nicolas's apartment had certainly been eventful, but he wasn't much further forward in finding Océane. What he did know now was that it was more urgent than he or even Serge had suspected that he find her. Perhaps he should have risked spending a little longer in the apartment to see if he could find anything that might lead to her.

It was five minutes before something occurred to him about the envelope into which he'd slipped the burned paper. There had been some kind of logo on it.

He stopped at a small square with a fountain in the centre, sitting on the bench by the fountain and taking the envelope out of his pocket. The address was the place he had just come from, but the addressee was Océane Fontaine.

There was a small logo in the stamp above the address, a stylised number 12, with small print underneath.

It said *Les Douze Mois*.

13

Les Douze Mois. The Twelve Months.

There was only one Les Douze Mois in Paris. It was an upmarket brasserie on the left bank. The menu on Les Douze Mois's website confirmed that it was as expensive as its address suggested. Mallory reckoned he could just about manage an entrée and a bottle of sparkling water before he maxed out his credit card. Of more interest was the banner image on the website, showing a suited maître d' with the hint of a raised eyebrow surrounded by four glamorous female staff dressed in black. None of the women was Océane, but they wore the same outfit that Océane had been wearing in the picture taken on Rue de Turbigo: black heels, black tights, black dress. Right down to the burgundy embroidered logo, a stylised number 12.

Mallory took the Metro from the station at Étienne Marcel to Saint-Michel–Notre-Dame. He climbed the stairs to the street and emerged into the sunshine that had abruptly graced the city with its presence while he was underground. Les Douze Mois was a short walk away along the bank. Mallory looked across the Seine at Notre-Dame, still in the

74

process of being rebuilt after the fire. On the river, a pair of glass-roofed boats passed each other at a leisurely pace, the tourists waving across the water. A group of teenagers was perched on one of the man-made islands between the bank and the Île de la Cité, sunning themselves and drinking cans of beer.

The exterior of Les Douze Mois was relatively unassuming, just the width of a standard ground-floor unit. The frontage was red-stained wood with the name of the brasserie spelled out in gold art nouveau-style lettering. Two pear trees flanked the entrance, in massive planters. As Mallory approached, the door was pushed open by a grey-suited doorman. He wasn't looking in Mallory's direction, just holding the door as an elegant-looking couple appeared and trotted out onto the street. The man, late forties, wore a dark suit and a blue shirt with a thin white tie. The woman, mid-twenties, was in a red blouse and black pencil skirt. The man in grey waited for the woman to clear the door and let it swing shut, rushing to get ahead of them and step out into the road, holding a hand up to stop traffic so the couple could reach their car without the inconvenience of having to wait thirty seconds.

Mallory approached the door, stopping when he heard urgent footsteps behind him. The doorman overtook him. For a moment, Mallory assumed he was rushing to get the door for the new customer, but instead he reached his post and then clasped his hands in front of him, in a way that signalled no door was about to be opened. He had jet-black hair with a fringe swept to one side and gelled. In contrast with his expensive suit, he had a weaselly look about him. He regarded with subtle distaste Mallory's jeans and hoodie and the beard that could possibly use a trim.

'*Bonjour,*' Mallory smiled, reaching a hand up to open the door.

The man in grey shook his head and answered in English. How did they always know? 'We are fully booked, I am afraid.'

'That's okay, I'll get a drink at the bar.'

'The bar is also fully booked,' the man in grey said with a smirk.

Mallory took a step back and scratched the back of his head. 'I was actually hoping to speak to someone who works there. She's a friend. Océane Fontaine. Do you know her?'

'Océane is not at work today. Who may I say was calling?'

Mallory focused his eyes beyond the man in grey's shoulder and pointed. 'Oh, there she is.'

The man reflexively looked around, and Mallory stepped past him and pushed open the door.

'*Monsieur!*'

The glass door swung open on an interior that seemed too large for the space suggested by the entrance. The walls and ceiling of the brasserie were covered with ornate art nouveau designs. Tables were carefully arranged to maximise space without giving the impression of being cramped, lined along each wall and down the centre of the room, divided by standing globe lamps like miniature lamp posts. There were mirrors running the length of the longest walls, giving the illusion of greater space. Tasteful piano music was piped from invisible speakers. The tables were all subtly different in style but seemed to be grouped by colours. White and blue tones in one corner, then shades of green, then browns and yellows. It took Mallory a second to notice there were twelve tables and put the theme together with the name of the restaurant.

Every month of the year was occupied, so perhaps the doorman had been telling the truth, and it wasn't just that he didn't like the look of Mallory. Mallory hesitated at the door, pausing to take in the bustle of the restaurant, and then felt a firm hand on his shoulder.

Without waiting for the doorman to say anything, Mallory automatically reached up and gripped the fingers of the hand, crushing them together. Then he pivoted slightly and guided him around to his side. His face was a mask of surprise and pain, but he didn't interrupt the piano music by crying out.

Mallory clenched his teeth and willed himself not to continue with the next motion every muscle was primed to put into action: tightening his grip to break a couple of fingers and punching him in the stomach for good measure.

Not smart. The fight in the apartment had hyped him up. He should have waited a little longer before coming here. The urge to throw this guy through the window was almost overpowering.

Instead, he released the hand and tapped the doorman on the small of his back.

'I'll just be a minute, mate. No trouble, don't worry.'

The man in the grey suit was too busy examining his reddened fingers to reply.

Mallory made for the bar at the far end of the room. The bartender watched him approach nervously. Perhaps he had seen what had happened to the doorman.

'I'm looking for Océane. Is she working today?'

'Who are you?'

'I'm a friend of her grandfather's. I need to speak to her about a personal issue.'

The bartender's eyes flicked from Mallory to the door on

the other side of the room. Mallory glanced back. The doorman had disappeared.

The bartender stuttered a little. 'I ... I will pass on your message.'

'I would really like to see her in person. It won't take long.'

Then the bartender's shoulders relaxed and he stepped back from the bar, his gaze shifting beyond Mallory.

Mallory turned and saw the man in the grey suit marching down the aisle between tables on the left-hand side, a tall gendarme a step behind him. Great. It probably wasn't hard to find a policeman on the street in this neighbourhood.

Mallory turned and kept his hands visible. The clientele had noticed there was an intriguing scene unfolding, and the chatter had hushed, leaving just the muted piano music and the taps of the shoes of the approaching men on the tile floor.

Mallory wasn't going to give them a show. He had made a mistake at the door, and he wasn't going to compound it by getting into a fight with an armed cop.

He turned and lifted his hands up. 'Just leaving.'

The gendarme let him go with a narrow stare, then stayed at the bar to talk to the grey-suited doorman, who was gesturing at Mallory and complaining in a fast chatter that he still had the restraint to keep to a respectable volume. Mallory walked past October, November and December. As he passed, the people at each table averted their eyes and found something to talk about with their companion.

Mallory chastised himself as he stepped out on the street. Right place, entirely the wrong approach. He should have known not to charge in there like that. He couldn't help it, though. The doorman had pissed him off. He could have played nice and left a message for Océane. Now he had needlessly burned a bridge.

But as he was walking past the alley running alongside the building, he heard a female voice call out.

14

'Direct approach,' she said in English. 'I like it.'

Mallory turned to see a woman in a black uniform standing in the alley, outside what he guessed was the fire exit of Les Douze Mois. Her face was very familiar.

Océane Fontaine was holding a pack of cigarettes in her right hand. She had taken one out and was holding it between two fingers, unlit, as she regarded Mallory. She had green-tinged eyeshadow and her black hair was pulled back in a ponytail, with a fringe in front. She looked like she had stepped out of a movie poster for a '50s French film.

'Who are you?' she asked, after she had examined him for long enough.

There was no concern in her gaze, considering she was alone in an alley talking to the strange man who had come unannounced to her workplace to find her.

'My name's Mallory. I'm ...' He considered for a second. 'I'm a friend of Serge.'

'*Grand-père*?' Océane's eyes narrowed. 'He sent you here?' From her tone, she didn't sound exactly thrilled about that idea.

Mallory shook his head. 'No. I was in town anyway and I said I would check in on you. He's concerned.'

Océane snorted and threw her head back. She switched the unlit cigarette to her left hand and tucked the pack into the small pocket on the front of her dress.

'He doesn't need to be. And I don't think it would be any of your business if he did need to be. Who are you, anyway?'

'I already told you that.'

'That didn't answer my question. *Grand-père* doesn't know anybody like you.'

Mallory took a deep breath and reminded himself about not burning bridges. 'I should have called first, I'm sorry if I've caused any hassle for you with . . .' He gestured at the fire door and the brasserie beyond.

'Henri?' Her eyes narrowed again, this time in amusement. 'Did you hit him?'

'No.'

She tilted her head in a way that seemed to say, 'Pity.'

Mallory cleared his throat. 'Anyway, I'm sorry. I met Serge and got on well with him. He was worried about you, didn't know where you were. I was going to be in town anyway, so I said I would check you were all right. No big deal.'

'Exactly. No big deal. So call him and tell him I'm fine, and that I don't need a babysitter.'

Mallory hesitated. 'Actually . . .'

'What?'

'I think you might have something to worry about.'

He expected her to tell him where to get off again, but she didn't. Maybe it was something in his voice that convinced her he knew what he was talking about. She seemed to tense up. She put the unlit cigarette between her lips. Took it out again and looked down as she spoke. A classic tell. She didn't want him to see what was in her eyes.

'What makes you say that, Mallory?'

'I'd like to talk to Nicolas about it.'

'I can't help you with that,' she said briskly. 'Is that what this is about?'

'I went to his apartment. He wasn't there.'

She kept her eyes on the ground. 'I don't know where he is if you don't.'

'Someone else was there.'

That made her look up. He saw a flash of anger in her eyes. 'Who?'

Mallory held a hand up. 'Not like that. It wasn't a woman. It was a man with a knife, and I don't think he was there for a romantic engagement.'

She blinked. 'What are you saying?'

'I think Nicolas is in trouble.'

She absorbed this, waiting for Mallory to say more. But he wouldn't, not yet. He wanted to know why she didn't seem as surprised as she ought to be when told a man with a knife was in her boyfriend's apartment.

'Are you going to light that thing?' Mallory asked, eyeing the cigarette.

She looked confused for a second, then shrugged. 'No. I'm quitting. It helps to stand out here and hold it. I don't light it.'

'Really?'

'Really. Also, in this place – no smoke break, no break.'

A tetchy-sounding voice sounded from within. 'Océane!'

She turned her head back to the fire door at the sound of the voice.

'My break is over,' she said.

'Can I give you my number?'

Océane stepped into the doorway as someone approached, blocking whoever it was from seeing Mallory. He guessed it was the guy in the grey suit, Henri. Her instinct that he might not like to see Mallory hanging around outside was probably correct.

'Meet me outside Notre-Dame this evening. Six o'clock.'

15

With a couple of hours to kill, Mallory found a quiet bar within fifteen minutes' walk of the cathedral. The place was a dimly lit tavern with a nook at the back where Mallory sat on a wooden bench and nursed a cold beer. After the encounter in the apartment and the run-in with the doorman, he wanted to give himself a little space to cool off.

It helped that he had a problem to chew over. He took out the scraps of paper he had retrieved and spread them on the table, laid out like puzzle pieces. He had gone to that apartment expecting something quite different to what he had found. Where was Nicolas Devereaux? Who was the Serbian? How did it all relate to what appeared to be a hit job?

He moved the scraps of paper around and tried to think of different interpretations of what they could mean, but it was no good. There just wasn't enough information yet. Perhaps Océane could provide him with more.

At twenty to six, he finished his drink, collected the scraps of paper and stood up. He was no further forward, but at least the bloodlust that had been building earlier had subsided. The break had been necessary, if not productive.

As he crossed the Parvis Notre-Dame on the east side of the cathedral, Mallory walked across a stone circle inlaid in the paving in the centre of the square. In its middle was an octagonal brass plate with a star and the engraved words POINT ZÉRO – DES ROUTES DE FRANCE. The marker denoted that this was the exact centre of the city. An auspicious spot for a rendezvous. As he crossed the stone, Mallory lifted his gaze from the ground to the towering spires of the eight-centuries-old cathedral that towered above the square.

On his previous visits to Paris, Mallory hadn't bothered to do the tourist stuff. He hadn't taken the lift to the top of the Eiffel Tower. He hadn't crowded into the Salle des États in the Louvre to jostle for position for a fleeting glimpse of the *Mona Lisa*. And he hadn't visited Notre-Dame. He had glimpsed these places briefly from time to time on his way to the next bar. These attractions had been there for hundreds of years, he reasoned at the time. There was always the next trip.

When he had seen the great cathedral in flames on the news a few years back, the scenes had given him a brief feeling of existential angst. Just because something had been there for eight hundred years didn't mean it would still be there tomorrow. Take nothing for granted. Tomorrow is guaranteed to no one and no thing.

From street level, it looked like the Parisians were well on their way to restoring this particular part of the past, albeit with a modern flavour. White canopies sheltered the unfinished sections of the roof. The new spire was yet to be erected.

Mallory chose a spot at the edge of the square near the Seine that afforded a clear view of the cathedral's main entrance. Océane had not specified where to meet at Notre-Dame, but he assumed she would mean somewhere around here. It was Point Zéro, after all. She would have picked Notre-Dame because she didn't want him to wait outside Les Douze Mois, and this was the nearest landmark in Paris that even the most clueless tourist would be able to find.

At 6.05, he spotted Océane approaching from the south. She was looking around for him. Mallory let her get to the front entrance of the cathedral and waited another minute. No real reason, just force of habit. Don't be too predictable.

She looked up from her phone at his approach. She was tapping an unlit cigarette against the pack.

'I'd be careful with that,' he said. 'They're a bit touchy about setting fire to things around here.'

Océane rolled her eyes. 'Very funny. I can see why *grand-père* likes you.'

'Because he has a good sense of humour?'

'Because he has an inappropriate sense of humour. Just like you.'

'I wasn't sure you would come.'

Océane tapped the unlit cigarette on the pack again. Mallory could see that the end of it was bent and frayed. She would have to not-smoke a fresh one soon. Her eyes flitted away from Mallory and across to the bank opposite the Île de la Cité.

'Let's walk.'

They navigated the sea of tourists, walking east, away from the cathedral. Mallory decided not to beat around the bush. 'Do you think you're still in danger from Nicolas?'

Océane stopped in her tracks and looked at him, confused. 'Danger? Why would you say that?'

Mallory considered his words. He got the feeling that being too candid about the source of his concern might be a bad idea. 'Serge mentioned that you said you thought he might kill you.'

'That interfering old . . .' She sighed. 'He read my journal?'

'He, uh . . . he didn't say.'

'I was being dramatic. I didn't mean he would literally kill me, just that he drove me insane. I can't believe he read my journal.'

'So you're not scared of Nicolas? He hasn't been violent or . . .'

'No! Never. I don't want to see him again, but he's harmless. A harmless idiot.'

'The man in his apartment wasn't harmless,' Mallory said, thinking about the way he had handled that knife.

'Yes, I wanted to know more about this. Who was he?' Océane asked.

Mallory described the Serbian, mentioned that they had had an altercation, without going into the details. He watched Océane's face carefully for signs of recognition as he spoke, but if the man sounded familiar to her, she had a good poker face.

'I've never seen anyone like that,' she said. 'Who do you think he was?'

'I think he may have been there for Nicolas. Or perhaps he was there because he knew Nicolas would be elsewhere. I think he was searching the place and I interrupted him.'

'You say he's a Serbian. How do you know?'

'I don't, but how many non-Serbians speak Serbian?'

'I don't think Nicolas knows any Serbians. But he knows a lot of people.' She tried to slide the cigarette back into its pack, noticed its condition and crumpled it in her hand instead. 'This man. Do you think he will come back to the apartment?'

'I think that depends if Nicolas comes back. Do you know where he is?'

She stopped and leaned on the railing, looking out over the Seine. On the opposite bank, an old man was playing a banjo while battery-operated monkeys danced in front of him.

'*Grand-père*. Is he all right?'

'He'll be better if you give him a call,' Mallory said, not hiding the disapproving tone in his voice.

'It's not as simple as that.'

'No?'

'*Grand-père* is a difficult man. A strong-willed man. Sometimes it is better to leave space.'

'What about Nicolas? Is he a difficult man?'

She snorted. 'Oh yes. But a different kind of difficult.'

'Tell me about him.'

They crossed the Pont Neuf to the right bank and sat down on the terrace outside a café. Mallory bought Océane a glass of Sauvignon Blanc and himself a bottle of Perrier. The drinks lay untouched while Océane told him the story of how she and Nicolas met.

It had been at the Cannes festival. Nicolas was some kind of party organiser. It turned out he was also an athlete.

'He almost qualified for the Olympic team. In 2012, when it was held in London. Were you there?'

Mallory considered for a moment. 'In 2012? I was floating around Syria. Didn't have time to keep up with the Olympics. What sport?'

'Pistol shooting. Marksmanship.'

Mallory raised an eyebrow. Suddenly, he remembered the photograph of Nicolas at the apartment. That was what he was doing. And then he thought of the other things he had seen. The photograph of the man with his face crossed out. *Chance. Proof of death.* A picture was starting to emerge.

Océane gave no sign of noticing that it had got Mallory's attention. 'He was really fun to be with. He had all these great friends, we were always invited to parties ...'

'You're talking in the past tense.'

Océane caught herself and then shrugged. 'We had a fight.'

'Because he's a difficult man.'

'Yes,' she said sharply. 'This is not my fault.'

Mallory held up his hands in mock surrender. 'I said nothing.'

'A few weeks ago ... he started ... he became different.'

Mallory opened his mouth to prompt her, but was interrupted by a wrinkled woman appearing at their table, proffering a plastic-wrapped rose.

'No, *merci*,' Mallory said, waving her away.

She persisted, turning to Océane, telling her she was a *belle mademoiselle*. Océane told her to beat it, less politely than Mallory. The woman scowled and moved to the next table.

'What do you mean different?' Mallory asked.

'It was as though he was replaced by someone else. He was stressed. Quick-tempered. We argued. And not like it was before, it was like he was always angry. Three weeks ago, I said I was leaving. I expected him to call me the next day, but he never did.'

'Did Nicolas ever mention somebody called Chance?'

'Chance?' she repeated. She wrinkled her brow, thinking about it, and Mallory noticed there was a thin white scar over her right eye, almost invisible until she frowned. 'No, I don't believe so. You think that could be the name of the man you found at the apartment?'

'I don't know. Doesn't sound very Serbian, though.'

He remembered the travel to-do list he had found. Reminders to meet Maxim at 7 p.m. and collect something else at 9 p.m. He asked Océane if she knew who Maxim was.

'Maxim is an idiot. He's Nicolas's dealer.'

'You know where he lives?'

'Somewhere in Pigalle. I went to his apartment once with Nicolas.'

'Don't suppose you have an address?'

She thought about it for a moment. 'It was off Boulevard de Clichy, I think. Near a club called . . .' She snapped her fingers, trying to think. 'Pink Panther. Around the corner from the Pink Panther.'

They were silent for a while. Mallory thought about everything he had learned since this morning. He had thought he was coming here to accomplish a simple task, to soothe an old man's concern for his only remaining family member. Now it felt like it was turning into something much more serious. He couldn't walk away now. Océane was safe and well . . . for now. But something was going on with her boyfriend. Something that involved a trained killer, who might show up again if and when Océane and Nicolas were reconciled. He had to get to the bottom of it. And, as he had told Serge, it wasn't as though he had anything else to do.

'I want to talk to Nicolas.'

Océane snorted. 'You're wasting your time. If he wouldn't tell me—'

'People tell me things,' Mallory said. 'Sometimes they

don't need to tell me with words. Trust me. I'm not walking away until I know what's going on here. Maybe it's nothing. Maybe the guy with the knife in his apartment was just a burglar. But I don't think so. And from what you've told me, it could come back to bite you when you least expect it.'

'I'm not sure I want to know,' Océane said, and Mallory thought he saw her shiver a little in the summer air.

'But you need to know. Forewarned is forearmed.'

Océane picked up her glass of wine, which she had barely sipped, and stared into it as though it could answer her questions. 'I don't get it. You met my grandfather once, you said you would do him a favour. This? This is way beyond a favour.'

'It's not just that. Somebody tried to gut me with a three-inch blade a couple of hours ago. I want to find that guy again.'

That was the truth, but it was only a part of the truth. Finding the Serbian wasn't just about retaliation, and his being here in the first place wasn't a selfless act, either. Not even close. He needed a mission, a way to keep himself on an even keel.

She was regarding him with curiosity. 'And what will you do if you find him?'

Triggered by her words, images flashed in front of Mallory's eyes like premonitions. Blood. Snapping bones. Stabbing blades.

He kept his expression neutral. 'We'll have a polite exchange of thoughts on what happened in Nicolas's apartment.'

Océane rubbed her eyelids and the bridge of her nose with her thumb and index finger. A police helicopter buzzed low overhead. Both of them glanced up at it, watching as it circled the square and banked south. The sound of rotors always took Mallory back to his old life. Dust and combat. Océane's voice brought him back to the present.

'How worried should I be?'

Mallory took a breath through his nostrils, weighing up the question.

'I think this is all about Nicolas. But I think you should be careful anyway. Can you go back to St-Jean-des-Pertes for a week or so?'

She shook her head hurriedly. 'No. Even if I wanted to, I have a job. If I take off, Guillaume will fire me.'

'I would be more comfortable if you considered that. I know your grandfather would be too. If—'

'Don't tell him.'

Mallory thought it over. Short of lifting her over his shoulder and carrying her back to Normandy on the next bus, he already knew he wasn't going to be able to compel her into going home. But perhaps he was being overcautious.

'You're not planning on going back to Nicolas's apartment anytime soon?'

'Absolutely not. I haven't heard from Nicolas in three weeks.' She waved her phone at him. 'No call. I'm not the kind of girl who eats ice cream and waits for a boy to take her back.'

'So you wouldn't talk to him if he did call?'

Her steely expression cracked, just a little and only for a second. 'I don't know. He would have to have a good explanation.'

'Who knows? Maybe I can get that too.'

She snorted. 'Good luck.'

'Don't go near the apartment,' Mallory reiterated. 'Where have you been staying?'

'With a friend from work. She lives in Opéra. She's nice.'

'She lives in the opera?'

'No. She lives in the ninth arrondissement.'

Mallory didn't know the city well enough for that to tell him anything. 'How far is that from Nicolas's place?'

'About three kilometres. One change on the Metro.'

'Okay. You should be all right. Keep your eyes open. Look out for anybody hanging around who doesn't fit in. Stay away from anywhere around Nicolas's apartment. If you see anyone you don't like, give me a call.'

Mallory took his phone out. It was a cheap Motorola he had bought in Caen and barely used since. He didn't know the number off the top of his head. Océane gave him her number and he rang it once so she would have it.

'Right. I need to find Nicolas and work out what kind of trouble he's in.'

Océane gave Mallory Nicolas's number too, mentioning that it probably wouldn't do him much good. 'He never picks up.'

'I'll give it a try anyway. Sometimes you get lucky. Do you know any of his friends?'

She shook her head. 'Everyone always knew him at the parties, but . . . no one close, not really. He didn't like to have many close friends.'

'Is he on social media? Facebook or anything?'

'He rejects social media. He teased me for using it, said it was a thief of time.'

'Quite a poet,' Mallory said. 'Anywhere else in the city he might go? Favourite pub?'

'*Pub?*' she repeated, giving him a withering look.

'Brasserie? Boulangerie?'

Océane shrugged. 'We go to restaurants and clubs, but all of that stopped a few months ago. He was just alone in the apartment after that.'

'It looked like he had packed for a trip. There's no one else he could be staying with? What about his parents?'

'He never mentioned them.' Her expression was pained. '*Dieu*. Mallory, you must think I know nothing about my boyfriend. The truth was, he didn't volunteer information. I liked that about him. Only now, it's a problem.' She raised her eyes to meet Mallory's. 'You think you can just track him down? This is a city of four million people. How well do you know Paris?'

He pretended to think about it for a moment. 'Pretty well. I've seen a few movies. *Ronin*. The Pixar one with the rat who cooks.'

'Outstanding.' Her voice was dripping with sarcasm.

Mallory smiled, enjoying her disdain. 'I have a little experience looking for people.'

'You were in the military?'

'Is it that obvious?'

'I don't know. It is to me.'

Of course, because she had been raised by a military man.

'I don't think he's in Paris, anyway,' Mallory said.

'What makes you say that?'

'I don't think anybody had been at the apartment in days.'

She was silent for a while. 'Mallory, I think what we had was over, but I don't want any harm to come to Nicolas.'

'You want peace of mind.'

'I suppose so.'

'So does your *grand-père*. Give him a call. Tell him I said hello.'

She sighed. 'I'll think about it.'

'Do. In the meantime, just do what I said, stay away from Nicolas's place, and I'll work this out.'

16

'*I'll work this out.*'

What had the arrogant Englishman meant by that? Océane wondered as she walked along Rue des Martyrs towards Marianne's apartment. Most days, she took Line 4 on the Metro after finishing work at Les Douze Mois. If it was a nice evening, or if she wanted to think about something, she liked to walk north across the city. It was a good way to absorb the buzz, to remind herself of why she had come here. Before the job, before Nicolas, before any strange men appeared to warn her about Serbian burglars with knives.

Whatever else you could say about him, Mallory had certainly given her a lot to think about.

As she walked, she tried calling Nicolas for the first time in weeks. It went straight to voicemail. She and Nicolas had rarely talked by phone even when they were together. Most of their communications had been through WhatsApp. She opened the app and found their conversation thread. The last few messages in their conversation had all been in one direction, from Nicolas. His final message had been sent on 15 July at 3.57 a.m., saying only, *Je suis désolé*. She hadn't replied.

She tapped in a quick reply now, saying that she needed to speak to him and to know where he was. A single check mark appeared to show the message had been sent. She watched the screen for a while, but the second check did not appear to show it had been delivered.

Holding the phone, she remembered the other man Mallory had wanted her to contact. She felt guilty that she had not thought as much about *grand-père* as she should have done in the last few weeks. She assumed that their tempers would cool and one day soon she would travel back to St-Jean. She would appear at the house, and they would joust verbally a little, and eventually things would be fine.

But the argument with Nicolas had dominated her thinking for the last few weeks. Marianne had said something infuriating the other day, but Océane knew now it was infuriating because it held a grain of truth.

'You're not talking to your grandfather, now you're not talking to your boyfriend. Ever think the problem might be you?'

Océane had squinted and taken her index finger from the wine glass in her hand to point at Marianne. 'Be very careful, or you're next.'

Marianne was a rake-thin blonde from Kentucky, studying in Paris for a year, and Océane had admired her directness in telling Henri to fuck off on her first day when he asked if he could stroke her legs. They had been friends since then; these two outsiders in the city.

She reached the Place Lino-Ventura, a triangular city park around the corner from Marianne's building. She knew she had to phone her grandfather, and not just because she had promised Mallory. Perhaps *grand-père*'s instincts about Nicolas had been right, in a way. He was wrong that Nicolas was a danger to her, but perhaps *grand-père* had understood something about him that she hadn't been able to see.

She definitely didn't want to make the reconciliation call from the apartment, though. Marianne had many virtues, but minding her own business was not one of them. Océane didn't want to spend the rest of the evening talking about her grandfather and what had led her to give in and make the first move after weeks of being adamant that hell would freeze over first.

Océane came to this little park often, particularly at this time of year, when it got so hot in the apartment. She liked to sit and read. There was so much greenery absorbing the noise of the city that it felt like being somewhere else entirely.

She took a seat on one of the benches. There was a brass plate memorialising a man called Sylvain who had died in the late '90s. She wondered if that person had liked to spend time here too.

She took out her phone and called her *grand-père*'s house.

She took a deep breath and held the phone to her ear as it rang on the other end, looking straight ahead at the traffic on Rue Victor Massé.

It rang eight times, and Océane was about to hang up when the call was answered.

'*Allô?*'

Océane opened her mouth to speak, but suddenly found her voice paralysed. Hearing her *grand-père*'s voice was unexpectedly emotional. Especially sounding like himself, not the angry yelling that had pursued her out of the door the last time they spoke.

'*Allô?*' An edge of irritation this time. He couldn't stand unsolicited calls.

'*Grand-père*,' she said simply, regaining the power to speak.

There was a long pause, and this time Océane was surer than ever that he was going to hang up. Instead, he said something unexpected.

'*Mallory.*'

Océane let out an involuntary laugh. 'Mallory,' she confirmed. 'He found me.'

Serge joined in with the laugh. 'He is with you now?'

'No, he ...' Océane hesitated. She didn't want to tell her grandfather where Mallory had gone. 'He had to go meet a friend. But he made me promise to call you.'

'If you see him again, tell him he is a *lightweight*.'

'Oh *grand-père*, you should not drink so much.'

'And how can I remember that, when there is no one here to remind me?'

The reproving tone in her grandfather's voice cut deep, but she sensed he was opening a door.

'I have some vacation days later this month. I could visit, if you don't think it would be inconvenient.'

'Inconvenient? You have always been inconvenient, Océane. But I miss inconvenience. That would be nice.'

She grinned. They spoke for another ten minutes, and as she sat in the park talking and laughing, Océane felt that a burden she hadn't noticed she had been carrying had been lifted. She felt gratitude that Mallory had forced her hand. He might be wrong about Nicolas, but he had been right about this. They made arrangements for Océane to come home at the end of the month, and Serge mentioned, slightly sheepishly, that she could help him 'get things organised'.

She knew what that meant. The little house would be a mess. Plates piled high in the sink, the laundry basket over-flowing. She didn't mind. It would be good to come back home, to take care of *grand-père* again.

Once she had said goodbye and hung up, she leaned back on the bench and rubbed the back of her neck. She had been putting that call off for weeks. Now she had finally been pushed into doing it, a weight had lifted. She felt sudden gratitude for Mallory's intervention.

She walked the rest of the way to Marianne's apartment, stopping at her favourite boulangerie on the corner of Rue Condorcet to pick up some pastries. Marianne did not drink, so this would be a good way to celebrate.

17

Mallory wasn't massively surprised to discover that the Pink Panther was a strip joint.

Pigalle was the home of the city's red-light district. When the Allies had liberated Paris in World War II, the Yanks had nicknamed it 'Pig Alley'. A sprawl of bars, lap-dancing clubs, sex shops and more, incongruously laid out in the shadow of the Sacré-Coeur on the hill above. Mallory had already passed the Moulin Rouge and a place identified as 'Sexodrome' with two-foot-high, red neon letters. A woman dressed in a short black skirt and a pink fur coat was handing out glossy flyers outside the Pink Panther. She grabbed Mallory's arm and tried to pull him towards the entrance.

'Best five minutes of your life in there, *monsieur*, guaranteed.'

Mallory politely declined. 'Do you know a guy called Maxim who lives around here?'

She repeated the name and smiled knowingly. 'Ah, so that's what you want.'

She gave him a street number, directed him to the second turn on the left and told him to have a good night.

Mallory reached the second turn on the left, a narrow alley, and slowed down. It was dimly lit, and he thought about taking the torch from his bag, and not just for light.

The woman in the pink fur coat had told him Maxim's number was 221, which was on the left-hand side, between a shuttered launderette and a tabac shop. There was a buzzer for 221. He pressed it and waited. Going by the neighbourhood and the look of this place, he wondered if Maxim would be foolhardy enough to open the door after dark. Then again, it sounded like his business relied on being available around the clock.

'Qu'est-ce que c'est?'

The voice was wary.

'Hi, my name's Jeff. Nicolas said I should drop by.'

The lock buzzed and Mallory pushed it open. The stairs were in darkness, but he could see a wedge of light on the first landing where a door had been opened.

'Come on up, my friend.'

Mallory climbed the stairs cautiously. At the top was a tall, skinny man with long, glossy brown hair, a scraggly beard and a plaid shirt that seemed a size or two too big hanging over his bare legs. Mallory could smell weed smoke wafting out of the doorway.

Maxim, if that was who the skinny guy was, turned and walked back inside, leaving the door open for Mallory. He hesitated. The last time he had walked into a Paris apartment he had almost been killed, and this place seemed much more like the kind of joint where that might not be a surprise.

It didn't look like there was anyone who might want to fight, this time. He took a moment to survey his surroundings, then followed Maxim into a small living room where there were two mismatching couches facing each other across an Indian rug on which a teenage girl wearing an Iron Maiden T-shirt sat cross-legged, snorting coke from a copy of French *Vogue* spread open on top of an upturned Amazon cardboard box. She glanced up at him as he entered and then went back to her task without comment.

'What can we get you?' Maxim asked.

'Something a little bit different.'

'Different. I am intrigued.'

'I'm actually looking for Nicolas.'

Maxim raised an eyebrow. 'Maybe he doesn't want to be found.'

'I think he's in trouble and I'd like to get him out of it. Do you know anything about it?'

'Trouble?' Maxim repeated. He put on a mock serious expression. 'Trouble is what I specialise in. What kind?'

'Not the kind of trouble you smoke or snort. Somebody's trying to kill him. A big man, likes to use a knife. Sound familiar?'

Maxim grinned again. Mallory knew it should irritate him, but somehow he found himself amused by this scatterbrained drug dealer. 'You're going to have to narrow it down.'

'Did he say anything when he came by the other night?' Mallory said casually.

'Last night?'

'Yeah, last night.'

'He wanted some ...' he glanced down at the girl on the floor. 'Of the usual. And something else.'

'Something else?'

'Some Valium. He said he wanted to be calm for something.'

'How did he seem?'

'Same as always. Great. I love Nicolas. Everybody loves Nicolas.'

'Did he happen to mention where he was going?'

Maxim scratched his head, took his time answering. 'No. Wait, yes.'

'Where?'

'A hotel.'

'A hotel where?'

'I don't know. I heard him booking it, asking for his usual room.'

Mallory thought about it for a minute and took his phone out to call Océane's number. Perhaps she would have an idea of Nicolas's favourite hotels, though it might be a long list.

'You can't do that,' Maxim said when he saw the phone in Mallory's hand.

Mallory's brow furrowed. 'Says who?'

'No, I mean it won't work. No signal in here.'

Mallory checked the screen and saw he was right.

'How did Nicolas do it then?'

Maxim looked confused, like he was working on a challenging crossword clue.

'When you heard him calling the hotel,' Mallory said patiently.

'Oh. He used mine.' Maxim gestured over at a landline phone balanced on one arm of the couch.

Mallory looked from the phone to Maxim. 'Mind if I have a look?'

'What's mine is my guests'.'

Mallory picked up the receiver and saw there was a screen. He pressed one of the arrows on the keypad and saw a list of recent calls. There was only one from the previous evening.

A call made at 7.51 p.m. to a number beginning with 334. Mallory hit the button to redial.

A light female voice answered on the first ring. '*Bonsoir*, Hôtel Marseillaise.'

Mallory smiled. '*Bonsoir*. Can you give me your address there, please?'

'Certainly,' the receptionist said. 'Number twenty-one Rue des Braves, Marseille. Would you like to book a room with us, *monsieur*?'

'No, thank you,' Mallory said and hung up.

Maxim was looking over at Mallory expectantly. 'Did you get what you need?'

'I think so. What's the fastest way to get to Marseille? Can I fly from Charles de Gaulle?'

'Yes, I think—' Maxim began.

'Not today.'

It was the girl in the Iron Maiden T-shirt who had spoken, for the first time. Maxim and Mallory looked over at her. She had taken a seat on one of the couches and was leafing through the magazine she had been using earlier.

'Baggage handlers are on strike today,' she said, without looking up from the magazine. 'Next flight'll be in the morning. You can probably get a train, though. They're not on strike until next week.'

Mallory was mildly surprised that she wasn't French. She spoke with a refined Edinburgh accent, sounding more bored and jaded than someone who's just snorted a couple of lines of cocaine should sound.

'How do you know?' Maxim asked, an amused expression on his face.

She thought about it for a moment and shrugged. 'I always

keep up to date with this kind of thing. I move around a lot. Sometimes Paris doesn't do it for me.'

Maxim snorted and gestured expansively at the window, which looked out on the graffiti-scarred alley wall opposite. 'If you are tired of Paris, you are tired of life.'

The girl raised her eyebrows, as though considering the point, and then shook her head and addressed Mallory. 'You want the Gare de Lyon. You better make it quick, though, I think the last direct train is half-sevenish.'

'Much appreciated,' Mallory said, then turned to Maxim. 'One last thing. Can you call me a cab?'

18

Océane stopped just outside Marianne's apartment building to take the call. She was surprised to hear Mallory's voice. It appeared that he had made fast progress.

'Marseille?' she repeated. 'Why would he go to Marseille?'

'I was hoping you could tell me that.'

Mallory was on his way to catch a train, so he told her he would call her as soon as he knew anything.

Océane knew something was wrong when she turned the corner to the final flight of stairs up to the landing and saw one of her red socks draped over the top step.

Frowning, she climbed the rest of the stairs. When she reached the top, she saw that all of her clothing and belongings were on the landing. They had been roughly stuffed into carrier bags and boxes. Her laptop was propped against the wall by the door.

Taking out her key, she moved one of the bags out of the way with her foot. She unlocked the door and opened it. Her bedroom door was open. Someone was inside.

'Marianne?' she called out.

Marianne appeared at the bedroom door, holding a bundle of clothes. The pale skin around her eyes was reddened. She had been crying.

'Marianne, what's wrong?'

Abruptly, Marianne dropped the bundle and marched towards her.

'Give me those,' she said, grabbing at the keys in Océane's hand. Océane dropped the phone and the keys on the carpet, flinching back at the unexpected attack. Marianne quickly bent and snatched the keys up from the ground.

'What are you doing?'

Marianne's eyes weren't on Océane's. She was looking beyond her, out of the door, like she expected someone to be standing behind her. 'Get away from here.'

'I don't understand, I ...'

'It's your fault. You're why he came here.'

'Why he ... you're not making any sense. Who came here?'

'The man with the knife. He said he would kill me if I didn't tell him where you were.'

'What man with the ...' and then she knew. The man Mallory had told her about. But despite what they had both thought, it sounded like he was interested in Océane. And he had been able to track down where she was staying.

Through an open window, they heard a loud male voice yelling in the street. Marianne flinched. Then there was the blast of a horn and a car driving away. Just an outbreak of ordinary Parisian road rage, nothing to do with this.

Marianne closed her eyes. 'Please go.'

'Did he hurt you?'

She turned her head to the side and pointed to a small red cut on the side of her throat. 'You see this? He put his knife here and said he would open me up if I didn't tell him where you were.'

'What did you tell him?'

She narrowed her eyes in disbelief, as though Océane had asked her how gravity worked. 'I told him where you were. Les Douze Mois.'

Océane realised she must have left the restaurant before this all happened. Had he gone down there looking for her?

'We have to call the police.'

'He said if I called the police he would be back.'

'I don't know what's happening. I don't know what—'

'Just go!'

Marianne physically shoved her back, out of the door. She slammed it shut before Océane could think to push back inside.

Océane looked around the small landing at her belongings strewn everywhere. She would need a car to move all of this stuff. And, more importantly, she would need somewhere to take it. She couldn't go to Nicolas's place, that was for sure.

She picked up her laptop from the floor and rummaged in one of the bags to find her toilet bag. Suddenly, she had swung from sympathy and concern for Marianne to anger. She was scared, but she didn't have to do this.

She knocked on the door sharply, clearing her throat.

'Marianne?'

There was no answer.

'Marianne, my phone is in there.'

There were footsteps on the other side of the door. And then a voice so loud that she must have pressed her mouth to the keyhole.

'Go. *Away.*'

'Marianne, I'm going away now. But you need to take my stuff back in, I'll get someone to pick it up in a couple of days.'

She was hoping that in a couple of days Marianne might have calmed down, or Mallory might have worked out what the hell was happening. But in the meantime, she agreed with her now ex-roommate. She wanted to get as far from here as possible.

19

Mallory watched the blur of the city through the window of the gunmetal grey Citroën as it hurtled south through the 10th arrondissement. The driver didn't speak, not even to greet Mallory or check his destination, but drove confidently, weaving in and out of traffic, cutting down side streets whenever a jam appeared ahead. Mallory divided his attention between the screen of the GPS showing their ETA and the streets passing by outside. Various signs flashed by, the names evocative: Dunkerque, Magenta, Voltaire.

While he had been waiting for his ride outside on the Boulevard de Clichy, he had checked on his phone and found that the bored girl in the Iron Maiden T-shirt had been exactly right. The first flight to Marseille didn't depart from Charles de Gaulle until 7.30 in the morning, and the last train left from the Gare de Lyon at 7.36 this evening, in less than half an hour's time. In theory, he knew where Nicolas was going to be for the night, but years of trying to pin down AQ commanders in Afghanistan had taught Mallory that when you have actionable intelligence, you need to move as quickly as you can.

The taxi driver dropped him on Rue de Chalon, on the north side of the grand station, with eight minutes to spare.

Mallory rushed through an almost deserted shopping mall adjoining the station and on to the concourse beyond. He bought a one-way ticket on the TGV to Marseille, one eye on the clock. The door alarms were sounding as he passed the barrier. He ignored a yell from the guard on the platform and put on a last sprint and dived through the closing doors. The door caught his shoulder and jammed for a second, then he squeezed through and the door closed behind him.

A stylishly dressed older woman with cheekbones you could cut sheet metal with gave him a disapproving look. Mallory pretended not to notice. He slung his backpack off his shoulder and stowed it in the overhead shelf, then collapsed gratefully into one of the vacant seats.

The world outside began to roll by slowly before gaining speed. The lights on the Victorian platform of the Gare de Lyon began to blur as they left the station, and then they were out in the open night.

The train rolled south across the bridge over the Marne. The city streets soon gave way to suburbs and then open country. Mallory felt like he had been on the move all day, and it wasn't over yet. He would be in Marseille by eleven o'clock.

Would Nicolas be there?

20

MARSEILLE

Nicolas was not where he wanted to be. In every sense of the concept.

On his previous trips south, he had stayed at the Hôtel Marseillaise a number of times, and was looking forward to resting in one of their luxurious suites. After all, it would be important to be able to relax a little ahead of the arduous task that awaited him.

Still, the standard room they had offered him was pleasant enough, he supposed. And perhaps it was no bad thing that he was economising. The travails of the past few months had made their impression on his bank accounts as well as his sleep patterns. The overnight drive had taken longer than he had expected. Road closures had sent him on a long detour, and he had decided to break his journey at a truck stop on the A6 south of Beaune and doze for a couple of hours with the seat tilted back as far as it would go. He had checked in at the Marseillaise in the afternoon. After a shower and six hours' sleep in a real bed, he felt a little more like himself. The task ahead was daunting, but the existential despair he had felt on waking with the grimy dawn light in a desolate truck stop had lifted a little.

The past few weeks had seen him lose his appetite, so he was pleasantly surprised that he felt hungry after his rest. Perhaps it was a sign that he was ready. It was like this when he was competing. The nervousness began to evaporate when he was close to the contest.

Nicolas decided to walk down to the Old Port to get something to eat. Perhaps tomorrow he should do something physical, to take his mind off things. The receptionist told him that there were tennis courts a short walk from here. Yes, some time hitting balls always relaxed him. If he could find a decent partner, a couple of sets of intensive play would occupy his mind for an hour or two.

Nicolas walked out of the hotel and made his way north through the winding streets, breathing in the salty tang of the night air. There was a Himalayan restaurant at the port he particularly liked. He had always enjoyed Marseille. It was so different in character from Paris. So much rawer. Océane had not been as enamoured, on their single trip here. She said she wanted to go home. He had laughed and said that it was like the zeal of the convert. She was more of a Parisian than he was, despite growing up in the countryside.

The night air was warm, almost too warm. Everywhere he turned, people were enjoying the evening. Groups of young people drinking beer, families dining at open-air restaurants.

Perhaps it was as simple as the change of scene, but the anxiety that had covered him like a blanket for weeks seemed to have lifted. Marseille, with its warmer climate and sea air, almost seemed as though it was another country; gave him the illusion of leaving his problems behind. But an illusion it was, because it was in Marseille that he would have to carry out his grim task.

If Nicolas was in need of a sharp reminder of that fact, he got it when he emerged from a side street onto the Quai de Rive Neuve and saw the boats in the marina lined up across the bay and the Quai du Port on the opposite side.

Nicolas swallowed and fought an urge to turn around and walk back the way he had come.

The job was not tonight, he reminded himself. Tonight he was free. He should not linger on the future.

Not for the first time, Nicolas wondered if he should have confided in Océane. Would she have understood? He thought not. Could he tell her what he had done, once it was finished and they were both safe? No. Perhaps there was no way that he could do this and then they could go back to the way things were. But that did not matter. She would be safe, and she would never know how close things had come to disaster. That was enough.

Nicolas leaned on the railing along the edge of the bay and forced himself to look at the rows of vessels, bobbing rhythmically in the calm waters. He was no longer hungry. The confidence and positivity he had tried to build over the course of the day had been shattered.

'Hey, *monsieur*!'

He turned around to see a young couple walking past, arms entangled. They were in their twenties: tanned and beautiful and as carefree as Nicolas had been ten years ago. The boy had raised his free hand to attract Nicolas's attention.

'Don't jump, you have so much to live for!' he grinned. His

girlfriend giggled and gave him a scolding slap on the arm, telling him to behave.

Nicolas made himself respond with a smile. The expression on the couple's face told him how unconvincing it was. They looked away and quickened their stride.

Nicolas turned his back to the marina and gazed up at the imposing basilica of Notre-Dame de la Garde at the top of the hill, its tower looming over the city like a sentinel. He lowered his gaze and looked up and down the quayside. The restaurants were bustling, the patrons spilling out onto the pavement. Excited chatter and music mingled in the citrus-scented night air. He was seized by the sudden sense of himself as a ghost, observing the living but unable to join them. Perhaps he should go back to the hotel. Perhaps he might sleep again.

As he was making up his mind, his phone buzzed in his pocket. He took it out and felt a stab of ice in his heart as he saw there was an incoming call. The number was withheld, but there was only one reason why someone would be calling him on this phone. He hesitated, wanting to ignore it. But he knew that ignoring the call would have consequences. Everything seemed to have consequences. He answered.

A male voice began to speak. It was colourless, emotionless. As always, the American was not interested in pleasantries.

'You are in the hotel?'

'Yes,' Nicolas said automatically, then remembered the importance of being scrupulously exact and truthful in his dealings with these people. 'I mean, I went for a walk. I am near le Vieux Port.'

'We're going to need you to move.'

'Okay. I will go back to the hotel. Is there ...' He caught

himself. It was a bad idea to question orders, to ask if there was a reason why he should be in a particular place.

'No. Leave the hotel. We have arranged alternative accommodation for you.'

'Ah ...' Nicolas began, and caught himself before asking why.

'Go to the Hôtel California on Rue Longue des Capucins. You are registered under the name Apparu. Not under your real name.'

Nicolas swallowed. That last comment had been a rebuke. He hadn't thought of using a false name, wouldn't have been able to when he was paying by credit card. But how had they known? Of course, he realised, they could have called the hotel and asked to speak to Nicolas Devereaux. And they didn't want anybody else to know he was there.

'Hôtel California, okay. Do I need to go now or ... ?'

'Immediately.'

'Understood. Thank you for—'

The call ended before he could think of what he was thanking the caller for.

Nicolas stood for a moment staring at the blank screen of his phone. He had no control over his own existence right now. What had he been thinking? Believing that it was in his gift to go for a walk, to stay at the hotel of his choosing, to select a nice restaurant for dinner. That life, those choices, belonged to a Nicolas Deveraux who no longer existed, at least for the moment.

Slipping the phone back into his pocket, he started walking quickly back in the direction of the Hôtel Marseillaise. The few spare words of the man on the end of the call started cycling through his mind.

Immediately.

As he turned off the Quai de Rive Neuve into the side street again, Nicolas realised that without consciously thinking about it, he had broken into a run.

In less than forty-eight hours, a man would die by his hand. If Nicolas failed, the consequences were unthinkable.

21

The train pulled into Marseille-Saint-Charles station at three minutes to eleven.

Mallory stayed in his seat while the other passengers debarked. This was the southernmost terminus, so the train wasn't going anywhere after this. When the carriage had emptied, he took his backpack from the overhead shelf and slung it over his shoulder. The carriage had stopped on an exterior platform, so the warmth of the night was a surprising contrast to the air-conditioned interior of the high-speed train. Mallory lingered at the doors to watch the tired passengers lugging cases towards the barrier, where some of them were greeted by waiting family. Mallory passed through the wide concourse beneath the vaulted ceiling. The station was on a hill, so he exited onto a grand staircase that led down to the streets to the city centre.

The Hôtel Marseillaise was located in one of the clusters of meandering side streets leading down from the Corniche, the coast road. Mallory worked out the route on his phone and set out walking briskly south, grateful for the opportunity to stretch his legs after the three-hour journey.

Marseille had a very different vibe from Paris. It was a lot warmer, for a start. It felt a little more like a Spanish resort town. As Mallory walked he passed rows of restaurants where people were eating and drinking at pavement tables. The tantalising aromas made his stomach rumble. He hadn't eaten anything since the sandwich right before he had gone to Nicolas's apartment. He bought a giro kebab from a street stall and ate it on the move. It was hot and spicy and filling, everything he needed.

Mallory considered how to approach Nicolas when he found him. From what Océane had said, he was in good physical shape. But she had also implied he was flaky, easily led. Whatever had brought him here, he would be on edge. He was far from home. He had been under pressure for many weeks already, if what Océane had said was correct. Perhaps he knew already the Serbian was out there looking for him, but if even he didn't know the details, he knew he was in trouble. Perhaps the uncertainty would be worse. Added up, Mallory was after a target that was liable to be jumpy, make rash decisions when cornered.

Hôtel Marseillaise was a four-storey sandstone building perched on a rise above a quiet stretch of beach that looked as though it had been freshly ironed. The name of the hotel was emblazoned in blue letters just below the roof, tastefully backlit by white lights. There was a suited doorman with a peaked cap standing to one side of a blue carpet that ran from the entrance down the short flight of marble stairs to the street. The pavement in front of the hotel looked like you could eat your dinner off it.

Mallory had viewed the hotel website on the train and had already worked out that it wasn't the kind of place you could just wander into and hang around the lobby. He had booked one of its cheapest rooms in the name Harrison. Cheap being relative. One night would cost a thousand euros, a hundred extra for a refundable rate. He had a couple of thousand in cash, savings from his well-digging and wall-building pay packets, but he didn't fancy blowing half of that on a posh bed for the night.

The doorman straightened as Mallory approached, and stepped onto the blue carpet in front of him. Mallory reminded himself about Henri, Océane's overly aggressive co-worker at Les Douze Mois, and how sometimes it didn't pay to be too confrontational.

'*Bonsoir, monsieur*,' the doorman said. He was wearing white gloves and gestured at a lectern at the side of the door. He asked if he could take Mallory's name.

Mallory gave him 'Harrison' and said that he had a reservation. The doorman glanced down at the notepad on the lectern. He made a notation on the pad and then stepped aside.

'Have a wonderful stay, *monsieur*.'

Mallory smiled acknowledgement and walked past the doorman. Booking a room had been the right call; it had got him through the door with no hassle. Definitely more successful than his attempt to wing it at Les Douze Mois. If he was lucky, he would even be able to cancel before the payment went through.

The foyer was floored in marble and everything else was brass and marble and verdant pot plants. A bow-tied staff member stood behind the reception desk, smiling as he approached. Mallory had long since learned the value of taking time to plan out his next steps. The train journey had been time well spent. He knew he couldn't just walk in and ask which room another guest was staying in, but he had a couple of ideas for how to get that information.

'*Bonsoir*,' Mallory said. He said he had a reservation for Harrison.

'*Anglais?*' the receptionist asked. When Mallory responded in the affirmative, he slipped effortlessly into English. 'Excellent. Welcome to the Hôtel Marseillaise. We have you in a standard room for one night, is that correct?'

'Perfect. Before I check in, I wondered if I could reserve a table in the bar. I'm meeting a friend who's also staying here.'

'Oh yes?'

'Nicolas Devereaux. In fact ...' Mallory checked his watch. 'Would you mind calling up and letting him know I'm here? I'm a little late.'

'Ah,' the receptionist said.

'Is there a problem?'

'I am afraid so. Monsieur Devereaux has checked out.'

Mallory let his surprise show. 'Checked out? I thought he was here for a few days.'

'That is correct, he was booked to stay with us until Thursday, but he informed us he was leaving earlier this evening.'

The receptionist had not consulted his screen as he was explaining this to Mallory. Suggesting either that he was a human computer, or ...

'Were you the one who checked him out?'

'Yes.' His gaze moved from Mallory to the clock on the wall. 'Perhaps an hour ago? Not long.'

'Did he happen to say where he was going?'

'I'm afraid not. He seemed –' the receptionist paused and

chose his words carefully '– preoccupied. He simply settled his bill and left.'

'He didn't ask for a taxi, anything like that?'

'No, although I did offer.'

Mallory could tell that the manner in which Nicolas had left had intrigued the receptionist. It was as though he were angling for information about the guest from Mallory, rather than the other way round.

'Do you have his number?' he asked Mallory.

'I do, but he isn't picking up.' Mallory glanced behind him, then leaned in conspiratorially. 'I'm a little concerned about him, to be honest. Nicolas has been having some personal issues. It's why he wanted to catch up.'

'Ah. That is unfortunate that you missed him. He did not mention the change of plans to you?'

Mallory knitted his brow. 'No. That's what worries me. He didn't give any indication as to where he was going? Do you know if he planned to leave Marseille?'

'He said only that he had been forced to change his plans. I am sorry, if there was any way I could . . .'

The receptionist stopped. He had thought of something. Mallory raised his eyebrows, waiting for him to continue.

'Actually, he did say something earlier. It wasn't when he was checking out, but before. He asked me if there was anywhere nearby to play tennis. I assume he wasn't going to play at this time of night, but . . .'

Mallory nodded. 'Good old Nicolas. He's a hell of a player, by the way. We call him the French Federer.'

The receptionist laughed politely and reached under the desk, back on more familiar ground now. He tore off a sheet from a pad and placed it in front of Mallory. It was a map.

Slightly classier than the giveaway hotel maps Mallory was used to seeing. It was branded with the hotel's logo and didn't have paid ads cluttering up the border. The receptionist took a fountain pen from the desk and circled the position of the hotel, then made two more markings.

'I told him the nearest tennis courts are here and here.'

'Right,' Mallory said. 'Well, like you said, he isn't going to be playing tonight. Maybe I can find him tomorrow. If he doesn't call me first. This is really helpful, I appreciate it.'

The receptionist beamed. 'Please don't mention it. I hope you can find your friend. And now, I will be happy to check you in. Do you require assistance with your ...' He looked down at Mallory's feet, then back up to the single piece of luggage, hanging from the strap over his shoulder.

'Thank you, but I think I'm going to stay elsewhere tonight.'

Elsewhere was an altogether less expensive – and less salubrious – establishment. Mallory found a place half a mile from the Hôtel Marseillaise that had a vacancy sign, still boasted of having colour TVs in every room, and cost €59 per night. He had felt a little guilty when he saw how crestfallen the receptionist had been when he informed him that he wasn't staying there, but a saving of a grand was enough to assuage that guilt.

When he opened the door to the room at the Hôtel d'Or, he fleetingly wondered if he had made a mistake. Greenish light from a sign in the alley outside penetrated the thin curtains, illuminating a room about the size of a small garden shed, a single bed with what appeared to be biscuit crumbs on it, and a carpet that looked at first glance as though it had some kind of random, intricate pattern. When he switched on the light, he saw it was a plain beige carpet with several years of overlapping stains and damp patches.

But Mallory had stayed in worse places. Much worse. A night under the stars in a ruined, roofless apartment building south of Kabul in the depths of winter sprang to mind, but there was ample competition. He stripped off his clothes, dusted off the top of the blanket, bundled up his hoodie to place as a barrier between his head and the pillow, and lay down, closing his eyes and trying to ignore the way the occasional gust of wind made the fire escape outside creak.

He was in the right place, at least. If Nicolas was still in town, he would find him tomorrow. Mallory set an alarm for six. He wanted to make sure he arrived at the courts early.

22

A6 AUTOROUTE, SOUTH OF BEAUNE

Océane knew one thing: she needed to find Mallory.

He was going to Marseille, so that was where she had to follow. Typical. She hated Marseille. It was grimy, the tourists behaved worse than they did in Paris, and it was absolutely too goddamned hot in August. But then again, anywhere that wasn't Paris sounded good right about now.

She kept thinking about the terror on Marianne's face. The accusing look that said this was all her fault. She knew that wasn't true, but she couldn't help feeling guilty, all the same. At first, she had searched online for a flight to Marseille, but there wasn't one until the morning. There was a baggage handler strike, and she wasn't confident that it wouldn't affect the next day's flights, either. She had long since missed the last train. So she had the choice of taking a hotel room or renting a car and driving.

She knew *grand-père* would have had a seizure if he knew she was planning on driving eight hundred kilometres through the night. He was understandably cautious about travelling long distances by car, given what had happened to her parents.

Then again, if *grand-père* had seen the look on Marianne's face, perhaps he would not quibble. Océane certainly thought putting as much distance between herself and Paris right now was a good idea. She would stop for the night halfway, perhaps somewhere around Lyon, and get up early for the rest of the journey.

She rented a blue Peugeot 208 from the Europcar branch at the Gare de Lyon. The attendant was clearly in the midst of his wind-down paperwork ahead of the branch closing, so he hurried through the process with her. When he asked when she would be returning the car, Océane wanted to say 'I don't know'. She took the lease until Friday. That should be long enough.

It took Océane the best part of an hour to get clear of the city, but from there the autoroute was quiet. As she put more miles between herself and Paris, she felt better. She hoped the man with the knife wouldn't go back to Marianne's place. She couldn't help but resent her friend a little, for turning her back on her. But then she thought about Marianne's red eyes, the small cut in the pale flesh of her throat, and she wondered whether she wouldn't have done just the same thing in her position.

Who was the man with the knife? Mallory hadn't gone into detail about what had happened in Nicolas's apartment, but he had left her in no doubt that he considered the Serbian to be extremely dangerous. Frightening Marianne was one thing, but if this man had concerned Mallory, Océane thought he must be dangerous indeed.

What the hell had Nicolas got himself into? What the hell had he got them *both* into?

Briefly, she considered calling *grand-père* and confessing that she was in trouble. But she dismissed the idea at once. Firstly, how could she explain this to him, when even she did not understand it? Secondly, it would worry him needlessly. What could he do to help? He was an eighty-four-year-old man with two bad knees and a heart murmur.

But then she considered that perhaps *grand-père* had already helped her, in a way even he did not fully appreciate. His instinct had been right. She had been in trouble, and he had sent Mallory. She didn't know anything about the dark-eyed Brit, but even the short time she had spent with him reassured her that he was a man who would not let her down, would not give up.

Suddenly, she knew that her relationship with Nicolas had run its course. It wasn't just because of this, or even the way they had fought for the past few weeks. It was that Nicolas was not the right kind of man for her. With Serge as her role model, how could he be? Nicolas styled himself as a man of action, but when it came to it, he was weak. The difference between a man like Nicolas who liked to talk about his prowess, and a man like Mallory with his quiet confidence, was night and day. Océane resolved that once this was over, she would make a clean break with Nicolas. She didn't need him.

She thought back to their first meeting, at that party in Cannes last autumn. Guillaume had sent her out there to oversee a pop-up café operation for which Les Douze Mois had paid €250,000. The café was set up on a raft floating on the Bay of Cannes. The pre-screening party for the premiere was held on that raft, and there their paths had crossed.

Nicolas was charming, intelligent, athletic. Too good to be true, her grandfather had said when she told him. Maybe he hadn't been wrong. Then again, she had been sceptical herself at first. When he mentioned he had narrowly missed out on representing France at the London Olympics, she had nodded politely and hadn't asked in which event. Later, she had discreetly googled him and found that he was a well-regarded competitor in pistol shooting. Actually, he was being modest. He hadn't lost out on his place in the 25-metre rapid fire pistol event because his replacement was better, but because he had broken his shooting arm snowboarding three weeks before the games.

The film premiere was for some forgettable drama starring one of the usual dinosaurs of French cinema. The kind of film that keeps being churned out because the government funded them and because the *maisons de l'image* were required by law to fill a certain percentage of their schedules with French-language films.

'What did you think?' Nicolas asked as the credits rolled, leaning in close.

She shrugged and answered honestly. 'I prefer superheroes.'

He had laughed and told her that not only did he agree, but the star of the film had told him the same thing earlier on. Would she like to meet him? A pleasantly drunken evening ensued in the company of Nicolas and the fading film star. The film star tried it on with Océane a couple of times, but he was smoothly diverted by Nicolas. Océane sensed that he wasn't looking out for her honour . . . or not just. And she was okay with that.

They went for dinner the next night. And the night after that.

From there, it was a whirlwind. Nicolas lived in Paris, only three stops on the Metro from Les Douze Mois. His apartment was much nicer than the cramped basement where she had been renting a room.

Eight months since their meeting, Océane still wasn't entirely sure what her boyfriend's job was. He seemed to have a portfolio of interests on the go that kept him in nice hotel rooms and Cristal. Or at least, he did until recently.

The change had been sudden. One day in May, he had been supposed to meet her after work and they were going to go out to a new club, but he had never appeared. Hours later, he showed up drunk and dishevelled, his clothes soaking wet from the rain. When Océane asked what had happened, he told her he didn't want to talk about it. The next morning he apologised and said he had had a bad night and had been mugged. After that, things had never been the same. The suggestions to visit expensive new night spots dried up. He started letting her pay for lunch when they went out. She didn't mind that, of course. She had been a little uncomfortable about him paying for everything before that, and so this was fine. For a while.

Things had come to a head when Nicolas left his phone on the coffee table when he went to the bathroom. It buzzed with a message. Out of curiosity – okay, she had to admit, she had been concerned about an affair anyway – she picked up the phone. There was a message from an unknown number, the preview flashing across the top of the screen. She only had time to see two words before she heard Nicolas saying her name, a tone of barely repressed fury in his voice.

She told him she had just been bringing the phone to him, but he snatched it away from her, telling her not to spy on him.

She lost it, yelling at him that if he wasn't acting so strangely, she wouldn't have to spy on him. He told her to get the fuck out of his place. She told him that she would, gladly. She snatched up her bag and coat and slammed the door.

That had been more than three weeks ago.

It was a little after 2 a.m. when Océane stopped at a rest area just north of Mâcon. She was struggling to keep her eyes open. She took a room at the hotel and turned the light out. It had been the longest day of her life. She was exhausted, and she expected sleep to claim her immediately. But instead, she lay awake, listening to the hiss of traffic on the autoroute, watching the blinking red light of the smoke alarm on the ceiling.

She was thinking about red eyes, and a red mark on a snow-white throat, and a faceless man with a knife.

And then she was thinking about the two words she had seen before Nicolas snatched the phone away.

The gun.

TUESDAY

23

MARSEILLE

Mallory was awake, showered and dressed half an hour before the sun began to rise over Marseille. He headed north, towards the tennis courts the concierge had marked out on his map last night. As he walked, the streetlights winked out and the sky changed from dark blue to purple to light blue. Even this early, the heat was already building, the port city coming to life. Mopeds buzzed in the distance, competing with the chatter of the seagulls circling overhead. The scents of brewing coffee and baking bread drifted out from cafés as he passed.

After Océane had mentioned that Nicolas had been a competitive shooter, Mallory had done a little digging. Nicolas had missed out on being an Olympian only by having the misfortune to get injured. His sport had been pistol shooting, not tennis, but Mallory knew that competitors at that level like to get an early start. The tennis court angle might not prove to be much of a lead, but it was all he had. If he was to find Nicolas in an entirely unfamiliar city, this was his best shot.

Best shot. That made him think about what Nicolas was here for. As soon as he had put together what Océane said with that picture of him shooting, he had been sure that Nicolas was here to kill someone. But who? Marseille had a seedier reputation than Paris. He already knew Nicolas wasn't averse to involvement with drugs. Could he have got in deeper than he intended to?

The first tennis club on the list was in the city's 3rd arrondissement, on the Boulevard National. There were already two players on one of the four blue-coloured hard courts as Mallory arrived. Unfortunately, he could be a hundred per cent positive that neither of them was Nicolas Devereaux. Mallory watched two athletic women bat the ball back and forth for a minute or two, and then checked the distance to the other club on his phone. The two clubs were half a mile apart, so he could patrol the distance between them and stand a reasonable chance of seeing anyone who turned up for long enough to play a set or hit some practice balls.

An hour later, he had completed six circuits of the ground linking the two tennis clubs, seen a dozen or so players arrive, drunk a cup of takeaway coffee, but he hadn't seen anyone who resembled Nicolas.

He spotted an attendant repairing one of the nets on the first court. The attendant watched Mallory as he approached, looking for the sports bag he wasn't carrying. Mallory told him he had arranged to meet a friend. He showed the attendant a picture of Nicolas. He examined it and shook his head.

'What about yesterday?' Mallory pressed.

'No . . .' he began, then reconsidered. 'Actually, a man like this did come by yesterday. He said he would be back, made a booking. Maybe you got the time wrong?'

Mallory asked the attendant if he would mind checking. Nicolas, or someone who looked like him, had booked a court at 2 p.m. under the name Fontaine. Too much of a coincidence not to be him.

'Listen, I'd appreciate it if you didn't mention it to him when he gets here. I'm embarrassed, totally my fault.'

The attendant told him no problem. Mallory wasn't entirely sure that he believed him. He decided to make sure he was here an hour in advance of two, just to make sure.

Which gave him several hours to kill. He had got his caffeine fix and some early-bird exercise, but he hadn't yet had breakfast. He decided to head down to the Old Port to get something to eat.

The Old Port was the hub of the city. There had been a harbour there for thousands of years, and the bustle pulled in citizens and tourists alike, day and night. There was a line of high-end restaurants and boutiques, but Mallory fancied something a little lighter on his wallet, so he walked east until the parked cars and mopeds were a little cheaper and the chains gave way to shops with hand-painted signs.

Based on the appetising smell, he chose a small café and bought black coffee and a couple of croissants. He took them outside to where there was a bench overlooking the marina and ate and drank while he thought about his next move. First, he tried calling Océane. He didn't have much to report so far, but at least he could tell her he had reached Marseille and had a line on her boyfriend. Or was it ex-boyfriend? At first, Océane had seemed like she couldn't care less what happened to Nicolas, but she had shown real concern when

Mallory had told her about the man with the knife. The call rang three times and then he heard a distorted recording of Océane's voice.

'*Salut! C'est Océane, laisse un message.*'

Mallory did as the message directed and said he had arrived in Marseille, and would try calling later. Perhaps Océane was at work, or perhaps she hadn't woken up yet. It was still early. He hoped that she would be safe at her friend's house. There was no reason to think otherwise, and yet ... He would try calling again in half an hour. He would feel better when he had spoken to her.

He balled up the paper bag the croissants had come in and tossed it into a bin ten feet away. He looked across the harbour at the hill. There was some kind of castle or cathedral on the crest of the hill. Mallory didn't know much about Marseille. The closest he had come to visiting had been watching *The French Connection*. That movie was half a century old now, but one thing he did know was that the city was then, and remained now, a magnet for trouble. He wondered what kind Nicolas had got himself into.

Mallory turned his thoughts to the other troublesome player with whom he had crossed paths. With everything else, he hadn't had time to think much about the Serbian. He closed his eyes and felt the morning sun on his face, listened to the lap of the water in the bay, the cries of seagulls.

Then, one by one, he tuned out his senses. Faded them out one by one until he was somewhere else. It was no longer Tuesday morning in Marseille, it was yesterday afternoon in Paris. He was not sitting on a bench at the Old Port in Marseille, but standing on the landing outside Nicolas Devereaux's apartment in Paris.

He visualised nudging the door open, walking through the doorway. The empty hallway. The scent of the flowers. The faint sound of traffic from the open window. The tingle at the back of his neck telling him that something wasn't quite right. The feel of the Maglite in his hand. In his mind's eye, he retraced his steps through the house, going slowly, trying to visualise everything he had seen.

Being in an intense fight is a little like being in a car crash. It can overwhelm the senses, blur memories around the incident. Mallory had used this technique after firefights in Afghanistan. It was his personal version of a debriefing. Rerunning the movie in his head, analysing what he had done right and wrong, looking for the things he had missed. Seeing the details he had been too distracted to linger on in the moment.

He tracked his path through the apartment. Glancing into the rooms, entering the living room first. The open window, the framed posters, the faint smell of burning, the items carefully arranged on the desk. The crossed-out face of the man in sunglasses.

Mallory rewound the tape in his head.

Back to the door, ajar. That had been wrong from the start. No one leaves the door to their flat open. He hadn't known that there was someone in there, but he had been on alert from the moment he'd stepped inside. Part of him was expecting to find a body. Nicolas, or perhaps even Océane. When the man had attacked, it had been a shock, but not a complete surprise.

Fast forward.

Standing outside the bathroom. He froze the frame in his head. The polished wood of the floor, the curtains swaying slightly in the breeze, the vase of flowers. He had known someone was there on some deep, primal level.

Mallory walked through the bathroom door again.

He saw the knife hand swinging for him. He froze the frame. He stepped out of the action again and surveyed the scene as a dispassionate observer, examining every detail. The Serbian had a day or two's five o'clock shadow. He was over six feet, with black hair. Late forties, perhaps. There was an old, white horizontal scar about an inch beneath his left eye. He smelled a little of smoke. Not the fruity odour of a vape, but actual cigarette smoke.

Now that he thought about it, Mallory remembered the man's fingers had been nicotine-stained. He had seen that when the hand was in front of his face, wrestling with the blade.

The blade. Mallory didn't need to dredge his memory for the details there, because he had it with him in his backpack. The Böker was a well-crafted and relatively expensive weapon. The Serbian had known how to handle it, too. While Mallory had been able to take the knife from him, it was with the help of a little more luck than he would have liked.

Who was the man, and why was he in Nicolas's apartment? The displaced items suggested he had been searching the place, but had that been his only reason for being there? The knife said that he had either come to use it, or was anticipating trouble.

And how did it fit with the burned note, and the theory that Nicolas was planning to kill someone?

He pictured the yellowed fingers again. The other time he had seen them close up, trying to tighten the strap of his satchel around Mallory's throat.

What was in the satchel? Something he had taken from Nicolas's apartment? Or perhaps the opposite. Mallory thought about the orderly way things had been placed on the desk. He had assumed a search. What if it hadn't been a search, or not just that? What if he had brought something *with him*?

The picture of the man with white hair, his face crossed out. If Nicolas was really planning to kill him, why would he leave this out in the open like that?

Mallory opened his eyes and let his senses ebb back. The warmth of the sun, the chatter of the seagulls, the lapping of the water.

It was after ten o'clock. Still a few hours to kill before it was time to go back to the tennis courts to see if he could find Nicolas. Mallory thought about returning to his hotel, but the idea of spending more time than necessary in the damp, airless room did not appeal. He started walking back the way he had come, in the direction of the marina. The sun was rising higher, heating the pavements and throwing glare from reflective surfaces. Mallory bought a cheap pair of sunglasses from a stall.

A raised voice attracted his attention as he walked along the quayside. He turned his head in the direction of the sound to see a deeply tanned woman in a minuscule turquoise bathing suit yelling at a workman who was carrying out some kind of repair on the engine of one of the boats in the marina. The workman raised his hands and said something too quiet to hear, but evidently it wasn't what the woman in the bikini wanted to hear. She got louder, the words coming too fast for Mallory to attempt to keep up. Another tanned figure in blue terrycloth shorts, the boyfriend, Mallory was guessing, was standing a few steps back from the woman, as though keeping his distance from a raging inferno.

Mallory smiled and moved on. The boats in the marina came in all shapes and sizes, from battered fishing vessels to gleaming yachts in what Mallory assumed were the more expensive berths. The closer to this part of the harbour, the more expensive the vessels.

Up ahead, he saw two men who looked like they were waiting to board one of the really big yachts. He paused a second and took a closer look. Something wasn't right. It was the middle of August; thirty Celsius already and rising. Everyone else out here was wearing swimwear or shorts and T-shirts at the most. These two were in suits and sunglasses. Even at a distance of a hundred yards, Mallory could see the light glistening off the sheen of sweat on the forehead of the closest one. And even without their climate-inappropriate attire, they didn't look like the kind of people who could afford to spend all day lounging around on a yacht.

Guards.

Slowing his pace, he studied the pair. Neither man was looking in his direction. One of them was turned to face the yacht. He seemed to be inspecting the activity on board, where two men in work clothes were stringing fairy lights around the open section of deck towards the bow. The other had his hands on his hips and was looking away from Mallory, down the street.

The second guard turned to look in Mallory's direction. Mallory, ready for this, looked away and continued walking. But before he looked away, he saw a flash of sunlight reflecting off something metal beneath the second man's jacket.

Plainclothes cops, or private security, he guessed. Maybe

the yacht owner was some kind of big cheese. Mallory didn't know much about the economics of yachts, but from the size of that thing, he decided whoever owned it would have to be a particularly *grand fromage.*

The guard turned back to look in the other direction again. His colleague lost interest in what was going on aboard and turned back to the shore. They seemed bored, not expecting any trouble.

Mallory was closer now, within fifty yards. His sunglasses allowed him to turn his head as though he was perusing the store fronts, while keeping his eyes on the two men. If they were any good at all at their jobs, they would notice him in a moment or two. Mallory was always noticeable to security personnel and police. In years past, before hipsters in every coffee house and record store on the planet had suddenly adopted the look, he had put it down to the beard and the military tattoos on his forearms. But even now, he drew those wary looks. He supposed that part of it was being a physically fit male, but he thought a lot of it was something more instinctive. Something innate in the body language and in the eyes. People whose job it is to look out for trouble homed in on him.

And often, he liked that.

Now that he was closer, he didn't think the two men were police. They didn't have the right official look. Again, Mallory couldn't put his finger on what it was. It was instinctive. He got an altogether different vibe from these two: they were on the other side of the law.

He liked that more.

Mallory saw movement in the corner of his eye and whipped his head round in time to see a kid on an e-scooter whizzing past him with about an inch to spare. He shook his head and watched as the kid continued along the street, waving at two teenage girls standing outside an ice-cream parlour. And then the rider made a mistake. He got a little too close to the gangway to the yacht. The bigger of the two guards stepped out into the scooter boy's path and roughly shoved him.

The kid yelped and swerved before losing his balance and tumbling onto the street. Mallory winced as he saw a bright red scrape on the kid's knee dripping blood.

'*Sors d'ici!*' the smaller guard yelled. *Get out of here.*

The kid looked up from his bloody knee, mouth open to protest, then apparently thought better of it. He settled for a surly glance and got to his feet, wiping the blood from his knee with his palm and checking his scooter for damage.

'*Maintenant!*' the first guard asserted.

The kid started pushing the scooter away, shaking his head. The teenage girls called after him, asking if he was okay. He ignored them and quickened his pace. The two guards watched him for another few seconds and then exchanged a glance. The big one said something and the other one laughed.

Mallory was almost abreast of them now. Something was rising in him. The overpowering urge to wipe smug bully smirks off a couple of sweaty faces. He struggled to contain it as he moved out a little bit to give the two men a wide berth. The yacht was even more impressive up close; had to be a two-hundred-footer at least. The hull was white, with an aquamarine stripe just above the waterline. Rectangular portholes outlined in the same colour lined the hull below the main deck. There were another two decks above that one, each set back from the one before. Near the bow was the yacht's International Maritime Organization number and its name, carefully painted in cursive.

Mallory stopped.

He read the name of the boat again, just to make sure he hadn't imagined it. The energy in him found its focus.

The name was *La Deuxième Chance*.

24

Mallory took his eyes from the painted name on the hull of the yacht to see that the shorter of the two guards had finally registered his approach. Distracted, he had got a little too close.

The guard was staring straight at Mallory. Without moving his gaze, he tapped his larger colleague on the arm. The bigger one turned to look at Mallory.

Mallory smiled. *'Joli bateau.'* Nice boat.

Neither guard returned the smile.

The big one swept his arm to indicate Mallory should keep walking. *'Avancer.'*

Mallory obliged. He passed by the two guards and turned his head to look at the storefronts again. He was just a harmless tourist, politely passing comment on a nice boat. Nothing to worry about. The angle of the light on the store windows showed the two men reflected. Both of them were still watching him.

La Deuxième Chance: the Second Chance.

Chance was a boat, not a person. Whatever Nicolas was

here to do, it concerned the luxury yacht currently moored at the berth behind him. Mallory was certain of it, and the fact that two heavies were guarding the gangway only made him more certain.

The reflective surfaces ran out as Mallory passed a bar that had no windows, just a decked area that spilled out onto the promenade. Mallory resisted the urge to look behind him. There was a coach parked at the next corner, a group of elderly tourists climbing carefully down and congregating on the pavement. Mallory weaved through the crowd and took a sharp turn onto the street that led north, away from the harbour. He quickened his pace and took the next left, into an alley that ran between two high-sided buildings. Washing lines spanned the gap three storeys above him, colourful garments and towels swaying in the breeze. A set of windchimes tinkled unseen in an open window above. He made another turn into the next alley and then stopped.

Ten feet from him was another person who was not dressed appropriately for the climate. A woman, this time.

She was slim and tall, wearing a grey suit, her blond hair tied severely back. There was no bulge beneath her jacket, because the gun was in her hand. As Mallory emerged, she trained it on him.

'*Arrêtez.*'

Mallory glanced back the way he had come, then thought better of it. It would take him a second or two to reach cover. Enough time for a moderately well-aimed shot to find its mark. Besides, he had the feeling reinforcements would be coming that way. Instead, he tried on a bemused expression. That sensation, the energy, was back.

The woman was watching him with an unblinking gaze.

Her eyes were a pale green, and they seemed to cut right through him with their intensity.

'Whoa. You can have my wallet, I don't want any trouble ... let me ...' He started to take his backpack from his shoulders, but the woman in the suit shook her head and adjusted her aim on Mallory.

She put her left hand to her ear, where Mallory could see a wire extending from under her collar. She spoke quickly to someone on the other end of the line. Then she dropped her hand and appraised Mallory.

'Who are you?' she said in English.

'I'm no one, I'm just here on holiday. From the UK.'

Mallory heard running footsteps from the alley. He had been right. The boys at the boat had obviously contacted this woman and told her to intercept.

Mallory turned slowly, not making any sudden moves, to see the smaller of the two guards from the boat sprinting up the alley. His gun was in his hand too. His face was red and as his jacket moved, Mallory could see dark sweat patches under the arms.

The guard could see Mallory already had his hands up, so he didn't bother to raise his gun.

Switching back to French, the woman holding the gun on Mallory asked the other one if this was the man who'd been staring at the yacht. He said that it was. He looked flustered and pissed off after having to run in the heat.

'Listen, I think there's been some misunderstanding here,' Mallory said, trying to sound scared. '*Je ne parle pas français.* I'm on holiday. Uh, *je suis en vacances*?'

'Who are you?' the blond woman demanded again.

'I'm Graham. Graham Chapman. From Leicester.'

'Why were you looking at the yacht?'

'What yacht?'

'The yacht back there. We saw you.'

'The big one?' Mallory asked. 'I just thought it was nice. It's a free country, I can look at—'

'Shut up,' she said.

The woman and the guard from the boat exchanged a few more words in French. The woman told the man to frisk Mallory. That told him that she had seniority.

'Against the wall,' he said.

Moving deliberately slowly, Mallory put his hands against the wall. The guard moved in and put his gun against the nape of Mallory's neck. He tensed. He couldn't risk trying anything in this position. Even if he moved faster than this guy, the gun could go off.

With his other hand, the guard started to pat him down. There was nothing in Mallory's pockets except a few euros and the key to his hotel room. The man took these out and examined them. There was no logo on the hotel key, so that was one less thing to worry about. He dropped the contents of Mallory's pocket to the ground and tapped on his backpack.

'Open this up.'

'My backpack?'

'Yes, your fucking backpack. Are you stupid?'

Mallory turned around, making it look as though he had to do that to get the backpack off. He kept talking, trying to sound terrified.

'Look, I didn't mean any harm. I don't want any trouble. I am very sorry.'

He noticed the woman was squinting at the military tattoos on his arms. Perhaps that was what had caught her attention. Or perhaps they just *really* didn't like anyone getting too close to their boat, like the kid on the scooter. Or perhaps it was the usual: Mallory looked like trouble.

He glanced from the man frisking him to the woman, who was holding the gun on him, making sure he had a good fix on their relative positions. When they found his passport, they would know he had lied about his name.

He placed his bag on the ground, carefully. Maybe there was still a chance he could walk away from this without further drama. And if there wasn't a chance? Maybe that would be okay too.

The man went down on one knee and ran his hand over the backpack, then glanced over at his partner to make sure she had her gun on him. She did, but Mallory could see she had loosened up a little since the other man had arrived and started frisking him. A common mistake. One person with a gun on you can be more dangerous than two. With two, the responsibility is divided.

Then, he reached into the bag. He pulled out the roughly folded change of clothing from the top of the bag. Then Mallory remembered what else was in there, besides his passport. He was still carrying the Böker knife from Nicolas's apartment.

'*Qu'est-ce que c'est?*' The crouching man pulled the knife from the bag and examined it. Clearly it was not what he had expected to find. He turned slightly to hold it up so the woman could see. She took her focus off Mallory to look at the knife.

A moment's lapse in concentration for both. But a moment was all Mallory needed.

He dropped his hands and kicked the crouching man in the head. The guard jerked back and sprawled on the ground.

The woman reacted quickly, but not quickly enough. Mallory scooped up the strap of his backpack with one hand

and threw it as hard as he could at her. The gun went off but the shot went wide as the backpack hit her in the face. Mallory closed the distance and wrestled the gun out of her hand. She tried to hold on to it, but he swung her around and let her momentum separate her from the gun.

He adjusted it in his hand and turned back to the other one, who was struggling to his feet and attempting to aim his gun at Mallory. He was still dazed, probably wouldn't have been able to shoot straight. Mallory didn't give him the chance. He shot him twice in the chest, the gunshots echoing like cannon fire off the close walls of the alley. He turned, ready for the woman to have recovered.

She had, but she was too smart to stick around. She was running towards the mouth of the alley. Mallory picked up his backpack and followed.

She was already two-thirds of the way down, weaving, expecting Mallory to fire at her. But Mallory didn't want her dead, he wanted answers. He swung the backpack over his shoulders and turned on the speed, closing the gap as the woman in the suit reached the end of the alley and turned sharp left, away from the harbour.

Mallory rounded the corner a second later into a wider side street. She was already out of sight.

Two smaller alleys led off in opposite directions. He could still hear retreating footsteps, but the echoes were disorienting. He chose one alley and took it, just in time to see the woman disappear around the corner at the far end.

Mallory charged up after her. If this woman was a local, she had a major advantage in the maze of backstreets. As Mallory neared the end of the alley, a heavy-set man with a moustache stepped out in front of him from a fire door, lugging a black bin bag. Mallory collided with him, sending him sprawling and the bin bag splitting on the concrete, shedding lettuce leaves and food waste everywhere. Mallory stumbled and regained his balance, picking up speed again, ignoring the angry yells from the moustached man.

He reached the end of the alley. This one opened out on a busy street. Two mingling streams of pedestrians moved back and forth. Mallory looked left and then right, searching for some sort of disruption in the flow of foot traffic that might tell him where the blond woman in the suit had gone. But there was nothing.

He tucked the gun in the back of his waistband before anybody saw it and studied the street, looking for any sign of her. Tightly packed stores and cafés and restaurants. The woman in the grey suit could have ducked into any one of them.

She was gone.

But maybe her colleague could provide some answers, even in death.

Mallory retraced his steps. There was no sign of the man with the moustache, but the burst bin bag was still where it had landed, the trash spreading out all over the ground. He turned back into the alley leading to where he had shot the other man and stopped when he heard voices.

There were people in there. The squawk of a radio. Police, maybe.

Mallory started to back away and then retreated towards the harbour. He followed the length of the building on the harbour side until he got to the alley that led back to where he had encountered the woman and her subordinate. There was a police car parked across the mouth of the alley.

Mallory hung back in the shadow of the building and watched.

Two men emerged from the alley. A uniformed gendarme and another man Mallory recognised – the second guard from the boat, the big man who had pushed the boy on the scooter.

It didn't look as though the gendarme was questioning him. The body language was that of two professionals discussing a delicate situation. The gendarme seemed a little agitated, kept gesturing in the direction of the alley. The man in the suit seemed to be sweet-talking him. He put an arm on the gendarme's shoulder, pointed at the alleyway, then shook his head.

Mallory glanced around. Across the street, there was a café with outdoor tables. He took a seat at one that was in the shadow of the awning and watched the alleyway. The two men continued talking, and then the guard went back into the alley. The gendarme stood by his car, fidgeting with his hands. He looked very much like a subordinate who had just been put in his place.

A waiter appeared. Mallory ordered a mineral water and watched. No more police cars appeared. No ambulance. After ten minutes, an unmarked grey van appeared and backed into the alleyway. Mallory couldn't see what happened with the van in the way, but that was probably the idea. Five minutes later, the van drove away again.

The man in the suit emerged and spoke to the gendarme again. He seemed to be calming the other man down. At length, the two of them shook hands and the gendarme got into his car and drove away.

Mallory didn't want to go back to the alley, certainly not yet, but if he did he had a pretty good idea of what he would find. The area would have been hosed down and the body of the man he had killed would be nowhere to be seen.

And the local police didn't seem too concerned about that.

25

Mallory took a zigzagging route back to his hotel. When he had put some distance between himself and the Old Port, he went into the first quiet bar he saw. The place was called Bar des 11 Coins. It had a red awning and football murals on the exterior walls, and as soon as Mallory entered he knew why it was quiet. No air conditioning. He paid for a drink and asked directions to the bathroom.

The cubicle had a broken lock, but it would give him enough privacy. He took out the gun he had taken from the blond woman. It was a Ruger 9mm. The man he had killed had been pointing the same kind of gun at him. It was possible that the people guarding the boat had been overzealous private security, but he didn't think that explained their eagerness to corner him and search him. He suspected that if he hadn't acted, he would have been taken somewhere away from prying eyes. Then he would probably have been beaten, interrogated and executed.

The two men at the yacht and the woman who seemed to be their superior had been mob, he was sure of it. They reeked of organised crime. The suits, the guns, but mostly the unshakeable confidence that they could act with impunity. The little scene he had witnessed with the gendarme only confirmed it. That, and the way the woman had been able to elude him so effortlessly, told him that these were locals.

Gangsters guarding a yacht. A yacht named *La Deuxième Chance*. Nicolas Devereaux had come here because of it. A man with a knife was mixed up in it. How did all this fit together? Mallory didn't have all the pieces yet, but he was sure they would form one picture.

After a little consideration, he decided to risk retracing his earlier steps. He headed back to the Old Port for another look at *La Deuxième Chance*. On the way, he bought a long-sleeve T-shirt from a tourist-tat shop. They were selling cheap fabric face masks with the French flag at the till, so he bought one of those too. Even having changed his look a little, he made sure not to get too close to the yacht this time. The security had been stepped up. Four men at the gangway, plus one patrolling the deck.

More fairy lights had been strung up. There was a stage at the bow, and audio technicians were setting up for a band. Mallory wondered what the party was in aid of, and who would be on the guest list.

He sidled around to one of the bars directly opposite the yacht, picking the one that looked least busy. Like many of the restaurants and cafés on this stretch, the front was open, with folding wooden shutters at the side that could be closed at night.

This place had lots of dark wood panelling and a long mirror behind the bar with an extensive range of cocktails listed on it in different colours of marker pen. Some kind of French electropop was playing at a volume that was just below obnoxious. Mallory took a stool at the bar and asked for a beer when a barmaid sauntered over. She was in her late thirties, with a bored expression that spoke of too many years pulling pints. Or half-litres, or whatever they had here. She turned to the nearest refrigerator and took out a bottle of Kronenbourg, snapping the cap off on a bar-mounted opener.

'*Merci*,' Mallory said.

Before she could turn away, he gestured over at *La Deuxième Chance*. 'Do you know what they're doing over there?'

She shrugged. 'Some big party. They've been in town since Sunday.'

'They drink in here?'

She nodded, and Mallory deduced from the face she pulled that she wasn't all that happy about it.

'Bad customers?'

'*Oui*. Not nice people, if you know what I mean.'

'I think I know,' Mallory agreed, and took a drink.

She leaned in close. 'I wouldn't go around asking questions about them. You never know.'

Mallory thanked her for the advice, and she moved off to serve another patron. He kept an eye on the yacht in the mirror. There were a number of men in suits, but none of the ones he had seen earlier. As Mallory watched, one of them was hassling another onlooker: an older, portly man in a Hawaiian shirt, beige shorts and socks with sandals. He wore a pair of binoculars around his neck, and was clutching them defensively to his chest, like a shield. He looked like a birdwatcher, except that the only birds to watch around here were obese seagulls.

Mallory watched, hoping the old guy wouldn't make a

mistake and try to get assertive with these dicks. He was relieved when he moved on without argument.

The birdwatcher was moving in this direction now. Mallory watched as he ambled towards the bar. He entered and stood at the bar, waiting to order. Mallory nodded and he smiled and said '*bonjour*' with enough of an accent to tell Mallory that he was an American.

'They give you some hassle?' Mallory asked.

'What?' He looked taken aback at first, then glanced over at the yacht. 'Oh. Yeah. Some people are ...' He paused and let out a heavy sigh. 'Unnecessarily difficult.'

'You sound like you get this a lot.'

'Oh, not a lot. Most people are only too happy to show off their boat. Some people, though ...'

Definitely not a birdwatcher. Mallory gestured at the binoculars. 'Are you like a ... yacht spotter, then?'

He shrugged amiably. 'Just a hobby. My wife says if I applied myself to my business the way I do to my hobbies, I could buy one of those things.' He laughed. 'She's wrong. *Waaay* wrong.'

'How much does a boat like that go for?'

He sucked his teeth. 'That one? You wouldn't get much change out of four hundred million bucks.'

Mallory let out a long whistle.

'That's not so bad,' he continued. 'It's the maintenance that kills you.'

Mallory bought a round. He had a few questions for the expert. Just casual curiosity, he explained.

After the old man left, Mallory waited for darkness to fall and took a hoodie out of his backpack. He put the hood up and risked getting a little closer, but not too close. He had learned that lesson earlier. The men at the gangway were occupied talking to a delivery man, which gave him a chance to take a good look at the yacht. The yacht-watcher, whose name turned out to be Elliot, had been only too happy to answer all his questions over a couple of beers. He had even used his phone to call up pictures and blueprints of comparable yachts, talking Mallory through the various features.

It looked like the preparations for whatever party was happening were almost complete. The note in Nicolas's apartment had mentioned the tenth, which was tomorrow. In twenty-four hours, he might need to get a little closer to the *Second Chance*.

He left the harbour and walked north, back towards his hotel. The streets seemed to huddle closer to one another away from the tourist areas, the lights sparser and dimmer. He saw hooded figures skulking in doorways, sizing up the passers-by. None of them decided Mallory was an easy target.

The receptionist beckoned him over as he entered the cramped foyer.

'*Monsieur!*'

Mallory went over to the desk.

The receptionist was a fierce-looking woman with short grey hair and rectangular spectacles. She didn't stand up as he approached. She was jabbing her thumb at a piece of paper in front of her. 'The room is a single rate. No guests.'

'I don't have any guests.'

'You must pay for a double room.'

'What are you talking about?' Mallory scanned the sheet of paper in front of him. It was a bill. *Simple* had been roughly crossed out in ballpoint pen and the bill now read *chambre double*. The room rate had tripled.

'You must pay,' the receptionist said again.

Mallory opened his mouth to say there had been a mistake, wondering if this was a standard shakedown in this establishment, when he thought of another possibility.

'Someone is up there?' he asked, pointing to the ceiling.

'That is what I said.'

'In my room?'

'Your girlfriend. You have to pay.'

Mallory held a finger up. 'I'll be back in one minute.'

He walked away from the desk, ignoring the protests of the receptionist. Carefully, he opened the door to the stairwell. The flight and a half he could see from this position were empty. No sound. He let the door close behind him on the spring and took his backpack off, lowering it to the ground. Reaching behind him, he gripped the handle of the Ruger he had taken from the gangster in the alley and drew it, clicking the safety off with his thumb.

Climbing the stairs quickly, treading lightly, Mallory covered each blind spot with the gun as he turned corners, listening for creaking floorboards, breathing. Every other landing light was out – lots of places for an assailant to lurk.

He reached the fourth floor. Some kind of Latin music drifted out of one of the rooms. His room was at the far end of the hallway. The door was closed.

Mallory kept the gun trained on the door and took the room key from his pocket with his left hand. He glanced down at it again to confirm there was no logo on the leather fob, just a room number. The woman from the alley couldn't have traced his hotel room just from this, could she? There were no identifying marks on the key itself, either. There had to be a hundred shitty dives in Marseille that used real keys instead of keycards.

But someone had found him.

He advanced down the hall, keeping close to one wall. The fire door at the end of the corridor was closed tight. He drew level with the door and stopped to listen. There was no detectable sound. He slid the key into the lock using his left hand, careful not to rattle it. There was a click as the lock disengaged. He pushed the door open quickly and stepped back, shielding himself with the jamb, then crouched low, ready to fire.

There was no one in the room. Just the single bed and the stained carpet and the neon glow from the sign in the alley outside through the grubby lace curtains.

Then he noticed the light was on in the bathroom.

He stepped into the room, keeping the gun trained in the centre of the top half of the bathroom door. He used his heel to close the room door behind him and approached slowly across the threadbare carpet, stepping around the loose floorboard.

Mallory could hear movement inside. The sound of something small and metal being placed on a surface. He could smell dampness in the air. There were beads of condensation on the wood frame of the door. Whoever it was had taken a shower, or at least run hot water for some reason.

The door was cheap, flimsy, like everything else in this place. Without wasting any more time, Mallory raised his right foot and slammed it into the door, just below the handle. The door exploded inward, smashing off the tiled wall.

There was a woman sitting on a chair at the sink beneath the mirror, her back to him, a towel wrapped around her. She screamed and jerked around.

Océane said, 'What the fuck are you doing?'

26

Mallory lowered the gun.

'I'm sorry, I thought ...' He stopped and held a hand up. 'Wait a minute. What the fuck am *I* doing? What the fuck are *you* doing? How did you get here? How did you find my hotel?'

Océane was angled back in the chair she had taken from the desk in the room. She put a hand to her chest to secure the towel. On the surface around the sink were the contents of her toilet bag.

'Can you give me a minute?' she snapped, gesturing at herself.

'Right, sorry,' Mallory said again, before he could catch himself.

He stepped out of the room and tried to pull the door closed. The wood around the handle had been destroyed, the handle hanging by one screw. He closed it as best he could and sat on the bed, waiting for Océane to finish.

There was a sharp voice from the bathroom. 'Can you give me my clothes?'

Mallory looked around the room. On the blindside of the door, Océane had placed a small case. There was a pair of jeans, a top and some underwear folded carefully on top of it. Mallory picked the bundle up and handed it around the remains of the bathroom door. The clothes were snatched out of his hand so quickly that the top fell to the floor and was quickly pulled inside.

A minute later, Océane emerged at the door. Her black hair was wet and shining in the dim light. She was rubbing it with the towel.

'This place is a shithole.'

'I've stayed in worse. And I didn't have the right credit rating for the place your boyfriend booked.'

'Did you find him?'

'We'll talk about that in a minute. Let's talk about you first. Start with how you found me.'

Océane's dark eyes flashed in anger. 'Why are you acting like this?'

'Acting like what?'

She threw her arms up. 'Suspicious! Like you don't trust me!'

'I don't trust you.'

Océane blinked, surprised.

'Take it easy, I don't trust anybody. But I got here last night. Since then, someone has tipped Nicolas off to avoid being where I expected him to be, and I've had a run-in with some people I think are part of the Marseille mob. Now you show up in my hotel room when you're supposed to be five hundred miles away. Drop the indignation and tell me what's happening.'

'I was scared, all right? You said I would be safe if I stayed away from Nicolas's place and you were wrong. Dead wrong.'

'What happened?'

'The man with the knife. The Serbian guy you said was looking for Nicolas. He showed up at Marianne's place.'

Mallory leaned forward. 'When you were there?'

'No, thank God. I don't know what would have happened. After I left you I called *grand-père*, then I walked around for a bit. When I got to Marianne's place, all of my shit was outside. She told me he came to the door looking for me and held a knife to her throat.'

'How did he find you?'

She shook her head. 'You're still talking to me like this is my fault. I don't know, okay? I don't know who he is, I don't know what Nicolas is doing, I don't even know who you are. But I couldn't stay in Paris.'

Mallory watched her as she spoke. She was certainly doing a convincing impression of someone who didn't know what the hell was going on. He was edging towards believing her. If it had been a concoction to cover up her involvement, she would have left fewer gaps in the story. But there was one question she definitely would be able to answer.

'All right, so you panicked. I told you Nicolas was heading to Marseille, and you knew I was following him, so you decided to come here. How did you find my hotel?'

'I knew Nicolas would have booked the Marseillaise, it's his favourite place. The man at the desk said he was gone, and that somebody else had been asking for him. I described you and he said yes. I asked if you were staying there and he said no. Then I asked what the cheapest hotels within walking distance were. It didn't take long to narrow them down.'

Mallory was impressed despite himself. 'Nice work. I didn't realise I was so predictable. You know, you could have just called me.'

'I lost my phone. I didn't have your number. I tried to find you on Facebook, but you weren't there.'

Mallory smiled. 'No, I'm not on Facebook. And I don't think the bastard from Nicolas's apartment is, either.'

'Who is he? What does he want? I don't know anything about what Nicolas is doing.'

Mallory thought of something. 'Maybe it's not about that. He doesn't want you for what you know about Nicolas, he wants you for leverage over Nicolas.'

'Nicolas? He doesn't give a shit about anybody but himself.'

'Is that really true?'

She said nothing for a while, looked down at the carpet then raised her eyes to his. 'I don't know.'

Mallory thought that she did: Nicolas did care about her, and he could understand why. He decided that that was what whoever had hired him was holding over him. That was how they were forcing him to do whatever he was going to do on *La Deuxième Chance* tomorrow evening.

'What is going on, Mallory? I feel like since I met you, the world has been turned upside down.'

Mallory stood up. He thought better on his feet. There wasn't much space in the room, but he began to walk in a circle. Océane's arrival had given him another piece of the puzzle. He didn't know who Nicolas was going to kill yet, but he thought he understood his motivation now: blackmail, not money. That changed things.

Océane watched him as he paced. She resumed drying her hair with the towel, saying nothing, letting him think.

He stopped at the window and pulled the net curtains back to look out on the bare alley wall and the neon sign.

He could see rats attacking a pile of refuse in the alley below, fighting over scraps.

'What exactly does Nicolas do for a living?' Mallory asked.

'It's difficult to say.'

'Why?'

'He describes it as a portfolio career. He does lots of things. He organises parties, corporate things, film premieres, stuff like that.'

'Sounds glamorous.'

'It can be. He's the kind of guy who walks into a drinks reception or a party and everyone knows him.'

'So he's connected.'

'Yes. He's like ... I don't know how you say it, an in-between man.'

'A middleman,' Mallory nodded. Perhaps here was a thread that could be pulled. He turned to Océane. 'Do you know much about the people he worked for?'

'No. It's as I said. He's a free agent, but he worked with lots of people.'

'Anybody dodgy?'

'Dodgy?'

'Shady. Illicit. Criminal.'

Océane's eyes turned down. 'I mean ... his business is parties, so ...' Her eyes lit up with an idea. 'Maxim, did you find him?'

'Yeah, and I don't think he's anyone to worry about. I'm not talking about him knowing where to get the best coke in town, that's a given,' Mallory said. 'I mean proper bad guys. Organised crime. Did you ever see anything to suggest Nicolas had mob links?'

'No. I mean, yes, drugs, but nothing like that. Not that I saw.'

'*La Deuxième Chance*. Does that mean anything to you?'

'It means the second chance. Why?'

'It's the name of a yacht. A yacht that's moored in the Old Port, right here in Marseille.'

It took Océane a moment to catch up. The realisation dawned in her eyes.

'*La Deuxième Chance*. That's what Chance means. So it's not a man, it's a boat?'

'A big bloody boat,' Mallory corrected. 'Earlier on I had a chat with an old geezer who knows a lot more about this subject than I do. He showed me how to check out the registration. It's registered in the Caymans under a shell company.'

'So who owns it?'

'I don't know, but I have some ideas. I was down at the port this morning, looking for Nicolas. I didn't find him, but I found two gangsters instead. They were guarding the gangway and they noticed me taking an interest in their boat. They weren't happy about it.'

'What happened?'

Mallory told her briefly about the alleyway, the woman in the grey suit and her subordinate, who had tried to take him in with them, the brief fight, the chase. Finally, he told her how he had watched one of the other guards remove the body with the acquiescence of one of the local police.

Océane listened, wide-eyed. 'My God. You killed someone?'

'It was him or me. It's not the first time I've had to make that choice.'

'And you think these people were with le Milieu?'

Mallory recognised the term. Le Milieu was the French equivalent of the Cosa Nostra.

'Yes, and they have something planned for tomorrow

night, on the deck of that boat. They're setting up for some kind of party.'

'And you think Nicolas is involved.'

'Exactly. It all fits. Parties is what he does for a living, and we know that he's here because of something relating to the word 'Chance' that's happening tomorrow.'

'Criminals don't just throw parties. Why would they do that?'

'Criminals are people too. Could be lots of reasons. An important birthday, a wedding, some kind of business thing. I don't know. But that's where it's going to happen, and we need to find Nicolas before it goes down.'

'So the man with the knife is one of them? He's a gangster?'

Mallory had been thinking about this ever since the encounter in the alleyway. It didn't quite fit. It was difficult to pinpoint, but the man in Nicolas's apartment didn't seem to go with the man and the woman in the alley. The alley had been no walk in the park, but at no time was he unsure that he could handle the situation. He could have taken them with both hands tied behind his back. The fight in the apartment on the other hand: that had been a fight for his life.

The disconnect could be put down to a difference in the ability of his opponent, of course, but his instinct told him it wasn't just that. The man with the knife didn't seem to be of the same kind as the people he had encountered in the alley. They were criminals and dangerous to an extent, but the man in the apartment was a killer, by nature and by training. It takes one to know one.

'I think he's someone else.'

Océane swallowed. 'If he knows what Nicolas is involved in ... could he have followed him here?'

Mallory had considered this, too. 'I think it's possible. And he knows what both of us look like, so we're going to have to be careful.'

Océane put her face in her hands. Mallory could understand her feelings. She had driven five hundred miles to get away from this man, and she might just have put herself in harm's way again.

'I think you should stay here until I find Nicolas,' Mallory said. 'Safer that way.'

She shook her head. 'Absolutely not. I'm coming with you.'

'I don't have time to babysit you. No offence.'

She didn't take the bait; instead she spoke immediately. 'How well do you know Nicolas, Mallory?'

The question caught him by surprise. 'I don't. You know that.'

'I've been his girlfriend for the past year. You really think there's no way I can contribute to finding him? You need me.'

Mallory opened his mouth to object, but she had a point. And the truth was he would be worried about her even without her coming with him. At least this way he could keep an eye on her. If anything dangerous happened, he could make sure to get her clear of the action before things kicked off.

'I don't suppose it would do any good if I insisted?'

Océane folded her arms and gave him a sceptical look.

'Try it.'

WEDNESDAY

27

MARSEILLE

Nicolas awoke to the sound of seagulls cawing outside his window. He had been dreaming about lying on a desert plain, vultures circling over him.

The Hôtel California was a significant downgrade from l'Hôtel Marseillaise. He wondered if it had been selected purely because it was all the way on the other side of the city from his original, apparently compromised, location, or if someone with a dark sense of humour had been thinking about the lyrics of the song; the idea of checking out whenever you wanted, but never being able to leave.

The hotel, despite its name, was owned and managed by a laconic Greek. He didn't ask any questions or offer any pleasantries. He had just looked up as Nicolas entered, taken the false name he had been provided with and handed him a key to a room on the top floor. Nicolas couldn't remember the last time he had stayed in a room this basic. There was no balcony, no bathtub, not even a minibar.

But he supposed he was not here for comfort. The task at hand loomed in front of him. Once that was done, he would stay here for another day and then he would be contacted with further instructions. He hoped that those instructions were to simply go home and forget everything, but he wasn't putting much faith in that. He already knew that *le patron* was not a man to take no for an answer.

He showered under the weak stream in the tight, mould-flecked cubicle, then dressed and went downstairs. There was no sign of any of the staff of the Hôtel California. The foyer was drab and depressing. No ceiling mirrors or pink champagne here, certainly.

He pushed through the creaking revolving door and stepped out into the sunshine. The fresh air was a welcome change from the damp, musty smell inside. He took out the cheap Android phone he had bought to use as a burner and saw that it was almost nine o'clock. He hurried to the park across from the hotel, not wanting to be overheard when the call came in. Not that any curious passers-by would suspect what the topic of conversation was.

At precisely 9 a.m., the phone rang. This did not come as a surprise. He had received several phone calls from his unknown employer, and each of them had arrived at the ordained time, practically to the second.

Nicolas answered, stopping himself at the last moment from adding '*C'est* Nicolas' to the greeting.

'Are you ready?' It was the American's voice again. All of a sudden, Nicolas's throat was dry. He swallowed, wondering how he could convincingly lie in answer to that question.

'I'm ready,' he said, his voice only quavering a little.

If the voice on the other end of the call registered it, he didn't comment on it. 'Change of plan.'

'Oh yes?' Nicolas said eagerly. Too eagerly. A cancellation? Had they changed their minds?

The hint of a snort. 'Not a big change. The caterer requires you to report at seven p.m., not seven-thirty. Some issue with transport. Nothing that should get in the way of our plans.'

'Oh,' Nicolas said. 'Good,' he added, unconvincingly.

'Your role is simple. Important, highly specialised, perhaps, but simple. Do you understand that?'

Early on, Nicolas had tried to protest, to argue. He no longer did that. 'I understand.'

'Think about your girlfriend.'

'I am.'

There was a long pause.

'She has been in contact with you, yes?'

Nicolas frowned. He wasn't confident that Océane would ever speak to him again. Even if she did, she would have no way to contact him this week. She didn't have this number, and didn't know he had left Paris.

'No. No, I haven't heard from her.'

'No?' The voice left a long pause. Eventually, he spoke again. 'All right.'

'Is there anything else?'

'No. Be at the rendezvous at seven p.m. We shall be watching. After tonight, your role is complete.'

Nicolas started to ask if the arrangements for tomorrow were still in place, but the line was dead.

He stared down at the blank screen of the burner phone. What had they meant by that question about Océane? Why did they think she would have been in touch? He decided it was nothing. A mind game. A way to threaten him and remind him of the stakes. He wanted to laugh. There was no prospect of him forgetting.

But it made him wonder. He installed WhatsApp. It took a few seconds to sync, and then he saw it.

One new message from Océane.

28

'So we have to be invisible?'

Mallory glanced over at Océane, who was walking by his side along La Canebière, the high street that cut through the old quarter of Marseille. He massaged an ache in his shoulder from a night sleeping on the floor of the hotel room before he answered.

'Not, not invisible. We just have to blend in.'

'We can't blend in,' Océane said, eyeing the crew of darkly tanned labourers clearing rubble from a ruined building across the street. 'We look like tourists.'

'Exactly,' Mallory said. 'You work with what you've got.'

'And what do we have?'

'We look like a couple. They're not looking for a couple.'

Océane glanced up at him over the rims of her sunglasses, one eyebrow slightly raised. 'You think we look like a couple?'

'Don't flatter yourself.'

The two of them had started early, walking the streets all morning. For the last hour, it had been growing hotter by the minute. With the temperature in the mid-thirties and no rain on the forecast, they couldn't make themselves inconspicuous with baggy hoodies or ponchos, so Mallory bought hats and sunglasses. As Océane had pointed out, they looked like tourists, but that was fine. There were plenty of those around. They covered different areas of the city, backtracking to check locations where Nicolas had been linked to, like the Hôtel Marseillaise and the tennis courts. They checked out parks and bars and cafés. They even passed by the berth where *La Deuxième Chance* was moored, making sure not to get too close to the security contingent at the gangway. The complement had increased since yesterday. Five men in suits now, instead of two.

At Mallory's suggestion, Océane bought a new phone from one of the many phone shops dotted around the streets. They swapped numbers and Mallory gave her an email address as well so they would be able to contact each other by alternative methods if they were separated again.

Mallory noticed another ruined building, fenced off from the pavement, and remembered he had seen another not far from the Hôtel d'Or. He asked Océane about it. She told him that there were a lot of buildings on the point of collapse in the heart of the city. A few years ago, people had been killed when their apartment building collapsed with them inside it. The contrast with the money that had been spent on the beach-facing parts of town stuck out to Mallory.

They saw a lot of the city, but they didn't see hide nor hair of Nicolas Devereaux.

Mallory was still learning the rhythms and idiosyncrasies of Marseille. It would take him weeks to get to know the city properly. But there were some things that were universal, and he had a good idea of where to start looking for the answers he wanted. Whether Océane liked it or not, the next part he would have to do alone.

Mallory waited until he could tell Océane was flagging. He had purposely not stopped for a drink or food in a while, so when she sighed and took a seat on a bench, he was ready.

'Look, I've got to sort something out that needs to be a solo thing. Why don't you go back to the hotel? Grab a drink, have a sit down, and I'll be back in an hour.'

'You promise?' she asked, giving him a sceptical look.

'Scout's honour.'

'Scout's honour?'

'It means yeah, I promise.'

Mallory saw Océane back to the hotel, checked the room was secure, and left her to rest her feet. He left again and stepped into the shaded alley that ran alongside it, removing his sunglasses. The fire escape from the hotel ran down the wall, and their room was at this end of the building. That had just been luck, but he was glad. It was good to have options if you needed to leave in a hurry.

He followed the alley to the other end and turned right, heading in the direction of the seediest neighbourhood they had passed through this morning. He was hoping to kill two birds with one stone here, and he didn't think he would have to go far.

The first bird to kill was a practical concern. Whatever happened tonight, Mallory wanted to be ready for it. The gangsters he had run into yesterday had obligingly provided him with a gun, but what he needed now was ammunition. Despite his exchange with Océane earlier, Mallory had never been a boy scout, but 'be prepared' was always a sensible motto. He didn't think the six remaining rounds in the

Ruger counted as adequate preparation. A towering, rail-thin man wearing a Che Guevara cap and selling MDMA at a street corner in the 13th arrondissement was happy to take Mallory's cash for information rather than his usual product.

'You're looking for a gun.'

'Not a gun. Bullets. Nine millimetre. Know anyone?'

Beneath the brim of the cap, the dealer's eyes were on everything other than Mallory. He watched doorways, passing cars, people standing at the bus stop. Mallory had an impression of the man as a tightly wound spring, ready to go off at a moment's notice. Judging by his slimness and his long legs, he was betting he would be able to outpace most of the local cops in a footrace. Then again, going by what Mallory had seen of the local police so far, maybe they wouldn't even try to catch him.

'Pierre's Bar, ask for Mathieu.'

Mallory found the place. It was less than a mile away. He followed the route the dealer had described, grateful for some time on his own to think. Nicolas was here in town and he was planning to kill someone on that yacht. The man in the picture? The way the face had been crossed out seemed to suggest that. But who wanted him dead?

Pierre's Bar was a forbidding joint on the docks; a one-storey windowless box with one opaque window and peeling whitewash on all the exterior walls. The kind of place that was probably a haunt for trawlermen and dockworkers, looking for hard liquor at a time most people were crawling out of bed and reaching for the coffee machine.

Inside, Mallory was pleased to find the light was dim and the awareness of the regulars was dimmer. Just a handful of hardened drinkers sitting at the bar gazing into space as they drank.

Mallory asked for Mathieu at the bar. The bartender was a tall man with light hair and watery blue eyes. He glanced in the direction of the nearest customer – a white-haired man who was at least ninety, crouched over a glass of red wine – before beckoning Mallory over to a door marked *Privé* at the side of the bar.

He opened the door for Mallory. It was a storeroom, low-ceilinged and musty. Cases of beer and wine stacked against the breezeblock walls. He motioned for Mallory to go in.

'After you,' Mallory said.

He shrugged and led the way. When the door closed, Mallory took a quick look around. There was a fire exit on the opposite side. Good. He didn't like walking into a room with only one way out.

'You're Mathieu?' he asked.

The man nodded. 'You are American?'

'Little closer.'

'Ah, from across the Channel, I should have known. What can I do for you?'

Mallory reached behind him and took out the Ruger. Mathieu flinched, then relaxed as he saw Mallory did not intend to use it.

'My apologies,' Mallory said, smiling. He tapped the button beneath the trigger guard and slid the magazine out. He took one of the 9 mm bullets out and held it up to the light. 'I need some of these, preferably with no questions asked.'

'No questions is my speciality,' Mathieu said. 'Any particular requirements? Armour piercing, hollow-point?'

'No, nothing special,' Mallory replied. 'How soon can I get them?'

Mathieu frowned and sucked his teeth, as though this was going to be a tough job. He walked towards a floor safe in the corner underneath the desk.

'I guess about ... five seconds?'

He tapped in the combination, opened the safe and took out three boxes of 9 mm ammunition.

'Enough?'

'I certainly hope so.'

Mathieu walked over to him, holding the boxes, then stopped.

'You know, there are some interesting people looking for a Brit today. They're very keen to talk to him.'

Mallory listened. He had been wondering how to bring this up, but Mathieu had beaten him to it. This was the second bird to kill.

'Oh yeah? Small world.'

'Small world indeed.'

'I shouldn't be selling these to you.'

'But you are.'

He smiled. Mallory handed him the money and threw in another hundred-euro note. 'I think it'll work better for both of us if neither of us mentions this, am I right?'

Mathieu grinned. 'I could tell from the look of you that I could do business with you.'

'One last thing. The big yacht at the Old Port. *La Deuxième Chance*. What's happening tonight?'

Mathieu watched him carefully. 'Something big.'

'Can you be more specific?' Mallory reached into his pocket.

'Put away your money. I don't know anything. But I know enough to stay far from it. You should too, my friend.'

29

Océane took a shower to rinse off the sweat and the dirt that had built up over the morning of trailing Mallory around the shittiest parts of Marseille. If she didn't know better, she would have assumed he was trying to wear her out. Mission accomplished, at least temporarily. The weak shower didn't help much, but at least she felt less grimy.

She changed into the jeans and blouse she had bought earlier and went to the window. Not that there was a view. This place was a far cry from the kinds of hotels Nicolas used to take her to. She wondered where he was holed up, sure that it would be classier than this place. Then again, Océane had seen nightclub toilets that were classier than this place.

She unplugged her new phone from the charger and spent a few minutes adding her apps again, suddenly remembering the message she had sent Nicolas the other day.

She installed WhatsApp and logged in. There were no new messages from Nicolas, but something had changed. Next to her message, there were two blue check marks. The message had been delivered and read.

She tapped out another message, saying that she knew he was in Marseille and she needed to talk to him.

One check mark appeared, and then immediately a second. They turned blue – he had read the message.

Océane took a breath as she saw a reply was being typed. A moment later a message appeared from Nicolas. An instruction to meet him in the place she didn't hate.

She got it immediately. On their single trip to Marseille, the one bright spot had been their visit to the Musée d'Archéologie Méditerranéenne. Océane had always loved ancient Egypt, ever since school, and their afternoon wandering around the exhibits had been the only thing she had enjoyed about the city.

She thought about waiting for Mallory to come back. He had said he wouldn't be longer than an hour, hadn't he? Then again, she was all but certain he had been eager to offload her. To not have to be a 'babysitter', as he had said.

'To hell with you, Mallory,' she said aloud, checking her reflection in the mirror as she tied her hair back into a ponytail.

She wore the hat and sunglasses she had bought earlier and followed the guidance Mallory had given her: sticking to the parts of the street that were in shadow where possible, keeping an eye on reflections, watching for people who seemed to appear in more than one place. Perhaps Mallory was paranoid, but she wasn't taking any chances after what had happened to Marianne.

The Musée d'Archéologie Méditerranéenne was north of the Old Port, in the 2nd arrondissement. It was housed in a huge classical building with three levels of grand archways and a central courtyard. She didn't know why Nicolas had suggested meeting here, but she assumed it was because so many tourists were milling around.

She bought a ticket and moved through the vast courtyard, looking up at the domed building at the centre. It was easier to take a look at the people in here than it was out on the busier streets. She didn't see Nicolas anywhere, though. It was so damn hot. She could feel perspiration gather at the back of her neck.

She stopped at the gift shop to buy a drink and stood in the shadows beneath one of the arches, watching people move back and forth on the courtyard.

When she felt a hand clutch her forearm, her heart lurched into her throat.

She turned to see Nicolas, the index finger of his free hand placed at his lips.

'I'm sorry. I didn't mean to scare you,' he said. Then his features contorted into frustration. 'What are you doing in Marseille?'

'I'm looking for you. What are *you* doing, Nicolas?'

He stepped away from her, into a sunbeam, and she wanted to gasp at the transformation in him. Nicolas looked as though he had aged ten years in the last few weeks. His skin was pale, his eyes reddened. His usually immaculately shaven cheeks were patchy with dark stubble. He had lost weight. More than that, though, it was his eyes. He was haunted.

'What's wrong?' she said, her voice softening. 'Whatever it is, we can fix it. I have a friend who—'

He was shaking his head. 'No. No one can fix this. You should not have come.'

Océane reached her hand out. 'Come with me. I have a friend who can help.'

He backed away from her. 'You should not have come. Go back to Paris.' He turned and started walking quickly away.

'Nicolas!' she called after him.

He didn't stop. She started running. He turned as she caught up, anger flashing in his eyes.

'There's something I have to do and if you don't listen to me—'

'What?'

'You could get hurt. Please, trust me. I love you.'

She swallowed. She dug into her pocket and pulled out one of the cards from the reception desk at l'Hôtel d'Or and a pen, quickly jotting the room number down.

'I'm staying here. Think about it. I know someone who can help.'

He didn't look at the card, but he stuffed it into his pocket. Océane was relieved that he didn't rip it in half on the spot.

'Go back to Paris,' he said again.

And then he was gone.

30

Mallory took a circuitous route back to the hotel. He had been wary already, but what Mathieu had said had told him he was right to be. He blended in with crowds whenever he could, kept his eyes on strategically parked cars and vigilant-looking men standing on street corners. Not for the first time, the coldly rational part of his brain told him that the smart thing to do was get on the next train out of this town and forget about Nicolas Devereaux and *La Deuxième Chance* and the mob. He had already done what he had set out to do: find Océane and put an old man's mind at ease.

But he knew that wasn't an option now. Océane was still in danger, and he had a feeling she was only going to be in more danger if Nicolas wasn't stopped from carrying out his mission on that yacht.

And besides, he had unfinished business with the Serbian. If Mallory could find Nicolas, maybe he could arrange a reunion.

When he reached the Hôtel d'Or, he saw he was just ahead

of Océane. From across the street, he watched as she got out of a taxi and went inside.

When he caught up with her as she was unlocking the door to the room, she had a surprise for him.

'You found him?' Mallory couldn't believe it. He had left her for no longer than an hour and in that time she had found Nicolas, and then managed to lose him again.

'I found him,' Océane replied. She tossed her bag on the bed and sat down, unlacing the boots she had bought that morning as a more practical substitution for the heels she had been wearing since she left work.

'He was in bad shape. I felt so terrible for all of the things I've been thinking about him.'

Mallory tried to keep the frustration out of his voice, with limited success. 'Why didn't you wait for me?'

'I'm sorry, I just got the message from him, and you had already been gone for a long time, and ...'

Mallory sighed. She had probably made the right decision. If she *had* waited for him, chances were Nicolas would have been gone by the time they got there.

'What did he say?'

'Just that there was something he needed to do, and that it would be over tomorrow. Mallory ... what are we going to do?'

'We stick to the plan. Whatever is happening, happens tonight. On *La Deuxième Chance*. I'm going to be there.' He stopped and pointed his finger at Océane. 'And you're not going to be anywhere near it. I mean it. These guys are bad news.'

'If they're bad news, then why is it okay for you to go and not me?'

Mallory checked the magazine, fully loaded with the new ammunition he had bought from Mathieu. He slipped it into the Ruger and tucked it into his belt.

'Because I'm worse news.'

31

Mallory found a department store in a *centre commercial* close to the Old Port that furnished him with everything he was looking for. He bought a survival knife, a set of canvas fingerless gloves, a pair of binoculars, black knee-length shorts, a black T-shirt and a light blue shirt with a check pattern. In the swimwear section, they had waterproof tote bags on special. He picked up one of those too. After a little consideration, he sprang for a backup air supply cylinder too. It was designed for scuba divers, so it wouldn't be the same high spec as the SASS devices he had used in underwater rescue exercises, but the principle was the same. If he needed to stay underwater for a little longer than holding his breath would allow, this would do it.

As he approached the Old Port, the daylight was bleeding out of the sky in the west and he could see the crescent moon already high in the dark blue to the east. Marseille was starting to come alive. In common with a lot of coastal cities, it took on an entirely different character at night.

Mallory had already picked out a good vantage point from

which to observe this evening's festivities. Forty yards along the harbour from where *La Deuxième Chance* was berthed was a long pier that jutted out into the bay. The boardwalk of the pier was lined with food stalls and brightly lit entertainment zones, but underneath was a dark expanse where the light from the moon and the bars on the shoreline only penetrated shallowly.

The organisers of the boat had taken the pier into account, but they hadn't gone overboard on security. They had two men patrolling the pier itself and another man posted at the gap in the railing where stone steps led down to the beach and the underside of the pier. Mallory wasn't going to use the steps.

Instead, he made his way to the end of the pier. The guards were moving about through the crowds, not in any particular pattern. Mallory kept to the darker spots and navigated past both of them with no trouble. The last attraction on the pier was a covered kiosk containing a mini videogame arcade. Beyond that, the pier widened out to a platform with some benches overlooking the bay. There were a handful of couples and families there, eating pizza slices and pointing up at the illuminated spire of the cathedral on the hill. Mallory walked to the edge, put his back to the railing and glanced back down the pier. Then he turned his head to look across to the yacht.

La Deuxième Chance was lit up like it was hosting a movie premiere. A purple carpet stretched out from the gangway and onto the quayside. On deck they were still making last-minute preparations. The guests would be arriving soon, no doubt.

Mallory looked back at the pier. One of the guards was

walking unhurriedly towards the quay, the other one had stopped and was standing with his back to the position of the yacht, watching anyone who pointed at it. He hadn't so much as glanced at Mallory when he passed.

Mallory's outfit was designed not to draw any particular attention. When he was satisfied no one was watching, he took the black baseball cap from his back pocket and fitted it over his head, then removed the blue shirt, balled it up and stuffed it into his waterproof tote bag. Lastly, he slipped on the gloves. They were designed for climbing: fingerless, with small spurs protruding from the palms. He waited for the nearest family to move off again and then, with a last glance in the direction of the guards, he swung his leg over the barrier and slipped down below the level of the boardwalk.

He got his legs around the nearest upright pillar and started to work himself down, using the spurs on the gloves to bite into the wood. At this end of the pier, it was a twenty-five-foot drop to the water. He climbed halfway down to where there was a horizontal beam. He positioned himself on it and adjusted his hat so that his face, the only part of him not clad in black, was in shadow.

He took a pair of binoculars from the bag and took a closer look at the *La Deuxième Chance*.

The guests were starting to arrive. Already there were people on the deck of the boat. Men in suits and women in stylish dresses. There was a band on the stage. It was difficult to make out over the competing music and noise from elsewhere in the harbour, but the instruments told him it was a jazz quartet.

Mallory didn't believe in suicide missions. More than likely, he would be boarding the vessel tonight, and the numbers against him would be considerable, but he wanted to make sure he knew as much as possible about the environment before he set foot in it.

There were two lifeboats at the stern and an enclosed section a little forward of that where Mallory guessed the sleeping quarters, galley and whatever other amenities the boat had were located. Probably a lot of amenities, judging by the size of the thing. Cinema, football pitch, concert hall, little home comforts like that. There was a narrow balcony behind the enclosed section that didn't seem to be patrolled, probably because there was no access to it other than through the interior. Mallory thought that was his way in.

There were plenty of men in suits who looked of the same ilk as the people he had had a run-in with yesterday, but some of the clientele were a little classier. Cars were arriving and emptying themselves of couples and small groups. At one point, a limousine rolled to the foot of the purple carpet and disgorged a group of women accompanied by a short, thin man in a linen suit with receding hair. They ranged from early twenties all the way up to late twenties. The man in the linen suit kept casting suspicious glances around at anyone who approached the group, like a store manager worrying about shoplifters.

Then there was a lull in arrivals, and the hubbub seemed to increase on board the yacht. The people there were getting into the swing of the party. The band got a little louder so that Mallory could now hear the music more clearly. The behaviour of the guards changed in the opposite direction. They turned their attention towards the shore. More of them appeared from nooks and crannies on the boat, talking to each other, communicating through the headsets. Mallory would have loved to know what they were saying, but the department store hadn't run to long-range listening equipment.

He didn't really need to hear them to get the gist, though. Somebody was arriving imminently. Somebody important.

Mallory took his phone out. The screen was already dimmed as far as it would go. He tapped it awake and sent a text to Océane.

> Mallory: *Everything ok?*

He watched the yacht for another minute until the phone buzzed softly in his hand to signal a reply.

> Océane: *Yes*
> Océane: *Have you found Nicolas?*

He tapped out the response, eyes moving between the screen and the yacht.

> Mallory: *Not yet, will keep you posted*

He put the phone back into the waterproof tote and zipped it shut, then resumed watching the yacht. He didn't have to wait long.

The outriders arrived first. Two black-clad men on motorcycles. Mallory would have assumed they were police, from the formation and the way they dominated the road, but a closer look through the binoculars showed that they were riding unmarked bikes. A moment later, a black SUV with tinted windows followed in their wake, followed by one more motorcycle. It was like a presidential convoy.

'Who's the VIP?' Mallory wondered aloud as he watched the SUV pull to a stop exactly at the foot of the gangway. The guards there looked uneasy, but stood to attention. Their eyes were on the riders. Mallory could see they were ready, waiting for something.

He knew one thing. The occupants of that SUV were not part of their group. They were wary of the new arrivals, on edge.

As Mallory watched, a bodyguard the size of a deluxe American refrigerator got out of the passenger side. He was wearing a black suit that struggled to contain his frame. He opened the rear door and another man got out. Was this the bigwig? No. He was young, his eyes were darting about, taking in the scene. The two of them approached the men at the gangway. They exchanged words. No smiles, no handshakes, no pleasantries, all business. Eventually, they came to some kind of agreement. The young guy from the back seat nodded and said something to the huge bodyguard from the passenger side. They went back to the SUV and opened the back door. They flanked either side of it.

A moment later, the VIP emerged.

Mallory raised the binoculars to his eyes. The VIP was much older than his flunkies, but he moved without effort. He had a mane of silver hair and wore a light grey suit with a white shirt. He was deeply tanned and wore sunglasses, though the sun had been absent for a while. A blond woman in a red dress who must have been a third his age hopped out behind him and took his arm.

The VIP stopped for a moment, a few paces from the gangway, and seemed to inhale the evening air. Long enough for Mallory to get a good look at his face. Hard to be sure, but he looked a lot like the man in the photograph in Nicolas's apartment. Then he started walking, pulling the blonde alongside him.

The guards at the gangway made way for him.

As the VIP stepped on board, another man, maybe a decade younger, appeared from the interior of the boat. He wore a black suit and a navy blue shirt. He approached the VIP, grinning, holding his hand out. The two men shook and embraced. Black suit turned and made a sweeping gesture, encompassing the yacht. Again, the body language said it all. 'Welcome to my humble dingy.'

Mallory had a pretty good idea of what was happening. These men were chiefs, but they were clearly from different tribes. This was a summit of some kind.

There was only one party guest yet to appear. Mallory slowly swept the binoculars over the rest of the yacht. He could see the crew hustling to make ready for casting off. Ropes were being untied, gates were being closed. The two tribes of flunkies were mingling, exchanging guarded conversation, keeping an eye on their respective charges. It looked like a powder keg.

And then Mallory found the loose match that might be struck.

On the top deck, there was a group of waitstaff in white jackets. Standing slightly apart from the crowd, one hand in his pocket, a faraway look in his eye, was Nicolas Devereaux.

At that moment, there was a muted announcement over the speakers. Mallory caught enough to work out that it was the captain announcing their departure. There was a ripple of applause from some of the guests, carrying over to Mallory across the water. The guards kept their hands by their sides and their faces blank.

The low rumble of the engines increased in pitch and the yacht started to move away from the shore.

32

Nicolas gripped the brass handrail in front of the bar as the boat started to move off. There was no need really, the departure was so smooth that many of the people on board didn't seem to have noticed they were sailing. But it felt good to have something solid to hold onto.

'You okay, *mon pote*?'

Nicolas turned. It was Gabriel, the preening cocktail waiter who had welcomed him on board as the newest member of the team.

'I don't like sailing,' Nicolas said. 'But I'm fine.'

'I could have guessed that. You look greener than this.' He held up a bottle of absinthe he had been using to make a cocktail. 'Don't puke on anybody, I don't think this crowd would react well.'

Nicolas smiled thinly and turned to look at the crowd on the mid-deck. Gabriel had no idea how badly this crowd was going to react in a little while. It was funny how easy it was to tell Cristofol's men from the party guests. With their dark suits and white, open-necked shirts, they were as rigidly uniformed as Nicolas's fellow waitstaff. A line of mono-chrome sentries guarding a multicoloured crowd.

And Fleuriot's men looked different again. The suits of the Parisians seemed more stylish, but not quite right for the weather. Most of them wore ties. They spent more time watching Cristofol's men than the crowd. So far, nobody was paying particular attention to Nicolas. Which, he supposed, was the reason he was here. One of them, anyway.

He flinched as someone put a hand on his shoulder, but it was only Gabriel. He had finished the order and the silver tray with five cocktails was on the bar.

'Some of these ladies look like they could make you feel better, you know what I mean?'

Nicolas attempted a knowing chuckle. It must have been unconvincing, because Gabriel's leer vanished. He pointed over at a group of three men and two women. There was an average age gap of at least thirty years between the sexes. 'That group, don't throw up on them.'

Nicolas took the tray and started to weave his way through the crowd. He searched for Fleuriot among the faces, without making it seem like he was too interested in any of the guests. The Parisian would be easily identifiable, with his silvery hair and the omnipresent sunglasses.

He still didn't know if he could go through with this. The final instructions had only come through this afternoon, and he understood why he had been selected for this job. Well, one of the reasons he had been selected, anyway. The other reason was lying at the bottom of one of the cases of cham-pagne that had been brought on board earlier.

The 'chance' encounter with Francisco at the restaurant. The old friend from Nicolas's days bartending. Only a few years ago, but it seemed like a lifetime. A script to be carefully followed. What brought Nicolas to Marseille? A vacation, how about you? A job. The big yacht at the harbour. They're paying big bucks. Nicolas had grinned. Let me know if you need any help. And then, like clockwork, two hours later a waiter had been injured in a serious moped accident. The phone call from Francisco ... would you be available? I need someone I can trust.

Nicolas shivered, thinking about how perfectly it had all unfolded according to the instructions the American on the phone had given him earlier. His employer was skilfully putting all the pieces in place for whatever game he was playing. Nicolas wondered how badly the waiter was injured.

He put it out of his mind. He had his own problems. If he didn't go through with this, he would be dead before the sun came up. He didn't doubt this, just like he didn't doubt they could find him wherever he ran to.

How had Océane followed him to Marseille? Who was this friend she talked about? Perhaps he should have lingered longer at the museum, asked her these questions, but as soon as he had seen her, he had known she was endangered merely by being close to him. He wanted to believe she would be safer here rather than back in Paris, but perhaps that was a fanciful wish. Perhaps they knew she was here already. Or perhaps they had orchestrated it so that she would be here.

Nicolas forced himself to stop thinking. Tonight wasn't about thinking. Tonight was about a very simple, horrible job.

He reached the group of five, trying to sound airy, confident.

'*Bonsoir, mesdames et messieurs.*'

The cocktails were removed from the tray without a glance

at Nicolas. That was exactly why he was here, of course. He was invisible. One of the blondes almost dropped her glass. Nicolas reached out and caught it before it overturned. She thanked him, giving him a wink.

'My hero.'

Nicolas lowered the empty tray and carried it by his side as he headed back to the bar. He left it on the counter and kept walking, carrying on down the stairs to the kitchen.

Below decks was a hive of activity, steam and noise and barked orders. Nicolas passed through, throwing out 'excuse me's until he reached the storeroom. The door closed behind him on a spring, the soundproofing so effective that it was like he had put on noise dampening headphones. He took out his phone and shone the screen light around to confirm he was alone, then moved to the stack of crates at the back. He hefted the top crates aside and opened the bottom one. There were six bottles of Perrier-Jouët champagne packed with ice. He reached under the bottles and dug into the ice beneath until he felt rigid metal.

A Stoeger STR-9S pistol. The American on the phone had told him they would provide a Glock 9. Nicolas, almost without thinking about it, had recommended this instead. A Glock clone, but with some improvements in design and ergonomics that Nicolas found advantageous. The American had listened to him.

He took the pistol from the crate. Vapour from the ice drifted across the metal of the barrel. It fitted neatly into his hand. He felt the aggressive checker pattern on the back of the grip bite into his palm. The familiarity of the tool had an oddly calming effect, when it should have been anything but. He ejected the magazine and checked it was fully loaded.

He straightened up and looked along the barrel, lining up with the three-dot fibre-optic sight. Dry-fired it. Replaced the safety and slipped the magazine back in.

Nicolas had followed every step to the letter, and everything had unfolded just the way the man on the phone had said it would.

The rest was entirely up to him.

33

Most people would be surprised at how cold the water of a Mediterranean bay can get on an August night, even after a blisteringly hot day. Mallory was prepared for it.

Getting into the water silently, swimming out to the yacht as it turned and getting on board hadn't been a picnic, but it wasn't the most difficult incursion into enemy terrain Mallory had ever attempted. The spurs on his gloves had proved just as effective for climbing one of the ropes trailing from the stern as they had for descending from the pier.

By the time *La Deuxième Chance* had completed its turn and settled into a brisk cruise out into the bay, Mallory had reached the top of the rope. He climbed over the railing onto the lowest level at the stern and hunched down so that he would not be spotted from the shore. The sound of the band and the crowd drifted over to him from the main deck. The music was some kind of uptempo jazz number. It wasn't the kind of tune that would find its way onto Mallory's playlists. Back in his old life, music had been part of the routine. Heading into a mission aboard a Chinook, he would blast hard rock and rap music through his ear buds while he studied maps and schematics. On the way back, he would unwind with something quieter. He wondered what would be a good choice for heading into this mission. Something nautical, 'Rockaway Beach' by the Ramones, perhaps. Or maybe NWA's 'Gangsta Gangsta' would be more appropriate, given the guest list.

Mallory estimated there were a couple of hundred people at the party. He was close enough that he could hear the murmur of chatter from here, even make out some of the words. Nobody sounded too boisterous, so far. But the night was young.

As the shore retreated at pace, Mallory felt safe enough to stand up and take a look around. There were two tarpaulin-wrapped shapes positioned on ramps off the edge of the boat. Mallory cut the ropes on one of the tarps and took a look. Beneath was a shiny blue and black jet ski. It had a futuristic appearance, like a kid's toy. It looked expensive. Everything on board looked expensive.

He dropped the tarp again and turned around. He was on a small platform that faced onto the blank wall of the interior cabins. There was a door with a keypad lock. At one end of the platform was a seven-foot-high steel gate; at the other, a flight of stairs to the next level. Mallory stood with his back to the railing and leaned himself over as far as he could without risking a tumble into the water. The platform was clear. From his observations earlier, the guards seemed focused on the main deck.

He climbed the steps to the next level, which was better lit than the one below. There was a long row of floor-to-ceiling windows that could open out to this upper deck.

Mallory moved to the edge and peered through the glass. The interior was in darkness, hard to make anything out inside. He used the railing to climb up on the roof. It extended about forty feet to the edge, curving a little in the middle. He knew there would be an unobstructed view of the main deck from the other side.

Keeping low, he moved quickly across the roof, feeling the motion of the boat pushing against him as it made another turn. He crouched and went into a crawl as he approached the edge and peered down onto the main deck. There were guards aplenty among the crowd. They were easy to spot, lone males in cheaper suits dotted around the edges of the party.

Sloppy. They were paying attention to all the people who had come on board the normal way, but they weren't looking elsewhere. The band was playing something Mallory was pretty sure he had heard Tony Bennett sing. People weren't really dancing, just standing around with their drinks, some of them swaying a little. One group in particular drew his eye: the only one with no women present. Six men, all in better suits than the guards.

The man with the white hair Mallory had seen emerge from the black SUV was there, along with his flunky. He was talking to his host in the black suit and navy blue shirt. It seemed as though there was an invisible forcefield around the group: there was no one within ten feet on any side. Mallory watched guests and white-clad waiters and guards alike adjust their paths to give the group a wide berth. They couldn't make it any more obvious who the senior personnel were. You could practically take them out with a drone strike with no collateral damage.

The man in the blue shirt gestured towards the enclosed

area and Mallory shrunk back as he watched the group walk towards him. The crowd cleared a path ahead of them.

They moved inside, just below Mallory, and the door closed.

He scanned the crowd again.

'Okay Nicolas, where are you?' he said under his breath.

It was like a live game of *Where's Wally?*, except his quarry hadn't had the decency to dress in a stripy top. No sign of him, though the way the crowd was moving around, it was difficult to be sure. There were plenty of waiters in white, but Nicolas was nowhere to be seen.

Mallory moved back to the other side of the roof, being even more careful to tread softly this time. As he had hoped, the lights were on in the big room at the back, casting the shadows of the blinds onto the platform. He took his phone from the waterproof tote and angled the screen it so that he could see the room reflected in the glass.

The two small groups were facing each other across a gigantic billiard table, though nobody looked like they wanted to play games. The windows were closed, but it would probably have been impossible to make out any conversation over the sound of the engine and the band and the party anyway. The tanned guy in the suit and the blue shirt was talking again. He was clearly the opposite number.

Perhaps Mallory didn't need to hear what they were saying. As he watched, the two chiefs exchanged words, both of them eyeing one another cautiously. Then, the hometown chief in the blue shirt walked unhurriedly around the billiard table, outstretching a hand.

The man with the white hair reciprocated and they shook solemnly. Blue shirt broke into a grin and clapped his guest on the back, before leading him back in the direction of the main deck.

It seemed like the meeting had been a success. Mallory wondered how long that would last.

Lying around on the roof wasn't going to get him any closer to finding Nicolas. He was going to have to get down there and in amongst the crowd. But how? He wasn't exactly in evening dress.

And then he saw an opening. One of the men from inside had hung back. He opened one of the glass doors and walked out on the platform, looking up and down. He gave a cursory glance over the side and then took out a pack of cigarettes and lit up. He stood by the door, looking back towards the harbour and smoking. In a couple of minutes he would finish, walk back inside and lock the door again. Mallory wasn't going to get another chance this good.

Mallory stood up slowly. The smoker was directly below him. All the time in the world to plot out the next three moves. Drop, disarm, disable. In fact, he only needed one. Mallory dropped on top of him, the smoker letting out a brief grunt before his head bounced off the deck and he was silent. Mallory took the smoker's gun from him and held it on him for five seconds, but he wasn't feigning. The crumpled cigarette was still between the smoker's teeth. He hadn't known what hit him.

Mallory dragged the smoker into the shadows at the far end and manhandled his jacket off. He ripped one of the sleeves from the guard's shirt and used it to tie the smoker's hands securely behind him. He removed the cigarette from his mouth before he gagged him with another strip of his own shirt.

'Too nice a guy, that's my problem,' Mallory said, addressing the out-cold gangster.

He slipped the jacket on and took a second to check his

reflection in the window glass, pushing his wet hair back with his fingers. He thought it would just about pass muster, if no one stared at him long enough to notice his other clothes were still wet from the bay. He took his phone and his gun from the tote and pocketed them.

Perhaps he could accomplish his goal without further drama; be in and out before anyone found the unconscious guard. If he could find Nicolas and talk him into backing off, the two of them could leave the same way Mallory had boarded. The yacht wasn't far from shore, and Nicolas was in good shape. With the backup air cylinder, Mallory was confident he could get him to shore and take him back to the hotel.

Mallory passed through the billiard room and into a tight corridor leading between cabins. The door at the far end opened. He tensed, but there was nowhere to go, so he kept walking, purposefully. One of the guards opened the door, saw him and hesitated. Mallory kept going and nodded to him. The guard returned the nod, presumably assuming he was with the other lot.

He stepped out onto the deck. The band had moved into a slower number. He searched until he found a familiar face from the summit. The group had split into two: white-haired guy's group near the band, blue shirt guy with his men over toward the starboard side.

Mallory did a double take and looked back.

There was no mistaking it. There, hovering by the stage, a few paces from the away team, was Nicolas.

Unlike the other waiters, he wasn't scurrying around carrying a tray of drinks. He was standing to one side, staring straight ahead intently. Mallory followed his gaze all the way back to the man with white hair.

He looked back at Nicolas. Mallory saw something familiar in his eyes and it took him a second to process what it was. He had seen that same look in the eyes of a would-be suicide bomber at a checkpoint in Mosul, years ago. Fear. Hesitation. Building resolve. Mallory could see the bar light glinting off the beads of sweat on his pallid face.

Nicolas started walking across the deck, making a beeline for his target. Nobody paid him any attention. Not the target and his men, not the home team, nor any of the dozens of armed men. Nicolas was part of the scenery. He put a hand in his pocket.

'Shit,' Mallory hissed through clenched teeth. He still didn't know who the man with white hair was, or why Nicolas had been sent to kill him. He had it coming, likely as not. But Mallory couldn't let it happen. Whether Nicolas was successful or not, he would be a dead man five seconds after taking that gun out. If that happened, Nicolas wouldn't be able to tell him what was going on, and there would be no way of knowing if Océane was still in danger.

He started to push through the crowd toward Nicolas. Guests scowled and muttered at him as he pushed roughly through, aiming to cut Nicolas off before he got to within striking distance of his target. If he could intercept him, talk to him, perhaps he could stop this turning into a bloodbath.

Almost there. Their paths about to converge, Mallory ducked around one couple, moved a guy in a silk turquoise shirt aside roughly, and then came face to face with someone who didn't shift.

Blond hair, green eyes. The green eyes narrowed, and then widened in recognition.

The woman from yesterday.

34

Nicolas was almost there. The remainder of Emmanuel Fleuriot's life could now be measured in seconds.

In a moment, he would pull the trigger and the die would be cast. Perhaps he would be able to escape as easily as his employer had promised, perhaps not. But he would, at last, know. No more waiting.

His senses seemed to dull as he moved through the crowd. Even the sound of the band seemed muted against the din of the blood rushing in his head. He was sweating hard. The smiling faces of the crowd seemed to mock him as he passed. As he got closer, a few of them seemed to notice him at last. A focusing of the eyes, a fading of the smiles.

A waif-like woman in a thin pink dress put a hand on his shoulder as she stepped out of his way, asking if he was okay. He mumbled that he was fine and moved past her. He navigated through a last knot of partygoers and found himself with a clear space of deck and his target, dead ahead. The empty space felt like a solid boundary. He hesitated on the edge of it for a moment, watching the four men.

The three lieutenants were grouped around Fleuriot. He was talking, maybe giving instructions of grave import, maybe just relating a joke that hadn't yet reached its punch-line. The other three listened with serious expressions. Nicolas saw that their eyes were on the crowd, even as they listened. They hadn't spotted him yet, but they would see him as soon as he made his move.

Nicolas played the steps in his mind's eye. Take out the gun, point it at Fleuriot's chest, fire twice. He would be six metres from the target. He had hit smaller targets from ten times as far, shooting from the hip. Missing was almost a literal impossibility. That wasn't what was in question. The question was, could he do it?

After he shot Fleuriot, there would be a second in which everyone was too shocked to react. In that second, he would run back into the crowd. He would drop the gun and take advantage of the fact there were two dozen other people on board dressed exactly as he was. He would make his way to the port side and his accomplice would be waiting for him by the lifeboats.

He had spent some of the evening searching the faces, wondering what his accomplice would look like. The other thing weighing on his mind: if he failed to carry out his task, the accomplice would become his assassin. It hadn't been spelled out to him, but it didn't have to be. He would be dead before he left the boat.

Nicolas took a deep breath and reached into his pocket. His fingers closed around the grip of the gun. The feel of a pistol in his hands wasn't just a comfort, it made him whole. He knew now that the shooting wouldn't be the challenge. Once he was in position and made the decision to shoot, muscle memory would take over. Action without thought. The challenge was taking the last few steps towards Fleuriot.

The band struck up another tune, a jauntier one this time, and it felt as though they were pushing him on.

He walked forward. Fleuriot kept talking, jutting his finger at the chest of one of his men. From somewhere further away, Nicolas heard some sort of commotion. He didn't bother to look. There would be a lot more commotion five seconds from now. He was utterly intent on what lay ahead. Finally, the man on the left side of the group caught Nicolas's approach in the corner of his eye and turned his head to look. It was too late. It was far too late.

Muscle memory.

Without conscious thought, Nicolas's body started to carry out the task it was made for. The world went into slow motion. He withdrew the pistol, sliding it smoothly out from under his jacket.

He angled his body side-on and pointed the gun square at Fleuriot's chest.

35

The blond woman took a sharp breath as she recognised Malloy, and her right hand immediately reached for her gun.

Mallory closed the distance and grabbed her left wrist, pressing his chest against her right arm beneath the jacket so she couldn't move. She opened her mouth and stopped when she felt Mallory's gun jabbing into her stomach.

'Drop it or you're dead,' Mallory whispered in her ear, then pulled back so that they were eye to eye. They were close enough that he could smell her perfume. Something that smelled subtly of citrus and money.

She grimaced, made a decision, and dropped the gun. The sounds of the party masked the sound of it hitting the deck, but Mallory felt the impact next to his foot. Without taking his eyes off the woman, he kicked it away into a forest of feet.

He looked over in the direction he had seen Nicolas and saw he had moved. He was barely ten paces from the man with the white hair.

The woman noticed Mallory's shift in attention and tried to grab for his gun. He lifted it clear and pushed her back, hard. She collided with a slim man in a white suit behind her and both of them crashed to the deck.

Mallory heard gasps from around him as the nearby party-goers reacted. One of the other guards had seen it too, and was already going for his gun. Mallory dived into the thick crowd in front of him and started pushing through. He had blown any chance of talking Nicolas down quietly, now he just had to try to get to him and find some way to get the fuck off this floating mob festival.

He kept his head down, hoping that the guy who had seen him wouldn't start indiscriminately firing into the crowd. Judging by the expensive suits and frocks, these people were a little too important to shoot at. He heard yelling behind him. Men shouting about a bearded man in a black jacket. The clothes at least wouldn't narrow it down too much in this crowd. It helped that people were starting to notice there was a commotion. Partygoers shifted position, tried to look for the source of the disturbance, and the churn covered his own movement. A space cleared ahead of him and he saw his target.

Unfortunately, his target had found *his* target.

Nicolas was standing opposite the small group of men that included the man with the white hair. The away team. As he watched, Nicolas pulled a gun from his pocket and pointed it at the VIP's chest.

No time to talk him out of it, no time even to yell a warning. Instead, Mallory charged forward, diving at Nicolas as he raised the gun.

He collided with him side-on as the gun went off.

The two of them collapsed to the deck, knocking over a champagne holder. The bottle impacted and lost its cork, firing off into the crowd like a rocket. Ice cubes scattered across the smooth wood of the deck like precious stones. Mallory looked up and saw the four men frozen in the same position they had been in a moment ago. As he watched, the three bodyguards started to reach for their guns while the man with the white hair pulled his jacket apart and examined his chest for a wound.

Nicolas yelled something that Mallory was pretty sure translated as, *What the fuck are you doing?*

'Get up.'

He hauled Nicolas to his feet. Two of the bodyguards were tending to their boss. He brushed them off angrily, pointing in Mallory's direction. The third was already running for them, gun in hand. As he raised it, Mallory instinctively shielded Nicolas, now asking himself what the hell he was doing.

But the guard's foot landed on a large chunk of ice and he skidded, throwing his arms up in a vain attempt to catch his balance. He landed on his back and Mallory grabbed Nicolas.

'Move it!'

Nicolas looked confused, either because he was being moved away from the bodyguards, or because Mallory's accent told him he wasn't one of them.

'Who are you?' he asked in English.

'Later. That way.' Mallory pointed at the closest railing. He had no idea what they were going to do once they got into the water, but he knew it was safer than staying on deck.

As though to prove the point, one of the guards chose that moment to risk taking a shot at them. The first Mallory knew about it was when he saw a man in a white tuxedo two feet from him grab his arm and collapse, blood blossoming on his pristine jacket.

Mallory gritted his teeth, feeling a weird exhilaration as the scene around him descended into panic. This was where he felt at home now. There were screams, yelled questions about what the hell was happening. Everyone was moving, but on the deck of a yacht, even one as big as this, there was nowhere to go. Mallory saw a woman trip on her emerald-green dress and fall headlong, only to be trampled by the hefty man who was behind her.

He heard shouts as the few guards who knew what they were looking for tried to direct the attention of the others effectively. Nobody knew what had happened. Somebody was shooting, that was enough to turn the assembled dignitaries into panicked animals.

They were almost at the railing now. Nicolas kept looking around, as though he had forgotten to bring someone with him. Mallory kept a hand on him, moving roughly forwards.

A gap opened in the crowd ahead and Mallory saw one of the mob soldiers. Mallory had the quick-draw advantage. He only had to watch out for the men with drawn guns, they had to filter out the rest of the crowd. Mallory raised his gun quickly and put two bullets in his chest as he was beginning to think about firing his own gun. He toppled backwards, his head smashing off the metal railing.

More screams, more shouts, more stampeding.

Mallory started to push Nicolas faster. It was on his lips to tell him to jump when Nicolas flinched backwards. Mallory immediately saw the reason as bullets thudded into the deck, cutting off their escape.

'Come on,' Mallory said, dragging him back into the melee.

Looking around as they pushed through the terrified horde, he could see that the men in suits had finally started to converge on them from almost all sides. They were being hemmed in, closer by the second. Mallory looked around and found they were in front of the stage. The band had evaporated, leaving overturned mics and abandoned instruments.

Mallory made for the door into the interior section where he had watched the two sets of gangsters meet earlier. There was a way out that way. He pushed Nicolas through the door. They ran past the billiard room and out onto the platform at the stern. Mallory overtook Nicolas and raced down the stairs.

'They saw us, they're coming!'

Mallory ignored him. He was busy ripping the tarpaulin off the jet ski he'd found earlier. The key was in the ignition.

Mallory grabbed Nicolas's arm and pushed him onto the back of the jet ski. He swung his leg over the front seat. He heard gunshots, saw new holes punched in the deck at their feet. One passed through the hull of the jet ski just below his leg. He hoped it hadn't hit anything important.

Mallory twisted the key in the ignition. The engine roared to life and he kicked the restraining bolt free. There was a moment of near weightlessness as they dropped down the ramp and plummeted toward the waves.

Mallory braced for impact and gripped the handlebars. He heard Nicolas gasp as they hit the water hard. It felt almost like impacting on sand, rather than water. The craft dipped and almost went under, then righted itself, then almost tipped, and finally came to rest. Mallory twisted the throttle and suddenly they were thrust forward.

Mallory had only ridden a craft like this once before, and it had been a less powerful model, but he was grateful for even that limited experience. He heard the cracks of gunshots as he upped the speed, putting as much distance between them and the yacht as quickly as possible. He weaved a little, but concentrated on increasing the distance. He knew exactly how difficult it would be to hit a moving target from the deck of a boat in the dark.

Gunshots popped like firecrackers in the distance. He heard Nicolas say something behind him, but it was impossible to make out over the roar of the engine.

'What was that?'

'We're dead,' Nicolas said, raising his voice.

They were three hundred yards out, now. Mallory started to turn in a wide circle, heading back for the harbour. He would put ashore further up, well away from the spot from which *La Deuxième Chance* had struck out.

'Don't worry about it, they have no chance at this range.'

'I'm not talking about them,' Nicolas said. 'You've killed us. They'll kill me and they'll kill Océane. And then they'll kill you, too.'

Mallory turned around. He couldn't make out Nicolas's features in the darkness. His face was a black void against the stars. His voice sounded like that of someone accepting the inevitable as he neared the end of a long, terminal illness.

'Who?' Mallory asked. 'Who'll kill Océane?'

36

Mallory slowed when they were a quarter-mile from the yacht. There were no lights on the jet ski, which was good. He wasn't worried about one of the men on the boat hitting them from this range, unless they had a military sniper on board, but he didn't want them to be able to follow their progress.

He steered for an area of the shoreline that was darker than the rest, away from the main strip. He estimated it was about half a mile down from where *La Deuxième Chance* had embarked. There was another pier: darker and more dilapidated than the other had been. Mallory steered between the piles and ran the jet ski aground on the sand of the beach.

He dismounted and waited for Nicolas to do likewise. Nicolas moved athletically, though his mind clearly wasn't on the here and now.

'Okay, we don't have long,' Mallory said. 'What do you mean they're going to kill you? Who was that guy on the boat you were about to shoot?'

'You're the man Océane told me about, aren't you?'

'Océane told you about me?'

'She should not have come,' Nicolas said. 'They're going to kill her.'

'Who's going to kill her? Mate, you need to start making sense soon.'

Nicolas put both hands to his face and rubbed down it. 'The man on the yacht I was supposed to kill; his name is Fleuriot.'

'And Fleuriot is some kind of big-shot gangster around here, right?'

'Not around here. He's a Parisian. The people hosting the party are from Marseille. Benoît Cristofol's gang. Different factions in le Milieu.'

'Some kind of mob summit then,' Mallory said. 'And you were supposed to shoot Fleuriot. Who hired you, this Cristofol guy?'

'I don't know.'

'You don't know? You were about to kill someone and you don't know who hired you to do it?'

'They approached me when I was having some money problems. They told me they could give me enough to bail myself out and then some. By the time I found out what they wanted – and why they wanted me – it was too late. They tested me. They made me ...' He was starting to hyperventilate, babbling. 'He has a house in the Alps and—'

Impatient, Mallory cut him off. 'How much are they paying you?'

Nicolas took a deep breath and composed himself.

'Half a million euros. They gave me two hundred thousand up front, enough to pay what I owed. Once I took that, they told me what I had to do. And they told me what would happen if I didn't do it. There was someone on the yacht who was going to kill me, I don't know what happened to him. I thought that was you.'

Mallory smiled thinly. 'There were a hundred people on the yacht who were going to kill you, you moron. They told you they had a way off the boat, right?'

He hesitated, then nodded.

'There was no way off the boat. They didn't have a man on the boat. They wanted you to kill Fleuriot and let Fleuriot's men take care of you. You know that, right?'

'I . . . I don't—'

'What about Océane? You said they'll kill Océane.'

'They will. It's how they knew I wouldn't try to run. They have a man in Paris, his orders were to kill her if I didn't kill Fleuriot.'

The Serbian. As Mallory had guessed, he hadn't gone to the apartment looking for Nicolas, he had been there for Océane. And he had almost caught up to her at her friend's place. Another piece of the puzzle. Mallory knew now why the trail in Nicolas's apartment had been laid out like that, too: the evidence linking him to Fleuriot was supposed to be found after Nicolas carried out his job and was killed.

'What? What are you thinking?' Nicolas said after Mallory hadn't spoken for a few moments.

'Nothing. Listen, don't worry about it. Océane is safe. You already know she's right here in Marseille, not in Paris. Those guys back there won't be able to trace her back from us, and no one else will, either. Only I know where she is, and that's not going to change.'

Nicolas's face, already not looking too healthy, seemed to drain of colour.

'What is it?'

'L'Hôtel d'Or,' Nicolas said slowly. '*Deux cent treize.*'

Mallory blinked. 'What?'

'She told me where she was staying. Room two-one-three.'

'Okay,' Mallory said tersely. 'But you didn't tell anyone that, did you?'

Nicolas didn't speak, but his face said it all.

'Nicolas?'

'She wrote it down on a card. I put it in my wallet. I meant to get rid of it, I swear ...'

With effort, Mallory controlled his voice. 'Nicolas. Where is your wallet?'

'It's on the boat. I left it in the locker when I got changed.'

37

Océane sat on the bed with her back against the headboard, watching the news on France 24 and trying not to think about how long it had been since Mallory had left. She had made herself a cup of coffee from the Nespresso machine, but it was much too hot to drink. Besides, she didn't need caffeine to stay awake.

She remembered his words when he left earlier in the evening: don't leave the room for any reason, don't try to call me, sit tight until I get back. The instructions were very clear, no room for ambiguity.

But what happened if he didn't come back? Mallory had promised her that he would find Nicolas and stop him from doing anything stupid. He was sure that whatever Nicolas was here to do was related to that yacht, *La Deuxième Chance*. But what if he was wrong? What if Nicolas was somewhere else?

She shivered as she thought about his appearance earlier in the day. He looked like a condemned man. Suddenly, she had gone from being angry at him to feeling guilty about walking out on him weeks ago. What if he had needed her? What if she could have stopped … whatever it was that was happening?

She let out a groan of frustration and punched one of the scrawny pillows. This was the hardest part. Not knowing what was going on in the first place, and now sitting here alone with the TV, even more lost.

She picked up her phone again, glaring at the blank screen.

'Don't call me, I'll call you,' she said, mocking Mallory's accent.

She picked up her phone and scrolled back through her WhatsApp threads. Messages from Nicolas, from Marianne, from work. She wondered how Marianne was doing. Maybe she should—

A soft knock on the door yanked her attention away from the screen of her phone. She started to get up, thinking Mallory was back already, and then she remembered.

Four knocks. Don't open the door, don't answer if you don't hear four knocks.

He had demonstrated by rapping his knuckles on the wooden desk in a specific rhythm: three quick knocks, then a beat, then a fourth knock.

Whoever was out there had knocked twice.

Carefully, Océane slipped off the bed, tiptoeing carefully across the floor to the door. There was no peephole, no way to look outside. She looked down. The room was dark, lit only by the television, and the corridor outside was brightly lit. She could see where the light cut through under the door, and she could see a shadow in the middle of it where someone was blocking the light.

Could somebody have got mixed up and knocked on the wrong door?

She flinched as there were another two knocks. A little louder this time, more insistent.

A male voice spoke. He said he was the manager, but his voice had a low, guttural tone, and he didn't sound that sure about what he had just said.

Océane shrank back from the door as he knocked again. Not a knock this time, the heel of a fist, pounding three times. She looked around the room frantically. She had bought clothes and a phone earlier, why hadn't she thought to buy something she could have used as a weapon? A knife or something. Her gaze alighted on the lamp beside the bed. She moved over to it and unplugged it, banging the base of the table as she did so.

The handle of the door started jiggling. She gripped the lamp, and then the handle stopped moving.

She heard voices outside the room. The man out there was talking to someone. A friend? The real manager?

A moment later there was a sudden thud, as though someone had thrown something at the wall. Océane took another sharp breath and looked around the room again. The fire escape was at this end of the building . . . but she would have to go out in the corridor to access it.

There was no other sound for a minute. No more voices.

Océane held her breath and put her ear to the door. She could hear someone breathing.

She put a hand to her own mouth, in case her own breathing was audible.

A creak outside, like someone had adjusted their weight on a loose floorboard. And then the door exploded inwards.

Océane was flung backwards, her motion stopped only when she hit the foot of the bed and collapsed in front of it. A man filled the door frame, silhouetted against the strip light in the corridor.

A big man. He didn't speak, but Océane knew with a deep certainty that he would have a Serbian accent. This was the man Mallory had told her about, the man who had threatened to open up her friend Marianne.

He wore a leather jacket and had dark hair tied back in a ponytail. His hands were by his side, balancing him after he had kicked the door in. Océane could see another man crumpled on the floor. This one had light brown hair and an open-necked shirt. He wasn't moving.

The hands of the man in the doorway were enormous. He wasn't holding a gun. He wasn't holding anything. Somehow, that made it even more terrifying.

Océane scrambled to her feet, clutching the lamp.

He stepped into the room.

38

The Hôtel d'Or wasn't far from the Old Port, but their escape from *La Deuxième Chance* had taken them another half mile in the wrong direction. Mallory hadn't had time to properly get to know Marseille in the two days he had been here, but he knew the rough direction to head.

Nicolas kept pace with him easily, his long legs carrying him along with a bouncing gait, like a jungle cat. He was neck and neck with Mallory, even though he was simultaneously looking up the location of the hotel on his phone.

'We have to get there faster,' he said.

'I know.'

'Océane—'

'I know,' Mallory said.

They ran through some kind of marketplace, the open-air stalls serving up loaded fries and paella and bratwurst and pastries; a generic Euro-smorgasbord of cuisines. A stout man wielding a giant stein of beer stepped out in Mallory's path as he passed a beer tent. Too late to move out of the way, Mallory collided with him at full pelt. The man was jolted into the upright supporting the awning over one of the stalls. He rebounded and fell the other way, dropping the stein. It shattered, sending an explosion of beer everywhere, as Mallory stumbled and fell into a display table of hand-crafted chocolate animals on the opposite stall.

Nicolas stopped and looked back. Mallory waved him on. 'Go, I'll catch up.'

He got to his feet, but before he could start running again, he felt rough hands grabbing his shoulders. He was pushed roughly to the side as a bulky storekeeper pointed at his destroyed chocolate bunnies and rhinoceroses and started yelling.

He murmured an apology, moving to sidestep the man.

Someone else placed themself in front of him, putting his hand on his chest and shoving him backwards, hard. Mallory, caught unawares, fell back and sprawled on the cobbles. That would bruise later. He felt a flash of anger, quickly followed by that familiar, addictive exhilaration, and got to his feet.

It was a friend of the man with the stein. He pointed at his friend, who was still on the ground, looking dazed, then turned back to Mallory, just in time to meet Mallory's fist full force in the middle of his face.

His nose exploded blood and he staggered back, trying to keep his footing, then fell into a third stall.

Mallory wrung his hand to work the pain in his knuckles out. He hadn't even thought about throwing that punch. The guy had pushed him down, so he had fucking thumped him as hard as he could. That was all there was to it. Dimly, a voice in his head told him he was lucky he hadn't broken his fingers. Another reminded him, very quietly, that these were civilians. But that voice was losing out to the din in his head.

A civilian can do as much harm to you as a professional, if he puts his mind to it.

Out of the corner of his eye, he saw something moving towards him fast. He ducked just in time to avoid someone hitting him with a chair. He had swung it with enough force that it hit a female bystander in the face. Mallory hooked his leg around the assailant's ankles and in the same motion, slammed his forearm into his face.

Mallory didn't have time for this. He started to move, looking in the direction Nicolas had gone to see where he was. There was no sign of him.

His attention was brought back to the immediate vicinity as he heard a yell of '*Connard*' in his direction. He didn't know what the hell that translated as, but going by the tone of voice, it wasn't anything good.

Two other young guys in pristine white T-shirts, who had no relation to any of the combatants so far as Mallory could see, were advancing on him, fists raised. An audience was starting to form as awareness of the fracas rippled through the crowd.

Somebody grabbed Mallory's shoulders from behind. Mallory slammed his elbow into an unguarded belly and twisted out of the way, standing back as the pair in white T-shirts approached.

The one on the left produced a folding knife. The sureness of his grip and the look in his eye told Mallory this wasn't his first time. He knew how to use that thing.

That was okay. Mallory had something he knew how to use, too. He reached back and pulled the Ruger from his waistband. He fired once in the air and then pointed it at the one with the knife. He blinked once, taking a long time to catch up, and then the eager look in his eye drained away.

Mallory backed against the wall of one of the huts, keeping his eyes on the crowd. Nobody was getting too close. That was good.

'Everybody get back,' he said, speaking loudly but keeping his voice calm and controlled.

He swung the gun around. The crowd started to retreat. He heard a couple of screams. That was good. No one knew who he was, what he was planning to do. That made it less likely they would continue to get in his way.

He took a step towards the two guys, keeping the gun on them. He jerked his head up in a 'get out of here' motion.

It translated. The two of them exchanged a glance and made a hasty retreat. A corridor had opened up as the crowd thinned. Mallory took it, running in the direction Nicolas had gone.

He had lost two minutes at least. He hoped Nicolas was making better time, and that he knew where he was going. More than that, he hoped they wouldn't be too late.

39

Nicolas burst through the foyer of the Hôtel d'Or, ignoring the outraged shouts of the receptionist as he barrelled up the stairs. He reached floor two and slammed the stairwell door open, sending it bouncing off the wall. One of the rooms had an open door ahead. There was a body lying outside it. He was too late.

As he moved down the corridor, he realised he might not be. The body on the floor was a man. Dark suit, no tie, a deep tan. Dead. One of Cristofol's boys.

But the door had been kicked in. He heard a sound like somebody trying to speak through an obstruction. When he drew level with the door, he saw it was Océane. She was being held against a wall by her throat by a big man. He knew who this had to be, and a cold dread seized him.

He didn't let it stop him.

Without hesitation, he launched himself into the room. The man turned, surprised, and released Océane. He put his hands up to grab Nicolas, but Nicolas ducked under his arms and got two punches in to the sternum. It felt like hitting a car tyre; no more give than that. The man got hold of Nicolas's shoulders and shoved him, then hit him with a punch of his own, deep in Nicolas's gut. It was as though all the air in his body had been sucked out of him. He staggered back. The big man followed up by delivering a hard, targeted kick to the side of the knee. Nicolas felt it give way and fell to the ground.

His assailant stepped forward.

And Nicolas grabbed the man's meaty ankle and bit it.

It had the element of surprise. But it also enraged his opponent. He yelled out and kicked at Nicolas's head. Nicolas managed to move just enough so that the blow was glancing, kicking against the floor to move out of range, feeling pain stab at his knee.

A scream from behind them made both men freeze for a second. Nicolas saw Océane swinging something small and white at the big man's head. As it smacked against his cheekbone and spilled brown liquid, the big man screamed. She had hit him with hot coffee.

Wiping at his eyes with one hand, the big man gripped Océane's shoulder with the other and threw her violently against the wall. Océane impacted hard enough to dent the plasterboard. She fell to the floor.

Nicolas picked himself up and lunged at the guy, grabbing him around the midsection and slamming them both into the wall-mounted television. It smashed off the wall and crashed to the ground. They glanced off the flimsy desk and crashed to the floor, Nicolas on top. Out of the corner of his eye, he saw Océane getting to her feet. She had a clear path to the door.

'Get out of here,' he yelled. 'Get—'

His instruction was cut off as the big guy worked an arm free and punched him twice in the chest. Nicolas crumpled and felt himself being thrown back like a paper doll.

Océane made it to the door and out into the corridor.

The big man got to his feet, reaching inside his coat. Nicolas knew that wasn't good. The lamp from the desk was lying beside him, cracked. He picked it up and threw it. The guy batted it aside, but the delay allowed Nicolas to scramble up and get in close, relying on his good leg. He was going to lose this fight, he knew that. But if he could stall the big man long enough for Océane to get away ...

The big man had a gun in his hand now. Nicolas recognised it in a glance. He recognised every gun. FNX-45 Tactical, elongated by a silencer. But he hadn't had time to point it in the right direction.

Suddenly, Nicolas felt a surge of hope. If he could somehow get the gun away from him, it would change the odds.

They struggled, staggering into the corner. The big man made no noise, but his eyes were locked on Nicolas's. His hand was still gripping the gun, his finger on the trigger guard.

Slowly, painfully, he started to force the gun back, back towards Nicolas's face.

40

Océane ran down the corridor as though there were wings on her feet.

From behind her, she heard something smash, a yell that sounded like Nicolas. He didn't have a chance. She had to find help. Maybe there would be a security guard, or perhaps there would be police out in the street.

She was in a daze, running blindly. She reached the stairwell door and thumped hard on it, trying to push it open. It took her a moment to register it was a pull handle. She got it open and spilled into the stairwell, losing her footing on the first short flight of stairs and tumbling to the landing. She could hear hyper-ventilating breaths and realised they were her own. Her throat burned from where the man had been choking her against the wall. She had been about to black out when Nicolas had burst in.

She rounded the corner to the next flight and screamed as she saw a looming figure with a gun in his hand, silhouetted by the stairwell light.

Not thinking, she kept running into the man, hammering on his chest, trying to get the gun from him.

He was too powerful for her. He grabbed one wrist, then the other. It was happening again. Now this one was going to kill her instead. He even knew her name, he was saying it, mockingly.

And then she realised it wasn't mocking.

'Océane, you're okay, it's me.'

The man stepped back into the light and she saw that it was Mallory. His black T-shirt was soaking wet. Blood was dripping down his face from a cut above his eyebrow. He was holding a gun.

'Nicolas,' she started to say, trying to focus on getting the words out, telling Mallory what was happening, where he needed to go.

She didn't need to tell him. He already knew.

'Stay here,' Mallory said as he moved her aside and sprinted up the stairs. As he reached the top, he flinched back and she heard sounds like someone knocking on a wall. It took her a second to realise they were suppressed gunshots. They were followed by louder reports as Mallory returned fire. The sound of a door opening hard enough to slam against the wall. Not the room door, the fire door? And then footsteps. Mallory's. Advancing cautiously but purposefully down the corridor.

There was silence for a minute. A door creaked open on the floor below and then quickly closed again.

Then she heard approaching footsteps again and huddled back around the bend, ready to run if it was the attacker. But it was Mallory.

'What?' she asked.

His face was grave.

'You better come with me.'

She followed him back up the stairs. The body of the man who had knocked on her door was still on the floor, and the fire exit door at the end of the corridor was open. She swallowed, a part of her knowing exactly what Mallory was taking her to see. She was prepared for it.

And then she stepped through the door of the hotel room and knew she really wasn't prepared for it. Could never be.

The room looked as though somebody had driven earth-moving equipment through it. The door was off its hinges where the big man had kicked it in on her. The bed-sheets were on the floor, blood and coffee sprayed across the white walls. The television was smashed, as was the mirror fixed to the wall.

The worst thing was what she couldn't yet see.

Sticking out from the other side of the bed was a pair of feet clad in black shoes. She took a step into the room and felt Mallory's hand on her shoulder.

'You don't have to look.'

'No.' She closed her eyes and swallowed. 'No, I think I do.'

It wasn't a large room. Three paces was all it took.

Nicolas was lying on his back, his eyes closed. There was a lot of blood. She couldn't see exactly where the wound was, but it was on the left side of his head.

'Is he . . . ?'

'Yes. I'm sorry.'

She forced herself to keep looking at him. She couldn't look away now, as much as she wanted to. This was her fault. He had died to save her. She felt Mallory's hand on her shoulder again and let him turn her away. He pulled her in close.

'It's my fault,' she said. 'I ran.'

'You were right to run. He would have killed you both.'

Océane sobbed against Mallory's chest. His T-shirt was wet, like he had taken a shower in his clothes. He smelled of seawater and, oddly, beer.

'Where is he? The man who did this?'

'He got out the fire exit. I'm guessing he didn't want to stick around for the—'

Mallory was interrupted by the sounds of approaching sirens. Gently, he pushed Océane back from his chest.

'The police,' she said. 'We can tell—'

'No. We need to get out of here. It's not just the police who are coming. And we can't trust the police anyway. Are you okay to move?'

Océane looked back at Nicolas's body.

'We can't do anything for him now. But we need to go.' Mallory's voice showed no trace of anger or irritation. He was telling her how it was. And as much as she wanted to stay with Nicolas, she knew that he was right.

She swallowed back a sob and nodded. 'Where?'

41

They took the same exit Nicolas's killer had used, descending the fire escape into the alley that ran along the side of the Hôtel d'Or. Mallory kept his eyes on the shadows and his gun in his hand, wary of an ambush from the Serbian. He was putting together the sequence of events. The people on the yacht had searched Nicolas's locker and found the hotel room number. They had sent whatever man they had in the area. It had been his final job, because he had been intercepted by the Serbian. Mallory remembered stepping over his body on his way into the room, seeing the ragged knife wound under his chin. Poor bastard probably hadn't seen it coming.

Mallory made Océane take her coat. The night was warm, but she was in shock. She bundled it around her and followed him as he moved quickly towards the mouth of the alley. He was pleasantly surprised that he didn't have to hoist her over his shoulder and carry her. God knows what she had been through if that bastard had found her alone. And now her boyfriend was dead. He recognised the look in her eye, though. She wasn't thinking, was just trying to get out of the situation. Shock can be a friend.

Mallory stopped at the edge of the alley. The sirens were getting closer. Even in a shithole like this, it appeared people called the police if they heard gunshots.

He took Océane's hand and pulled her out on the street, heading towards the sirens.

'Keep walking, don't look up,' he said. 'Not too fast.'

He put an arm around her shoulder. They were just a couple out for an evening stroll. Not panicking, not fleeing the scene of a major crime.

The noise of the sirens built in volume; whiny, peremptory. The first police car rounded the corner at speed, blue lights blazing. With less fanfare, he could see other vehicles arrive. Black SUVs, motorcycles. Cristofol's men, looking for the people who had crashed the party.

'Keep walking,' Mallory said.

The car flashed past them, neither of the cops inside looking at them. It travelled the length of the street and pulled up outside the front of the Hôtel d'Or. Another car appeared from the opposite direction.

Mallory calculated the timings in his head. Two minutes for them to get upstairs and find Nicolas's body. Maybe they would send someone around the back, in which case they would work out that someone could have got out by the fire escape. Either way, it would take a few minutes.

They turned onto the next street and Mallory saw a bus idling as a solitary passenger climbed on. Mallory squeezed Océane's hand and pulled her forward. As they ran, he pulled the brim of his cap down and murmured to Océane to keep her hood up. He had no idea if French buses had CCTV, but he wasn't taking the chance.

Mallory asked for two tickets to Roucas Blanc, which was the destination on the side of the bus. The driver grunted a figure and he handed over a twenty euro note, hoping that would cover it. It seemed to.

They sat in the middle of the bus, which was almost empty. It pulled off, frustratingly slowly.

Another police car appeared ahead of them. Mallory turned his face away from the window as it blew past. The bus made a yellow light and picked up speed.

'He was big.' Océane's voice was steady enough, but with a brittle edge. 'Was he the one who … ?'

'The Serbian. The guy I met in Nicolas's apartment,' Mallory said. 'I saw enough of him as he was leaving by the fire escape.'

'Who is he?'

'I don't know. But I don't think he's finished with us.' The bus started to slow for the next stop, and they passed a bank with an ATM outside. 'Time to get off.'

'Already?'

They alighted at the stop and Mallory scanned their surroundings as the bus drew away. This street was quieter. No other traffic. He could still hear sirens, but they were more distant. He turned to Océane. 'Do you have any cash?'

Océane shook her head. 'I have my card.'

Mallory pointed at the ATM. 'We should take out as much as we can. We don't want to leave a trail if we can avoid it.'

Océane withdrew the maximum from her account, 600 euros, and Mallory did the same. Then they walked down an alley to the next main road and flagged down a cab.

Mallory had found another hotel in the 6th arrondissement on his phone.

Then he thought about it from the perspective of the people looking for him. It was the kind of place he would expect someone fleeing from the Hôtel d'Or to go. Across town, equally low-rent and unobtrusive. He remembered how Océane had been able to find him yesterday.

'*Vers où?*' asked the driver as they got into the back seat. He wore a flat cap and had thick five o'clock shadow.

'*Un moment, monsieur,*' Mallory said.

'Anglais?'

Mallory sighed and nodded as he narrowed the map on his phone a little. He found a boutique hotel that was a mile closer, in a neighbourhood called Saint-Victor. He gave the name of the place to the driver.

'Artemis,' the driver repeated. 'Nice.'

'Doesn't sound very French,' Mallory commented. 'Greek goddess of hunting, right?'

'Marseille used to be Greek,' the driver said. 'About two thousand years ago. *Massalia.*'

He pulled out onto the road, seemingly happy to leave the history lesson there, which suited Mallory. He settled back into the seat, keeping his eyes on the streets as they passed by.

'Why didn't we wait for the police?' Océane whispered.

'Because I make it a habit never to trust the police in a strange town. And this town in particular hasn't done anything to persuade me I'm being overcautious.'

'We could have told them what happened.'

'We could have told them all sorts of things until we were blue in the face. At the end of the day, you've got the two of us in a room with two dead bodies and no other suspects. That's bad enough. When you add in the fact that every gangster in the city is looking for me and Nicolas, you've got some real problems.'

42

Artemis was a grand stone building not far from the Abbey of Saint-Victor that gave the neighbourhood its name. Mallory asked for a room on the first floor. Easy to leave in a hurry if necessary, harder for someone else to sneak in unauthorised. The room was a suite, with a master bedroom with a four poster and a couch bed in the living room. He told Océane to take a shower and wash the blood off while he gave the place a once-over.

The rooms on this side had balconies that overlooked a central courtyard. More secluded than the street, which was perfect. There was no one down in the courtyard, just an illuminated fountain cycling through various coloured filters. It would be simple enough to hang from the balcony and drop, should they need to make an escape by alternative means.

Mallory drew the curtains and checked over the rest of the room quickly, opening the cupboard and the drawers. There was a connecting door to the adjacent room. Mallory knocked softly on it and listened. When there was no sound from the other side, he took his pick set out. He beat the lock in seconds and opened the door onto a darkened apartment that was the mirror of this one. He closed the door, leaving it unlocked, to give them a second exit route.

Océane emerged from the bathroom ten minutes later, dressed again in the same clothes, with a wet patch on the shoulder where she had scrubbed the blood out of her shirt. Her hair was wet, and she was rubbing it with a luxurious-looking white towel.

Mallory handed her a miniature bottle of whisky from the minibar.

'This'll help.'

She looked at the bottle for a second, then wordlessly took it from Mallory's hand and necked it. The bottle could have contained tap water for all the reaction it caused.

'It's my fault,' she said. Her voice was composed, she didn't look on the verge of bursting into tears. It was as though she was stating a fact.

'It's no one's fault. Nicolas got himself into some trouble. He didn't deserve what happened to him, but he started the ball rolling.'

'How can you say that?' she snapped.

'Listen. The only thing he cared about at the end was saving you. And he did it. He didn't die in vain.'

Océane held Mallory's gaze for a long moment, as though trying to gauge whether he was lying to make her feel better. Then she threw the towel haphazardly in the direction of the bathroom and walked across the room to the glass doors that opened onto the balcony.

'Leave the light off and don't get too close to the edge,' Mallory said.

She stopped in her tracks and turned back to him. 'You're telling me what to do?'

'Yes, I am. And if you want to not get killed, and not get *me* killed, you'll listen.'

She tossed a Gallic curse at him under her breath, but she kept the light off when she walked out onto the balcony. Mallory followed.

The night air was still warm. The buildings around them muted the normal sounds of a lively city after dark. The horns and sirens and shouts sounded a long way off.

'Océane, we're safe here for now, but we need to get to the bottom of this.'

She glanced down, confused. 'What?'

'It's a figure of speech. We need to work out who used Nicolas to take a shot at this Fleuriot guy.'

She didn't answer him, just stared across at the windows on the opposite side of the courtyard. Mallory reminded himself that she was a civilian who had probably never encountered much in the way of violence. Now she had witnessed her boyfriend's murder, and almost been killed herself.

'How's your neck?' he asked, softening his tone.

She took her right hand from the railing and touched the spot just above her collar bone.

'He was going to kill me. He didn't threaten me, didn't ask any questions, he just wanted me dead. How can a person do that?'

She turned around. Mallory could furnish her with a few different answers to that question, but he didn't think any of them would be helpful. Instead, he examined her throat. The bruising was already showing up: a fierce dark haze around her throat, but her voice no longer sounded as husky. The heat of the shower had probably helped with the swelling.

'He won't get a chance to do it again,' Mallory said, feeling a swell of anger as he studied the bruising. 'I'll make sure of that.' He meant it. Usually, he took pains to avoid situations where he might lose control, give into the darkness. With this guy, he was going to relish it.

She looked down at her feet. 'What happened tonight, Mallory? When you went to the yacht?'

Mallory went over the events of the evening. Watching the yacht, the well-heeled clientele, the less salubrious guests. Getting on board and finding Nicolas just in time to stop him from killing the man with the white hair and sunglasses. No, killing wasn't the right word. Assassination was the word.

'Who do you think he was?'

'Nicolas told me his name is Fleuriot. Some kind of boss in le Milieu, from Paris. He was a guest. The other crew on the boat were local, from Marseille. They were making a big fuss, but they were wary of Fleuriot and his men. I think it was some kind of summit, or maybe a big deal.'

'But why would Nicolas shoot this person?'

'Somebody was blackmailing him, telling him he had to do it or they were going to kill you.'

'But why Nicolas? He's not a hitman. He was a party organiser.'

'How many party organisers do you know who can hit a small target at a hundred yards under pressure?'

She shook her head. 'No. It's different. Shooting was a sport to him, he wasn't interested in hurting people.'

'I believe you,' Mallory said. 'He had the skill, but that wasn't why they chose him. He was a clean skin. He wasn't a hitman, and nobody had any reason to suspect the threat would come from someone like him. That's why they picked him. They used you as collateral.'

'You said you stopped him from shooting. Why?'

'Because I knew he would be dead five seconds after he pulled the trigger.'

'The man who came to kill me tonight. The Serbian. He's working for the people who hired Nicolas?'

'Almost certainly.'

'But why was he at the apartment in Paris? Why did he come to Marianne's place? If they were using me to blackmail Nicolas, why would they kill me before he had done what they wanted? It doesn't make any sense.'

'That's what I can't work out,' Mallory said.

He thought about the yacht. The oblivious partygoers, the guards, the men in suits. Two different tribes of men in suits. In as much as he'd had time to consider it, he had decided Cristofol, the Marseille chief, had hired Nicolas to take out a rival. Set Fleuriot up by inviting him to peace talks. But then he remembered his earlier thought about the Serbian. How he could have been leaving something in Nicolas's apartment, rather than taking something.

'It wasn't Cristofol's people.'

'What?'

'Why would they invite a rival gang on board and kill him there? If they want deniability, they wouldn't do it on their turf. And if they just wanted to kill him out in the open, they would do it themselves.'

'You're not making sense.'

Mallory ignored her, kept talking. 'Whatever that was on the yacht, none of them expected what happened. Both sides were shocked. Nobody was prepared. That's part of the reason we managed to get out of there. I think we're looking for a third party.'

'A third party?'

'I think someone wanted to start a war. A war in which you and Nicolas would be collateral damage. And they just might have got what they wanted.'

Mallory got up from the chair and went back inside the room. He picked up the Ruger, slipped out the partly spent magazine and replaced it with a fresh one.

'What are you going to do?'

'I'm going to do something that doesn't come naturally.'

'What?'

'I'm going to see if I can make peace.'

'What about the gun?'

'There's an old saying. The original's in Latin, and I can't remember all of it. I'm not sure what it would be in French. In English, it's: "If you want peace, prepare for war."'

THURSDAY

43

MARSEILLE

Twelve minutes after one in the morning and the Marseille nightlife showed no signs of quieting down. Mallory weaved across the pavement to avoid stepping on a skinny teenager who had either tripped coming out of a bar or been helped on his way by the fearsome-looking bouncer stepping over him.

Walking into enemy territory was always risky, but a person could minimise the risks by taking certain precautions. The most important rule was the one he had used on the yacht: always be ready to run, and always have somewhere to run to. Beyond that, it was mostly about blending in and keeping your eyes open.

Mallory walked in the shadows, away from the shining signs of shops and bars, staying out of the brightest areas. He kept the brim of his hat down. In ten minutes, he saw a handful of men standing at corners and sitting in parked cars that he might need to be concerned about. None of them saw him.

What he was looking for was one of his pursuers on his

own, away from prying eyes. He hadn't seen what he was looking for yet. He would have to risk getting a little closer to where things had started.

He passed the open door of a club playing blaring techno music and adorned with sickly green neon and turned into one of the darkened backstreets. He covered the length of it quickly, keeping his head down, slowing as he reached the hard line of glaring streetlights marking the boundary between the backstreets and the quayside of the Old Port. Every instinct in Mallory's body was telling him to stay far away from this part of the city. Every action he had taken since escaping *La Deuxième Chance* had been geared towards putting as much distance between himself and the hosts of that party as possible.

But now here he was, on the stretch of quayside at the marina near where *La Deuxième Chance* had been moored until earlier in the evening. He looked both ways and stepped out into the light.

There was no sign of the yacht in the spot where it had been moored yesterday, or anywhere nearby. Mallory found an awning over a closed restaurant and moved under its shelter. He backed against the wall and surveyed the immediate area, quickly spotting four sentries posted near where the yacht had been moored. They had to be Cristofol's men. He knew they would be on the lookout for someone matching his description. By now, they would know that Nicolas, the other man they were looking for, had been found dead in a hotel room, along with one of their colleagues. Mallory was betting that was all the information they would have.

He thought about what Mathieu, the man who had sold him the ammunition, had said yesterday. *They're looking for you*. Mallory knew that they would be looking a lot harder now, and the Serbian would be too.

He had been keeping an eye on the news updates. There were some reports of two men being found dead at the Hôtel d'Or, but nothing on *La Deuxième Chance*. Mallory had half-expected reports of a massacre on board the yacht, but evidently the two sides had managed to restrain themselves. Even the Marseille cops wouldn't be able to cover up an entire ship of the dead.

The four Cristofol sentries were positioned in a rough square formation. They obviously had orders to stay put and keep an eye on the mooring. It didn't look like there was any way to approach one of them without the others seeing, which was a problem. Still, there would have to be a break or a change of the guard at some point.

As he watched, the man closest to him took his phone out and read something off the screen. He put the phone back in his pocket and looked up in Mallory's direction. Mallory shrank back into the darkness, but then realised the guy wasn't looking directly at him. He followed his gaze and saw that he was watching the mouth of the alley from which Mallory had emerged earlier on.

A moment later, a woman strode from the alley. A dark suit, blond hair tied back. The woman from yesterday, the one he had seen again on the yacht.

She walked unhurriedly over to the man who had received the message. The other three saw her and straightened. She was clearly a person of authority in Cristofol's organisation, but Mallory had surmised that already. They exchanged words and the subordinate pointed his finger at one of the others. The other three men closed the distance and stood around the woman. They were still too far away to make out any of the words. The woman listened and then nodded. She said something and then turned around and walked back the way she had come. Mallory watched her, then looked back at the four men. They were now in a close circle talking to each other. Which meant they weren't looking in his direction.

Mallory slipped out of the shadows and quickly walked in the direction of the alley.

The woman was almost at the far end. Mallory quickened his pace. The sound of his footsteps were covered by the loud music from the club at the far end.

Mallory emerged from the alley into the green wash of the neon light and saw the woman get into a black Citroën C3 parked on the opposite side of the road.

He slowed and walked a little way along the pavement, watching the woman in the car and trying to stay out of her eyeline as she pulled her seatbelt on. She looked down and her face lit up with blue light from her phone. Probably checking in with the boss.

Mallory decided he wasn't going to get a better opportunity. He cast a last glance around to check there was no one watching, then crossed the road quickly, opened the passenger door and got in.

'Hey!' she said sharply, looking up from her phone to tell him he had the wrong car.

She froze when she saw Mallory's face. She made to reach inside her jacket, and then stopped when she saw the gun pointed at her stomach.

'Give it to me, left hand.'

She hissed a frustrated curse between her teeth and did as

he asked. He took the gun from her, a Glock, and tossed it in the footwell in the back seat behind the driver's seat.

'Drive.'

She didn't blink. Didn't make any move to obey Mallory's order.

'*Un homme mort*. You are a dead man.'

'Maybe so,' Mallory said. 'Which would be bad news for you, because it means I've got nothing to lose.'

That gave her pause. Mallory gestured at the road ahead with his free hand.

'*Allez.*'

The woman turned the key in the ignition, casting a last glance at the mouth of the alley as they moved away from the kerb.

Over the last couple of days, Mallory had got to know this part of the city pretty well. He wanted to get away from the areas where there were a lot of people around. 'Take the next left and keep on that road. You understand?'

The woman gave him a look of contempt. She didn't answer, but she took the left. This route would take them away from the heart of town, and he hoped, away from the greatest concentration of police and Cristofol's men. But it paid to be clear about his expectations.

'Don't try anything. You crash the car, try to signal somebody on the street, anything, I'll shoot you and I'll run. I'd rather not do that, so keep doing what you're doing and we're going to be fine.'

She gripped the steering wheel tightly and her jaw was set, but if she was tense, it didn't filter through to her driving. Mallory felt a modicum of sympathy for her. Nobody likes being caught out when they're supposed to be on high alert.

'Do you have a name?' Mallory asked.

She glanced over at him, her eyes burning with disdain, then stared back at the road.

'Corinne.'

'Corinne Cristofol, right?'

She looked back at him, this time too surprised to show disdain.

'I thought so,' Mallory said. 'Unusual to see guys like that take orders from a woman.'

She rolled her eyes. 'You think I'm only here because I'm the boss's daughter?'

'No, I think the boss knows you can handle yourself. He's right. You were smart to run yesterday, and you're being smart now. I prefer dealing with smart people. People get hurt when you're dealing with idiots.'

'What do you want?'

'I just want to talk. And then, if you haven't done anything stupid, I'd like you alive at the end of our talk to take a message back to your father.'

Corinne snorted. 'You want to *talk*.'

'Yeah.'

She glanced over at Mallory, a little curious now.

'Who are you?'

'Who do you think I am?'

'One of Fleuriot's people. We did not know he used foreigners.'

'I'm not with Fleuriot. What do you know about me?'

'I know you lied about your name in the alley the other day. I know you killed Simon there. I know you were watching *La Deuxième Chance*. I know you got on board and left with the other man. The assassin.'

'His name was Nicolas. Was he on your radar?'

252

'Radar?'

'Was he known to you?'

She buttoned her lip.

'I'm not trying to catch you out here. I'm just trying to work out what the hell is going on, just like you are.'

She hesitated, and then shook her head. 'No. We found his belongings and a card with his hotel and room number. He killed one of our men there. Or you did.'

'No, he didn't, and neither did I. Someone else killed them both.' Mallory thought it over for a minute. 'You were looking for me and him. What were your orders? Kill us?'

Mallory thought he caught the hint of a smile at the edge of her mouth.

'That's not it, is it? Your father wanted us brought in, right? He wanted to question us.'

'That's correct. *Then* he would kill you. Do you know anything about Benoît Cristofol?'

'Should I?'

'If you knew anything, you would not joke.'

Corinne kept driving. They gained altitude, circling around the eastern edge of the port. Mallory told her to take the road that wound beneath the Basilique Notre-Dame de la Garde. The floodlit stone walls of the basilica towered above them, the lights of the city and the port laid out before them. The woman kept her eyes on the road, didn't glance at the view.

'You seem on edge,' Mallory said.

'I'm fine.'

'It's not just because I'm pointing a gun at you, is it?'

No response.

'That little party earlier this evening. Fleuriot's people are your competitors, right?'

Corinne gave him a side eye and looked back at the road. Mallory had to give her credit. She believed she had to cooperate if she wanted to stay alive, but she didn't seem overly rattled.

'What was it? Some kind of big deal on the cards?'

A slight twitch in the eye on the side Mallory could see.

'Ah, that's it. Seemed like you were all getting pretty friendly, until somebody tried to take a shot at Fleuriot.'

'It was fake. Fleuriot wanted to make it look like that. That's what you were there for, to get in the way and save him.'

Mallory took a moment to recall the moment, to visualise the moment he had tackled Nicolas. The shock, the sudden fear in the eyes of the man with the white hair.

'I don't think Fleuriot knew anything about it. I think someone else wanted him dead, and for it to happen on your boat so you would get the blame. Someone wanted to cause a war. Have they been successful?'

Corinne said nothing. It started to rain, sudden splashes of water quickly obscuring the windscreen. She activated the wipers and kept driving.

'Take the next left,' Mallory said as he saw a turn-off coming up to the descending road that would take them back toward the port. She obliged.

'I'm guessing you're going to have trouble with Fleuriot's people. They still in town?'

Mallory wasn't sure if he imagined it, but he thought her jaw tightened.

'Things are calm, for now.'

'They always are before the storm.'

She looked over at him and the look in her eyes told him

everything. Anger, but fear beneath it. Perhaps both sides had held off in the immediate aftermath, but a reckoning was coming. Unless Mallory found a way to head it off.

'I'm going to give Cristofol what he wants,' Mallory said.

A raised eyebrow.

'Part of what he wants. Tell him I want to talk to him. I'll meet him as soon as he's available.' He held out a card, on which he had written the number of his burner phone. When she didn't move to take it, he dropped it in her lap. 'Call me when you've spoken to him, I'll tell you where to be.'

They stopped at a set of lights at the foot of the hill. Mallory opened the door and stepped out, covering the gun from onlookers with the door until he had got fully clear. Then he pocketed it and slammed the door as the light turned green.

'Nice talking to you,' he said through the open window, then he turned and walked away.

44

Océane had tried to follow Mallory's advice and get some sleep, but every time she closed her eyes, she saw the face of the man who had kicked open the door and almost choked her to death. To hell with sleep. She couldn't imagine sleeping ever again while that man was still out there.

So instead, she tried to make herself useful in Mallory's absence. Once again, he hadn't told her where he was going. He had just assured her, with his usual airy confidence, that he would be back in a couple of hours. Océane opened her laptop and searched the news websites. No updates on the story about two murders at the Hôtel d'Or. To the outside world, it looked like nothing big had happened in the city tonight.

What had Nicolas got her into? She wondered if she could access his messages to see if there was anything there. She went to Gmail and typed in his email. She tried a series of passwords. Her name. The name of his high school. His first car. Nothing worked.

Even if she had been able to get into it, chances were it

would be useless. Mallory had only told her a little about the people Nicolas had got involved with, but she didn't think they would be foolish enough to commit their instructions to writing.

What about his communications with her?

She opened WhatsApp again and scrolled back to the start of her conversation history with Nicolas. When they had first met. According to the log, their first contact had been at 16.51 on 16 September last year. Nicolas had sent her a link to a restaurant by the Pont Neuf. The accompanying message: *This place looks shit. Want to go?*

She smiled when she read the message, and then felt an immediate stab in her heart as she remembered Nicolas wasn't here any more.

She felt a tear run down her cheek. She wiped it away and took a second to compose herself. She started scrolling through the message history. Nicolas wasn't an obsessive communicator by any stretch of the imagination, and neither was she. The messages had been regular in the early days, dropping off a little when they moved in together and could talk to each other in person instead.

Océane skimmed every message as she tapped the cursor to advance through the days and weeks of disjointed conversations and jokes and updates, looking for anything that could hint at what had happened to Nicolas, when things had started to go wrong. It was a little unreal, reading the words of her dead lover, reading exchanges relating to lunches and parties that she had almost forgotten about.

The first hint was on 22 May. So strange, being able to date it that precisely.

The message at sixteen minutes past midnight was a reply

to Océane's suggestion that they go for a late dinner after her shift at Les Douze Mois finished.

Je suis occupé

He was busy? At midnight? What did that mean?

Océane knew what had happened from there. She scrolled through the exchange of messages. She had lost her temper. Looking back, she knew she could have handled it better, but he was a jerk in his replies too. He had seemed different from that point. The next argument had been in person, and so had the argument after that.

Leaving aside their brief exchange yesterday, the last reply she had sent was more than three weeks ago, on 15 July at 19.11. She remembered tapping it out as she sat on one of the stools in Marianne's kitchen, telling him shortly that she would come over the following morning to pick up her stuff.

Nicolas hadn't responded. She'd collected her things in a couple of boxes – there hadn't been time for her to build up all that many belongings – the next morning. At least he hadn't changed the locks, she remembered thinking at the time.

There were only three messages from Nicolas after that. The first two asking her to respond, the final one an apology.

What had happened in May? She sat back in the chair and massaged her eyes. She was physically exhausted, but she knew that wouldn't translate into being able to get to sleep. The rain was getting harder outside. She could hear it bouncing off the metal balcony, pattering onto the awning directly below them.

May, what happened in May?

That made her think of work. Table *Mai* was the trouble table. No one knew quite why, but if there was a jerk or an order screw-up or a complaint, more often than not it would come from a temporary Monsieur or Madame Mai. It was the table with the worst view and the least leg room, so perhaps it just made the customers grumpy.

Suddenly, she opened her eyes.

Les Douze Mois.

She was thinking about work. About the tables. About another customer. Not Monsieur Mai. Monsieur Janvier, a few days ago.

The day she met Mallory. The day before the man with the knife tried to find her at Marianne's house.

She felt her skin crawl.

Monsieur Janvier. She could see him in her mind's eye. Dark eyes, greying hair, but in good shape. An amused air about him, as though he knew something she didn't. And he had known something. He had known Nicolas.

She had completely forgotten about the conversation until now. That was normal. She spoke to dozens of customers every week. Very few stuck in her memory. And what had happened over the next few days hadn't given her much time to think about anything but the present.

But Monsieur Janvier knew Nicolas, and he was amused and evasive when she asked how he knew him. Suddenly, she was sure this was the person who had employed Nicolas to kill the man on the boat. And that meant that most likely he also employed the man who had come after her.

Océane took a sharp breath as she heard footsteps outside on the landing. She was sure she wouldn't have registered them under normal conditions, but she was on edge, attuned to every new sound. The footsteps got closer, then stopped.

Three knocks, then a beat, then a fourth knock.

She approached the door, still cautious.

'Océane, it's me, Mallory.'

Relieved, she moved the chair away from where she had wedged it under the handle. She opened the door, not sure what to expect.

But Mallory appeared to be fine. A little bedraggled from the rain, but none the worse for wear.

'What happened? Did you get anywhere?'

Mallory stepped inside the room and closed the door, threading the chain again and pushing the armchair back against the door.

'I had an interesting conversation with one of our friends.'

'One of the gangsters?'

Mallory nodded. 'I don't think they knew anything about what was going to happen on the yacht. They seem to think it was a false flag attack. They think Fleuriot – the mark Nicolas was supposed to kill – set it up. I think it was some kind of—'

'Mallory, I have to tell you something.'

He stopped, mid-flow. 'What?'

She told him about the encounter with Monsieur Janvier three days ago. The man who had known Nicolas, and had asked some questions.

'I think that's it,' Mallory said. 'He's involved. Describe him to me.'

Océane furrowed her brow as she tried to recall all the details of the day. It was difficult, when you saw so many customers day in, day out, your brain doesn't store details the way it might in another context. It helped that he had asked about Nicolas. That made him stick out. It was the only reason she had remembered him.

'He was, I don't know, maybe fifty? A little older or

younger perhaps, it was hard to tell. He was in good shape, tall, I think. He wore a suit and a dark shirt.'

'Was he French? Could you tell?'

'No. I don't think so. Swiss, maybe.'

Mallory thought about it. Nicolas had mentioned a house in the Alps.

'And the day you met him . . .'

'Was the day you found the man with the knife in Nicolas's apartment. The day he came looking for me at Marianne's.'

'I think you've cracked it,' Mallory said. 'It's all about this guy. Up until then, he was focused on Nicolas. Something changed after he met you. He sent the Serbian to either get something from you, or . . .'

'To kill me.'

'Yes. And tonight was about tying up loose ends. He wanted to kill you and Nicolas as soon as Nicolas outlived his usefulness.'

'Why? I had nothing to do with this. Nicolas didn't tell me what he was doing.'

'Because you're a loose end. And you've met him. Maybe he's worried about being identified.'

'I'm not sure I could,' Océane said. 'Like I said, he was just another Monsieur Janvier at first. I think I remember what he was wearing and so on, but I couldn't swear to it. Maybe if we could explain that—'

'These don't seem like the kind of people who are open to reasonable explanations. We need to know who Mr January is. For one thing, it might get the Marseille gang off our backs.

'If only there was—' Océane stopped and slapped her palm in the middle of her forehead. Because of course there was a way to go back and take a better look at him.

'The security cameras. He'll be on video.'

Mallory grinned. 'Can you access it?'

'I don't know. I haven't even spoken to them. They'll be pretty mad that I didn't show up for work today, but ... Henri. I can ask Henri.'

'Who's Henri?'

'Assistant manager. I think you met him the other day.'

'Oh, Henri. Yes, Henri and I met.'

'He's always had a little thing for me. He'll do it, if he can access the footage.'

'If we can get a picture of this guy, it might give me a little more leverage with Cristofol's people. Can you get hold of him now?'

Henri, too, had sent her WhatsApp messages; had sent them to almost every female staff member. Mostly inappropriate memes and inuendo. A moment later, Océane was on the balcony, starting a voice call. She wondered if he would still be awake.

'Océane? Where the hell have you been?'

She heard tinny music in the background. He was probably vaping outside of a bar somewhere. She put the call on speaker so that Mallory could listen in.

'I'm really sorry I didn't call. I had a family emergency. I had to go ... I had to go to see my uncle.'

'Where are you?'

She saw Mallory staring at her, slowly shaking his head.

'Lyon,' she said, the lie coming easily.

'When can you come back? Guillaume is really mad at you, he said—'

'Tell him I'm really sorry.'

'He's really mad,' Henri said again, sounding doubtful. 'In fact, he said—'

Océane cut in. 'I need you to do me a favour. I don't want you to get into trouble, though.'

There was a long pause before Henri spoke warily. 'What kind of favour?'

45

The picture of Monsieur Janvier was low quality, blown up from a grainy CCTV image, but was in colour, which was a plus. It showed a man remarkably close to the description Océane had given. She had been right on almost every detail, except that he had been wearing a light blue shirt, not a dark one.

Mallory didn't recognise the man in the picture. There was no reason why he should. But something about him told Mallory this was the guy. He just had to hope that someone else would recognise him.

There were a number of people he could contact. People who could run a facial match in databases inaccessible to the general public. People who might even recognise the face without having to check. If he survived the next hour, Mallory would consider reaching out to such people. But he wanted to show the picture to someone else first.

The text message came in at 2.27 a.m. It was short and to the point.

7 a.m. Send location.

He smiled. It showed that either Cristofol's people wanted to talk, or at the very least that they were taking him seriously. They hadn't messed around trying to manoeuvre him into a location of their choosing. They were allowing him to choose the place where they would meet. That meant he had given them enough reason to suspect it might be worth talking.

He sent a holding reply, to tell them he would be in touch soon.

Mallory didn't bother trying to sleep for the few hours he had available. From prior experience, he knew he could go another day minimum without sleep and still function fine.

Instead, he ordered two espressos in the hotel bar and sat out at one of the tables on the street, thinking through every aspect of the upcoming meeting. He already had a location in mind, but he didn't want to give them any time to scout it out in advance.

At 5.50, an hour before dawn, Mallory pulled his jacket on and put the gun in his pocket.

He nudged Océane awake gently and gave her instructions. Stay in the room until noon. If he wasn't back by then, he would be dead. She was to go to the bus station and buy a ticket back to Normandy. She would be as safe there as anywhere.

She told him she would do it. He believed her. One thing he knew about Océane Fontaine: she was unsentimental about cutting her losses and walking away from a bad situation.

He took a bus that dropped him within half a mile of the location, on a road named Chemin du Littoral, and covered the rest of the distance on foot.

Number 301 Chemin du Littoral was the headquarters of a company manufacturing elevators which had recently gone out of business. Mallory had chosen it because of that – and because of what it backed onto. The warehouse and offices were in a long, single-storey building with aluminium siding, and sat behind a small car park and a low fence.

Mallory approached the building from the rear, coming in from the harbour side through the shipping container park between the warehouse and the bay. He had spent a couple of hours scouting locations and this one ticked all the boxes: the people he was meeting with would have to approach from a single direction, but he would have a number of routes of escape without the danger of being backed into a corner.

There were three vehicles in the car park, as well as a couple of skips overflowing with junk. Mallory took up position behind one of the skips and took a look at the street beyond the fence.

As he had expected, there was someone there already. A black SUV with two men inside watching the building from across the street. Looking further up it, he could see a lone man on the corner. He was there to keep an eye on incoming traffic, which was non-existent at this hour.

There was an uncommon stillness in the air. They were a couple of miles out from the centre of town, but it felt a lot further.

Mallory took his phone out at 6.58. There were no new messages.

The two men in the car exchanged words. One shook his head. The man on the corner glanced back at the car.

At seven on the dot, another SUV appeared, approaching from the opposite direction from the sentry on the corner. It was travelling fast, as if the driver wanted to show he was taking the job seriously. He slammed on the brakes as they reached the spot where the other SUV was parked. The two men in the first SUV were already getting out, straightening up, looking around like secret service agents in a movie.

The passenger door and one of the rear doors of the second SUV opened and two similar-looking men got out. The driver stayed where he was.

It really was like witnessing the arrival of a dignitary. Mallory wondered if the SUV had bulletproof windows and run-flat tyres, like the US president's state car, the Beast.

The four men spoke quietly, though the morning air was so still that Mallory caught a few words. He didn't need them. He knew exactly what they were talking about. Were they being stood up? Were they walking into an ambush? Mallory was pleased. He wanted them on edge, but not too on edge.

At 7.01 he sent the message he had prepared.

Drive through the gate. One vehicle only.

He watched the four men plus the one on the corner, wondering which one the message would come to. It didn't come to any of them. Instead, one of the rear windows in the SUV rolled down. The window on the side where no one had got out. The closest man bent to talk to somebody inside and then nodded.

The four men didn't get back in the car. All of them, as though in response to a signal, took their guns out. One of them stayed on the pavement. The other three started walking towards the gate. They weren't making any attempt to look inconspicuous. There was no one around to ask questions. They had their guns up, waiting for a reason to fire. Mallory was reasonably impressed by the way they covered potential angles of attack.

He heard the rhythm of the SUV's motor change and it started to crawl forward in the wake of the three men on foot.

The first one reached the gate, examined it, then hesitantly pushed it, as though he expected it to electrocute him. It didn't. The gate swung inward, and the three men stepped inside. The car gradually drew in after them until the tail was fully inside. Then it stopped, engine still running. The blacked-out windows reflected the burning orange of the dawn sky. The sunrise was straight ahead, as Mallory had planned, so the three of them had to squint and shade their eyes.

Mallory sent his final text:

Stay where you are. Do not advance.

They were closer now, so he could hear what the voice in the back of the SUV said this time. Calling a name: Samuel.

The closest flunky bent down to the window again, not taking his eyes off the car park. He listened and nodded. He spoke in a low tone to the other two. Everyone stayed put. No one put their guns away.

Mallory stepped out from behind the skip.

The three men tensed, but didn't move. Most importantly, they didn't immediately start firing. That was a good sign.

'I want to talk to your boss,' Mallory said. 'Ask him if he would like to get some fresh air.'

The man closest to the SUV – Samuel – turned to the window again, but the door was already opening. The man Mallory had seen on the yacht last night got out. He had changed out of the black suit and blue shirt, and was wearing a cream linen suit now. He had come better prepared for the dawn than his henchmen. He was wearing thin sunglasses.

The door on the opposite side opened and his daughter got out. Corinne hadn't bothered with the costume change, she was still wearing the same clothes from earlier.

Cristofol sized Mallory up, taking advantage of his first chance to get a good look at him.

'Monsieur Cristofol,' Mallory said.

'Who are you?'

'I'm someone who might be able to fix your problem.'

The three men around Cristofol simultaneously looked at him for direction. If he noticed the coordinated show of subservience, he betrayed neither satisfaction nor distaste. He put his hands on his hips and took a long look at Mallory through his dark glasses.

'What were you doing on my yacht?'

'I was looking for the guy who was planning to put a bullet in your guest. I found him in the nick of time.'

He seemed to consider this for a long moment. 'This man is dead now.'

'Yes.'

'Did you kill him?'

'No.'

'Did you kill our man at l'Hôtel d'Or?'

'No.'

'Who are you working for?'

'I'm self-employed. And this particular job I was doing as a favour for a friend.'

'You mentioned something about my problem,' Cristofol said. 'Tell me, what is my problem? Other than you.'

'I figure you're a day or two from open warfare breaking out on the streets. Fleuriot's men are still in town, aren't they? And more are coming.'

Cristofol gave an insouciant shrug. 'What happens, happens.'

'What if you can persuade them they're blaming the wrong people?'

The gangster turned and looked at his daughter again. Corinne raised her eyebrows briefly and Mallory knew he had a temporary ally on the other side.

He raised his voice and addressed Mallory without turning to face him. 'I'm listening.'

'Take a look at your phone,' Mallory said.

Cristofol hesitated, then took the phone from his pocket. He opened the message Mallory had just sent. There was no text, just a picture. A picture of a man in a suit in a Parisian restaurant.

The man in the linen suit stared at the image for a long time. His expression was impossible to read, but Mallory thought it was interesting that he hadn't immediately dismissed what he was looking at.

'Where did you get this?'

'I think it's the man who took out the hit on Fleuriot. I think he wanted to cause a war between you and the Parisians. Could be French, but probably Swiss. Employs a Serbian who likes sharp edges. Do you know who he is?'

Cristofol was silent for a moment. Something seemed to change in his body language, a slight stiffening of the shoulders. He put the phone back in his pocket after a moment. He took his sunglasses off and squinted at Mallory.

'This problem. You said you could fix it. Illuminate me.'

'You've seen what I can do. I don't go looking for trouble, but I can handle myself.'

Cristofol's eyes were amused. 'I suspect that is not the whole truth.'

Against his will, Mallory was starting to like this guy. But he kept his face straight and ignored Cristofol's observation. 'If you tell me who this man is, I can help you take care of him.'

'What makes you think we need help?' he said, glancing at the handful of men around him.

'What would have happened if I hadn't been there last night?' Mallory asked. 'Fleuriot would be dead, and you would be at war already. What would have happened if I hadn't come here this morning? You wouldn't have a lead on the person who's really behind this. Sometimes an outside contractor can be of use.'

Cristofol stared back at him, his face betraying nothing. Finally, he spoke. 'As an outside contractor, what kind of reward are you expecting?'

'It'll cost you nothing. Not money, not respect, not inconvenience. All you have to do is *not* do something.'

'You want us to leave you and the girl alone.'

'Exactly.'

There was a pause again. The bodyguards shifted uneasily while Cristofol stared at Mallory. At length, he looked down at the phone again, betraying nothing.

'You killed two of my men,' Cristofol said, then looked up.

'Self-defence,' Mallory said. 'Nothing personal.'

Cristofol seemed to consider this, weighing the matter up dispassionately. 'You will kill this man for me, or die trying?'

'I don't plan on that second option.'

Cristofol slid the phone into his pocket and folded his arms. He looked up at the dawn sky. Then over at his daughter. She raised an eyebrow. *Your call, Dad.*

He turned back to Mallory. 'I'll think about it. Why

don't you come with us in the meantime? We'll make you comfortable.'

Mallory smiled.

'You have my number. I'll expect a call when you've made your decision.'

46

Mallory took the long way back to the hotel, doubling back a couple of times and cutting through a bustling flea market to make sure he hadn't been followed. The tactics were second nature. He barely thought about what he was doing as he went through the moves.

His mind was on the meeting with Cristofol and his people. Had they believed him? He wouldn't have bet on it up until the point he showed them the picture of the man from Les Douze Mois. Cristofol hadn't given away much, but he could tell that had been a turning point. The atmosphere changed at that moment. Whoever the man was, he was known.

Mallory was back at Artemis just after eight o'clock. He passed through reception without engaging with any of the staff and took the stairs up to the first floor. He checked his phone as he climbed. Nothing from Océane, nothing from Cristofol's people. He wasn't surprised by the latter. It would probably take them a while to make their own enquiries, check his information, decide on an offer. Even without all that, they wouldn't want to seem too eager.

The first-floor corridor was empty apart from a trolley at the room two doors down from Mallory's. He glanced in as he passed and saw the maid changing the bed. He advanced down the corridor. Soft moans were coming from one of the neighbouring rooms. Someone having an early good time.

He gave the four knocks and waited. There was no response.

The hairs rose a little on the back of Mallory's neck. He knocked again. Four times. Harder.

No response. The *Ne Pas Deranger* sign was still hanging on the handle.

Mallory glanced up and down the corridor to make sure he was still alone and took his gun out. He tapped his keycard and opened the door.

The room was empty.

He listened. The sound of a breeze. Traffic noise. He moved through into the bedroom. The bed was missing its duvet. The balcony door was open, the silk curtains waving slightly in the breeze. He could see a figure in one of the chairs, unmoving.

He moved quickly to the balcony and stepped outside. Océane was in the chair, wrapped up in the duvet, her eyes closed. As he was reaching out to touch her, her eyes sprang open and she screamed.

Mallory immediately held both hands up. 'It's okay, it's me.'

'Why didn't you knock?' she yelled.

'I did,' Mallory said. He stepped back and put the gun down on the table. He gestured at the courtyard, all the windows. 'I thought we said stay inside in daylight.'

'*You* said that. *I* needed air.'

Mallory resisted the urge to berate her for compromising her security. She had had a tough couple of days. She had probably needed the fresh air, and the rest.

'How long were you asleep?'

She checked the screen of her phone for the time and sighed. 'Not long. I was dreaming about Nicolas. We were at a party and all the other guests were wearing black masks. I think it was going to be a nightmare. Perhaps it's just as well you woke me up.'

'With what you've been through ... it's going to be tough. Maybe we can get you something to help you sleep.'

She shook her head. 'I don't want to sleep. Did you meet Cristofol?'

Mallory sat down in a chair next to her. Océane had draped a bath towel over the balcony. It obscured her from prying eyes, but it would probably draw attention in a place like this. He would move it in a minute.

'I think I got his attention.'

'And he believed you?'

'Hard to say. I offered to take care of his problem if he backs off us.'

'And the man who killed Nicolas?'

'He's a different problem. He definitely isn't with them.'

They were silent for a moment. The sounds of the city drifted over the red-tiled rooftops and filtered, muted into the courtyard. Mallory heard footsteps below and glanced over the balcony. Just a hotel worker, scooping up some glasses that had been left at one of the outdoor tables.

'What can we do?'

'Nothing,' Mallory said. 'Except wait.'

Her eyes went to Mallory's phone on the table. 'And if they don't call?'

'My guess is, if they don't call by this afternoon, then they're not going to call.'

'And what will we do then?'

'We'll leave. I'll get you back to St-Jean. You should be safe enough there. If your grandfather doesn't mind, I'll stick around for a week or so, just to be safe.'

Océane bit her lip and looked at the sky. It was cloudless; a deep azure blue.

'I don't know if I can do that.'

'Go home?'

'Go home. Go anywhere. I don't want to know he's out there, looking for me.'

'People only look for so long. Sooner or later, you move down the list. Eventually, you drop off it.'

'You sound like you know this from the other side.'

'I do. I used to hunt people down. People slip through the net. It's inevitable.'

'Who did you hunt?'

'Bad people, mostly. Sometimes they weren't bad, but we needed them.'

There was another pause. Océane carefully stood up and leaned over the balcony to check there was no one there. She pulled the duvet off and started to go back inside.

'I think they'll call,' Mallory said.

'Why?'

'What happened last night took them by surprise. I don't get the impression they're the kind of people who like surprises. I've given them a cost-free chance to take this bastard out. It's win/win for them. I succeed, they get rid of a thorn in their side. I fail, they've lost nothing and tie up a loose end.'

Océane looked back at him for a moment and then turned and went inside. Mallory followed. It was dim in here after the bright sunlight on the balcony. She was lying on the bed, turned away from him.

'Are you okay?' Instantly, he regretted the stupid question.

'Sure.'

'I'm going to sort this, Océane.'

She wiped her face, and when she spoke again, her voice bore only the slightest hint of emotion.

'I feel guilty,' she said. 'Do you understand that?'

'You have nothing to feel guilty about.'

'Nicolas is dead. I'm sorry about that, but I'm still angry at him for what he's done to me. It's selfish.'

'Not selfish. Just honest.'

She didn't say anything for a minute. When she did, her voice sounded drowsy. 'Will you watch the door?'

'I've got the door, Océane. Don't worry about it.'

'*Merci*,' she murmured.

Less than a minute later, she was sleeping again. Exhaustion had finally won the battle. Mallory was glad. She needed the rest. Gently, he pulled the sheet over her. He went back out on the balcony, sitting back from the edge, and waited. He should have been tired. He wasn't.

They called at 3.02 p.m. A private number.

'Am I speaking to the man who can solve my problem?'

Mallory recognised Cristofol's voice.

'It's me.'

'We have a name.'

'That's good news for both of us,' Mallory said.

There was a low chuckle. 'I'm not sure that it is. We have a problem, *Monsieur Big Talk*.'

'I knew that already.'

'No. We have a name. We even have a location. But it

won't do you any good. You will not be able to touch this man, no matter how skilled you think you are.'

Mallory leaned forward in his chair.

'What's the name?'

47

APPELBURG, SWITZERLAND

'Monsieur Rousseau.'

At the sound of his name, the man with eyes the colour of granite turned from gazing out of the window to look back towards the door. It was Fabian, as always. The slim American was standing in the doorway. His clothes and perfectly groomed appearance gave no hint that he had been awake all night.

Rousseau stood up and turned away from the view. 'News?'

'The Marseille police have yet to identify Nicolas Devereaux. They suspect there is a link to a local faction of le Milieu, so ...'

'So they are being discreet, in the hopes that they do not upset their paymasters,' Rousseau finished, smiling. 'As I thought. Has Petrovic reported since this morning?'

Fabian nodded. 'He just called. He has been unable to locate Océane Fontaine or the British man.'

'"The British man",' Rousseau repeated, raising an eyebrow. 'You haven't identified him?'

Rousseau enjoyed how irritated that made Fabian look. His right-hand man's unflappability was one of the reasons he was so good at his job, but Rousseau couldn't deny it was satisfying watching him squirm.

'As yet, we have been unable to establish his identity, or his link to Devereaux.'

'And our two other parties? How does the rapprochement look?'

'Dead,' Fabian said immediately, on surer ground now. 'Although Devereaux escaped the yacht, the attempt itself seems to have been enough.'

'Good. Perhaps, in a way, it's better that the attempt did not succeed. Speculation mounts on both sides. The Marseillais think it was a false flag attack, the Parisians think it was a botched hit.'

'Exactly. The cold war between the two gangs appears to be warming up.'

'Good,' Rousseau said. 'Tell Robert that his department may proceed as planned.'

Fabian nodded. 'Will there be anything else?'

'Who did we find to join us for the hunt tomorrow morning?'

'His name is Erich Baumann. He's become something of a recurring problem for Widmer.'

Rousseau glanced out at the balcony that overlooked the town below. Widmer was the police chief down there. He had been reluctant to send candidates up to Rousseau's house at first, but he seemed to be becoming more enthusiastic about it.

'Good candidate?'

'Twenty-eight years old, reasonable shape. Completed his twenty-one weeks' *Militärdienst* in 2015.'

'Good, sounds like he'll fit in. That will be all.'

As Fabian turned to go, Rousseau called him back.

'Yes, sir?'

'Keep looking for information on our mysterious inter-loper, will you? And make sure Petrovic lets us know when he has found either him or the girl.'

Fabian acknowledged with a curt nod and left the balcony, heading in the direction of the main office.

Rousseau went over to the sliding glass doors that led out to the deck outside his quarters. He leaned on the railing and gazed down on the town. The sun had passed its apex. It shone off the wet rooftops, and Rousseau could see that some of the narrowest streets in the east were already in darkness. The black seemed to be seeping up from the streets themselves.

On Alpenstrasse, the main thoroughfare through the town, Rousseau noticed a young child in a red coat pointing up at him. Too far to tell if it was a boy or a girl. Rousseau raised a hand to wave. The child waved back. His mother, tall, wearing a beige coat looked up and hurriedly pulled the child along in her wake, quickening her pace.

It seemed as though the unexpected intervention of the Brit had not interfered too greatly with the course of events. Perhaps it had even been of benefit. But he was a question mark. An unknown element. Rousseau had been around long enough to be wary of elements he did not understand. Without understanding, there is no control. He wondered if Fabian, adept as he was, had been guilty of tunnel vision in this case. They had assumed that the Brit was an associate of Devereaux. Perhaps someone he had met through his busi-ness or in his athletic career, but so far Fabian and his team had turned up no candidates. Perhaps he wasn't known to Devereaux. Perhaps he had become involved through the girl, Océane. They had last been seen together, after all, before Petrovic had fled the hotel where he had killed Devereaux. Perhaps they were still together.

Probably safe enough to forget about them. After all, the goal had been achieved, albeit by unintended means. The pact was dead. The Parisians and the Marseillais were at each other's throats, and the deal contingent on enmities continuing would go through. Océane Fontaine and her British friend would most likely try to distance themselves as far as possible from this.

But then again, Rousseau had not built his business on assuming things would be safe enough.

He took out his phone and called Petrovic's number.

He answered on the second ring.

'It's me,' Rousseau said. 'Where are you now?'

'Marseille. The old town.'

'Any leads?'

In lieu of an answer, there was a stony silence. Rousseau knew none of his other employees would risk being so disrespectful. He didn't believe the thought would occur to the Serbian. That wasn't the way he was made. Rousseau admired that about him.

'Unfortunate,' Rousseau said. 'Do you think our uninvited guest is still with the girl?'

'Yes, they're together.'

Rousseau thought about it. The targets knew Petrovic was in Marseille, and that Cristofol's men would be looking for them too. They would almost certainly try to leave; perhaps return to Paris, or even go to the UK. He would have Fabian make some calls, ask their local partners to watch the airport, the train and bus stations.

'I'll see what we can do from here, but in the meantime ...'

'Yes?'

'When you do find them again, kill the man first.'

48

'Who is he?'

Océane was sitting on the edge of the bed, watching Mallory. The look in her eyes said she was genuinely curious as well as anxious.

Mallory took a moment to process the information he had just received over the phone. It was actually helpful to have someone here to talk it through with. Perhaps it would kill two birds with one stone and take Océane's mind off her ordeal last night.

'His name is Rousseau.'

By all accounts, Cristofol, the man Mallory had just been speaking to, was a pretty hard nut. And yet, the way he had talked about Rousseau betrayed a sense of respect. Perhaps more than respect. Fear.

'The details are a bit sketchy, but it sounds like he was in the military, and then in the Kommando Spezialkräfte: the Swiss special forces command. He worked as a mercenary in Iraq for a while in the early 2000s. After that he dropped off the radar. Our friend in the Marseille underworld thinks he's set himself up as some kind of multinational crime lord.

Assassinations for hire, drugs, arms dealing, providing support to terrorists. You name it: if it's happening in Western Europe and it's bad, this guy's got a hand in it.'

'This is Monsieur Janvier?'

'Mr January. It sounds like it, and if my contact comes through for me, we're going to be able to confirm it soon.'

'But it doesn't make sense. What could he possibly have wanted with Nicolas?'

'Nicolas was a tool to him. He fulfilled three important criteria: he had the necessary skills, he could get on board that yacht without being suspected, and he could be coerced into doing the job.'

'So all of this ... he did this to stop a deal between the Parisians and the Marseillais? But why?'

'Most likely, he has an interest in the deal not going ahead. People like this don't hesitate to cause whatever chaos it takes to improve their bottom line. I've seen it before. It's easier to kill someone than take the small risk that anything will come back to bite them.'

As soon as the words were out of Mallory's mouth, he knew he should have worded them more sensitively. Océane looked pale. Mallory sometimes forgot that others didn't come from his world. They couldn't shrug off an attempt on their lives like normal people shrug off a bad day at the office. Or understand a world where one person would kill another simply to nip a potential problem in the bud.

'Don't worry, we're going to persuade them otherwise.'

'How?'

Mallory's phone buzzed. It was Mac, his contact in the CIA. He had helped him out occasionally in the past, and there was no one better connected.

As usual, Mac's Brooklyn tones sounded equal parts amused and scolding. 'Ernst Rousseau, huh?' he said without preamble. 'You sure know how to pick enemies, Mallory. How did you get into this?'

'The road to hell is paved with good intentions. This started off as a favour.'

'Well, you can let me know how it finishes, if you're still breathing.'

Mallory turned away from Océane to continue the conversation. He wasn't sure if Mac's words had been audible, but they would not have helped Océane's mood.

'You got anything for me?'

'Yeah. Not sure how much good it'll do you, though.'

'Is he somewhere in France?'

'Rousseau has boltholes all over the Continent. Paris, Berlin, Rome, even your neck of the woods. Looks like Brexit hasn't gotten in the way of organised crime, huh?'

'Mac . . .'

'All right, all right. The intel is pretty fresh. It looks like he's back at his main home right now.'

'Switzerland?'

'Yes. And that's bad news. Have you ever heard of a town named Appelburg?'

Mallory thought about it. 'Can't say that I have.'

'It's small, tucked away in the Alps about sixty miles outside of Bern. Rousseau has a house there.'

'Doesn't sound too bad.'

'Some say he has a whole town there. He runs the place like some kind of personal fiefdom. Word is the local cops are all on the take, they're like his personal security force. And his house isn't just some deluxe chalet on a five-acre plot. It's practically a castle, on the mountain above the town. Only way up is by cable car or helicopter.'

'Why haven't I heard of this guy before? He sounds like he's a self-made world leader.'

'That's pretty much what he is. Without all the inconveniences of elections or media scrutiny. You haven't heard of him because that's the way he wants it.' He paused while Mallory absorbed this information. 'Look, man, I don't know what your beef is with Rousseau, but unless it's absolutely necessary, take it from me. Don't go there.'

'Too late. You know me. I like a challenge.'

49

The Lyon train departed from the Gare de Saint-Charles just before six in the evening. From Lyon, they would change for Geneva, and from there make the last connection to Bern – as far as the rails would take them. The plan was to rest there for the night, then rent a car in the morning for the rest of the journey to Appelburg.

Mallory had considered putting Océane on a bus to Normandy, but she had quickly shut that idea down. She wanted to come with him. She needed to see this through.

Mallory left Océane in a café alongside the station, selecting a table that was in the back, by the fire exit. He walked across the road to the station, climbing the grand staircase. There was a wide, polished concourse beneath a high arched ceiling. Small knots of evening passengers made their way to the platforms, eyes on the departure board. Mallory had a twinge of unwelcome déjà vu, thinking about the last time he had entered a big railway station at night, and what had happened. He lingered at the entrance and surveyed the concourse. It was quiet enough that it didn't take long to evaluate the people standing around.

Since the advent of smartphones, Mallory had found it was a lot easier to spot a stakeout. No one people-watches any more, unless they have a reason to. No one even stares into space aimlessly. It means that anyone paying attention tends to stick out. Right now, all eyes were either on the departure board or on a handheld screen. More importantly, there was no sign of the Serbian.

Mallory crossed the open space to the ticket machines and used cash to buy two through tickets to Bern. He turned to give the concourse another once-over, and then raised his eyes to the departure board. Ten minutes.

He slipped the tickets into his pocket and went back outside, descending the grand staircase and crossing the road. He had left Océane in a little Italian café that was tucked between a newsagent and a dry cleaners. A bell chimed as he pushed the door open. Océane looked up as he entered. The place was as quiet as when he had left her a few minutes before. They had it virtually to themselves. Océane hadn't touched the cup of lemon tea that was sitting in front of her.

She widened her eyes questioningly as Mallory approached.

'All clear,' Mallory said in answer. 'You ready?'

They left by the front door and approached the grand staircase again. But this time, something was different. There was a man at the top of the steps wearing a leather jacket. He had no phone in his hands. He was watching the trickle of passengers as they lugged suitcases and backpacks up the stone stairs.

'What is it?' Océane asked, and followed Mallory's gaze. 'Is he looking for us?'

Mallory hesitated. He was watching people, that was for sure, but it could be he was waiting for a travel companion.

And yet, it didn't feel quite right. He didn't look like one of Cristofol's men. Not enough of a tan, never mind the way he was dressed.

Mallory checked his watch. The train left in six minutes. They probably had time to avoid walking past him.

'Come on.' He took Océane's hand and pulled her with him as he walked along the street running along the east side of the station, keeping the man at the top of the stairs in the corner of his eye. If he had noticed them, the man gave no sign, keeping his own gaze on the people on the steps.

There had to be a side entrance to the station. They reached the corner, where the railway bridge crossed over the intersecting street above them. There was an arched station entrance below the bridge with a single globe lamp at the apex. Two minutes.

'Come on.'

They ran for the entrance. It led into a low-ceilinged corridor. The only other company was a busker strumming his guitar, not bothering to sing along. They hurried past him and up an escalator. At the top, Mallory stopped to orient himself. He pointed the direction to Océane and they hurried to the train. They reached it as the door alarms were sounding and squeezed on board as they closed.

As the train started to pull out, Mallory watched the passengers on the other side of the platform waiting for the next train. All of them were looking at phones, looking down the track or looking at each other. All except one. A man in a leather jacket was facing the opposite direction, looking straight at Mallory's train. As they passed, their eyes met.

It was the man from the staircase.

50

Rousseau's phone rang at six o'clock. It was Fabian, calling from his office on the east wing. A call, as opposed to a visit in person, meant this was urgent.

'I have news.'

'The girl and her white knight have been attended to?'

'Not yet, but we know where they are. Or at least, where they're headed. One of our partners confirmed they boarded a train at the Gare de Saint-Charles just a few minutes ago.'

That piqued Rousseau's curiosity. 'Destination?'

'They took the TGV from Marseille to Lyon, but they purchased tickets to Bern. I think—'

Rousseau felt something he hadn't felt in a long time: surprise. It wasn't an unwelcome sensation. 'That they're coming here?'

'It's a possibility.'

This had been the last thing he was expecting. He had expected them to flee Marseille, but this ... 'How much background did we assemble on Devereaux's girlfriend?'

Fabian paused for a second while he thought about it. 'Not much. She's nobody.'

'Where does she live?'

There was a pause. 'As you know, we traced her address in Paris and—'

'No, where is she from?'

There was a pause. It was unlike Fabian not to have the answers at his fingertips. 'I ... believe there was a link to a town in Normandy.'

'Normandy.'

'She grew up there. If I recall correctly, her parents are both deceased.'

Rousseau considered the information. Bern was a long way from either Paris or Normandy. He didn't think the girl had chosen their destination.

'It could be a coincidence, sir.'

Rousseau took a moment. Out of all the directions they could choose to go, they were coming this way.

'It could be,' Rousseau agreed. 'But I think it's too much of a coincidence to ignore. And if they really are coming here, then we were right to treat this man seriously. Perhaps we even underestimated him.'

He asked Fabian to send him the details of the train journey, then hung up and dialled Petrovic's number. The gravelly voice sounded on the other end of the line. He was in an echoey space. Rousseau could hear crowd noise and some kind of electronic announcement.

'Where are you?'

'Still here.' At times, the Serbian's taciturnity could be an irritant.

'Change of plan. Our two fugitives appear to be making their way here, to Appelburg.'

Petrovic answered only with a grunt. There was no point

speculating aloud with Petrovic about the chain of events that seemed to be leading Océane Fontaine and an unidentified but dangerous man to his doorstep. It would be like trying to hold a fulfilling conversation with a pit bull. Rousseau moved him on to easier questions.

'They're making a connection in Lyon. The onward train to Geneva is at eight thirty-eight. Can you intercept?'

'Yes. I have a car. I will join the train from Lyon.'

'Good. I'll expect your call directly.'

Rousseau hung up and called Fabian back.

'I want to know more about the Brit. Somehow, he has not only identified me, but located me. I don't need to tell you how unacceptable that is.'

Fabian cleared his throat. 'No.'

'Find out who this man is.'

51

'Your boyfriend seems intense.'

Océane looked over at the girl in the seat across the aisle; one of the few other passengers in the carriage. She was young, early twenties perhaps. She had dark hair, about the same length as Océane's, and wore a black T-shirt and pristine white Converse trainers. She was speaking English in a Dutch accent. Océane leaned out and peered down the aisle in the direction Mallory had gone. They had changed trains at Lyon. The only shop open had a lousy selection of sandwiches, so Mallory had gambled on waiting and buying something on the train. Océane hadn't been hungry, but she had bought one bottle of soda and one of vodka, and was nursing her second paper cup of a half-and-half mix. It was taking the edge off. She wished she had a cigarette. She would be smoking this one for real.

'He's not my boyfriend,' Océane said, though from the way the girl was looking at the bottle of vodka on the table, she decided she wasn't making conversation just because Mallory had interested her. 'Do you want a drink?' she asked.

The girl nodded enthusiastically, and suddenly seemed a little older than Océane had guessed. She shrugged and poured some vodka into the other cup, handing it over. Maybe she wanted the drink a little too much, but who was Océane to judge?

She handed the cup across the aisle and the girl took it, her hand shaking a little. Océane smiled and turned away, hoping this would not turn into a longer conversation.

She rested her head against the window and watched the world whip by outside, bathed in the last glow of the sunset. The sky on the horizon was dark enough that she saw Mallory's reflection appear in the glass. She turned as he slipped into the seat across the table from her. He laid two baguette sandwiches and two bottles of water on the table, pushing one of each across to her. She pointed at her drink.

'I'm not hungry.'

'First rule of survival,' Mallory said. 'Eat when you get a chance.' He was taking a folding road map of Switzerland out of its shrink wrap, the other purchase he had made at the station.

Océane made an effort at a laugh. 'You sound like *grand-père*.'

'Do I?' He didn't look up from studying the map. 'I did get the impression he was a very sensible man.'

Océane snorted. 'You're very like him in some ways. You were in the army?'

Mallory looked up this time, an amused glint in his eye. 'I have a few more braincells than that. Royal Navy. SBS.'

Océane had heard of the SBS. As elite as it got. Most men she knew would want to boast about their exploits in such a field, but Mallory spoke as though he was talking about an unremarkable career in the civil service.

'You retired recently?'

'Mmm,' Mallory agreed and turned his attention back to the map, tracing a finger along the path of a main road. 'Although, sometimes it feels very long ago.'

'You were in Iraq?'

'Iraq, Afghanistan, some of the other beauty spots.'

'Why did you leave?'

Mallory was silent for a moment. 'It was time.' He looked back at her. 'How are you doing?'

She noted the change of subject but decided not to comment on it. Besides, Mallory's question had suddenly given her a lot to think about. As he must have known it would.

'I'm all right, I think. All things considered. Do you think that makes me heartless?'

'Not at all. I think it makes you a survivor.'

Océane took a drink of her vodka and soda. 'You seem to know something about that.'

Mallory shrugged, as though he had never given the matter much thought. 'I'm not dead yet, I suppose that's something.'

'What do you plan to do when we reach Appelburg?'

'You know what I plan to do. End this.'

'How?'

'I'll do what I'm trained to do. I'll evaluate the target and work up a strategy.'

'You plan to kill him, this Rousseau?'

Mallory's eyes flitted away from her, checking again that there was no one in earshot. Océane noticed that the Dutch girl seemed to have moved elsewhere while they had been talking.

'If it comes to it,' Mallory replied. 'Maybe I won't have to. Maybe he's a reasonable man and this can all be resolved over a chat.'

'You really think so?'

'No, not really.'

Océane held his gaze for a long moment. Long enough for it to mean something, more than just what they were talking about. She was slightly amused when he looked away first, breaking the moment. The fearsome Monsieur Mallory. Unafraid to stare down gangsters and thugs, but avoiding the gaze of this slight woman.

She hadn't had time to really look at him the first time they had met. He had presented as one more tough guy, but with an edge that she couldn't deny she had found attractive even then. In the last few hours, she had seen different sides to him. For a start, he was the opposite of those men who are all talk but crumble when the going gets tough. For another, he was a thinker. He always seemed to be one step ahead.

There was a darkness behind his confidence and his sarcasm, though. A sense that he was holding something in check. She couldn't decide whether that intrigued her or frightened her.

She sat up in her seat. 'How do we get there from Bern?'

'There's a bus, but it might be better to see if we can rent a car,' Mallory said. 'We'll find a place to sleep tonight, head on to Appelburg first thing in the morning. I want to go in during daylight, with the rest of the traffic.'

Océane took another sip of her vodka. A place to sleep sounded good. An anonymous hotel, hundreds of miles from the man with the knife and the gangsters. She thought about a comfortable bed, maybe a hot bath. Perhaps it wouldn't be the worst thing in the world, spending some more time with Mallory.

52

Mallory was grateful that the train was quiet as he studied the map and searched for more information about Appelburg on his phone. He looked up at one point to discover he and Océane were now alone in the carriage. It was a little stuffy, the AC on the blink. Océane had dropped off, her head resting against her bunched-up hoodie pressed against the window. On the other side of the glass, dark fields and forests rushed by. They had travelled hundreds of miles north. The air out there would be cool, refreshing after the oppressive heat of Marseille. He wished the windows opened, but these modern trains were bloody airtight. You could probably run them through the Channel without a tunnel.

He stood up and massaged an ache in his neck. He now knew enough about Appelburg and the surrounding area to be a tour guide, he reckoned. He decided to take a break and go for a walk to the other end of the train. He headed against the direction of travel, feeling the motion of the train rocking gently from side to side as it ploughed through the night northwards. The other carriages weren't much busier than the one he and Océane were in.

As Mallory opened the link door at the end of one carriage he could suddenly hear track noise and the wind whipping past. He smelled a familiar, sweet odour a moment before he saw the source. A young guy in jeans and a hoodie was standing in the passage between two carriages, leaning on the top of the window he had pushed down and looking out at the night, a smouldering joint in his hand. Mallory had seen him when he boarded at Lyon, chatting to a Dutch girl with dark hair. Ten full seconds after Mallory appeared, the kid noticed he wasn't alone.

He turned his body abruptly to face the intruder and tried to hide the joint behind his back.

Mallory held a hand up in apology. 'It's okay. Don't mind me.'

The kid grinned sheepishly and brought the joint back out. 'I get travel sick.'

'Whatever works,' Mallory said.

The kid took a long drag and exhaled. 'Where you headed?' He had a German accent, Mallory thought. Interrail vibes.

'Geneva, for the moment,' Mallory said. 'You?'

'Geneva, then Zurich. I'm Franz,' he added, extending his hand.

Mallory shook, deciding not to offer a name if Franz didn't press him for one. He didn't.

The two of them leaned against opposite walls and were quiet for a moment. Maybe it was the second-hand weed fumes, but Mallory welcomed the opportunity to exchange pleasantries with a stranger. Someone who wasn't planning to kill him or in need of protection from him.

The kid suddenly remembered his manners and held the joint toward Mallory. 'I'm sorry, do you ... ?'

Mallory held a hand up in polite refusal. 'Thanks anyway. I don't want to get too relaxed right now.'

The kid raised an eyebrow. 'Lady friend back there, huh?'

'Just a friend,' Mallory said. 'What's your story? Doing the Grand Tour?'

'Kind of.' He gently tapped his backpack with his foot. 'This is my life right now. I broke up with my girlfriend last year, during all that craziness. I don't care what you say, a year confined to a one-room apartment in Berlin will break up anybody. I started looking for a new place and then I stopped looking.'

'How do you mean?' Mallory asked, intrigued.

The kid swept the hand with the joint in it around in an expansive gesture. 'This is my place now.'

'This train?'

'No, all trains. The Continent. I move around.'

'Interesting. What do you do for money?'

'Same thing I did before.' He put the joint in his mouth to free his hands and pulled a scratched and sticker-emblazoned laptop out of his bag. 'I can work from anywhere, so why not *be* anywhere?'

'I like it,' Mallory said. Thinking about it, it wasn't too different from his own existence for the last year or two. Although it sounded like Franz here had had a quieter time of it.

'I saw you and the lady earlier at the station,' Franz said. 'Where is she now?'

Mallory was suddenly wary. He had mentioned Océane twice. 'Why do you ask?'

300

Franz held his hands up defensively. 'Oh, I didn't mean anything. Your friend asked about her.'

Mallory straightened up, the hairs on the back of his neck standing to attention.

'My friend?'

Franz nodded. 'The big guy. Eastern European, I think. He's got kind of intense eyes. You don't know him?'

Mallory turned and started moving back the way he had come, breaking into as close to a run as he could manage in the narrow aisle.

A ticket collector emerged at the door at the other end of the carriage. A large man, taking up almost the width of the narrow doorway.

'*Arretez*,' he said, giving Mallory a suspicious look as he charged towards him. '*Billet?*'

'I'm sorry, I'm in a hurry,' he said, brandishing the ticket.

The ticket collector widened his stance to take up more space and snatched the ticket from Mallory's hand, making a show of examining every line on it. Eventually, with a slightly regretful look, he handed Mallory back the ticket and stood aside. He said something in French that Mallory assumed was a remonstration about running on his train. Mallory passed through to the next carriage. The officious ticket man had cost him ten seconds, but a physical altercation and its aftermath would have cost him a lot more.

He reached the quiet carriage a minute later, drawing a sharp breath when he pushed open the door and looked ahead, to the table seat where he had left Océane.

The seat was facing away from him, but he could see the body was lying at an unnatural angle in the seat, one hand hanging out in the aisle. He moved forward and saw a leg was crumpled beneath the seat. There was a dark red pool of blood on the floor beneath.

Mallory caught a whisper of movement in the corner of his peripheral vision and looked down the aisle as the door opened. The Serbian. A gun in his hand.

And then he wasn't thinking.

The red mist descended.

53

A European railway carriage is roughly twenty metres long. Running at full tilt, a fit man can cover that distance in under four seconds. In four seconds, a trained shooter can empty the magazine of a standard automatic handgun at an approaching target.

If he doesn't panic.

Mallory wasn't thinking about any of these considerations. He wasn't thinking about the bullet that had passed an inch over his head an instant ago. He wasn't thinking about the shard of door frame the bullet had sent cutting into the left side of his cheek.

He was thinking only about a limp arm and a pool of blood.

Océane. Dead.

Dead by the hand of the man at the other end of the carriage.

Without conscious thought, Mallory was running towards him. He saw the muzzle flash twice. The attached silencer dampened the reports to dull thuds. The Serbian had wasted time trying to aim at the moving target, instead of firing as quickly as he could. His eyes widened as he realised he wasn't going to get another shot off. Mallory didn't know if he had been hit and he didn't care. Nothing was going to stop him.

The Serbian was tightening his finger on the trigger again as Mallory slammed into him. The gun discharged again, but this time pointing up at the ceiling. Mallory grabbed the Serbian's wrist and twisted it around, trying to break it. The other man moved with the motion, saving his wrist but letting go of the gun in the process. Mallory smashed him into the wall, and then took a headbutt. The impact of the hit knocked him back a little, and his opponent pushed him backwards – hard. Mallory fell back over the seat across the aisle, grabbing one of the seatback grips to keep himself upright.

The Serbian had taken a step back, going for his gun again. Mallory ducked as he fired again, the shot passing above his head and punching through the window behind him. Mallory charged back across the aisle and shouldered him into the opposite window, making sure he was too close for the gun to be effective. The night air whistled through the hole in the glass behind him, the noise of the wheels on the tracks adding a lower-pitched undertone.

Mallory punched the Serbian in the gut. He doubled over and Mallory grabbed his gun hand at the wrist and slammed his forearm across his knee, trying to break the bone like a branch. He didn't feel the bone give, but the impact was enough to jolt the gun out of the Serbian's hand and make him grunt in pain.

He was off balance now. Mallory gripped him around the upper body and threw him across the aisle, smoothly continuing the movement to grab the gun from the floor. The

Serbian was picking himself up from the floor between the seats but froze as he saw Mallory had the gun in his hand.

'You're a fucking dead man,' Mallory said. 'But first you're going to tell me what Rousseau wants.'

The voice was utterly calm in reply. 'It is you who is a dead man. And it is because that's what he wants.' The words were heavily accented, but they were the first words he had said in English to Mallory.

'Why? Why kill the girl? She couldn't hurt you.'

'I do not ask questions.'

'No,' Mallory spat. 'Your kind never do.'

A thin smile appeared on his face. 'It is a shame I had to kill her so quickly. No time for anything else, eh?'

Mallory didn't know if that was an attempt to rile him up or not, and he couldn't care less. He aimed between his eyes and pulled the trigger.

The hammer clicked on an empty chamber.

As the Serbian launched himself forward, Mallory realised he had been suckered. The bastard had known he was out of ammo, and had used the gun to give himself time to recover. He had been ready for this.

The Serbian had both hands around Mallory's throat now, forcing him against the window with the hole in it. Not just trying to choke him, but trying to crush his throat. Mallory saw blackness at the edge of his vision. He felt the window start to crack and give at his back.

He tried hammering at his attacker's head with his fists. Not good enough. They were too close together for him to get enough power into each swing. The Serbian's eyes were staring into his in determination and expectation. Mallory knew then that this man wasn't just paid to kill with his hands, he enjoyed it. Mallory started to feel himself starting to pass out. He forgot about trying to pound his opponent's head and reached down, dug into his hip pocket. The pencil he had been using to draw on the map. He worked it out, gripped it, and put everything he had into swinging it into the Serbian's neck.

It didn't pierce the skin – the lead was too blunt and Mallory didn't have enough space – but it made an impact. His assailant blinked in surprise, taking one hand off Mallory's throat to hold to his own.

Mallory shifted his weight, pushing him back a little and kicked him hard in the shin.

The other hand loosened on his throat now as the Serbian grunted and stepped back. Mallory pressed his advantage. If the fucker got his hands around his neck like that again, it would be game over.

The Serbian was bringing his hands up again, reaching for Mallory's shoulders. Mallory used the backs of his hands to bat both arms out of the way and then jerked his head forward, butting him straight in the nose with his forehead.

He still didn't yell in pain, but the pissed-off groan had a more frantic edge this time. That was three good hits in a row for Mallory, time to go on the defensive for a moment. He ducked as the Serbian threw an unfocused punch that had so much force behind it that the plastic casing on the wall cracked at the spot his head had just been. He moved forward, grabbing him around the midsection and flinging him into the window. Weakened by the bullet hole, it smashed. The track noise and the rush of the wind increased.

The Serbian's fingers grabbed at Mallory's face and head, unable to get purchase on his short hair. He managed to get the crook of his elbow around Mallory's head and swing him around so Mallory's upper body was out of the smashed window. He was trying to throw him out. There was no way to tell how fast they were going, but from the way the wind was cutting into him, Mallory was betting that someone hitting the tracks below would end up looking like the contents of a tin of corned beef.

He managed to brace himself on the edge of the window frame. The window was safety glass, so there were no shards. Instead, it had shattered into icy crystals that clung around the edge beyond the gaping hole that Mallory was hanging out of.

The Serbian hissed a curse between clenched teeth. He had both hands on Mallory's chest now, pushing hard. Mallory glanced ahead of them and saw that there was a steep rise coming. Unless this was suddenly going to turn into a funicular railway, he knew what that meant. Whether or not this bastard succeeded in pushing him all the way out, he was a goner.

He took hold of the Serbian's shirt with his left hand and then released his grip on the frame, feeling himself start to be pushed backwards as he did so. He grabbed a handful of the shattered glass and slammed it into the Serbian's face.

The pushing stopped, and Mallory pulled himself back into the cabin using the Serbian's shirt as his opponent scratched at his eyes.

The train's horn let out a mournful moan. Mallory ducked a blind punch and manoeuvred to the side of the Serbian, got a grip on his shoulders and pushed him head first through the window. It didn't match the force with which Mallory had been pushed out earlier, when their positions had been reversed. It didn't need to. Only the Serbians head and shoulders protruded through the window.

A split second later, the train entered the tunnel.

Mallory instinctively closed his eyes and mouth and turned his head as a torrent of blood exploded back from the window. Most of it went outside, but when Mallory wiped the warm sticky mess from his face and opened his eyes, he saw plenty of it had spattered the inside of the carriage.

The assassin's truncated corpse slumped down beneath the window, his hands still trembling as his body caught up with what had happened to his head.

Mallory staggered, almost fell backwards and sat down on the seat opposite. The roar of the wheels on the tracks had doubled in volume inside the tunnel. A moment later, the train exited the other side and the noise dropped. He could see the moon over a hilly landscape.

He put his hands on his face again.

'Shit.'

He had won this fight – just. But in another sense, he had lost it before it had begun. Océane was dead. Her killer had followed her soon enough, but it was Rousseau who had given the order. If it was the last thing Mallory did, he was going to make Rousseau pay for it.

Unwillingly, the analytical part of his brain started working. There was no time to mourn.

He opened his eyes to the scene of carnage. There was no cleaning this up. He would have to get off the train and let the authorities come to whatever conclusions they could. Before he left, he had to see Océane again. He couldn't leave her the way this bastard had.

Struggling to his feet, he wiped blood off his face with

the bottom of his T-shirt, getting as much off as he could. Mallory cast a last disdainful glance at the headless corpse sprawled over the seat and turned to look back down the aisle to the opposite end.

Her body was slumped on the chair, the dark hair covering her face. The front of her shirt was stained red below where her throat had been cut.

Mallory gritted his teeth and approached. Her backpack was lying on the seat beside her. The blood had spattered all over her white Converse trainers.

Wait a second . . .

Mallory gently touched a hand to her forehead and pushed her hair back. Before he could finish, the door at the end of the carriage opened.

54

'Mallory, what the hell happened?'

Océane's brown eyes were wide as she opened the door to see Mallory crouching by the body.

He blinked, making sure this wasn't some kind of stress-induced hallucination. He looked at Océane's face. Looked down at the black lace-up boots she had been wearing since he had found her in his hotel room in Marseille. It wasn't a hallucination. She was alive. But in that case …

Mallory looked back at the body slumped in the seat. He pushed the dark hair hanging over the face aside. He saw the features of the Dutch girl he had seen earlier. Océane looked down and screamed.

'Who is she?'

'It's Mel,' Océane said. 'She turned up with a beer after you went for a walk. We had a couple of drinks, she wanted to talk about her boyfriend. I felt sick and went to the toilet, when I came back …' She glanced at the body and averted her eyes quickly. 'He thought it was me.'

'Yeah,' Mallory acknowledged, resisting the urge to say, *him and me both.*

Océane turned back to him. 'You got him?' Then she noticed a window was smashed and there was a pair of feet sticking out from one of the rows at the back. She took a step forward.

Mallory put a hand on her forearm to hold her back. 'You don't have to worry about him.'

She saw enough to take his word for it and turned away. 'What do we do?'

Mallory checked his watch: 9.55 p.m. If they were on time, they were forty minutes from Geneva.

'We get off at the next stop and go from there.'

Océane glanced back at the body.

'What about Mel?'

Mallory shook his head. 'We can't do anything for her. She's gone.'

He felt the urge to grab Océane's arm again and pull her out of there. They needed to get as far away from this carriage as possible, and hope nobody found the bodies before the next stop. He hesitated and then gently moved the body so the girl was lying on her back. He closed her eyes with his fingertips.

'Let's go,' she said quietly.

Mallory grabbed his backpack from the shelf and pulled his hoodie on over his bloody T-shirt. They moved along the carriages, heading in the direction of travel until they reached the front of the train. Fields and trees outside the window. Mallory tried to remember if there were any more stops before Geneva. He thought there was one, maybe two. Right now, they were still in France.

'When we get off, I'm going to find a way to get you back home. I go alone from here.'

'No way,' Océane said at once. 'They want to kill me. It should have been me, not Mel.'

'You're not safe.'

'I'm not safe anywhere, but I'm safer by your side.'

Mallory opened his mouth to protest, but she had a point. Every time Océane had been in trouble, it had been when he was elsewhere.

She smiled, because she *knew* she had a point. 'I'm sorry we both got dragged into this.'

Mallory was about to reply to that when he heard rapid footsteps. A train guard advancing along the carriage towards them. He wore the standard green uniform and hat. Mallory tensed, but as he got closer it was clear the guard's eyes were fixed on the locked door to the driver's cab. He was pale. Beads of sweat stood out on his shoulder.

Mallory and Océane exchanged a glance as the guard hurried past them, mumbling an *'excusez-moi'*.

He took a key out and opened the door to the cab, quickly closing it behind him after giving a furtive glance back the way he'd come.

'Do you think he found the bodies?' Océane whispered urgently.

'Either that, or he just had to deal with a really difficult fare dodger,' Mallory said. 'It might be okay, they might go on till—'

A screech of brakes and a rapid deceleration put paid to that hope.

'What's happening?'

'They're stopping the train. Must be procedure. They'll call the police and lock us all down.'

'What are we going to do?' Océane asked.

'We're going to get the hell off this train.'

55

Mallory and Océane moved to the next carriage, which was a little busier. The air was cooler, the air conditioning was functioning in here. Passengers were looking up from their laptops and phones, exchanging questions about what was happening. None of them had any awareness of what had occurred further down the train. There was an announcement over the PA informing them that there would be a short delay due to a technical fault.

They exited at the far end of the passage. There was no one in the join section between carriages. Mallory glanced through the windows in the next set of doors to check there were no other guards coming and then smashed the emergency door release panel and pressed the button. The door slid open over a four-foot drop to the tracks. The night was cold, but the fresh air was welcome.

Without waiting to be directed, Océane sat down on the edge and dropped off. There was a stretch of fields with hills in the distance on this side of the train, thick pine woods on the opposite side. Not a difficult decision.

Mallory and Océane ducked under the body of the train and crouch-walked to the other side. Mallory glanced up at the carriage as they hustled into the cover of the trees, but the seats at the windows above them were mostly unoccupied. The only passenger he could see was staring straight ahead, probably at the electronic update board that was currently lying to the passengers about how long they were going to be stuck here.

'Where are we?' Océane asked as she ran alongside Mallory through the pines.

'Somewhere between Culoz and Seyssel,' Mallory said, making a rough guess based on the time. 'We haven't crossed the border yet.'

'Do you know where you're going?'

Mallory glanced up at the tree canopy. It was overcast, so there were no stars to orient himself by, and dawn was hours away. He closed his eyes and listened.

'Mallory?'

He shushed her and concentrated. Running water, not far away. If that was the Rhône, keeping it on their right would take them north, towards the Swiss border.

'We're going this way.'

'Which is where?'

Mallory glanced back the way they had come, he could still see thin slivers of the night sky in between the trees, which meant they hadn't come far enough.

'Let's just put some distance between us and the train before we get into the full revised travel itinerary, okay?'

She sighed and followed as he took off running again. Océane was obviously in good shape. She kept up with him with seeming ease as he covered around a mile of ground through the forest. When the trees started to thin out and snatches of night sky began to appear ahead, he stopped and listened. There was a low hum of traffic ahead of them.

'Okay, take a break,' Mallory said.

'You would make a good drill sergeant, you know that?'

'There's no need to get insulting, Océane.'

She sat down on a fallen tree trunk, took a deep breath and blew out, the first sign of exertion she had shown. It was a good thing she was able to run, Mallory thought, it was a skill they would both need. She wiped a thin sheen of perspiration from her forehead.

'What do you think they'll do? The staff on the train.'

'They found two dead bodies in the back carriage. By now the police will probably have arrived or be on their way. The passengers will have to be questioned before they're allowed to continue their journey.'

'What about us?'

'It won't take them long to work out someone left the train. There are cameras in the gangway connections, maybe the carriages too. When they get around to piecing everything together they'll work out what happened: the Serbian killed the girl, and then I killed him.'

'So the police will look for you.'

'Yeah. Won't be the first time. They'll only have the security footage to go on, though. We paid cash for the tickets. No names.'

They sat there for a moment. Mallory thought about the next steps. Having to throw out one set of plans and come up with a new set on the hoof was familiar territory to him, as it was to any soldier.

After a couple of minutes, Océane stood and rolled her

trouser leg up to massage a bruise on her shin, probably received from running through the woods. 'So what now?'

'Same plan,' Mallory said, 'but with a few changes. We're still going to Appelburg.'

'Rousseau must know we're coming now.'

'Rousseau knew we were coming before; that was why that bastard was on the train. All that's different now is we know he knows.'

Océane turned and looked back the way they had come, as though she could see through a mile of closely packed pine trees with X-ray vision. 'Well, we can't get back on the train.'

'No. And I think it would be wise to avoid public transport entirely. Which means we need to get ourselves a car.'

'Maybe we can rent one in Seyssel.'

'Maybe,' Mallory said.

A few minutes later, they emerged into a clearing that was sheltered from above by thick leaves. Mallory dropped his bag and started picking up dry branches from the ground.

Océane's brow furrowed as she watched him. 'What are you doing?'

'We're going to stay away from the roads tonight, they'll be too quiet. We'll wait until the morning when there's more traffic.'

'You want to *camp*?'

'Yes. You have a problem with that?'

Ten minutes later he had a fire going. The leaves above were thick enough to hide the flames and dissipate the smoke. Océane took the bottle of vodka out of her backpack and offered it to Mallory. He took a gulp, enjoying the way it burned his throat, then handed it back.

The night was quiet. Occasionally, the peace was

broken by the muted calls of owls or the sound of other nocturnal animals moving through the bushes. Nothing larger than a fox, Mallory was pleased to note. If anyone came this way, they would hear their movements and see their flashlights a long distance away. He knew this was the smartest play. Anyone looking for them would be concentrating on the roads just now.

Mallory pulled a hoodie from his backpack and tossed it to Océane. 'Put that on, it'll keep you warm while you sleep.'

She shook the creases out of the hoodie and put it on. 'Sleep sounds like a good idea. At least we have fresh air. Do you think more men like that one will come for us?'

'Get some sleep,' he repeated, ducking the question. He sat down across the fire from her. The flames had died down but the embers were glowing with warmth. 'I'll be right here.'

'My guardian angel,' Océane said, then let the smile fade from her lips as she met Mallory's gaze. 'Is there any way you could be ... over here?'

'Océane—'

Before he could finish, she walked around the fire, leaned in and started to kiss him full on the mouth. Surprised, Mallory responded. She kissed harder. And then almost without thinking about it, he was pushing gently on her upper arms. Pushing her back.

'Océane, I don't think this is a good idea.'

She frowned, the faint scar on her forehead creasing. 'It's a perfect idea.'

He shook his head. 'You've been through a lot. We need to take it easy.'

'Don't tell me what I've been through,' she snapped, the romance well and truly evaporating.

Mallory opened his hands in apology. 'Look, I'm just saying, not a good idea.'

'God, do you have any idea how patronising you sound? What's it to you, anyway? Nicolas and I were broken up a long time ago. You didn't even know him.'

'No, but I know you. You're displacing.'

She narrowed her eyes.

'You're not even tempted?' Océane asked. 'You are. And yet you won't. Just my fucking luck. A gentleman.'

Mallory leaned against a tree with one hand and rubbed his eyes with the other.

'First time I've been accused of that. Océane, you can call me patronising all you want, but complicating ... this ... isn't going to do you any good right now. Believe me. This is not the time or the place.'

'And when would be the time or the place?'

'Tell you what. If we survive the next couple of days, and if you still want to give it a go in a few months, give me a call.'

'You'll have the same number?' she asked.

'You'll know how to get hold of me,' he said. 'If we survive the next couple of days.'

Océane sighed and lay down on her side of the smouldering embers. 'All right. Sweet dreams, you bastard.'

FRIDAY

FRIDAY

56

APPELBURG, SWITZERLAND

Rousseau watched as Frei and Keller took one ankle each and dragged the bloodied body of the young man roughly across the grass and onto the gravel path. Erich Baumann had been a disappointment. He had been armed, he had had time to prepare, but still he had lasted less than twenty minutes in the garden.

Rousseau shook his head as they pulled the body inside the maintenance door. The corpse would go to the basement and be disposed of later. Rousseau holstered his gun and started to walk back to the house. He stopped when he saw Fabian standing in the doorway ahead of him.

'What's wrong?' Something had to be wrong. Fabian had a squeamish distaste for the occasional dawn hunts. He wouldn't be out in the garden unless there was a reason.

'Petrovic is dead,' he said flatly.

A week ago, perhaps as little as a day ago, the statement would have come as a surprise to Rousseau. Over the past few hours, his opponent had taught him to expect the unexpected.

He walked past Fabian and into the changing room, lifting a fresh towel from the pile at the door and wiping the light sheen of sweat from his face.

He tossed the towel in the used bin and told Fabian to elaborate.

Fabian related how Petrovic had been found dead on the TER from Lyon to Geneva, minus head.

'He took his *head* off?' Rousseau almost wanted to laugh.

'It appears there was a fight and at some point Petrovic's head was forced out of the window as the train entered a tunnel, and, well . . .'

'You don't have to draw me a picture. The girl on the train was not Mademoiselle Fontaine?'

'No. She was a drifter. A drug addict, probably a prostitute. Either Petrovic mistook her for Fontaine, or perhaps the Brit killed her.'

'Are we on good terms with the police?'

'Sadly, we do not have as strong contacts with the police in Auvergne as in other regions. However, I have been able to ascertain some details. The train was stopped four kilometres south of Seyssel, Haute-Savoie. The police are searching for a man answering the description of our friend. Images have been released to the press. It's definitely him.'

'And we may have lost our best chance to stop him on the way.'

Fabian cleared his throat. 'The police are searching for him at transportation hubs. And of course, our local people will ensure appropriate checks are carried out on anyone approaching Appelburg, should they make it this far.'

Rousseau thought it over. 'Keep me posted.'

Rousseau took off his gun belt and shed the rest of his clothes, then stepped into the showers at the far end of the changing room. Erich Baumann hadn't caused him to build up much of a sweat, but the hot water and the steam would let him think.

This adversary would not be picked up by an alert transport cop. He may not even be stopped by Rousseau's own, better-paid police. He was coming here, and it was beginning to look like no one was going to stop him.

And part of Rousseau relished the prospect.

57

Mallory dozed lightly, never quite surrendering to sleep. Occasionally, he would hear sounds in the night and snap fully awake, but none of them sounded human. Alertness wasn't the only thing on his mind. Océane had been right: he had been tempted. Plenty tempted. He didn't think there was a chance in hell she would think he was a good prospect once her head was straight, but it was certainly a thought.

At first light, he nudged Océane awake and told her it was time to get moving. She moaned and reluctantly opened her eyes, shivering in the morning air.

Mallory found a gap in the tree canopy and used the position of the sun to tell him which way they needed to go. In less than twenty minutes, they were close enough to the road to hear the hum of regular traffic.

Océane had been unusually quiet since she had awoken. When Mallory heard a long sigh from behind him, he turned around. Océane had stopped. She had her back to him, looking into the trees.

'What?'

She turned around and held her hands up, as though surrendering. 'This is pointless. This Rousseau guy knows you're coming. He'll kill you.'

Mallory folded his arms and leaned on the nearest tree. There had been a lot of tension building up, of one kind or another. Perhaps it was as well to let off some steam now. 'Thanks for the vote of confidence.'

Océane held his gaze and shook her head. 'You don't even care, do you?'

'Of course I care.'

'You act like you don't go looking for trouble. You know what I think?'

'No, I don't. I haven't the slightest clue what goes on in your head.'

'I think that's *bullshit*. You adore trouble. You feed off it. I've been sticking close to you because I'm scared, but maybe I just need to walk away.'

Mallory let out an involuntary laugh, knowing immediately he was pouring fuel on the fire. 'Why don't you? That's what you're best at.'

Océane blinked, disbelieving. She opened her mouth. Closed it. Decided on a reply. '*Excuse me?*'

'You heard me. Your grandfather, Nicolas. Any time it gets a tiny bit difficult you run away. That's how you deal with life, by dodging it. Well, some things you can't run away from. This bastard had Nicolas killed. He tried to kill you and me. I'm not letting that go.'

Océane stared back at him for a long time before she spoke. 'Let's get to wherever we're going, then you can go and do whatever the hell you want, Mallory.'

'Sounds like a plan.' He turned and started walking away, not looking back to check if Océane was following.

They walked until the traffic noise got louder and they could see vehicles flashing back and forward on both sides of the road. They kept a few rows of trees between them and the road as they moved at a fast clip.

When he heard Océane's voice, he allowed himself a small smile of satisfaction that she had spoken first. It was petty as hell, but some people brought that out in him.

'What's that over there?' she asked.

Mallory turned and followed her gaze. The sky had lightened. He saw a single house on the edge of the road. One light on in a downstairs room. There were two cars in the drive. All of a sudden, stupid point-scoring went out of his head. The mission was back on.

'It's what I've been looking for.'

One of the cars was a shiny Tesla, plugged into a dock that looked just as new as the car. The other was a worse-for-wear pickup truck with rust around the wheel sills and a crack on the windscreen.

The door was answered by a wary-looking middle-aged woman wearing black slacks and a white blouse. She peered suspiciously over the rims of her cat-eye glasses, first at Mallory, then at Océane.

'Puis-je vous aider?'

Mallory waved a greeting, trying his most non-threatening smile. He stood back and let Océane do the talking, as they had agreed.

She explained that the two of them had broken down three kilometres away, but they had to get to Geneva urgently for her niece's christening. She added in a detail about their clothes being in a suitcase in the other car. Could they possibly borrow one of the cars? They would, of course, pay for the trouble.

The woman listened, glancing now and again at Mallory. The suspicion did not leave her face. When Océane had finished, she started talking rapidly. Mallory only picked up a few words here and there, but he got the gist. She was telling Océane that they most certainly could not borrow the Tesla, and she didn't even know if she would consider parting with the wreck.

'What did she say?' he asked Océane.

'She says the truck is unreliable. We might break down and not bother to bring it back to her.'

The woman was regarding them with narrow eyes, like a poker player waiting for the outcome of a hand.

'How many euros do you have left?'

'About three hundred, I think.'

'Tell her that truck is on its last legs. We'll buy it from her for two fifty and she doesn't need to worry about us getting it back.'

Océane started to translate, but the woman was already snatching the sheaf of euros from Océane. She gave them a hurried *au revoir* before starting to close the door. Mallory put a hand up to stop the door.

'Madame . . .'

'*Oui?*'

'The keys?'

Ten minutes later, they were on the road headed north, Océane behind the wheel.

'That was a nice touch, saying our dress clothes were in the other car,' Mallory said. 'Sold the story.'

Océane waved a hand dismissively. 'I just thought of it while I was talking. You did good too, haggling with her.'

'Are you kidding? She was desperate to offload this thing. I'm betting her husband will wake up in an hour and wonder where his pride and joy went.'

Océane smiled briefly at the thought.

The truck drove better than it looked. It had no problem keeping pace with the other traffic. They passed through a small town and a road sign told them they were fifty kilometres from Switzerland.

'You can drop me once we get over the border, if you want,' Mallory said. 'I can make my own way from there.'

Océane didn't respond, keeping her eyes on the road. Mallory said her name, wondering if she had heard him.

'It's fine. I don't have anywhere else I need to be right now.'

Mallory hid his smile behind his hand and cleared his throat. 'Fine by me.'

There was a well-thumbed road atlas in the glovebox. He took it out and plotted the distance by road to Appelburg. After they crossed the Swiss border, there was another two hundred and fifty kilometres or so to Appelburg via Bern. He didn't anticipate any problems for most of the trip. The danger would come on the approach to Appelburg, as the roads narrowed and the choice of routes diminished. After the train, Mallory knew that Rousseau was forewarned.

That changed things.

58

At the border at Douane de Bardonnex, the road split into lanes, each with a kiosk checkpoint. A series of three painted yellow steel arches spanned the crossing. The arches made Mallory think of McDonald's, and that reminded him they hadn't eaten since last night. Then he forgot about his stomach as the barrier in the lane they were in started to lower ahead of them.

'I'll do the talking,' Océane said as they slowed.

'I thought you said we could drive straight through,' Mallory said as he watched a uniformed Swiss border guard approach from the kiosk.

'Sometimes they do spot checks,' Océane said, winding the window down. 'Customs, not passports. This has to be the laxest border in the world. Relax, it's the Swiss. They're cool about everything if you mind your own business.'

There was another possibility, Mallory knew. Perhaps the French police had had a tip-off. Perhaps they had been alerted to their likely direction of travel and border guards had been instructed to stop cars with one male and one female. Perhaps he should have hidden in the boot.

No, that would have been stupid. If this was indeed a random spot check, then a man hiding in the boot would not be the sort of thing that was waved through, passport or no passport.

Mallory took his gun from the pocket in the passenger side door and cocked it. He positioned it back in the door pocket, ready to grab, and kept his right hand in position.

'Keep it in first gear with your foot on the clutch,' he said. 'Handbrake off. If I say drive, floor it.'

Océane turned to give him a look that asked if he was nuts. She couldn't ask him out loud because the guard was now in earshot.

The guard approached Océane's window on the driver's side. He was short and stocky, dressed in navy chinos and a close-fitting jacket with his job title in three languages written on the front: *Grenzwache, Garde-frontière, Guardia di confine*.

Océane was ready with one of her most dazzling smiles. It was as though she had snapped her fingers and made three days of stress and sleepless nights disappear. She greeted him in French and commented on the weather. Mallory gave a wave to acknowledge the guard and looked ahead, considering options.

If the guard detained them, it would only be for one reason. Therefore, they couldn't allow themselves to be detained. He was glad this was a loose border. They weren't expecting drug smugglers or suicide bombers.

Ahead of them was the customs checkpoint kiosk. The barrier had been lowered on the lane that they had been guided into. The barrier was painted aluminium, didn't look too solid. Mallory didn't think it would stand up to their pickup truck driving straight at it. No spike strips on the road or anything like that. Low security. This was just a bit of bad luck.

The guard asked Océane a couple of questions. As he listened, his gaze roamed over the interior of the car, lingering on Mallory for a little longer. Mallory smiled in what he hoped was a relaxed, non-threatening way.

The guard said something to Océane, pointing at the rear of the truck.

The guard told them '*Une seconde*' and walked around the back. Océane and Mallory exchanged a glance. He looked ahead at the barrier, checked they were still in first, slipped the gun into his hand. The guard was armed, but Mallory hoped that he would back down if Mallory was quicker on the draw. He didn't want to be forced into a kill-or-be-killed situation with an innocent border guard.

The guard approached again. He stopped at the window again, this time crouching a little to look past Océane and at Mallory. He seemed to be pointing at his hand. Shit. Had he somehow intuited that Mallory was armed?

'*Monsieur.*'

Mallory didn't move. He tried to look confused. He didn't have to try too hard.

The guard was staring hard. Was the butt of the gun showing above the door pocket? Mallory glanced down. It was concealed from the guard's line of sight, he was sure of it. But maybe he suspected there was something there. If so, it would be better to make the first move.

Mallory's right hand started to move towards the pocket, and then stopped.

If the guard suspected he was armed, why the hell hadn't he pulled his own gun?

'*Monsieur.*'

As he spoke again, Mallory realised the guard was gesturing at his left hand, not his right. Or specifically, his left wrist.

Mallory raised it slowly to show him the watch. 'This?'

The guard snapped his fingers before extending his palm over Océane's lap. Mallory unfastened the watch and handed it to him. The guard took the watch and withdrew his hand. He held it up to the light, weighed it in his hand, then handed it back to Mallory.

'You must declare watches, even for personal use.'

'Seriously?' Océane asked.

The guard smiled for the first time. 'Welcome to Switzerland.'

Océane apologised, the relief a little too evident in her voice. The guard gave Mallory another suspicious look and then straightened up, waving them through. The barrier rose. The car jolted as Océane forgot they were in gear and stalled it. She gave Mallory a sheepish look as she restarted the engine and pulled through the barrier.

And then they were in Switzerland.

Mallory glanced over his shoulder as they picked up speed. The officious border guard had retreated to his kiosk, wasn't looking at them.

'The one thing the Swiss give a shit about you importing, huh?'

'I think it was you,' Océane said. 'You look like trouble.'

Mallory thought it was a fair enough point. He didn't argue. 'Something tells me getting into Appelburg will be a little more challenging.'

'Why? It's not a border.'

'That's not the way I hear it.'

59

They stopped for fuel a couple of miles inside the border. The filling station was alongside a two-storey concrete strip with a café and a mini supermarket on the ground floor and flats with balconies along the top. Mallory thought about waking up every morning with a view of HGVs refuelling and decided his current lifestyle was the right one for him.

When the truck's tank was full, they bought food and water from the supermarket, then settled in for the long haul.

Mallory reviewed the links about their destination he had saved on his phone while Océane drove. Appelburg was a picturesque mountain town, a little too far off the beaten track to get the volume of tourists that other Swiss towns attracted.

It wasn't quite the level of preparation he would have liked for an assault on enemy terrain, but between that and the map, he now had a decent idea of the territory. As his contact had told him, Rousseau's house was on a ridge overlooking the town, like a castle. He seemed to rule the place like a monarch, too.

Reading between the lines on local news reports,

Rousseau's influence was all over Appelburg. He was frequently pictured with the mayor at civic events. He seemed to plough money into the town so that it remained prosperous and affluent without chasing the tourist dollar. It was a smart tactic. Pablo Escobar had done the same thing. Make people love you as well as fear you, and you're protected by more than just your paid guards.

Judging by what both Cristofol and Mac had said, the local police force was bought and paid for, which was why approaching via the main road was out of the question. To be safe, they would have to take the smaller road that wound three miles south of the town. They would leave the car and approach Appelburg across country, which would involve fording the river that passed through it at some point.

Assuming that went smoothly, they would have to be even more careful when they reached Appelburg. The police would be looking for them.

And then they had to get to the house itself, which was approachable only by cable car or helicopter. Mallory didn't have access to a Wildcat or a pilot, so it would have to be the cable car. But how to get on board undetected? Security would be tight. As with so many of the operations he had run in Afghanistan, some things were impossible to know in advance. You had to prepare as best you could, but be ready to adapt when boots hit sand.

He enlarged the Google Earth satellite view of the grand house and sketched out a schematic of the place on the back of an invoice he found in the glove box, working out an idea of the interior going by what he could see from above. There was a large garden to the rear of the house, taking up the rest of the mountain ledge. It had a lot of foliage, a lot of stonework. Stone staircases and small buildings and what looked from above like statues.

He widened the scope to take in the distance between the town and the house, the twin cables linking the two places. If he could get on board that cable car by hook or by crook, he was confident he could find Rousseau before he could evacuate.

He was so deep in concentration that he didn't hear Océane's question. When he felt her eyes on him, he asked her to repeat it.

'Why do you have a watch anyway?'

Mallory looked at the watch that had almost got them detained at the world's laxest border and shrugged. 'To tell the time with.'

'Most people don't have them any more. You tell the time with your phone.'

'It was a gift. From someone in my old unit.'

'Do you think about those days a lot?'

Mallory considered the question. It wasn't a simple yes or no, that was for sure. 'Some days ... some days it feels closer than others.'

They passed through Bern, skirting the edge of the old town. It looked like a pretty model railway set scaled up in size; lots of trees and red-tile roofs and the spire of the cathedral towering over its surroundings. They joined the A6 autoroute and started to bear south-east for the final leg of the journey. Appelburg wasn't that far from Bern as the crow flies, but that's the thing with the Alps – nothing is ever as the crow flies. It was mid-afternoon now, the sun past its peak and beginning its lazy descent towards the peaks of the mountains. Océane unwrapped one of the baguettes they had bought after crossing the border and ate quickly, steering with her other hand.

Mallory kept his window rolled down, enjoying the mild fresh air after the heat and clamminess of Marseille. On their left, the vast expanse of Lake Thun stretched out, the calm water like a giant mirror, reflecting the mountains and the blue sky.

Then the mountains began to close in on the road. An hour after leaving Bern, they passed a sign for Gänsern, the last town before they reached Appelburg. 'We'll stop there,' Mallory said.

'You need to get something to eat?'

'Not a bad idea, but we need a few other things, too.'

A couple of minutes later they saw the sign welcoming them to Gänsern. It was small but perfectly formed. They passed a church and a hospital and rows of wooden chalets. Océane parked in a petrol station nestled between the road and the bank of a fast-flowing river and topped up the tank while Mallory crossed the road. Every town in the alps had an outdoor store, and this one was no exception. Mallory was hoping he would find the equipment he needed to give himself a fighting chance when they reached Appelburg.

The store was a big, barn-like structure. Like everything else he had seen so far in Switzerland, it was gleaming inside and out. A beaming blond woman greeted him as he entered.

He walked the aisles, gathering anything that might come in handy and carried what he had chosen to the checkout, where the woman greeted him again. There was a board behind the counter with guns and rifles carefully displayed. He gave them a longing look, but he didn't think even Switzerland was laidback enough to sell a tourist with no ID an AK-47. He would have to make do with the Ruger until something better came up.

He paid for the equipment with the last of his cash and went back outside. The mid-afternoon sun was warm on his skin, the aggregate in the pavement surfaces sparkling in the light. Océane was waiting by the car, watching the river as it rushed past.

'You get everything you needed?'

'No,' Mallory said. 'But it'll have to do. Let's go.'

60

The first obstacle was further out from Appelburg than Mallory had anticipated. Had it not been for a curve in the road and a line of waiting cars three miles from town, they would have had no notice at all.

Océane pulled onto the hard shoulder where the road curved around a sheer wall of rock. Mallory got out and walked towards the blind corner. He reached the end of the line of cars and carefully stepped out so he could see the hold-up. As he had guessed, it wasn't an accident, it was a police roadblock. Two squad cars with their lights blinking flanked the road. As Mallory watched, one officer waved the car at the front through while one of his colleagues moved on to speak to the next car in line.

They were checking every car passing east to Appelburg. He wondered what excuse they were using. The Swiss didn't seem like the kind of people who liked an excess of authority.

Mallory backed out of line of sight again and jogged back to where the truck was parked. Océane was looking out of the windscreen at him with expectant eyes.

'Turn around,' he said as he got in. 'We'll have to take the other road. It was a couple of miles back.'

Océane made a quick turn in the road, then floored it. They reached the junction in under three minutes. She executed another quick turn and they were on a smaller road, gaining altitude. Mallory checked the map and saw that this road began to veer sharply away to the north in about a mile. He looked up at the road for a place to stop. The pines encroached on one side, steep hillside on the other. When he saw a gap in the trees ahead, he told Océane to slow down. There was a narrow logging road ahead. Océane turned onto it and steered along a few hundred yards of rutted dirt track, then pulled into the side of the road by a pile of timber. The wood was shrouded in a thick layer of moss. Like the trees had been felled, stacked and then forgotten about.

Océane pulled the handbrake on and turned the engine off, looking at Mallory expectantly as silence filled the car.

Mallory studied the map again. The direct route would take them through the thick forest. 'From here, we walk.'

Cristofol had been right, Mallory thought as they moved south through the woods. A full-on frontal assault would fail. It would take a small army to capture Appelburg. Perhaps Cristofol had the manpower for it, but it would be impossible for them to spring any kind of surprise attack. Before any attacking force encountered Rousseau's guards, they would have to deal with the police. Police who could legitimately call in official support.

No, this was the only way to do it. Low footprint, asymmetric warfare. Still, it was a little more asymmetric than he would have liked. He would have felt a lot more confident going into this with the men from his old unit. Or even just a handful of them. Westwick and Donno, perhaps.

Mallory felt the familiar pang of regret that this was an impossibility. He knew Donno would get himself over here within twenty-four hours if Mallory picked up the phone to him. He had briefly considered doing so on the train, while evaluating the task ahead, but he knew that wouldn't be fair to Donno, or to his family. Not after everything that had gone down last year and before. He thought about Westwick often, too. Westwick would know exactly how to attack this location, and he would know how to handle himself when they got in there. But Westwick was dead, and Mallory couldn't shake the weight of his responsibility for that fact.

'I'm glad I bought new boots.'

Grateful for the distraction, Mallory glanced over at his walking companion. He had stopped being surprised that Océane was able to keep up the pace without complaint. When he had commented on it after they left the train, she had brushed off the compliment, saying that being on your feet for a twelve-hour Saturday shift at Les Douze Mois put most other physical trials in the shade.

'So this Rousseau guy pretty much owns the town, huh?' Océane said.

'That's about the size of it. *Someone* was paying those cops to check incoming cars.'

'Sounds like the mayor back home in St-Jean.'

That reminded Mallory of the day this had all started, a lazy sunny afternoon that felt a million years in the past. 'Remy's dad, right?'

She looked at him with surprise. 'You know Remy?'

'We had words. Your grandfather sent him packing.' He

felt her eyes on him and held up his hands in defence. 'It was all him, I really didn't go looking for trouble there.'

'I believe you. I hate Remy, his father too.'

'Didn't have the pleasure of meeting Remy senior.'

She snorted. 'Those gangsters you talked to back in Marseille are probably more morally upstanding. You know he charges extra "town insurance" to the businesses? Says it's the only way they can fund the police.'

'Interesting,' Mallory said, thinking about how it was the same all over. Dickheads fattening their own wallets by walking over the little people. Only the scale was different.

In a few minutes, they reached a wide river. Mallory knew it had to be the Appelbach, the river that flowed through Appelburg and snaked close to the road back to Gänsern, the town where they had stopped on the way. The river was deep, and around forty feet wide here, but Mallory could see that it narrowed a little upstream and a formation of rocks had caught some felled trees and created a calmer spot. They waded through at that point, holding their bags aloft.

Mallory was soaked through up to his chest, and Océane almost to her neck when they reached the opposite bank. He pulled his shirt off to wring it out, then turned his back as Océane did the same, ignoring her amused look. He watched the river as it rushed past after meeting the obstruction here. It was a pity the current was running away from Appelburg. Maybe they could have built a raft and floated all the way past the roadblocks, otherwise.

'When we get close, I'm going to need you to hang back.'

'I thought we were sticking together,' Océane said.

'We are. To a point. But if I'm going in there, I need someone on the outside. Somebody who can make sure there's an exit.'

'Why do I think you're just saying that to shut me up?'

Mallory kept his face straight. 'I try never to do anything just for one reason.'

'Okay,' Océane said. 'You want to make sure there's an exit. That means we need to find a way to get the car into town. Or find another car.'

'Agreed. We'll work something out once we get the lie of the land.'

They reached the edge of the woods after walking for twenty minutes. Mallory signalled for Océane to stop and crouched low, moving to the edge of the treeline. Close by, there was a thick fallen tree that was overgrown with foliage. Mallory left Océane waiting there while he moved right up to the edge of the cover to take a closer look.

61

Their route had brought them to a point north-west of Appelburg. Beyond the trees was a grassy plain that gently sloped down to the edge of the town. Under the blue afternoon sky, Appelburg looked like an idealised screen-saver image. It was a picturesque mountain village built on the slope up to the mountain. It reminded Mallory of the picturesque parts of Bern they had glimpsed on the journey, but built on a slope, the town clinging to the foothills like a set of stairs.

At the top of the town, the incline became too steep for houses and got progressively steeper until there was a couple of hundred feet of almost sheer rock, and then a plateau where Rousseau's chalet loomed over the town below. Chalet seemed like the wrong term. For Mallory, the word conjured images of cosy little wooden buildings with peaked roofs. Rousseau's place was more like a sprawling alpine hotel. It was a series of linked buildings built out of stone, steel, glass and wood. The side that overlooked the town was fronted by a wide decked area where, Mallory assumed, the man of the house could look down from on high, like a monarch surveying his kingdom.

Mallory felt a tug of déjà vu. In some ways, it wasn't so different from some set-ups he had encountered in Afghanistan. Tribal warlords ruling over their patch of earth with impunity. It was jarring to think of a man like Rousseau operating in the middle of Europe, but he supposed that was a very modern assumption. Perhaps Switzerland was the ideal place for a warlord to stake his patch. Neutrality. Laissez-faire. If you don't cause them any trouble, they'll leave you alone.

Mallory thought it was about time somebody caused some trouble.

He took a deep breath of the air. It was noticeably clearer, fresher. There were grey clouds in the east. Rain was on its way.

From a distance and with the naked eye, Appelburg was idyllic. A nice, if expensive place to spend a weekend. Mallory took the binoculars from his pack and took a closer look. As he had expected, Rousseau was prepared for an attack. There was a bigger police presence than he would have expected from a town of this size. Marked cars and uniformed officers on the streets. The men guarding strategic corners were either plainclothes or they were Rousseau's personal security. Every incomer would be seen and assessed.

Raising the binoculars again, he took a closer look at the imposing house on the mountain. Sleek, modernist edges jutted out. The sun glinted off the glass and steel. On the deck at the front he could see a table and a single chair, unoccupied. That suggested Rousseau's living quarters were at that end of the building.

There was a single guard on the decked area, this one making no secret of what he was. He wore a black uniform and gloves and carried a semi-automatic rifle. There was another one on a platform on the roof. On the left-hand side of the house was the cable car terminal. Mallory followed the lines down to the terminal at the bottom, which was located on the eastern edge of town.

The cable car set-up was similar to others Mallory had seen. Two steel cables and two cars, each counterbalancing the other as the large bull wheels at each terminal pulled them up and down the mountain. The terminal at the ground was guarded by three men, all wearing the same black uniform as the man up at the house, all carrying guns. No way anybody unauthorised was sneaking on board that way.

What, then? Frontal assault? He could take out the three guards and hope that the cable car wasn't too complicated to operate. But then Rousseau would have time to station men at the top, and he would be a sitting duck for however long it took the car to make its way up the mountain.

He looked back up at the house again. There was a black Bell helicopter on the helipad; no doubt Rousseau's personal taxi for when he needed to fly to Geneva or Bern. How long did it take to accumulate so much wealth? Mallory wondered. Where was the motivation to acquire more when you already had all this?

Turning around, Mallory peered back into the woods. Océane was leaning with her arms on the trunk of the big fallen tree. Her gaze was questioning, but she didn't say anything. He turned back to look at the town and the house and the cable cars and all those men with guns standing between him and Rousseau.

His own words echoed mockingly in his head: *I like a challenge.*

He put the binoculars back in the pack. This was a decent

position to watch from, but it was too risky to keep Océane around. He left the pack at the edge of the trees and went back to the fallen trunk.

'What did you see?' she asked.

'I once shook the prime minister's hand when he flew into Basra for one of those daring photo-ops. He had less security around him than this guy.'

'Is it possible? Can you get to him?'

Mallory thought about it. He didn't honestly know the answer to that question. But they had come this far already, and there was no guarantee that walking away would be any safer in the long run.

'It's going to be a little harder to make it up there than I thought.' He braced himself for the inevitable argument. 'And we need to—'

Mallory stopped mid-sentence. Out of the corner of his eye, he saw movement in the trees, less than fifty yards away. He vaulted the fallen trunk and ducked back under cover with Océane. Her eyes were wide, questioning. He put a finger to his lips.

He risked a glance over the top of the trunk. Two men, approaching through the trees. He reached for his pack to take the Ruger out, and then with a sinking feeling, remembered he had left it at the edge of the treeline.

Had they seen him?

He heard the sound of someone moving through the undergrowth. And then he got his answer.

'Come out with your hands up.' The voice was coming from no more than twenty yards away, and he spoke in English. 'I know you're there.'

62

Océane was terrified, Mallory could tell from the look in her eyes. But she wasn't panicking. That was good. He thought quickly. He was in a tight spot here, no question. But it might be possible to save Océane.

'Listen to me very carefully,' he said, speaking in a low whisper. 'They saw me, but I don't think they saw you.'

She reached out and grabbed his hand, squeezing so tightly that it was actually painful. Gently, Mallory moved her hand away from his.

'In a minute, I'm going to walk out there with my hands up. They might shoot me right away, but I don't think so. Either way, you hide under here. No matter what happens, you don't move, you don't make a sound. Wait until you're sure they've moved away from here.'

'Mallory—'

She was interrupted by another order. 'Come out. We're not going to shoot as long as you cooperate. We know you're there.'

The voice didn't sound any closer. Mallory wasn't

surprised. They had the drop on him, why would they risk coming in close? How many of them were there? He had seen two, but what if there were more?

'Listen to me. I can handle myself, but I need to go out there alone.'

'They'll kill you,' she said, her eyes wide.

'Maybe, maybe not, but right now we can let me get caught or we can both get caught. It's a no-brainer.'

'But—'

'We don't have time to argue, so shut up and listen. This is what you're going to do. You're going to wait until you are absolutely certain they're gone. They'll want to take me to their boss if they don't shoot me on the spot. When you know they've gone, go back to where we left the truck. Take it and get the hell out of here. Don't go back to St-Jean, don't go back to Paris. I want you to go to England, Birmingham. There's a pub on Kent Street called the King's Arms. Ask for Donno. Tell him everything, he'll make sure you're okay.'

'I'm going to count to three,' the voice said, sounding a little irritated. He wasn't bluffing. He knew Mallory was there. 'Then we start shooting.'

'I can't just leave you,' Océane said.

'You can. It's not a choice. They get me or they get both of us. You have a good chance this way.'

'One.'

'But what if they just kill you?'

'I've taken the gamble before. Where did I tell you to go?'

'Two.'

Océane shook her head, but he could see in her eyes that she knew this was the only way. 'Birmingham. The King's Arms. Ask for Donald.'

'Donno.'

'Donno.' She moved in and kissed him quickly. 'Don't get killed.'

Mallory gave her a wink. Then he stood up with his hands raised.

'*Th—*'

'All right, I'm coming out.'

63

Mallory stood up slowly, hands raised. They were uniformed police officers, not the black-clad guards he had seen through binoculars, patrolling the inner sanctum. One was stocky with beady eyes, the other was tall and blond-haired. Both of them were pointing handguns at him. One positive thing: only two of them.

'Guys, I don't know what this is about. Is this private property, or ... ?'

'Over here.'

Mallory carefully walked around the trunk and approached the two cops. They hadn't seen Océane, otherwise they would have called out for her to stand up too. That was good. It would be better if he could get them to move away from here and let her run.

'We know who you are,' the blond-haired cop said. He was the one who had been doing the talking. The other one regarded Mallory with a nervy expression. He was the one to worry about. He was out of his depth, scared. He was the more likely of the two to start shooting.

'Who am I?'

'The man Mr Rousseau is looking for.'

'He's your boss, huh?' Mallory said.

The blond-haired cop had the self-awareness to look offended by that. He gestured back towards the rough path through the trees from where they had emerged. 'Start walking, keep your hands up.'

The other cop interjected with a few words in French. He spoke quickly and his accent was too unfamiliar for Mallory to catch what he was saying. The other one said, 'Are you armed?'

Mallory shook his head slowly, trying not to let his expression show how stupid a question that was. If he had his gun, they wouldn't be having this conversation. Again, he chastised himself for leaving the Ruger in the backpack when he went back to speak to Océane. And then he put it out of his mind. Regret was a distraction: he had to focus on the situation as it was, not as he would like it to be.

'Okay,' the first cop said. 'Walk.'

Mallory obeyed, moving slowly and deliberately. These two jokers were on edge, not used to taking a potentially dangerous suspect in. That could well prove to be a good thing, but in the meantime, it meant they were more likely to be trigger-happy. He was particularly worried about the stocky guy, who looked like he'd spent the last twenty-four hours drinking espressos.

He glanced around, looking for opportunities. If they weren't going to shoot him, they would cuff him and take him somewhere else. The police station, probably. From there he could be handed over to Rousseau. They were walking along a narrow path between trees, but there weren't any thick bushes around. If he ran, they would shoot, and stand a decent chance of hitting him.

'No sudden moves,' the blond-haired one said, and Mallory felt the gun jab into the small of his back, prodding him forwards.

Mallory kept walking. He had no intention of making a move while they were still putting distance between them and Océane. He kept talking, wanting to keep them off-guard as well as masking any sound Océane might make when she ran for it.

'Come on fellas, this is all a misunderstanding.'

'Shut up,' the blond cop said, and pushed him again. He was being very stupid, getting too close. Putting a lot of trust in the fact that he was armed and Mallory wasn't.

He heard the other one speak in French, complaining that he didn't have a signal. The other one said they would radio in from the car.

As Mallory was translating in his head, he saw sunlight glinting off metal ahead. The path widened out into a gravel turning circle where a police-branded SUV was parked. A gravel road led away from them on the other side of the car.

'I don't know what this is about,' Mallory said, starting to turn as they reached the turning circle.

The blond cop walked around in front of Mallory, keeping his gun on him. The other cop moved towards the car. He opened the door and took out a radio, muttering something into it Mallory could not hear.

'We're looking out for a man who's planning to cause some trouble in Appelburg,' the blond cop said. 'A man who matches your description.'

'I don't know what that's about, but you've got the wrong guy.'

He stared back at Mallory, sizing him up. 'I don't think so.'

'Where are you taking me? Don't you need to read me my rights if you're arresting me?'

The hint of a smile at the corner of his mouth. 'Not in Appelburg.'

Before Mallory could respond, the air was split by the sound of a flock of birds taking flight from the treetops above. The two cops stopped and stared back the way they had come.

'Is someone with you?' the cop asked, his eyes on the woods. Both of them were looking into the trees now, searching for a threat out there. Neglecting the threat right here.

'No,' Mallory said quietly. 'I'm just hiking, like I told you.'

The stocky cop said something. It sounded like a question. The blond cop looked at Mallory and then nodded. The stocky cop started retracing his steps.

The blond cop got closer. Tantalisingly close, gun trained on Mallory, but glancing back after his partner.

'Who's with you? How many are there?'

Mallory opened his mouth as if to answer. Then he grabbed the barrel of the gun, twisting down hard, and used his grip to yank the cop towards him, slamming his forehead into his nose as hard as he could.

The cop jerked backwards and fell down. Mallory kept hold of the gun and turned it around in his hand.

He heard running footsteps, and the other one coming back, calling out a name. Mallory spun and saw him emerge from the path, raising his gun. Mallory was faster. He shot him three times in the chest, watching to make sure he fell, and then turned around just as the blond cop launched himself at him. He didn't make it. Mallory got the gun in position so it stopped the cop's forward motion by digging into his chest, then he pulled the trigger, point-blank. There was a muffled bang and the cop grunted and staggered back. Mallory took a step forward and shot him again in the forehead.

Above them, the birds moved on again with a fluttering of wings, and then silence descended once more.

64

Océane kept running flat out until her lungs burned in her chest. She cast the occasional glance behind her as often as she dared, but there was no sign of anyone following her.

Small comfort. There had been no sign when those men appeared out of nowhere and cornered her and Mallory.

Her mind was racing. Mallory would know how to get away from those men, wouldn't he? He had made a calculation that this was the best way to keep them both safe, that was all. But then she remembered the grave look in his eyes. The instructions he had given her and made her repeat. He knew there was a real possibility that he might not survive the day.

She didn't bother wasting time thinking about how she was supposed to get to England. Getting out of this area was going to be enough of a challenge.

As she reached the river they had crossed twenty minutes before, she slowed and stopped, her legs and lungs grateful for the break. She turned and watched the dark verticals of the thick forest behind her. There was no sign of any of the men, no sound other than the rush of the water.

And then she heard distant gunshots.

Her breath caught in her throat. She waited, listening to the sound of her own heartbeat thudding in her head.

Two more gunshots, in quick succession. She flinched and then waited, but there were no more.

Had the sound come from the direction in which she had been running? It was difficult to tell.

She crossed the stream at the same place Mallory had used and tried to work out which way would take her back to the pickup truck. The woods looked so different now. She reached into her pocket for her phone, knowing there would be no signal, but hoping somehow Mallory had found a way to send a message.

It was gone.

At some point in her panicked run, the phone had slipped out of her pocket. Now she was in the middle of nowhere with no phone and no help.

And then she saw a familiar landmark. A felled tree that was so recent that the split wood was still fresh. It wasn't far from where they had parked.

A couple of minutes later, she found the dirt track. The rusting blue pickup truck was right where they had left it, beside the pile of moss-covered timber. She exhaled in relief and reached her hand into her pocket, her fingers curling around the key. And then she froze.

A man in a black uniform with a gun holstered at his side walked out from behind the woodpile. He was facing away from her, looking at the truck. Quickly, she stepped back into the cover of a thick tree and crouched down. She risked peeking out. The man was still there. Now she could see there was a second set of tyre tracks in the dirt. His car was obscured by the woodpile. He put one hand to his ear and spoke, too quietly for Océane to hear what he was saying.

She watched until he moved away again. An engine started up, and for a second Océane felt a surge of hope that he was driving back to the main road. The hope evaporated as she saw that he was just manoeuvring the vehicle backwards, lining up nose to tail. As she watched, he took a hook line from the back of his SUV and attached it beneath the bumper of the truck.

If she was going to find a way out of here, she would have to go back.

65

Both of the dead police officers were carrying Glock 19s. Mallory emptied them, kept the ammunition, and tossed the guns into the woods. Two less firearms he had to worry about. He went back to where he had left his pack and took the Ruger out. He tucked it into the back of his belt, promising he wouldn't leave himself without a weapon again until he was a thousand miles from this place.

He dragged the two bodies under the cover of a stand of bushes and then looked back the way Océane had run. She would be long gone now, he hoped. He thought about retracing his steps to the car to make sure, but he dismissed the idea. He should have left her in Gänsern. Bringing a civilian along on a mission like this was always a recipe for disaster. She would have protested, but Mallory should have known better. He took his phone out, but there was no signal. Perhaps he could send a message when he reached town; tell her he was okay and that she should stick to the plan.

He raised his gaze to the sky to orient himself and worked out the direction back to the edge of town.

He checked the load in his gun one more time, slung his backpack on and started walking towards Appelburg.

It took Mallory all of five seconds to decide that Plan A wasn't going to work.

Two more guards had appeared at the bottom terminal for the cable car, and he could see at least one at the top terminal, where Rousseau's chalet clung to the side of the mountain like a five-million-dollar barnacle. Even if it hadn't been for the guards, it didn't look like the car was seeing regular traffic. There was no scope to sneak on board in a crowd or bluff his way on.

There was never only one way to approach a target, though. It was just a matter of finding the least-worst option.

He raised the binoculars to his eyes again and found the river where it flowed through town at the lowest point. He raised them slowly, scanning the roads and the houses until they gave way to the mountainside, rising up to the house itself. It was built into a natural cleft in the slope, about two thousand feet above the town and the same distance again below the summit. Most of the building was constructed on a relatively flat section, with the eastern wing extending out over a sharp drop on a cantilever.

The slope beneath the cable car line was steep, but under normal circumstances it wouldn't pose a reasonably fit person much of a challenge. The problem was that the path of the cable car was cleared of trees. Nowhere to hide. He could see floodlights at the base of the slope. Attempting to scale the mountain on that approach, day or night, would be like trying to walk out on the pitch at Wembley without anyone noticing.

To the east, the slope became a cliff about two-thirds of the way up, stretching all the way up to the ledge where the house stood. The approach to that side was closed off by a fence at the bottom. There were no lights on the hill or the cliff on this side.

As he watched, a black and white police SUV drove past, taking its time. Mallory took a closer look through the windscreen at the driver and passenger. A patrol.

When they had disappeared behind a row of houses, Mallory took a closer look at the cliff, letting his eye travel from top to bottom several times. It had been a while since he had done any serious climbing, but he knew the summer of digging wells would stand him in good stead. Perhaps he had always known he would have to go the hard way, that was why he had selected the equipment he had back in Gänsern.

He opened his backpack and examined the inventory he had hoped he would not have to use: a sixty-metre nylon rope, cams, high-friction rubber climbing shoes. It had been a while, but he thought the ascent was within his capabilities. It would have to be. It was the only way to get to Rousseau.

He stayed in position and kept watching for another hour. The sun descended behind the mountain, bathing the landscape in a burning red glow. Night wasn't far off, but the shadow of the mountain meant that the darkness began to swallow Appelburg early. The street lamps were already on, highlighting the curving roads like lights on a Christmas tree. It was pretty in the summer; it would be stunning in the winter.

A single journey was completed in the cable car. A lone man wearing a suit jacket, jeans and glasses. The guards checked his ID before they let him on. The same police vehicle made three more passes, at regular twenty-minute intervals.

As soon as darkness fell, Mallory moved as close to the fence as he could safely get, which was an empty car park across the main road through town. It didn't look as though this part of the town had been marked out for any special attention. Compared to the manpower on the roadblocks Mallory had seen and the guards on the cable car, security was relatively light here.

Mallory took up position on the edge of the car park and waited for the police SUV to appear. He had spotted it at other points on its circuit, and it had kept to a predetermined route for the whole hour. Sloppy, like the two he had killed earlier. A sloppiness born of complacency, no doubt. The circuit took it through the heart of town, up to the line of picturesque shops and boutiques on a rise on the north side, then back around on one of the roads skirting the edge of town. He noticed they slowed down when passing the cable car, probably assuming that this was the most vulnerable point. So far, they hadn't slowed at the fence.

There was a foot patrol as well. This one varied and was less predictable. Mallory had seen at least three distinct pairs of guards walking this length of road while he had been sur-veilling. They weren't police. These were Rousseau's private guard. They carried AR-15s strapped across their chests, like airport security. They were dressed in black with black base-ball caps. Mallory took a closer look through the binoculars. There was no insignia on their clothing. They were wearing stab vests. In contrast to the police, they seemed more alert. They didn't seem to talk much, kept their mind on the job and their eyes on their surroundings. One of them even rat-tled the chain-link fence as he passed by, pausing to examine it for breaches. At least that told Mallory it wasn't electrified.

The fact it was twelve feet high and topped with razor wire, together with the sheer cliff anyone getting past it would face, probably meant electrification was deemed overkill.

Mallory checked his watch after the foot patrol had passed. The police drive-by would be due in a couple of minutes and then he would have at least a ten-minute gap. More than he needed. He checked over his equipment again as he waited for the car. He hoped it would be enough.

The headlights of the police car lit up the bend in the road before it appeared. Mallory shrank into the shadows and watched as it drove past. When the tail lights were out of sight, he picked up his bag and took off across the road at a run. There were signs along the fence in French and German saying, *Warning – Private Property, Armed Guards.*

He took the wire cutters he had bought from the store in Gänsern from his pack and quickly snipped enough links in the fence to pull back a hatch big enough to crawl through. As he was replacing the fence so it wouldn't be noticeable from a distance, he heard footsteps approaching.

There was a fifty-yard stretch of open grass from the fence to the trees. There wasn't enough time to cover the ground in time. Instead, Mallory lay down in the cover of a solid concrete fence support.

It wasn't the patrol this time. Just three men in civilian clothes, walking past and chatting about one of their wives. Mallory held his breath. He didn't doubt that the townsfolk were incentivised to report suspicious activity. Rousseau probably had his own version of 'See something, say something'.

Mallory waited until they had disappeared, grabbed his bag and ran for cover. Once he was safely in the darkness at the foot of the climb, he made a final check of his equipment:

the rope, half a dozen climbing cams, gloves, two spare magazines. He had the Ruger strapped to his belt in a holster, and the hunting knife on the opposite side. He had already slipped on the climbing shoes.

The slope was steep, but he made quick progress, moving up through the trees, scrambling up sections of rock that occasionally rose up from the ground like giant steps. The pines were thick here, blocking out the light.

He gained height quickly, the town below already looking like a model village when he glanced down. In less than an hour, he had reached the foot of the cliff. It rose almost vertically.

Mallory had planned the climb after careful examination through binoculars. It had the advantage of being in a sheltered area of the mountain that couldn't be seen from the house, and the going was straightforward for the first eighty per cent. But then there was the last twenty per cent.

There was a sheer wall for that section that seemed utterly devoid of handholds. Passing it would entail zigzagging to where there was a long vertical crack in the rock – what climbers called a chimney. The only way to traverse it was to brace his back against the opposite wall and inch his way up. If he could manage that, it would take him all the way up to where the cantilevered platform jutted out over the void.

Mallory flexed his hands in the fingerless gloves, cast one last glance behind him and began the ascent.

66

The first section was as straightforward as Mallory had hoped. He covered sixty feet in a few minutes, pausing twice to fit climbing cams into suitable fissures and attaching the rope. It got a little tougher than it looked after that. He lost ten minutes backtracking and taking a different route past an expanse of smooth rock. Around the halfway point, he wedged his feet in a gap and took a break as he watched the police car make its slow circuit below, the headlights giving him a feel for how high he had already climbed. Taking account of the steep incline and then the cliff, Appelburg was at least fifteen hundred feet below now.

The luminescent dial on the watch that had almost caused a diplomatic incident told Mallory it was twenty past nine as he reached the start of the chimney. It was a two-hundred foot-high vertical scar in the otherwise smooth rock wall, roughly three feet wide, with a ledge at the bottom. He pulled himself up onto the ledge and took the opportunity to rest his arms. Digging wells was one thing, but it had been a long time since he had used the muscles needed for rock climbing.

Looking straight up, he could see the underside of the canti-levered deck on this side of the house.

Physically, this was a challenging climb, but at least the difficulty came from the terrain. He had done his time fighting in the mountains in Afghanistan. The climbing was tough enough without Taliban mountain men dropping grenades on you. At least he didn't have to worry about that here.

He flexed his hands, savouring the break from gripping and pulling himself up. He could see the road winding past by the fence a long way below. As far as he could see, there was no frenzy of activity, no men with flashlights moving through the woods. Looking further, towards the town, he could see tiny people walking around, cars that looked like Matchbox toys moving unhurriedly through the streets.

It felt like a vulnerable position, all the same. He knew it would be difficult to spot a man wearing dark clothes against the cliff face at night, but if someone did see him, there was nowhere to go. He glanced over the edge at the vertiginous drop and reminded himself that there was one way to go. It just didn't appeal. In the town below he could just make out the sound of the carousel in the main square, a half-familiar tune. As he watched, he felt a drop of rain hit his forearm. Looking up, he saw the stars had been obscured by cloud. More rain fell. Not a deluge, but he should get a move on in case it got heavier.

He thought about Océane, wishing there was a way to find out if she had got away. He hoped she had made it to the pickup truck and was halfway back to the French border by now. If things went down like he expected, Rousseau wouldn't be able to go looking for her after tonight.

Break over. Mallory slipped another cam into a fissure

in the wall and tugged it to check it was secure. The mechanism expanded, pushing against the inside of the fissure, providing a solid anchor point. The advantage of cams over pitons was that he didn't need to hammer them in, potentially giving away his position. He clipped the rope to the cam and pulled himself up to the start of the chimney. This would be the toughest section. Once he was committed, he would have to cover the entire height without stopping. There were no ledges, probably no way to attach another cam before he reached the top. If fatigue hit him halfway up, he was screwed.

The fissure stretched up so high above him that he couldn't tell where it terminated. Earlier in the day, from his vantage point across the road, this had seemed like a pretty manageable climb. A challenge, sure, but nothing too daunting. With his feet braced against one wall and his back against the other, staring up at a seemingly endless vertical climb, it looked a whole lot different.

Mallory tugged on the rope to check it was still hooked to his belt and started inching up.

After ten feet or so, he got into a rhythm, taking vertical steps up with his feet flat against one side of the chimney, then shimmying his back up the opposite side. Further and further he moved, trying not to think about what would happen if he slipped. The rope was attached at the ledge below, which meant it would catch his body, but only after he had hit the bottom of the chimney and bounced off.

The action started to become almost hypnotic. Right foot up. Left foot up. Back up. Repeat. He lost all sense of time. He no longer noticed the cool night wind circling around him in the narrow space, the occasional flecks of rain blown onto his face by the light wind. He stopped thinking about the space below him or the space above him. The world was reduced to this three-foot wide space and the action. Right. Left. Back.

A voice sounding when surely there could be no voice snapped Mallory out of his trance-like focus on the climb. He stopped, made sure he was firmly braced, and looked up. The top of the fissure was less than twenty feet above him. Above it he could see the wooden boards and steel struts of the cantilevered platform on the left of his field of vision, the clear night sky on his right. He couldn't hear anything. Had he imagined the voice?

No. He heard it again. Muted, because the speaker wasn't raising his voice, as well as the fact that it had to travel through three inches of wood and twenty feet of thin air.

A one-way conversation. Someone talking into a phone, or a radio. Mallory heard leisurely footsteps now. A guard. Perhaps they stationed one up there at night.

Mallory inched up a little further. The conversation stopped, but the pacing continued. From the footsteps, he was walking in a slow circle, directly above Mallory. Mallory started moving again, trying to keep the scrapes of the soles of his shoes against the wall to a minimum.

Almost within reach of the top, a loose piece of the rock wall dislodged as Mallory put his foot on it. He managed to scrabble and plant his foot on a more solid patch, but a fist-size chunk of rock dislodged and plummeted straight down. Mallory gritted his teeth and braced himself as he waited for the rock to hit bottom. After what seemed like an eternity, it cracked into the floor of the chimney, before rebounding out and down the rest of the descent.

The footsteps above stopped.

67

As the sky darkened above the tree canopy and the shadows began to deepen to black, Océane began to worry that she was hopelessly lost. When she saw the first lights winking through the trees ahead, hope had swiftly been followed by fear. The lights meant she was close to Appelburg. By now, she knew she would have to pass through the town to get back to the road. If she kept to quiet streets, it might be possible. Perhaps there would be some kind of transport back to the town they had stopped in earlier. What was its name again?

Océane slowed her pace as she approached the edge of the treeline. The woods on this side of Appelburg were on a gentle incline, and there was a wide grass plain between the trees and the first houses. Océane watched in the wooded gloom for a few minutes. The streetlights were on, the first lights in the houses coming on too. It looked peaceful from here. She reassured herself that it would be safer to traverse the streets now that evening had fallen.

Ten minutes later, Océane was walking down one of the narrow cobbled streets that seemed to lead towards the heart of the town. The shop windows were so clean and neat that they could have been dressed for a movie. Nicolas had taken her to Disneyland Paris last Christmas, and the spotless windows and glittering window displays reminded her of the artificiality of Main Street USA. All that was missing was hidden speakers playing jaunty music.

It wasn't all old-world charm, there were modern conveniences tastefully blended in. Streetlights on the quieter streets dulled until a pedestrian approached, and then lightened. Tasteful display screens interspersed ads for local businesses with picture-postcard images of Appelburg.

A light rain began to fall. Océane put her hood up and tried to keep to the shadows beneath the awnings. Dusk was well under way, hastened by the clouds, but she would be more comfortable when it was fully dark. She remembered what Mallory had said about this place. It wasn't just the men who worked for Rousseau you had to look out for – it was the police as well. Thankfully, she hadn't seen too many of those so far. Just a single police car parked at a junction she had changed course to avoid.

She tried to keep to the side streets, where it felt safer. No police officers, and none of the men in the black uniforms. Just normal people: mothers and children lingering in front of shop window displays, groups of well-dressed men moving between bars. She caught herself thinking it was the kind of place Nicolas would like, and banished the thought as she felt a wave of sadness well up within her. It was followed by a stab of guilt when she remembered making a move on Mallory last night. She had been a little insulted at the way he had rebuffed her at the time, but now she was glad that he hadn't—

Océane tensed as she heard the sound of an engine working hard. She shrank back beneath an awning as she saw a black SUV drive past the end of the alleyway. Whoever was driving was in a hurry to get somewhere. She lingered by the shop window. This was a boulangerie. Artfully crafted pastries were arranged in the window. They were so perfect that they almost looked like they were made out of plastic, just for show. The whole town felt a little like that, come to think of it.

'Maman.'

The child's raised voice pulled her away from the window. She turned around to see a mother and a little girl, perhaps eight years old. Like everyone else on the street they were well dressed, the mother in a long beige coat and brown leather boots, the child in a matching outfit. They were both blond, but the little girl had artfully woven pigtails. She was looking straight at Océane. Instinctively, Océane smiled back at her. Then she realised the little girl wasn't smiling. She was regarding her like the prize in a treasure hunt. She was tugging her mother's arm, trying to pull her attention away from the window of a shoe shop. One of the changing advertising screens was fixed on the wall beside the window. It showed a sunset over the town with '*Bienvenue à Appelburg*' printed along the bottom.

As Océane watched, the screen changed. It didn't show an advert or a publicity image now.

She had to blink before her eyes would believe what she was looking at. Blown-up images of her face and Mallory's: *Attention! Dangereux!*

68

Mallory braced his feet and looked down. He couldn't make out the bottom of the vertical shaft he was wedged at the top of, just a black nothingness.

Above him, the footsteps started again, approaching the side of the deck. Mallory heard a soft creak from the barrier as it took some weight. The guard was looking down. Thankfully, his position meant he wouldn't be able to see Mallory unless he climbed over, hung by one hand, and shone a torch directly at him. Mallory was pretty sure he wasn't about to do that.

The air was so still that Mallory could hear the man above breathing.

The ache in his thighs and shoulders was more noticeable now. The vertical drop below him became a more present concern. Then there was another creak and two more footsteps away from the edge. Then the voice again. Speaking English, in what sounded like an Italian accent.

'It's Alessandro. Do we have any cameras under the south deck?'

Mallory's blood ran cold as he listened.

'I don't know. I heard something. I'm going to check it out.'

Mallory had been hoping the falling rock would have been dismissed as nothing, but it sounded like this guy was on the ball. Which meant Mallory had no option but to try to get up there while there was still only one man waiting for him.

Gritting his teeth against the ache, he started to move upward again, going even more painfully slowly to avoid making any noise.

After a few seconds that felt like an eternity, Mallory drew level with the top of the fissure. This was the beginning of the long plateau on which the house and grounds were built. At the top of the fissure was a shelf beneath the level where the deck above was fixed to the mountainside. He forced himself to stop. It would be easy to screw this up and slip, and then the man above would hear a much more suspicious noise when fourteen stone of flesh and bone slammed off the ledge below.

Mallory got his feet into position with the top of the fissure and then eased his back up until he was almost sitting on the ledge below the deck.

Back on a flat surface, his muscles seemed to sigh with relief. He could barely feel his arms. His body wanted nothing more than to lie down and recover for a few minutes. But his mind knew he didn't have that luxury. He closed his eyes and breathed in, willing the pain and the fatigue away. The climb became a distant memory. It was time to devote all focus to the next move.

Mallory looked up. It was a little easier to see up here. The floor of the deck was about ten feet above his position. The nearest support was bolted to the cliffside, almost low enough to reach when he stood up. Carefully, Mallory did, conscious of the placement of his feet and the narrowness of the ledge on which he was perched.

He heard the voice again.

'No, nothing ... yeah, probably nothing. All right. See you at changeover.'

Finally, a break. There was still the matter of that single guard, though. He examined the wall, next to him, squinting into the darkness, then felt along it, looking for a crack wide enough to take a cam. There were none. It felt as smooth as poured concrete. The next move would have to be made without the security of a rope. If he fell, he would drop two hundred feet if he was lucky. Ten times that if he missed the ledge at the bottom of the fissure. It was academic, because either drop would do the job.

He examined the closest support arm for the deck above. It jutted down at a forty-five-degree angle from the edge of the deck to meet the cliff wall. It was wooden, formed of two thick beams bolted together with a six-inch gap, and then bolted to the rock of the cliff, directly above the shaft he had just scaled. The bolts between the two beams looked strong. They would have to be.

Mallory reached to his belt and took out a carabiner. He put his weight on his right foot and reached up to see if he could clip it around the bolt and get his rope secured. He was just short of being able to reach it. He grimaced and put the carabiner between his teeth. He glanced down at the drop, then at the beam. There was only one option, and he would only get one chance at it.

He tensed for a second, then committed. He launched himself off the ledge and for a moment he was airborne, the void beneath him, his hands reaching for the beam. His left hand caught it, then his right, and he had time to wonder what would happen if the beam was less sturdy than it looked. But then gravity asserted itself and his whole weight was on the beam. It held. He hung there, suspended over the drop. The momentum of his jump carried his legs out in a swing, and then his body settled back, causing the beam to creak softly.

Footsteps again, approaching.

Quickly, Mallory took the carabiner from between his teeth and clipped it around one of the bolts connecting the two beams. He attached his rope, securing himself to something solid for the first time in twenty minutes.

The footsteps stopped directly above him.

Without thinking, Mallory took one hand off the beam and reached further up its angle, towards the join with the edge of the deck.

At the moment he did so, the wood above him splintered as the guard fired a burst of automatic fire through the deck.

Mallory hung over the void, looking at the bullet holes that had been punched through the thick wood above the spot where he had been hanging a moment before. Beams of light shone through into the gloom, like miniature spotlights.

He heard the guard adjust his weight. He was listening, for a moan, a thud, anything to let him know he had hit something alive. For the first time, Mallory had the advantage. The guard above him didn't know if he'd hit someone, missed someone, or if there never had been someone in the first place, and he'd just messed up his boss's decking.

The voice again. 'It's Alessandro again. I think you better send somebody up here.'

Mallory swung himself out, moving more confidently now

he knew that the rope was secured. His fingers found the edge of the deck and he gripped it with one hand, then the other. He could see straight up at the edge, now. There was a wrought-iron barrier topped with a wooden railing.

From this angle, he couldn't see the guard, but he could see his shadow. Carefully, he reached up and gripped one of the upright supports, waiting to snatch his hand back if he heard movement. He let go with his other hand and reached down to check the position of the Ruger strapped to his belt. If he could pull himself up and draw immediately, he could take this guy out. He gripped the uprights and pulled himself up, getting one foot on the edge of the deck where it protruded.

And then he knew it was too late to take his gun out.

There was a creak on the boards and a face appeared directly above him as the guard peered over. He was early forties, greying hair under a black cap, lines at the corners of his eyes. There was an instant of surprise on his face. Mallory used it.

He forgot about reaching for his gun and pulled himself the rest of the way up, getting his other foot planted on the edge. As the guard was bringing his rifle to bear, Mallory let go of the railing and grabbed him by the front of his jacket with both hands.

And then he straightened and leaned back, like a high diver executing a reverse dive.

For a moment, the two of them hung, perfectly balanced on opposite sides of the railing.

Then the guard shrieked as he realised what was happening, and Mallory, with a helping hand from gravity, dragged him all the way over the railing.

The two bodies fell from the platform. Mallory's stomach

flipped as he dropped and then the slack in the rope ran out and he stopped sharp. The guard continued, screaming all the way down until the thud of impact silenced him.

Mallory's momentum swung him towards the cliff wall. He used his feet to contact the rock, then hauled himself back up as quickly as he could.

Five seconds later, he was climbing over the barrier and over onto the deck. He saw a tight cluster of bullet holes. Other than that, the platform was still empty.

But it wouldn't be for long.

69

Close up, the house was even bigger than it had looked from the bottom of the mountain.

This wasn't the first time Mallory had mounted an attack on an enemy compound, but it was the first time he had attempted it solo. He couldn't be sure how many guards Rousseau kept on duty at the house itself, but he had counted six when surveilling the place earlier. It was safe to assume there could be more. He still had the element of surprise to an extent, because even though they knew an attack was coming, they didn't yet know how far he had penetrated. But he would need more than that. Asymmetric warfare works by giving a numerically superior enemy multiple fronts on which to focus.

On the journey here, Mallory had spent some time zooming in on the Google Earth view of the building from above, plotting out where each room was likely to fit. He had drawn his own schematic, and he hoped all the skills developed in those years of extrapolating the layouts of compounds in Afghanistan and Iraq would translate here. Same shit, different continent: there were only so many ways to skin a cat. The big advantage he had was that unlike Taliban and al Qaeda commanders, Rousseau and his men would not be accustomed to having to repel an attack on their compound.

What he thought might be Rousseau's living quarters were on the top floor of the opposite side of the house. He hoped Rousseau would be there at this hour. There was no way he was getting up there without being seen, so he would have to make sure there was enough to keep the guards busy.

This end of the building was single-storey and flat-roofed. Glass doors faced out onto the deck. Inside there was what looked like a banqueting hall. There was a long, polished wooden table and a row of neatly stacked chairs against the wall. He knew from the bird's-eye view that on the opposite side of this wing was some kind of garden. Statues and miniature ponds and neat hedges. The back of the house extended out there to make an L shape at the end of the wing, and there was a fenced-off area containing dumpsters. Mallory was guessing that was the kitchen. It would make sense, as that part of the house would open onto both the banqueting hall and the more intimate dining room that looked out over the town.

Mallory climbed up onto the railing where it joined with the wall of the house, once again standing over a sobering drop. He took a second to steady himself, then jumped up and gripped the edge of the roof. He lifted himself up just enough to draw eye level with the rooftop and check it was empty, then hauled himself up the rest of the way.

No longer sheltered by the bulk of the house, the cold night air cut into him, the wind surprisingly strong. Gusts of rain swept across him as he moved across the roof. The helipad on the top of the main part of the house was lit up with spotlights. He could see a single guard up there, facing in the other direction. Keeping his eyes on him, he moved to the opposite side and peered down into the enclosed garden that was framed by the house on three sides and the rise of the mountain on the fourth.

There was a guard down there, just outside the door to the banqueting hall.

As he watched, the guard below straightened and put his finger to his ear, listening and then replying in German mixed with some English. He caught enough to know that they were trying to get hold of Alessandro, the guy he had just thrown off the deck. There was a pause and the guard said, 'Okay.'

The guard below stayed put. Clearly, he hadn't been instructed to leave his post. Someone else would be looking for Alessandro. They wouldn't find him, but it would be difficult to miss the bullet holes in the deck. Things were about to escalate.

Mallory took one of his last two climbing cams from his belt and weighed it in his hand, judging the distance to a gravel path that led between two rows of thick trees. He threw it sideways, like a skimming stone, and it clinked across the gravel before being lost in the shade of the trees. The guard's head jerked up, looking towards the source of the sound. He raised his gun and trained it on the spot where the path disappeared into shadow.

He tapped on his earpiece and spoke into his headset, then started moving towards the path.

Mallory slid his knife out from its sheath and waited for him to pass directly below him. The guard's eyes were fixed on the spot on the path where the anchor had hit.

He slowed his approach and tapped a switch on the barrel of his rifle. A thin but powerful beam lit up the bushes and the path. The light glinted off the metal of the cam. He took a step closer.

Mallory dropped from the roof. He landed on top of the guard's back, forcing him forward onto the ground. Instinctively, the guard let go of his rifle to put his hands out to break his fall. Mallory was already grabbing him across the bridge of the nose with his left hand. He jerked his head back and then slashed the knife across his throat.

The guard was bleeding as he hit the ground, gagging and clutching at his neck. Mallory pushed him onto his back and took the rifle from him. The guard gasped again and then was still.

Two down.

Mallory took the AR-15 and checked the magazine and found it fully loaded. He lifted the headset from around the dead guard's head, wiped the blood spatter off the mouthpiece and fitted it into his own ear. Lastly, he unstrapped the guard's Kevlar vest and pulled it on over his head. Courtesy of Rousseau, he had just benefited from a major equipment upgrade.

Mallory turned towards the house and saw that the door to the kitchen was right by the bin enclosure. At the same moment, he heard a voice in his ear. Speaking English this time.

'Get some people up here. I think Alessandro is dead.'

There was no point dragging the dead guard into the bushes. They knew he was here.

It was time to open up a second front.

70

Rousseau heard the sound of gunfire from the east wing. He had been following the updates from his guards for the past twenty minutes, and he knew that if he could hear gunfire, the intruder must already have taken out several men at the exterior. He was mildly disappointed to hear hints of panic in the voices of some of his employees. He did not expect that from the calibre of men he had hired. Perhaps it was inevitable. Give a man a gun and a well-compensated but boring job and he quickly becomes soft.

That was one reason for the hunts, to keep everyone sharp. But, as he had suspected, the petty thieves and rapists gladly provided to him by the Appelburg police force were inadequate preparation for the real thing.

Rousseau turned away from the picture window and opened one of the hardwood lockers that lined the wall. He took out a Kevlar vest and an AR-15. So be it: a hunt with an element of uncertainty.

Fabian appeared at his door as Rousseau was checking the load in the rifle. He was flanked by two of the more capable men: Volkov and Keller. Volkov was a hulking Russian; one of Rousseau's informal talent scouts had encountered him working for the Wagner Group in Syria and recruited him. Keller was slighter in build, and came with far fewer air miles. Rousseau had personally elevated him from the Appelburg police force.

'Mr Rousseau,' Fabian said. 'The helicopter is ready to leave. We're going to escort you to the roof and we aim to be in the air before there's any danger of the attackers penetrating the building.'

'Just one attacker,' Rousseau said. 'It's the man from Paris and Marseille. And he's already in the building.'

As though to prove the point, another muted exchange of gunfire broke out.

'Mr Rousseau,' Fabian said, stepping aside and gesturing towards the door.

'We're not going anywhere.'

'Mr Rousseau, this is a developing situation. We have to get you to safety.'

'This is safety,' Rousseau said, shrugging off his jacket and tossing it over a chair. He strapped the Kevlar vest on and picked up the AR-15. 'Come. We will repel this invasion.'

He looked up and saw that Fabian and Volkov both seemed disquieted. Only Keller was unmoved by events.

'Is there a problem?' Rousseau asked, looking from Fabian to Volkov.

'Mr Rousseau, we can't let you ...' Volkov stopped, realising what he had said. 'That is to say, your safety is my priority.'

'Unless I'm very confused, Volkov, it's not up to you to *let* me do anything. Or to decide what's best for me.' He shifted his gaze to Keller. 'Who can't we raise?'

'Alessandro. He was on the south deck. Lukas is a confirmed kill, he was in the garden.'

'Then we still have four men downstairs, plus the four of us.'

'Four?' Fabian repeated.

Rousseau walked three paces to the locker and selected another rifle. He checked it was loaded with the safety on, and tossed it to Fabian underhand. He recovered in time to catch it in an ungainly way.

'Let's go.'

Fabian opened his mouth to protest again, but this time Keller put a hand on his shoulder. 'Mr Rousseau is right, we'll take this scum out.'

Rousseau was pleased. He knew that some of the more experienced men had voiced misgivings about Keller, but there was a glint in his eye now that he recognised. He was relishing this. The entirely correct response.

This mysterious man had already caused some damage to his staff complement and to his building by the sounds of things, but both could be repaired. If the intruder helped to remove some of the dead wood, he would have done Rousseau a favour.

Rousseau stopped by one of the touch panels in the hallway and used his fingerprint to wake the screen. He turned the lights off, darkening every room in the building, leaving only the low-level floor lighting. The mysterious attacker was making impressive progress, but Rousseau was on home territory, and he intended to use that advantage.

There was another burst of gunfire from downstairs and a cry of pain.

'What the hell is going on down there?' Fabian said through gritted teeth. 'Have you found him on the cameras?'

Keller nodded. 'He came in through the kitchen. We lost him in the hallway. I told you we needed blanket surveillance on the interior.'

'I vetoed it,' Rousseau said. 'It's a home, not a government building. And besides, nobody was supposed to penetrate this far.'

Another burst of gunfire.

Rousseau stopped and listened. 'That's coming from the main hall.'

'No way out back there,' Keller said. 'We've got the bastard.' He tapped on his earpiece. 'Who is firing on the intruder in the main hall?'

He listened and looked back at Rousseau. 'It's Thomas.'

'Tell him to keep him cornered.'

71

Océane had moved away from the main streets of Appelburg, seeking quiet side streets and fewer people. She walked briskly, every muscle wanting to break into a run, but knowing that would only draw attention. She kept her head down, avoiding eye contact with any of the pedestrians.

Occasionally, there would be a gap in the buildings and she would glimpse the mountain and the big house looming over everything. She wondered about Mallory. If he had indeed escaped his captors, had he found a way to get up there?

The rain continued, occasionally threatening to become heavier before letting off. Her clothes, already wet from crossing the river, begin to weigh down on her. She was cold, and she had no idea where in town she was.

She found herself on a street of larger houses. They were of a uniform design: wood frames, generous plots, basement garages accessed by a ramp. There were no other pedestrians on the street. Suddenly she wondered if she had made a mistake by avoiding crowds. She glanced at windows on both sides of the street, imagining residents peeking out at her from behind wooden venetians and off-white curtains.

She heard running footsteps behind her and turned, her heart jumping into her mouth. A middle-aged jogger trotted past her, his face red, sweat beading on his forehead. He held up a hand in acknowledgment as he passed, his gaze focused directly ahead.

Océane put a hand to her chest and breathed out. As she watched, the jogger started to slow as he approached the next intersection. A moment later, she saw why. A black SUV rounded the corner and stopped. A hand reached out of the passenger window, waving him down. The jogger slowed and stopped, leaning down to speak to whoever was inside.

Océane moved off the pavement and into the shadow of a large pine tree in one of the driveways. She strained to hear, but could only make out the low murmur of the jogger's voice, no distinct words.

They had to be asking if he had seen either of the two '*dangereux*' visitors. She didn't dare look. Was he pointing back in the direction where he had just passed a lone woman? Her pulse quickened again and she began to feel light-headed. She looked around her at the blank windows of the houses, then down the ramp towards the garage beneath the house she was outside.

She narrowed her eyes and looked closer. The door of the garage seemed to be ajar.

Raising her gaze to the house again, she saw no sign of life. She walked down the ramp, quickening her pace as she heard the sound of the SUV's engine approaching. She reached down to the bottom of the garage door and pulled it up, just enough to crouch under it.

Inside, she tugged the door down and listened. The SUV's engine approached, unhurriedly, and then continued on its way.

Océane breathed a sigh of relief and took a moment to evaluate her surroundings. There was a small window in the door that let in streetlight, and she could make out a green Renault and neat shelving units on one of the walls. On the opposite side was a short set of wooden steps up to the house.

She moved away from the garage door and tried the door of the Renault. It was locked. She turned away from it and scanned the shelving units, searching for anything she could use to break into the car. A plan started to form. She could climb into the boot, wait until the owner of the car drove her out of here. The perfect way to avoid patrols.

She searched the shelves for a crowbar or something that might help her get the boot open and found a large screwdriver, but then stopped to think. Even if she managed to break the lock, it would probably be noticeable. And what if the owner of the car wanted to put something in the boot before they set off? No. This was a bad idea.

She turned away and looked back at the stairs to the house. Maybe there would be a spare key up there. She moved to the foot of the stairs and then hesitated again. She had no idea if anyone was at home. Perhaps it would be better to wait until dark.

She looked back at the car. Her ticket to freedom hung tantalisingly out of reach.

And then she stopped thinking about anything else as the door at the top of the stairs was thrown open.

72

Rousseau and his men moved down the stairwell to the ground floor, clearing each corner as they descended.

They reached the ground floor and advanced down the corridor towards the main hall. Rousseau took the lead. He could feel how uncomfortable his guards were, not used to following the man they were supposed to be protecting.

There was a firefight under way ahead of them. Staccato bursts of gunfire alternated in stereo. The main hall was the core of the complex. A cavernous space the size of a basketball court, with a towering vaulted ceiling. It had played host to many a grand event over the years. Perhaps it did so even now.

They reached the tall hardwood doors that opened onto the hall and lined up on either side: Rousseau and Keller on the right, Volkov and Fabian on the left. Fabian was shrinking back, holding his rifle like it was something disgusting to touch. Worse than useless. He would be a liability when they entered the maelstrom.

Rousseau shook his head and gestured back the way they

had come. 'Fabian, go back to the control room. We're going to flush him into the garden.'

Fabian opened his mouth and then restrained himself from thanking Rousseau. Instead, he just nodded and turned away, running back down the corridor.

Volkov watched him go, naked contempt in his gaze, and then turned back to the closed doors into the main hall. The gunfire continued, most of it coming from one direction. Multiple guns, so that meant the intruder, if he really was only one man, was on the opposite side.

Rousseau glanced at Keller, then Volkov. He held up his left hand with three fingers raised, then curled the fingers one at a time.

Three.

Two.

One.

Volkov kicked the doors open and stood back.

Inside, they saw Müller and Frei crouching behind one of the leather couches that had been overturned. There were two men lying dead in the centre of the floor beside the big fireplace at the centre of the room. Rousseau recognised one as Thomas. The other was probably Schmid, though his face wasn't visible, so it was hard to be sure.

Signs of destruction were everywhere. Bullet holes in the whitewashed walls and the exposed pine beams, blood seeping into the joins in the parquet floor. One of the ten-metre-wide picture windows had been blown out.

'He's over there,' Müller yelled back at them, pointing at the wide pillar in the north-west corner of the room. Volkov craned his head around the edge of the doorway to look in the direction the other man was pointing, just for a second, and immediately jerked back as a single gun-shot rang out.

He fell on his back, his head landing beside Rousseau's right foot. There was a clean bullet wound in the centre of his forehead. A very good or very lucky shot. Rousseau looked back out at the two dead men in the centre of the room, and thought about the three or four other corpses that must be scattered around.

Definitely not luck.

'Who are you?' Rousseau yelled out into the doorway.

There was no response.

'There's no way out of there. If you surrender, we will take you alive.'

Still nothing. He glanced at Keller. 'Give me a grenade.'

Keller hesitated, then handed him a grenade from his belt. Rousseau peered into the room as the intruder traded bursts of gunfire with the two remaining men. He turned to look back down the corridor, where Fabian had reached the door that would lead through to the east wing. Rousseau considered the next move. He would toss the grenade in the intruder's direction while he was distracted. Even if it didn't take him out, it would let him and Keller enter the hall and form a pincer movement with the other two men.

'Fire a burst over there,' he told Keller, indicating the position of the intruder.

But before anyone could move, there was a thunderous explosion from the east side of the building.

73

The small boy at the top of the stairs blinked. He was about five or six years old. Straw-coloured hair and grey-blue eyes. Océane could see kitchen cupboards and an aluminium cooker hood behind him. The low hum of a microwave sounded off to the right-hand side. He stared back at her, not scared or surprised, just regarding her with interest, like a shiny insect beneath a rock he had picked up.

She heard a male voice speaking Swiss-accented French from behind him.

'David, what's wrong?'

Océane froze. As she watched, a man appeared behind the little boy.

He was tall and wiry, with the same straw-coloured hair as the boy. His eyes narrowed and he took a sharp breath when he saw Océane. He put a hand on the boy's shoulder and, gently but firmly, pulled him back from the top of the stairs. He took the boy's place, filling the door frame. His body blotted out most of the light spilling down from the kitchen, so that his face had disappeared into shadow when he spoke.

'David, get my phone. It's beside the microwave.'

The boy didn't move, still trying to peer past his father to the strange woman in the basement.

'Please, don't tell anyone,' Océane said, hating the desperation in her voice. 'I don't want to cause you any trouble.' She took one step up towards him, then stopped.

The father looked down at his son. '*David.*' The repetition of the name in that tone was an instruction. The boy knew to act on it, moving quickly away.

He straightened and took two steps down the stairs, closing the distance between them.

'I have no choice. I'm sorry.'

'You do have a choice. I won't tell anyone. Just let me go and you'll never see me again.'

The boy appeared again, the phone in his hand. The screen had woken, uplighting his cutely chubby face in blue.

The father took the phone.

Océane took another step closer. 'Please.'

The man said, 'I need to call the police,' but made no move to do anything with the phone. He sounded almost apologetic about what he was going to do. Then his focus shifted and he saw the screwdriver in her hand. He took a sharp breath and reached his hand out to the boy, drawing him behind him.

Océane glanced down at the screwdriver and realised what he was thinking. For a split second, she wondered what Mallory would do. Only three stairs separated them. But then she looked at the man's eyes, then the boy peering out from behind his father.

Océane let her arm drop. Her fingers uncurled and the screwdriver bounced off two stairs before tumbling off the edge to the concrete floor of the basement.

'I'm sorry,' Océane said. 'I didn't mean to scare you. I just want to get out of this place.'

The man stared at her for a long time, then closed the distance between them. He grabbed her hand, the one that had held the screwdriver. She tensed, but then felt him placing something in her hand. A car key. He waved a hand at the green Renault below in the garage.

'You broke in and stole my keys. We're out right now, I won't find out until later.'

It took her a moment to catch up. 'But ...'

The man raised his gaze to the ceiling, like he was talking about God. 'Rousseau is looking for you, right?'

She hesitated, then answered, 'Yes.'

'My brother had a business in the town, until Rousseau decided it should close.' He gestured a hand up at the ground floor. 'Did you see that tree out there? That's where he hung himself in the winter.'

'I'm sorry,' Océane said. She looked down at the key, then back up at the man who suddenly seemed twenty years older. 'Thank you.'

'Please don't damage the car. You can leave it parked in Gänsern.' He thought for a moment. 'But if you do damage it, write it off.'

Océane smiled and clutched the car keys. She turned and ran back down the steps into the garage. She unlocked the green Renault and started the engine. As she was wondering how to open the garage door, it started to swing soundlessly up. She looked up at the stairs to the house and saw the man looking back at her, his hand on the boy's shoulder.

As she was pulling out of the driveway, she heard a dull thump, as though something heavy had been dropped in the distance. As she pulled out onto the road, she saw black smoke rising into the evening sky above the mountain, an orange blaze at its base.

Mallory. He was still alive.

She sat there with the engine running, staring up at the pillar of black smoke.

It couldn't be more than five minutes' drive from here to the edge of town. She was in a civilian car. If they still had roadblocks, it would be easier to bluff her way past as a lone woman, and then she would be on the road, home free.

And Mallory had told her to go; to walk away. That was what he wanted, wasn't it?

74

The explosion was deafening. The house shook so violently that Mallory thought for a second the whole building was going to break up and start tumbling down the mountain. Dust and parts of the ceiling rained down all around.

He thought, 'Finally.'

On the way through the vast kitchen he had cut the gas hose at the back of the big range cooker and left a blowtorch burning on the far side of the room. The elapsed time had clearly allowed a big build-up of gas.

Mallory took full advantage of the chaos. He stepped out from behind the pillar and started running towards the other side of the hall. One of the shooters on the opposite side had been blown off his feet and was holding a hand to his head. The other was distracted by the wall of flame in the corridor outside. Without breaking stride, Mallory shot the one on the ground and then the other as he turned back around. He saw movement at the doorway and fired another burst as he quickened his pace, making for the glass wall on the opposite side.

He adjusted his aim and fired a short burst into the plate glass from floor to ceiling, covering his face as he slammed into the window and smashed through.

The glass fragmented and he hit the floor on the other side, covered in a dusting of crystals.

This was not going to plan for anyone. The idea had been to get in fast, find Rousseau and take him out. Best case scenario, he would have time to get proof of death. Cristofol had said he wanted Rousseau's head on a platter. Mallory assumed he hadn't been speaking literally, and that a photograph of the body would suffice.

But that was all looking less likely as the minutes ticked by. The men Mallory had engaged so far were well-trained private contractors. If they knew what they were doing, they would be getting their boss the hell out of the house. Perhaps he was already gone. Mallory knew the most likely escape route was by helicopter, rather than cable car. He had to find a way to get up on the roof. Perhaps it wasn't too late to intercept Rousseau.

Mallory heard a muted burst of gunfire behind him and turned around quickly. There was no one there. Thick, black smoke was filling the corridor. He felt a grim satisfaction. His opponents were jumping at shadows.

He reached the end of the corridor and moved down an unlit narrow staircase, covering each corner. He reached the bottom ready for another attack. It had been two or three minutes since he had seen a guard. Surely there were some down here in the bowels of the house? He found himself in another low-ceilinged corridor. Green floor-level lights lined the corridor on one side, the only source of illumination. He could still hear yells and movement above him; the occasional loud crash as the fire destroyed more of the building. The smoke hadn't permeated down here yet.

He heard the sound of a door slamming above him and stopped, waiting to hear footsteps on the stairs. There were none. Instead, he heard a lock engage. He hoped he hadn't climbed into a hole with no way out. Being trapped down here as the house burned down on top of him didn't sound like a good time.

Mallory advanced down the corridor. The strip of green floor lighting seemed to stop at a blank wall thirty yards away. As he got closer, he heard a click and realised the wall was a door. It slid aside and he felt fresh air on his face. He could make out grass and thick bushes outside. There was no one in sight. The mechanism must have been triggered remotely. A safety mechanism reacting to the fire? Or something else?

Either way, there was a locked door and a burning building behind him and one exit. Not a lot of choice.

Mallory walked cautiously towards the doorway, then picked up speed as he got closer. He was running by the time he made it outside. As soon as he passed through the doorway he started weaving, expecting a volley of gunfire. If there was someone waiting to pick him off, he didn't want to make it too easy.

But there were no gunshots. He was in the garden behind the house. There was a low wall straight ahead of him. He continued weaving until he reached it, then vaulted it and crouched down in the bushes behind it.

As he watched the house, the door he had emerged from slid closed again. He had been guided outside.

All of a sudden, Mallory knew how a laboratory rat must feel.

75

Mallory took advantage of the pause to reload, switching the almost-empty magazine out for the last fresh one he had. He could hear sounds drifting up from the town below. The music of the carousel, mingling with the discordant wail of distant sirens. The clouds had cleared and the moon was full, illuminating the garden like it was under floodlights. He could smell the burning building. A large column of dark smoke obscured most of the sky to the east.

Raising his head, he took stock of his surroundings. The garden was a sprawling area to the rear of the house that occupied almost as much space as the house itself. The satellite image had given him an idea of what was out here, but a limited one, because it was in two dimensions. He saw now that the garden spread over multiple levels. Platforms and raised daises and stone stairs were scattered around seemingly at random.

First order of business: get to the high ground. He moved forward, trying to keep aware of any movement, any sound that might give him a warning.

Large stone statues populated the space. Angels and gods and mythical beasts. He passed a wide pond with a familiar-looking cluster of concrete in the middle. It took him a second to recognise it as a three-dimensional map, the European countries spreading out with Switzerland at the centre.

He moved towards the nearest set of stairs. They were stone, flanked by classical balustrades, and led up to what he guessed was supposed to look like the ruins of a Greek temple. Another statue was silhouetted against the blue and purple of the night sky. This one was male. A naked, muscular figure stretched back, poised to hurl his stone javelin.

Mallory reached the top of the stairs and quickly sized up the platform. He missed his night-vision goggles. It made immediate certainty much more elusive. But he was pretty sure he was alone up here.

The platform was lined with more stone balustrades. He crouched behind one and looked down on the house. The entire eastern side was engulfed in flame. The west side, from where he had just emerged, was in darkness.

Mallory saw a whisper of movement in the corner of his eye and turned quickly. A figure had appeared in the gap between two rows of hedges. Without hesitation, Mallory squeezed off a burst of fire. He was on target. But the figure didn't flinch. A moment later, a spotlight winked on.

The figure between the hedges was a crude mannequin, held up by a metal post.

It took Mallory a second to understand. This wasn't just a garden, it was a shooting range.

And the distraction meant only one thing.

Mallory hurled himself to the ground as an answering

burst of fire exploded in a line across the top of the stone balustrade where he had just been standing.

He held still until it was over, then peered up at the stone-work. There was no damage on this side, other than a small channel carved along the edge of one of the supports where the bullet had glanced by. That meant the shots had come from directly ahead of him. Mallory pointed the barrel of his gun between the supports and fired another burst, hoping to hear a cry of pain. No joy.

The air was still. Mallory's senses were attuned to catch the smallest noise, the tiniest movement. Meanwhile, his mind was re-evaluating his opponent.

The way he had been herded out here; the configuration of this garden, it all confirmed a theory that had been percolating. The enemy wasn't hiding behind his guards. This was a game, and Rousseau was an enthusiastic participant.

Mallory rolled to the side and low-crawled to the opposite edge of the platform. There was a ten-foot drop to a fountain pool. He risked raising his head, ducked down again. No shots. He gripped the edge of the barrier and vaulted up and over, dropping to land on the foot-wide paving that surrounded the pool.

He moved quickly to the corner of the platform above him. If he was lucky, Rousseau wouldn't have had the angle to see his escape route. He might still think Mallory was up there.

Mallory reached the edge and watched. There was a light breeze. The tall bushes near the perimeter wall were swaying slightly. And then Mallory saw something. Against the movement of the thick leaves, a dark shape that didn't move with the wind. He trained his gun on it and at the same moment, it moved. Mallory and the figure fired at the same time. He jerked back as bullets smashed into the corner and passed through the air where his head had just been.

He had got it wrong earlier. He wasn't a lab rat in a maze, he was game in a reserve.

Mallory had misunderstood his adversary in one crucial respect. He was expecting Rousseau to hide behind his walls and his men; to run at the first sign of trouble. Only now did he wonder if perhaps he had been *allowed* to get this far. He hadn't got within thirty feet of Rousseau yet, but the man's actions as a commander told him a lot. He was relishing this. Enjoying the challenge, savouring the hunt. An unwelcome realisation bubbled up in Mallory's mind: the two of them were on the same wavelength on this, if nothing else.

Mallory glanced around the corner again. He could see no movement. Was the shooter still there?

He was straining his eyes looking into the darkness when the soft rustle of clothing behind him told him he was facing in the wrong direction.

76

Rousseau watched as Keller made his way around the perimeter. He estimated his man's chances at no better than twenty-five per cent. Keller was good, but whoever the intruder was, was better. He was a born killer. Rousseau felt a mild tug of sadness at the men he had lost tonight, but it was masked by the exhilaration he felt at finding a worthy adversary.

All of this, the garden, yes, but really, the whole business, was set up to keep that thrill of the hunt alive. It had fulfilled its purpose up until now, but there was always that ersatz, aspartame quality to it. There was no real danger. Until now.

When Keller had vanished into the shadows, Rousseau turned his head to look at the last position from which he had seen the intruder's muzzle flash. He was boxed in over there. Rousseau knew the spot well, from training and live fire exercises. It was a deceptive position. It felt sheltered, but it was closed off on the western side, and Keller would be able to approach most of the way from the east without being seen.

Rousseau moved across towards the staircase, keeping

below the level of the hedge. He didn't doubt if he raised his head a few inches, it would be taken off.

His plan was to get into position at the south-west corner, by the fountain. He should be able to make it there without being spotted, and it would leave him far from the last position the intruder had seen. He would wait for the intruder to take out Keller, and then he would move in.

A smaller explosion echoed from inside the house. He didn't let it distract him. There would be plenty of time to take account of losses when the night was complete. Perhaps the fire in the east wing wouldn't spread to the rest of the house. Even if it did, there would be plenty of time to reach the cable car and evacuate. He barely cared about the destruction of the house. He had many houses. How many nights like this had he had? Very few, and none in the past twenty years.

He watched the dais where the intruder had been positioned. He had seen no movement, heard no sound for minutes. Keller should have reached him by now. Perhaps he was more careful than Rousseau had given him credit for; perhaps he was waiting for his moment to strike.

He waited another minute. Two.

Hesitating for a second, he touched a finger to the button on his headset, making sure they were still on the closed channel.

'Where are you?'

There was silence.

Rousseau began to feel an unfamiliar frisson. It took him a second to recognise the feeling: unease.

'Keller,' he said. 'Do you have him?'

The voice that replied wasn't Keller's. It was cold and unforgiving.

'He had me. But then he didn't.'

At that moment a bullet smashed into the wall just above Rousseau's head. He flinched and looked out into the darkness. The intruder knew where he was. How? He searched the blacked-out shapes of the garden against the clear sky, looking for movement.

Another bullet hit the wall. He was trying to flush him out.

Rousseau took stock of his situation. This was getting more interesting. He decided to fall back to the house.

He took out his phone and tapped into the app. It felt a little like cheating, but what good was home advantage if you didn't use it? He tapped into the array of lights on the north side, skirting the mountain. They would create a five-second light show, sufficient to distract the intruder's attention long enough for him to run for the house and regroup.

The lights flashed on, the blast of music started, Rousseau started to move.

And then something stopped him in his tracks. Keller was hanging from the light array, blood dripping down the length of his body.

It was only a second's hesitation, but it did the job the intruder intended it to do. Rousseau felt the impact of the bullets before he heard the gunshots.

The vest stopped most of the bullets, but he was hit in the upper left arm. At least once, maybe twice. He started running, hearing another burst of gunfire. This time the intruder didn't find his target. The door was open. He rushed through and slammed his good hand on the emergency door close.

Shit. He had underestimated this man. This *monster*. He would find a way in here, and Rousseau was wounded, bleeding badly. He looked down and saw there was blood pooling on the floor at his feet, just in the few seconds he had rested here. He was hit on his left side too, just below the Kevlar. He tightened the straps, wincing at the pain. It would help the vest to staunch the blood flow a little, buying him a little more time.

The cable car. It was the only way down.

But the intruder knew that.

77

Mallory barked a curse into the cold night air. He had had Rousseau dead in his sights and thought he could count on another half-second of surprise. But Rousseau had moved much faster than he had anticipated. He thought he had hit him, though.

Even from this distance, he could see the door Rousseau had vanished through was the same reinforced job as the other exterior doors. It also had the same thumbprint lock. He looked up at the guard he had killed a few minutes before, hanging like a scarecrow from the lights.

He sighed and took out his knife.

A minute later, the guard's thumb opened the door lock. Mallory pocketed the severed digit and raised his rifle. The interior was dark. The doorway at the end of the corridor was open, dim light filtering in from beyond. If he was right, the big room beyond would open out onto the deck, where the cable car terminal was. Perhaps he could catch Rousseau on the way. Even if he had reached the car, it would probably be possible to engineer an accident on the way down.

The room beyond was a wide, open space, like a ballroom. Floor to ceiling windows lined the opposite wall, covered with opaque curtains that let through the glow of the town below. At one end of the room, the curtains were blowing a little in the breeze.

Mallory pushed the curtains out of the way and moved through the doorway. There was a trail of blood drops on the decking, registering as a red so dark it was almost black in the dim light. He could see a pair of thick, taught lines against the sky, as though tethering the house to the town below. The cable car terminal was around the next corner. Rousseau had clearly decided to abandon his fortress.

Mallory stepped outside. The trail extended along the deck, the blood drops spaced evenly apart, before disappearing around the corner. Rousseau was wounded, but still moving, and therefore still dangerous.

Mallory moved forward, careful not to make any sound that would give away his position. He kept his rifle trained on the corner, ready to fire. He reached the corner and stepped out.

The cable car was in its station, the door open. The windows were at waist height, so it was impossible to know if it was empty from here.

There was something wrong.

Mallory glanced down and saw that the trail of blood drops extended about halfway from his position to the cable car door and then stopped. Which meant—

Mallory cursed out loud as he looked up in time to see a dark figure on the roof of the terminal, breaking the black and blue line of the building against the sky. He fired, too late. A muzzle flash lit up the sky and Mallory felt bullets smack into his vest and tear into the unprotected flesh of his arm. He fell down, dropping the rifle. The figure, with difficulty, slid down from the roof and landed with an ungainly thump on the deck, almost losing his footing.

Rousseau did not look in good shape. He was tired, in a lot of pain. His right hand held the gun on Mallory, steady, but his left hand was clutching his side, where he had been hit. Blood was dampening his sleeve from a wound higher up on his arm. He was in worse condition than Mallory, if anything.

Mallory didn't feel much like gloating. He had been hit at least twice in his right arm. On the shoulder and just above the elbow. That arm was useless to him now. Even if Rousseau was obliging enough to let him crawl over to his dropped weapon, he would have to shoot left-handed.

Rousseau saw Mallory staring at the wound and looked down at it, then back at Mallory on the ground. His expression was almost comradely.

'Tonight ...' he stopped and took a breath, with difficulty. 'Tonight hasn't gone well for either of us, my friend.'

Mallory gritted his teeth through the pain. The fact that this guy was about to put a couple of bullets in his head was bad enough. That he wanted to act like best buds beforehand was adding insult to injury.

Rousseau shuffled closer, limping. Despite himself, Mallory found himself impressed that the fucker had managed to climb up onto the roof for that ambush. It must have taken some resolve.

'Why did you come here? I hope the Marsellais paid you well.'

Mallory shook his head.

'No? The Parisians, then?'

He seemed genuinely curious. It bought Mallory time. Out of the corner of his eye, he had seen something he just might be able to use. Rousseau's aim had been all over the place. One of his bullets had smashed through one of the barrier supports, leaving splintered wood sticking out.

Rousseau had stopped. His gun was unwavering, but he was clutching his side as tightly as ever.

'Don't you want to tell me? It doesn't matter now.'

Mallory coughed. His mouth tasted of blood. 'Talk and you'll let me live, is that it?'

Rousseau's lips twisted into a sad, almost kindly smile. 'I won't insult you. But I would like to know.'

'Nicolas Devereaux,' Mallory said slowly.

Rousseau looked confused. 'You knew him?'

'No, just a friend of a friend. You messed with the wrong people.'

'Ah. An occupational hazard as ...' Rousseau winced and gripped his side tighter. He cleared his throat. 'As I'm sure you understand. It was nothing personal, of course.'

'Whatever you say.'

'That's why you came here. Not for the Parisians, not for the Marseillais. It was the girl, wasn't it?'

Mallory didn't answer. He was focusing on the loose railing where the bullets had shattered it.

'She came with you, didn't she? Before ...' Another wince and intake of breath. 'Before all this, she had been spotted down there, in town. I'm afraid she's dead or captured by now.'

'Go to hell,' Mallory said from between his teeth.

Rousseau looked a little disappointed, as though he had expected more from his opponent.

'I fear you will arrive first, my friend.' He took a final step closer and pointed the gun at Mallory's head. 'Do you have any last words?'

Mallory coughed again and nodded his head. He moved slowly, acting even more in pain than he was, like he was just trying to get to a sitting position.

'I do.'

Rousseau leaned closer.

Mallory snapped off the jagged piece of wood and slammed it hard into Rousseau's waist, just below the vest.

He screamed as the spear of wood punctured the opposite side from his existing wound. Involuntarily or otherwise, he pulled the trigger, but Mallory had already moved. He hauled himself to his feet, ignoring the pain, using the embedded stake as leverage and sending another scream from Rousseau's lips.

'Happy landings.'

Mallory gripped Rousseau by the shoulders and used every last remaining ounce of his strength to push him back against the railing. Back and up and over.

Rousseau let go of his wound, his bloody hands clawing at Mallory's face, but it was too late. He was past the point of no return. He toppled over the railing and tumbled head first into the void.

Mallory had already collapsed on the deck by the time he heard the distant thud of Rousseau's body hitting the rocks hundreds of feet below.

With an effort of will, he forced himself to stay awake. The exertion of the last minute had accelerated the damage. His vision was swimming in and out. Blurred and darkening. He tried to focus on the pain in his arm. The blood was flowing quicker now. He tried to grip the wound to staunch the flow, but his fingers were weak.

He could smell burning wood and plastic, feel the night air warming around him. He didn't know if he could make it, but he didn't want to die up here.

78

Mallory staggered forward, light-headed.

The cable car stood ready and unoccupied at the station, its doorway open and ready to receive. Whoever guarded the terminal had either abandoned their post or he had killed them already. The rifle felt like it weighed as much as he did, but he clutched it like a drowning man holding onto driftwood. He stumbled forward, dimly telling himself this could be a trap, that someone could be lying in wait inside, and being surprised to realise he no longer cared.

The control desk was unguarded. He tried to focus on the labels on the controls. Mostly mechanical switches and buttons. Fighting to focus his eyes, he found one labelled FERMER and another with COMMENCER LE VOYAGE. He flipped both switches and a soft, regular pinging sound began, ushering him towards the car.

The car rocked slightly as he half-stepped, half-fell through the doorway. He collapsed on one of the leather seats circling the interior and closed his eyes as the door clicked shut. The bleeding wasn't stopping. Was getting worse, if anything.

He closed his eyes and, what seemed like a second later, felt a judder. He opened his eyes again to see that the cable car had completed its journey down the side of the mountain. The door hissed open.

Mallory had to try three times to stand up. Everything felt heavier than it had even a couple of minutes before, back at the chalet. He could hear sirens, raised voices. He steadied himself on the door frame and then started walking, no longer thinking clearly about where he was or where he was going, just understanding that he had to move.

He stepped out of the station and squinted his eyes against the million-watt glare of the moon.

The sirens and the voices seemed to have stopped, replaced by a dull, woolly thudding sound.

He felt his arm again and strangely there was no pain, though his fingers were wet and sticky with blood. He took three steps onto the grass slope. He could see people down there. They would see him soon. That was bad.

But why was it bad?

Mallory couldn't remember.

He had been concerned about something a minute ago, and now he couldn't remember what that was. Everything was fine.

In fact, he was just going to sit down for a minute.

Everything was fine.

79

'Mallory!'

Océane slid her fingers between his shoulders and the grass and tried to shake him. She barely managed to move him. He was still alive, she knew that because he kept mumbling that everything was fine, but his eyes stayed closed, and he betrayed no sign that he knew she was there.

The wound on his arm looked very bad. She pulled her sweater off and tied it around his upper arm as tightly as she could. The blood immediately soaked through the material, but she thought it would make a decent tourniquet. She glanced over her shoulder. The police hadn't spotted the car yet, but they soon would.

She looked back down at Mallory. There was a faint smile on his face. She slapped him hard across the face once, twice ...

Mallory's left hand grabbed hers at the wrist before she could strike a third time. His eyes were bleary. He hadn't acted consciously, his body had done it for him.

'Whu ...'

Océane hissed: 'Everything is *not* fine. They'll kill us if we don't get out of here.'

Mallory blinked twice and examined the tourniquet on his arm.

'Can you walk?' Océane asked.

'I don't know,' he mumbled. 'Help me.'

She put an arm around him and with great effort hauled him to his feet.

'The car is right over there, can you . . .'

Mallory blinked again and struggled to focus.

'This way,' she said, pulling him along with difficulty. He was leaning his whole, not-inconsiderable weight on her, and she was barely holding it.

Painfully slowly, she half-helped, half-dragged Mallory towards the green Renault. She had left the lights off and the driver's door open. She let him lean against the car as she got the rear door open.

That was when she heard the raised voices. A group of uniformed police had spotted them and were running towards them.

Mallory was fumbling with his rifle, his eyes still not focusing. He had heard them, but she doubted he could hit the broad side of a barn right now. She pushed him towards the car door.

'*Merde*. Get in!'

80

The first bullet smashed through the rear driver's side window, passed about an inch in front of Mallory's face, and then punched its way through one of the support uprights on the opposite side. It also brought Mallory's senses a little more into focus.

'Go,' he said, weakly swiping at the back of the headrest in front of him with his left hand. He tried to shout the instruction, but it came out even weaker than his hand movement. Luckily, Océane didn't need to be told.

The engine roared to life and she floored the accelerator. The Renault's tyres spun on the grass on the shoulder, then caught purchase on the road surface and before Mallory knew it, he was flung back in his seat with the sudden acceleration.

His arm was hurting like a son of a bitch again, which was probably a good sign. Océane had wrapped a good, tight tourniquet around it, but he knew he had lost a lot of blood. If he didn't get to a hospital soon, he wouldn't have to worry about any of the bullets coming any closer.

That was a concern for the future, though. Right now, he didn't have time to bleed to death.

Wincing at the pain in his arm as he turned, he peered out of the back window. The grassy slope and the stand of pine trees was receding quickly, but he could already see two cars swinging onto the road in pursuit: one police car with lights blazing, one black SUV.

'Where we headed?' he asked Océane without looking away from the road through the rear window.

'I don't know,' she yelled back. 'Away from them!'

Mallory glanced back. Océane was gripping the wheel. The needle on the speedometer was climbing past 90 kph.

'They'll still have a block on the high road,' Mallory said, turning back around and resting the barrel of the rifle between the two rear headrests. Left-handed, he fired two single shots through the glass. 'Take us through town.'

'Through town, are you crazy?'

Mallory didn't answer. He was too busy trying to draw a bead on the lead car; the police car. He switched the selector to full auto and fired a burst, missing, but causing it to swerve and lose a little speed.

A sudden swerve threw him to the side and he screamed out in pain as his wounded shoulder hit the door.

'Sorry!'

'I'm fine, keep going.'

The Renault took a tight corner, at least one of the wheels lifting off the ground, and then they hit the cobbles as Océane drove them down the slope towards the main road through the centre of Appelburg. Mallory could see pedestrians scrambling to get out of the way. Océane leaned on the horn to clear those who were slower on the uptake.

'Watch ...' Mallory started as he saw a police car emerge from a side street and move to block the road.

Océane didn't brake. Instead, she adjusted their path slightly and put her foot down, aiming for the gap.

The gap wasn't quite big enough to let them through unscathed, but it was just wide enough that they smashed the front bumper off the police car and continued, barely slowing.

'Nice one,' Mallory said, impressed. He had thought the gap was too tight.

Océane yanked the wheel again and they cornered onto a smaller street running off to the left. Stalls lined one side. People scrambling to get out of the way. All except one.

A uniformed cop was standing in the middle of the road, taking aim.

'Duck,' Mallory said.

Océane was already doing it, just as a bullet smacked into the centre of the windscreen.

Mallory wasn't sure what happened next. He was flung back in his seat by sudden acceleration, another lightning bolt of pain hitting his wounded arm. The cop, who had been taking aim to fire again, suddenly stopped, his eyes widening. He tried to move, too late. The bonnet of the Renault hit him mid-dive and Mallory felt the impact hard enough to jar his arm again as the cop tumbled over the car and landed sprawled in its wake.

'Nice driving,' he said with surprised approval.

Océane looked up at him in the mirror, somehow managing to look irritated. 'I hit the wrong pedal!'

Finally, they reached the end of the alley and seconds later they were on the low road leading out of Appelburg. Mallory had given up counting their pursuers. There were a lot of them. They seemed to be falling back to a regular gap of a couple of hundred yards. Mallory knew why that was. They weren't trying to catch them any more, just make sure there was no avenue of retreat.

'Mallory, this is just going to run us straight into the other roadblock.'

'Keep going,' he said.

They reached the outskirts of town and the road opened up in front of them. Tall pines lined the road. Mallory heard Océane curse and felt the car begin to slow. He turned around to face the direction of travel. A large articulated lorry had been parked across the road about a quarter of a mile ahead. In front of it were three black SUVs and a dozen or so men: uniformed police officers and Rousseau's private contractors.

'What do I do?' Océane yelled. 'We can't get past this.'

Mallory looked around the interior of the car. The Renault was almost new, still with the showroom smell. That meant it was in great working order, as solid and fuel efficient and roadworthy as it would ever be. But what it wasn't was a tank. They weren't getting past that roadblock.

He looked ahead at the road as the block loomed closer. Trees and the river on one side, the steep rise of the hill on the other. A dozen vehicles hot on their heels. They were completely hemmed in. The trap was ...

'Airtight,' Mallory said quietly.

'What?'

'Don't try to get past it,' Mallory said. 'Slow down a little.' His eyes searched the line of trees on their left-hand side. The blurred vision wasn't making this any easier.

Then he saw it. The river, glinting starlight back at them through the trees.

'Take a left, quickly.'

'Left? There is no—'

Then Océane saw what he meant.

'Seriously?

'Seriously.'

She committed to it without being asked twice, yanking the wheel to the left and plunging them through the gap between two trees. Mallory had a second to see the puzzled faces of the men at the roadblock and then they were bumping down a forty-five-degree hill, narrowly missing pines as Océane weaved left and right. Mallory could see the river through the trees ahead of them.

It had to happen eventually. Océane clipped one of the trees and they heard toughened plastic smash and metal shear. The Renault's momentum kept it going. A loud crack told Mallory that the front axle had gone. They weren't driving anywhere else in this car. Hopefully, they wouldn't need to.

The Renault reached the bottom of the slope, crashed through the bushes on the riverbank and rolled straight into the water. They dipped almost fully under, water spraying through the bullet holes in the glass, and then the current spun the car around backwards and they glanced off a couple of big rocks as the river started to carry them away.

Océane let go of the steering wheel and unbuckled her belt.

'We need to get out.'

Mallory shook his head. 'It's all right, leave it.'

She opened her mouth to tell him that it wasn't all right and then realised what he meant. They were still being pulled along by the current, but they weren't going under. The car had righted itself and they were bobbing down the rapids in a makeshift raft. Water was seeping in, but slowly. The Renault was new. Great seals on the doors to ensure efficient climate control. Lots of air inside. It would hold for a while, maybe long enough.

Océane laughed in surprise and angled her neck so she could look up the hill in the direction of the road. It was no longer in sight, lost behind the trees. They were being drawn inexorably away from the road and Rousseau's men. If the car didn't sink, they might be able to float all the way back to Gänsern.

'How did you know that would work?'

Mallory suddenly felt very tired again. The sharp pain from the wound in his arm had numbed to a dull ache.

'I didn't,' he said simply.

And then he slumped down in the seat, and it felt like he was being pulled gently into a dark tunnel. From somewhere in the distance, he heard a soft, French-accented voice saying his name, over and over again, like a lullaby.

THREE WEEKS LATER

81

ST-JEAN-DES-PERTES, NORMANDY

They didn't make it.

Not all the way to Gänsern, anyway. The Renault managed to drift about five miles downriver before the seals let in enough water for it to finally start sinking. Soon, the river had swallowed enough of the car that the water began streaming in through the bullet holes in the windows.

Later, Mallory had only vague memories of Océane pulling him to the riverbank. She said that part was easy, with the current supporting his weight. Dragging him out of the water and onto a sandbank had required a lot more effort. The rifle had been swept away as they clambered out of the window of the sinking car, which turned out to be just as well.

There were police on the road, but Océane saw from their uniforms that they were from Gänsern. Later, they told her multiple drivers on the road had called in to report a floating Renault, just downstream from an apparent warzone in Appelburg.

They got Mallory to hospital in double time.

While Mallory was unconscious, Océane had to answer a lot of questions. She kept it simple: they had visited Appelburg for a holiday and got caught up in some kind of gang war. She didn't know what it was about, they had just unwittingly strayed into the middle of a terrifying situation. The stern-eyed Swiss detective had listened, asked occasional questions, but he didn't seem particularly suspicious. Océane could sense she was just a small detail in a much larger investigation

When she told Mallory about it, he knew it was a good thing she had spoken to the police first. It hadn't taken much for her to convince them that she was an innocent civilian caught in the crossfire, because that was exactly what she was, even if that wasn't the whole story.

The detective paid a visit to Mallory in his hospital room when he regained consciousness late in the evening. Mallory acted more dazed and confused than he actually was. The painkillers slurring his speech helped with that. The detective asked about Mallory's military tattoos before he left, promising to come back in the morning.

He probably had come back, but Mallory had made sure to be long gone by then.

Three weeks on, Mallory was feeling a lot better.

The emergency medical team in Gänsern had done a great initial job of patching him up, and rest, food and exercise had done the rest. He had started going for morning walks; leaving while it was still dark and returning as the sun was coming up.

It was still dark now as he watched the gîte across the road.

It was a one-storey cottage with grey stone walls. It had

been a farmhouse a hundred years ago. Now it was a holiday let, empty this week. Or at least, it was supposed to be empty. Mallory watched as torchlight occasionally appeared through the shutters. This place was on the edge of town, wasn't overlooked by any inhabited homes. Still, the intruders were being sloppy. At least they had thought to leave the truck around the back.

Mallory checked his watch. They had been in there ten minutes now. Wouldn't be much longer. He walked around to the lane that ran around the back of the gîte and took up a position beneath a sprawling beech tree that blacked out the ground beneath with its leaves. The sun was starting to come up, almost ready to appear above the eastern hills.

Mallory kept his eyes on the open back door until he saw movement.

Two figures appeared, each carrying one end of what looked like an eighty-five-inch television. That would be a perk of the job. The real point of the exercise was ensuring the owner of the property got the message about security.

Mallory cleared his throat and stepped out from beneath the shade of the tree.

'I hope you're going to remember to turn off motion smoothing. Makes films look crap.'

The figure at the back almost dropped the television. The one at the front gripped it tightly and looked over in Mallory's direction.

He took one hand off the TV and a moment later a torch beam appeared, sweeping around until he found Mallory. Mallory held up a hand to shield his eyes and stepped forward. There was a gun in his pocket if he needed it, but he didn't think Remy and Hugo were armed. Their boss, the mayor, would discourage that. It's never smart to let imbeciles play with guns.

'I thought we told you to get out of town,' Remy said. He glanced at Hugo and the two of them lowered their bounty to the ground carefully. 'This is none of your business.'

'My mistake. I thought you had made it my business when you asked for help with all of these burglaries.'

The two of them exchanged a glance. Then they turned back to Mallory. Remy let out a forced laugh, but even from across the road, in the half light, Mallory could see the fury in his eyes.

Remy started walking towards him, Hugo in tow, as always.

'You don't have the old man to hide behind this time.'

Mallory didn't respond.

Remy broke into a run as he charged towards Mallory. He was ten feet away when the headlights lit up the alley. The light threw him off balance, almost as though it was a physical blow. He turned and looked to the source of the light, shading his eyes. Chief LeGrande chose that moment to turn on the police lights as well as the headlights.

'What is this?' Remy yelled.

'It's me helping the police with some trouble in town. Least I can do, as a visitor.'

The doors on either side of the car opened. LeGrande and his deputy got out, guns drawn.

'*Arrêtez! Mettez-vous à terre!*'

Hugo, his hands up already, started to slowly get down on the ground, muttering the word *merde* to himself over and over.

Mallory eyed Remy, who was still on his feet. 'I'm not fluent in French, but I think he wants you to get down.' He pointed at the dirt road in front of his feet.

Remy lost it. He set his feet, pulled back his fist and swung it towards Mallory's face. Mallory, fully expecting the strike after provoking it, sidestepped easily and caught the fist in his left hand, wincing as the impact travelled through the healing wound in his upper arm.

'Thank you,' he said quietly, then smashed his own fist into Remy's face.

Belatedly, Remy obeyed Chief LeGrande's instruction and dropped into the dirt.

That was just enough. Mallory didn't have any trouble restraining himself from going further, but he knew he would have had a tension headache all day if he hadn't done that.

The two officers approached, yelling out instructions to the men on the ground. As his partner attended to handcuffing them behind their backs, LeGrande regarded Mallory.

'What did you say to him?'

'What you said. Just trying to help.'

The cop raised a suspicious eyebrow.

'Remy's father will put some pressure on you, you know,' Mallory said. 'Difficult to sell "town insurance" when it gets out your son's been doing all the burglaries.'

'Let him try. When the rest of the town finds out about this, I think we're going to be looking for a new mayor.'

'Maybe I should run for the office,' Mallory said, deadpan.

LeGrande replied, equally deadpan. 'Your help is welcome. But perhaps you can move on now.'

Mallory turned and took a moment to admire the golden glow on the crests of the hills. 'I'll be out of here by this afternoon. But I'm having breakfast with friends first.'

*

The sun was fully up by the time Mallory reached Serge's house, a paper bag stuffed full of pastries from the boulangerie braced between his good arm and his chest. His shoulder hurt like a bastard after stopping Remy's punch. It had probably set him back a couple of days. But it had been a hundred per cent worth it.

The smell of freshly brewed coffee greeted him as Serge opened the door. He gave Mallory a quizzical look. Mallory answered with a nod. Serge grinned and patted him on the shoulder. The bad shoulder. Mallory winced and followed him inside.

After breakfast, he said his goodbyes and Océane walked him out to the street. His taxi was waiting.

'Where next?'

Mallory rubbed the wound on his upper arm. 'Nowhere near a bloody mountain for a while, that's for sure.'

She lowered her eyes coyly. 'You'll still have that email address in a couple of months?'

'Same as I said before. If I'm alive.'

She went up on her tiptoes and kissed him on the lips, then dropped back down again.

'Try to be.'

Mallory smiled. 'If I ever needed an incentive ...'

The taxi honked its horn. Mallory rolled his eyes.

'Goodbye, Mallory.'

'*Au revoir*, Océane.'

He threw his backpack into the back seat and got in beside the driver, a leathery-tanned older man with a tweed cap.

He looked Mallory up and down and addressed him in English. How did they always know?

'Where to?'

'The bus station at Vire, mate. No hurry.'

The driver put the car into drive and rolled away from the kerb. Mallory turned around to see Océane waving, a light breeze blowing her summer dress and her long hair as she blew a kiss after him.

Mallory returned the wave and turned around, a grin on his face.

It was a big world, and he was going to see more of it. But something told him he would be back here someday.

AUTHOR'S NOTE

One of the best things about fiction is the way it allows both writers and readers to explore the world on the page.

In my first novel, *Cold Justice*, I sent Mallory overseas, to South Africa and the United States. For the second book, I wanted to move a little closer to home. The plot for *Red Mist* allowed me to return, at least in my imagination, to one of my favourite countries in the world: France.

I spent seven years of my youth there, in a town called Saint-Lô, in Normandy. It was a wonderful place to grow up: getting into mischief and annoying the local farmers, most of whom wouldn't hesitate to come after troublemakers with a shotgun. Running through maize fields, camping out in the woods, getting into scraps and making friends. Nothing lasts for ever though, and as I grew older I knew I wanted to see more of the world, just like Mallory does.

I drew on the experience of those years to create St-Jean-des-Pertes, the village where Mallory first encounters

Océane's grandfather and hears the tale that will draw him into a dangerous adventure that spans the Continent.

France is a land of contrasts, and I wanted to demonstrate that by taking Mallory and you, the reader, on a journey from the tranquil countryside of Normandy to the bustling cities of Paris and Marseille and beyond, and weaving a thrilling tale on the way.

France is also a country, like anywhere else, that has its problems with drugs, gangs and organised crime. I wanted to drop Mallory into that world, and show how his military skills translated to the challenges he finds there. As you know by now, Mallory is a guy who finds it hard to stay out of trouble, and I wanted him to find plenty of trouble in this book.

Rousseau, the villain, was one of my favourite characters to write. It seems that many of the real-life villains in our world today are like him: wealthy, powerful men who lurk behind the scenes and pull strings, using ordinary people as their pawns.

And of course, no matter how much of a lone wolf Mallory likes to think he is, he always manages to be drawn into the problems of others. I loved writing Océane, and I think you'll love her too. She's a flawed person who goes on her own journey, discovering reserves of strength she never knew she had. She's also another challenge for Mallory. He's comfortable in the heat of combat, but when someone's depending on him, that's an extra challenge that nobody trained him for.

Mallory will be back, and I hope you will be, too.

ACKNOWLEDGEMENTS

It won't be a surprise to learn that much of my life has been stranger than fiction. I've travelled the world, met the very best, and sometimes worst, of humanity. That's the truth.

People are a constant fascination to me. I love getting into their brains to understand their motivations and actions, and it's no different to the characters I write in my fiction books. I'm loving every minute of storytelling, and Mallory has allowed me to go deep, to explore memories but also see the world through different eyes and experiences.

Writing fiction has been a real gift and I've had a lot of help along the way. Thank you to Gavin Bell who continues to guide me on my thriller-writing journey and knock it out of the park. Thank you to everyone on the *Red Mist* team at Little, Brown/Sphere, particularly: Charlie King, Catherine Burke, Lucy Malagoni, Gemma Shelley, Kirsteen Astor, Tom Webster, Sean Garrehy, Sarah Shrubb, Hannah Methuen, Tamsin Kitson, Charlotte Chapman and Oliver Cotton. A special mention and thanks to Thalia Proctor who worked on my first book, *Cold Justice*. She is sorely missed by the whole team.

Thanks to my editor Ed Wood. Your guidance and input have been invaluable, Mallory would be lesser without you.

Thank you to my agents at YMU. Jordan Johnson, we're clocking up the miles together, man – exciting times! Thanks also to Mary Bekhait, Holly Bott and Lizzie Barroll-Brown and my literary agent, Amanda Harris. We're just at the beginning of Mallory's adventures, where in the world next?! The sky is the limit. Thank you, team.

To my family: Emilie, Oakley, Shyla, Gabriel, Priseïs and Bligh … words fail me sometimes. Thank you. You are everything. And to Terry Batt and Uncle Tony, you have my back and I'll be forever grateful.

To Mallory's fans across the world: thank you for the reads and the listens and the likes. You push me on to the very best I can be.